BOOK ONE

QUARANTINE

theLONERS

LEX THOMAS

QUARANTINE
theLONERS

BOOK ONE

EGMONT
USA
NEW YORK

EGMONT
We bring stories to life

First published by Egmont USA, 2012
443 Park Avenue South, Suite 806
New York, NY 10016

1 3 5 7 9 8 6 4 2

www.egmontusa.com

Library of Congress Cataloging-in-Publication Data
Thomas, Lex.
Quarantine / Lex Thomas.
p. cm.
Summary: When a virus deadly to adults infects their high school, brothers David
and Will and the other students soon break into gangs that fight each other
for survival and the hope of escaping their quarantine.
ISBN 978-1-60684-329-1 (hardback) — ISBN 978-1-60684-330-7 (e-book)
[1. Survival—Fiction. 2. Gangs—Fiction. 3. Interpersonal relations—Fiction.
4. Virus diseases—Fiction. 5. High schools—Fiction. 6. Schools—Fiction.
7. Science fiction.] I. Title.
PZ7.T366998Qud 2012
[Fic]—dc23
2011039460

Printed in the United States of America

1

SOMEONE MUST HAVE BITTEN OFF HER NOSE.

David remembered her. Julie Tanaka. She used to be gorgeous. He'd spent an entire semester of biology class fantasizing about her. She was perpetually tan and had a physique that always rendered David speechless. But now she looked like an old sewer rat. The tip of her nose was gone, like a piece of string cheese with the end chomped off. Her arms were spindly, and her bony joints jutted out like thorns. Her skin was brittle and dry. Her white hair was dirty and frayed. David studied Julie's eyes. They were full of hate. She seemed hungry to get a little payback for what over a year in this place had done to her.

She'd get her chance any minute now.

David surveyed the quad. Hundreds of kids stood along the

perimeter, staring up at the massive gray veil that obscured the sky. The dim daylight that passed through the translucent canopy cast dull shadows down David's lean face. He took stock of his competition. Some kids hopped up and down; some stretched their muscles. Others wrung their hands. They were grouped by hair color. The blue-hairs stood together at the south wall, the reds at the east opposite the yellows, and so on all around the quad.

But David had no group. He had only his brother, Will, at his side. A familiar rumbling echoed in from the distance. It was almost time. Anxious chatter got drowned out as the rumbling grew into a quickening thunder. The gray sky began to wobble and shake. The noise settled right above the quad, and the canopy convulsed like the ocean's surface in a violent storm.

David shouted a staccato command at Will. "Southeast corner!"

He could barely hear his own voice over the swelling roar above. It didn't matter. Will knew where to meet. David still reminded him every time. And he always got back the same exasperated nod from Will.

David trained his eyes back on the gray canopy and saw what everyone was waiting for. A thirty-yard incision split it open from the outside, revealing a brilliant slash of aqua-blue sky. Kids too timid to step foot onto the quad leaned out of windows and doorways for this brief contact with the outside world. Many of them stretched their arms skyward. Some of them sobbed. Others clapped their hands together in prayer. They came for this moment only, to catch a glimpse of the blue sky, to feel the warmth of the sun. They didn't have the courage to participate in what would happen next.

A black military helicopter eclipsed the view of the sky and lowered its giant cargo through the opening. Pallets of food, water, and supplies were lashed together into a single block the size of a school bus. The mass of supplies breached the slash and hung there, suspended by a cable forty feet above them.

The cable detached with a *plink*. The block of pallets fell. It cracked into the ground and broke apart, scattering supplies all over the quad. As the helicopter retreated, an unseen mechanism mended the slit in the gray canopy. The kids on the perimeter bolted toward the mound of supplies. Colors collided. All around David kids kicked, clawed, and stomped each other to get at the food.

David never thought high school would be this hard.

2

DAVID THREW HIS GIRLFRIEND'S PHONE INTO

the toilet. It sank to the bottom of the bowl, two years down the drain. The bathroom door was locked behind him. The door muffled the blasting music and drunken shouting of the house party on the other side. He couldn't deal with all those people out there yet, he had to wrap his mind around what he'd just seen.

An hour ago when Hilary had forgotten her phone in his Jeep, he shouldn't have checked her text messages. But he did. And there it was, a text from Sam Howard asking her what kind of panties she was going to wear that night.

David wrapped his hands around the cold porcelain of the sink in front of him. He wanted to rip it out of the wall. If David hadn't checked that stupid pink phone, then he never would have known. Maybe that would've been better. Then he wouldn't have driven to this shitty party at Sam's house and spotted Sam and Hilary together at the end of a long hall full of sweaty people. He would have spared himself the sight of Sam covertly palming Hilary's ass, and Hilary swatting it away, blushing and smiling. She liked it.

There was a knock on the bathroom door.

"Occupied," David said.

"It's me," Hilary said from the hall.

David popped the lock, swung the door open, grabbed Hilary by the wrist, and pulled her into the bathroom. He kicked the door closed.

"Hey! What's with the rough stuff?" Hilary said, and jerked her arm free of his grip.

The closet-sized bathroom was cramped with two people. Her face was only inches from David's and she looked more beautiful than ever. She had one of those impossible faces, the ones that only seem to exist on magazine covers. And her body, Jesus. David had always told her that if she ever posted a naked picture on the Internet, all of the comments would be angry claims that she was Photoshopped.

"Are you having a good time?" David asked.

"What are you doing here? You don't come to parties."

She scrunched up her nose like she was grossed out. It was the way she flirted. She faked like she thought you were a weirdo. David used to see it as a challenge. But this time, she wasn't pulling it off. He studied the way her lips fidgeted, the way her eyes wanted to look away from his.

"You got a text," David said, and he nodded toward the toilet.

She looked at her pink phone in the still water.

"I just got that phone, asshole!"

Her outraged expression went calm and controlled as she continued to stare at the phone. She must have realized she'd been caught. She pursed her lips. They were wet with a berry-colored gloss. Her makeup was prom-night perfect. She'd gone all out tonight, but it wasn't for him.

"Sam Howard? Sam fucking Howard?" David asked.

She let out a tense breath and raked her fingers through her hair.

"We need to talk, David."

"No, you need to talk. Tell me why."

"I don't know. It just happened."

"Really? You're giving me the *it just happened* excuse?" David said.

Where was I'm sorry? David thought. *Where was* I love you and I made a horrible mistake?

"You had to know this was coming," Hilary said.

David stared at her. He couldn't believe what he was hearing.

"Are you serious? You're gonna tell me this is my fault?"

"You know, this past year was hard on me too," she said.

"It was hard on you that *my* mom died? Oh, real sorry about that."

"This is why I haven't been able to talk to you. You won't listen," Hilary said.

"No, I'm listening. Tell me how it's okay that you slept with one of my teammates."

"I'm not happy when I'm with you, David!" Hilary said. "What do you want me to say?"

That hurt.

"This whole time I thought you cared about me," David said.

"I do. I've been there for you. Through the funeral, through everything. Every day. You know I was."

"And then every day, you snuck off to bang Sam?"

"No," she said. "I've only been seeing Sam a couple weeks."

"Only?" David laughed in disbelief. "What do you even see in that jackass?"

"He's got big dreams," she said without hesitating. "He's going somewhere."

"Wow. Who the fuck are you?" David said.

Hilary jutted out her jaw in that certain way she did when she was about to boil over.

"I didn't change, David, you did! What happened to the guy who gave a shit?"

"I'm right here."

"Yeah? 'Cause I only see the quarterback who quit the team in the middle of the playoffs, the one who stopped hanging out with all our friends. I waited for you. I honestly thought you'd pull your shit together and try to be happy again."

Hilary leaned forward, pointing at him.

"But then I realized that you want to be miserable," she said. "You don't ever want us to hang out with anyone, you spend all day alone, you work extra night shifts at the supermarket, all so you never have to move on."

"You're too good to date someone who works at a supermarket?" David said.

"I'm too good to date a loser."

Her words were a kick to the balls. At first it was pure shock, then the shock gave way to a terrible, clenching ache that hurt worse and worse with every second.

Hilary's venom seemed to drain out of her. Her posture became awkward, and she backed toward the door.

"I'm sorry," Hilary said.

She opened the door and left.

David emerged from the bathroom ten minutes later with his chest out and his shoulders pulled back. He pushed through the crowd in the hall, ignoring the watchful eyes around him.

He stepped into the living room. It was large with reddish wooden walls, like a cabin in the woods. The high ceiling had two large skylights, blacked out by the dark night above them. The wood floor was scuffed and brown and tilted to the east. There were two couches and two recliners, all pointed toward an obscenely large big-screen television, not a flat screen, an old six-foot-tall black box that dominated the room and played a muted NFL game on its burned-out screen. The music was fast and harsh but was nearly drowned out by everyone talking over each other. He saw guys using thin excuses to touch girls, and he saw girls flawlessly acting like they didn't know what the guys were up to. People were clustered into separate groups all across the room. There were almost as many new kids as familiar faces, transplants from all across Colorado, thanks to the job boom in Pale Ridge. David watched as a new kid orbited the different groups like a party satellite, hoping to penetrate one of the circles. All the kid was looking for was a little approval, just a slight parting of a circle or a nod of acceptance. He hovered around one group after another until the message sank in. They all knew he was there, and they weren't going to let him in. The kid shuffled out of the room, straining to look casual, red keg cup clutched in hand, in search of other circles that might be less selective.

There was a time when David had ruled high school parties. Back when he was team captain, when his mom was alive and Hilary was his girl. David hadn't come to a party in nine months. In late November, his mother died in a fatal car accident. It felt unreal to David. She'd left for a two-day business trip to Cincinnati and then blinked out of existence. After that, almost everything in his life seemed unimportant.

Especially parties like this. David ignored the urge to walk to his car and drive home. That would only prove Hilary right. And she was wrong, he was no loser. Maybe he had let things slip a bit. But he was the same guy. He could face this party, no problem; he just needed a drink.

David slogged to the kitchen. It was stuffed with people and hot from all the bodies. The floor was covered in a slippery grit of beer and grime off the bottom of people's shoes. He weaved through the mass of tipsy kids, toward the collection of open liquor bottles clustered on the kitchen counter.

David had his eye on a half-empty bottle of cheap vodka. He reached for it. A pudgy hand got to it first and gripped the plastic bottle with a crunch. He locked eyes with Alan Woodward, one of his former teammates, a fat-faced kid who was built like a brick chimney. Alan's cheeks were flushed red. They were always that way, whether he was making a tackle or sleeping in class.

"Dave-o," he said with a raspy, halfhearted laugh. "You're the last guy I expected to see here."

"I'm turning over a new leaf," David said.

"Uh . . . how's it going?" Alan said, still holding on to the vodka bottle. He leaned on it like a crutch.

How's it going? That was a loaded question. Where did he start? Did he go with *Hilary just dumped my ass in the bathroom*? Or did he go all the way back to when he and Alan stopped hanging out? When he stood in front of the whole team in the locker room after winning regionals and told them that his heart just wasn't in it anymore and he couldn't lead them to state. Alan had been the most devoted of his teammates, bringing guys by the house to try to change David's mind, saying that they believed in him and that Coach Barter said they had a real chance of winning their first state championship. He remembered Alan telling him that focusing on the team might be just the thing David needed. David remembered thinking that Alan didn't know what the hell he was talking about, none of them did.

"Things are going pretty good," David said, still eyeing the vodka.

"Yeah?" Alan said.

"Sure," David lied. "Ready to drink you under the table."

Alan stared back at David with a smile.

"You serious?"

David grabbed two wet shot glasses from the sink and plunked them down in front of the vodka bottle.

"Let's go shot for shot, we'll see who's serious," David said.

Alan clamped down on David with a bear hug. He held it for too long, but David didn't mind. A hug was exactly what he needed.

"You're not gonna grab my ass, are you, buddy?" David whispered.

Alan burst out with a laugh. David smiled. Alan had a great

quality of laughing at almost everything. He'd laugh so hard, it looked painful. Alan let go, still smiling.

"I'm so glad to see you, man!" Alan said.

Alan poured out two shots in a hurry. He gave a glass to David, and David took it gladly.

The booze burned his throat, then spread warmly into his stomach. He wanted more.

"WHOO!" Alan said, and slammed his glass down on the counter at the same time as David.

"Again," David said, loosening up his shoulders.

"You're out of your mind if you think you can outdrink me," Alan said. "This shit's in my blood. My grandfather was Siberian."

"You know how many times I've heard this bullshit?" David laughed. "You're gonna end up puking in the bushes, just like always."

"Oh, now you're talking war, Cappy!"

Alan poured two more shots.

David hadn't heard anyone call him Cappy in forever. Just hearing the name brightened his mood. As he downed that vodka shot, and the next, and the next, David laughed with Alan over little things. Inside jokes he'd forgotten, awesome games they'd had, epic touchdowns he'd thrown. He'd turned his back on all of those memories when he walked away from the team. Back then he was a leader. He knew how to win.

He wasn't a weird guy restocking yogurt with sad graveyard-shift coworkers at Safeway. He was captain of a team of guys who would fight for him. They'd been like family to him, and he'd shut them out.

Vodka soaked David's brain. A fuzzy warmth dulled his senses. He made a grab for the vodka bottle. It bounced out of his hand and skittered across the counter. Alan brought his fist down hard and crushed the plastic bottle.

"Killed it!" he said. "C'mon. There's a keg outside. The rest of the team's out there too . . . in case you're planning on any big announcements."

David looked at Alan, confused. "What are you talking about?"

"I don't know," Alan said. "I just thought maybe if you're back, like old times . . . then you're back. You know?"

Back? Like back on the team? David couldn't believe he was actually considering it, but for the first time in a long time, that sounded . . . really good.

What the hell?

"Yeah," David said. "I'm back."

Alan punched David, jaw agape.

"You'll come to practice on Monday morning? For real?" Alan said.

"I'll be there," David said. Just by saying it he suddenly swelled with strength. Why couldn't he do it again?

Alan raised both fists in the air, *"Yes!"* He grabbed David by the sleeve and pulled him away from the counter. "You gotta let me break the news!"

David followed Alan through the warm forest of bodies, toward the sliding glass doors to the backyard. Just as they got to the doors, Alan saw someone he knew, and he stopped to lock the dude in a bear hug. David didn't pay attention to who it was; he was looking at Sam.

Half the football team stood around the deck as Sam hazed a younger teammate, forcing the kid to chug a beer. He tripped the kid, making him flop face-first onto the ground. Some of the team laughed, and Sam's face transformed at the sound of it. He had the delighted expression of a child receiving a surprise present. As the kid tried to get up, Sam pushed him back down again with his foot. Sam looked to the team for a bigger reaction. Fewer of them laughed this time. Sam snapped at the kid to get up as if it were the kid on the ground's fault that the gag didn't land a second time.

David remembered when Sam was the one being hazed. Last year, a senior, Carson Lacy, spread IcyHot all over the inside of Sam's jock strap. Someone had done the same to David his first year—it was standard. You ran to the showers and washed it off. Not Sam. Later that day, in the weight room, while Carson did bench presses, Sam threw a twenty-pound dumbbell down between Carson's legs. Carson ended up losing a testicle. In the end, Coach Barter just looked the other way, because David quit soon after. The team needed a quarterback, and Sam was the only other one.

"Hey, sorry. Let's do this," said Alan.

Alan patted David on the shoulder and walked out to the deck. David followed slowly. The deck was as wide as the house, went back a good twenty feet, and it was thick with kids. The sky was just a touch lighter than black. The area was lit by the low, warm light of novelty chili-pepper string lights around the perimeter of the deck. A drunk girl on the grass fell and knocked over a copper fire pit. Flaming logs toppled onto the ground and coughed up a cloud of sparks. She lay laughing on the damp grass, beside the cooling embers.

David felt more out of control with every step toward Sam. An image flashed in his mind of Sam and Hilary in bed together. Hilary throwing her head back in ecstasy, her lips quivering, her blonde hair whipping across her wild eyes, Sam's hands moving up her.

Sam laughed about something. David hated Sam's fake smile. He hated his pig nose and that ridiculous dimple in the middle of his chin. The closer he got, the more he was certain that Sam was the cause of all his misery. He blamed Sam for losing Hilary; he blamed him for his mother dying, for the year of grieving that followed. He put it all on Sam. Through the haze of all those vodka shots, it was clear as day.

"Look who showed up to rage tonight!" Alan said to the guys. "He's got some big news!"

Sam saw David approach; his face flinched.

David's old teammates hollered back halfheartedly. A warm *Hey, old friend* kind of smile blossomed on Sam's face, but David was sure there was panic in his eyes. Sam walked toward David, his arms spread out for a manly hug.

"This party just got killer," Sam said. "What's the big n—"

David interrupted Sam by bashing his forehead into Sam's teeth. Sam let out a grunting whimper and fell to the floor. David kicked him, then he kicked him again. Sam spit blood onto the keg. David tried to drive his foot straight through Sam's body, to make up for all that David had lost.

The team rushed forward and grabbed David. They wrenched his arms behind his back. Alan stood there in shock, staring at David like he was crazy. Spit was falling out of David's mouth in ropes. It took four guys to drag him into the kitchen. He saw the outdoor crowd's disgust, their fear of him. He saw Sam on the ground, holding his bloody mouth; and just before the people in the kitchen blocked his view of the deck, he saw Hilary's face in the crowd outside. He swore she was smiling.

3

DAVID DIDN'T WANT TO GO TO SCHOOL.

Monday's morning light taunted him through the windows of his bedroom. He'd spent all Sunday in bed, nursing a wicked hangover and beating himself up for having drank so much that night. Why couldn't he have just gone home after Hilary broke up with him?

His hangover was gone, but he felt even worse today. What he'd told Alan wasn't drunken bullshit, it was true. He did want back on the team, he did want to lead them again. But he had obliterated his chances of that ever happening when he attacked Sam. As half the defensive line dragged him through the party, he'd heard whispers spill out from the crowd. *He's a maniac. . . . He just snapped. . . .* When his former teammates tossed him onto the brick walkway and slammed the front door in his face like he was a stranger, he knew that he had severed whatever was left of their bond.

This day was going to suck. Sam would want payback. Everyone was going to be gossiping about him. If it were up to him he'd skip today. But he had to go. Today was his little brother's first day of high school.

David peeled back his flannel sheets and stood. His room was in shambles. There were used plates and glasses on the floor along with piles of dirty clothes, free weights, and one overflowing trash can. He couldn't believe he had gotten used to living in such filth. He resolved to clean it up the minute he got home. David pulled on a frayed T-shirt that was draped over a lamp, and then some dark jeans from the floor. He'd had these clothes since football season of last year, and they still fit. He slipped on a black hooded sweatshirt and pulled the large hood over his unruly brown hair. David dug his feet into his favorite beat-up sneakers and took the stairs down two at a time.

He stepped into the kitchen and smelled burned food. The room was small, with counter space and a breakfast nook taking up most of it. The walls were painted the color of marmalade, and the lace curtains his mother had made cast floral patterns across the floor. His little brother, Will, stood in front of the fridge. He was short and stringy, and he drank orange juice out of the carton with the refrigerator door wide open. Smoke plumed up from a pan on the stove. David ran to it and switched off the burner.

"What are you doing?" Will said.

There were pancakes in the pan, dry and brown on top, charred black on the bottom. "You're gonna burn the house down," David said. He took the pan off the stove and walked it to the trash.

"Whoa, whoa, there's nothing wrong with those," Will said.

"They're incinerated."

"I like 'em crunchy," Will said. He took the hot pan from David. David shook his head. There was no use arguing. Will was too stubborn.

Will slid the stiff, blackened disks onto a plate. David moved to the counter and opened Will's epilepsy medication. He shook out some pills.

"Already took 'em," Will said. David gave Will a puzzled look. "Dude, if I managed to remember taking my meds for three weeks on the trail, I think I can manage myself from now on."

Will sat down at the kitchen table with his burned breakfast. It had been their father's idea to enroll Will in a three-week leadership expedition called Wild-Trek. He'd left for Utah kicking and screaming, but when he'd come back four days ago, he was more confident than David had ever seen him.

"So you take one trip with Chazz the Scoutmaster—"

"He's a wilderness instructor," Will said.

"Right. One trip with him, and you're a brand-new man, huh?"

"Somethin' like that."

"So you're probably not scared about this being your first day of high school or anything."

"Nope. I'm gonna rule that place. It's just another challenge for me to overcome."

Will had been talking in aphorisms and affirmations since he got back from his trip. David had to admit, he was a little jealous of Will's newfound positivity.

"So, what happened out there at this big sausage fest?" David asked. "Did you guys give each other a lot of back rubs and stuff?" David did his best meathead voice. "You climbed that rock like a champ today, Chazz. C'mere and lemme lube up your thighs.'"

Will laughed. He had black flecks of char on his teeth. Will had their mother's sharp, angular features, not like David who had a rounder, fuller face, like their dad's.

"It wasn't a sausage fest. There were girls," Will said.

"There were girls? Or there was *a* girl?"

"No. There were girls. It was a coed trip."

Will blushed. David laughed. "Now it all makes sense! You come home all smiles, and you clean up your act. There definitely was a girl. What is she, like, a hippie chick?"

"Don't worry about it, it's none of your business."

"Did you make out with her? I hope you at least tried, you don't want to get stuck in the friend zone."

"I don't want to talk about this," Will said.

"I'm going to need her phone number."

"Shut up."

"Ooh, and her e-mail address. I've gotta send her pics of that time you cried watching *Finding Nemo*."

Will threw a burned pancake at David like a Frisbee. It bounced off his shoulder. David laughed. Teasing aside, he was happy for Will. His little bro was growing up.

"How was that party the other night? I thought you were dead up there yesterday," Will said.

David deflated at the mention of the party. What could he tell him? That the party was all right, until he committed social suicide?

"It sucked," David said.

"You know you have to start taking me to these parties. You promised you would once I started high school."

David didn't have anything to say. Will was so pumped, so enthusiastic to start his high school life. David hoped that he hadn't ruined it for Will already, because whatever horrible reputation he had created for himself this weekend, he might have branded Will with it too, just by being his brother.

Above their heads, the blue sky was limitless. David drove Will to school in his old '95 Jeep Wrangler. It had no doors and no roof, just a roll cage and a windshield. The road raced by beneath them. The wind whipped through David's hair and then fluttered down the back of his shirt.

David had no idea what was in store for him once he got to school. He tried to relax and appreciate Colorado's natural beauty all around him. It was true what they said, fresh air made a world of difference. The trees were shifting to the yellow, red, and auburn shades of fall. Even though the road was entirely within the cool shadow of the mountains, the turning leaves seemed to radiate warmth. David watched a single bird above as it flew in the opposite direction of its flock.

"Oh, I forgot," Will said. "Dad called. His trip is canceled, he's coming home tonight."

"What? How could you forget to tell me that?"

"Dunno. Just did."

It was great news. David couldn't wait for his dad to be back. His dad had to travel for work, and when he was gone the house felt so empty. But when he got back, it always felt like a home again.

"How long is he going to be home?"

"He said a week."

David smiled, more at ease than he'd been all morning. Will straightened his clothes and made sure the zipper was cinched closed on his book bag as he had already done twice since they left the house. Will seemed a little more nervous than he'd let on.

"You want some advice about high school?" David asked.

"Sure."

"I'll tell you what Mom told me before my first day."

Will's eyes went wide. He listened without blinking.

"She said be nice to everyone, but if someone is mean to you, be mean to them right back."

"I like that," Will said.

McKinley High School crested over the horizon and stared back at them with its countless, tinted eyes, baring its white column teeth. The main building was a giant gray brick on a pristine, manicured hill. The Pale Ridge city council decided they needed a new, larger high school to accommodate the town's growing population, so they tore down the old one and put this behemoth up in its place. The closer David got to the new school, the larger he realized it really was. By the time he pulled into the parking lot, the tremendous building seemed large enough to fit four of his former high schools inside of it.

David navigated the expansive school parking lot until he found a spot. Rows upon rows of cars gleamed in the sunshine. He and Will got out of the Jeep and joined the sea of kids who drifted slowly through the grid of parked cars, toward the school. David drew his black hood up over his head.

"This is gonna be a fresh start," Will said, staring at the towering three-story block of a building.

"That's right," David said. But he didn't believe it. He felt as though he was walking into a trap. They reached the end of the parking lot. The flow of students bottlenecked at the pavilioned front doors, causing the herd to pack in close and shuffle forward as one big mass, like a crowd entering a concert. David saw Alan standing by the front door, talking to Anthony Smith, Rhodes Dixon, and Brad Hammond, three of Sam's best friends from the football team. Alan made eye contact with David, then stiffened and looked away quickly. That was not good. David stopped walking forward.

He had a strong urge to get back to his car and drive away. He swore he could hear people whispering his name through the fabric of his hood. All of his fears about being jumped or shunned or mocked over Saturday night weren't theoretical anymore. They were real. David's hand closed around his car keys in his pocket.

"Dave," Will said from afar.

Will was ten feet ahead, standing still in the slow-moving crowd and looking back at David. His face was twisted in concern. He looked like he knew just what David wanted to do at that moment.

"You're coming, right?" Will said. His voice cracked as he spoke. David knew that look in his eye. For all his brave talk, Will was scared to walk through those doors alone. He needed his big brother.

"I'm coming," David said.

David and Will walked into their new school together.

Inside, the hallways smelled like paint fumes. The lockers looked fresh out of the factory, the floors didn't have one scuff or stain yet. Everything shined, colorful and bright. The place was so huge it was disorienting.

It took David almost fifteen minutes to locate his first-period classroom. He went inside. The classroom was empty except for Mr. Meyer, his English teacher from last year. Mr. Meyer was a nice guy in his late twenties. His face looked younger than that, but his unfashionable clothes and his weird beard proved that he was a teacher.

"Mr. Meyer? You're teaching world history now?"

"David, hey, man. No, there's no first-period class here."

"1807, right?"

"1807-E or 1807-W? I think you want E. That's the East Wing."

"What the hell, this place is ridiculous."

Mr. Meyer laughed, "Totally, but I guess we're stuck with it. They gave us maps to hand out, lemme get you one."

Mr. Meyer walked to his desk at the far end of the room.

"So, how was your summer, man?" he asked, and rummaged around his desk.

The whole school shook.

A wretched noise erupted from the east end of the school. Books toppled off a shelf above Mr. Meyer and pummeled down onto him. David lost his balance and fell back against the door frame. There was screaming in the hallway. A fog of black smoke plumed up the hall and enveloped him. Shrieking kids fled past David, running through the soot and airborne debris.

Coughing, David scrambled up to his feet and away from the doorway. He scanned the room for Mr. Meyer. His teacher was lying on the floor with books scattered all over him. David ran over to help him up and grabbed his wrist. Mr. Meyer's body spasmed. He vomited up a bloody mass. David jerked his hand away in shock. He met his teacher's terrified eyes for an instant. Mr. Meyer tried to scream but made no noise.

"Stay back," he mouthed silently.

Mr. Meyer's body clenched again, and a second bloody lump came hurling out of him. It sprayed David with a muddled stew of blood and clumps of organ and strings of sinew. Within seconds, Mr. Meyer was dead. There was so much blood. David's legs buckled. He expected blood to come spewing out of his mouth too, but no vomit came. David's mind raced. He started shouting, not even full words, just shouting at the top of his lungs.

Kids were spilling into the classroom from the hallway. They were climbing over each other to get away from the east end of the school.

The hair of every student he saw was falling off in clumps. David reached up and painlessly pulled a handful of hair right off his head. He rubbed the hair between his fingers, trying to process what was happening.

Where was Will? David suddenly stood up. He barreled into the hallway and lunged through a crowd of students, fighting the current toward the hallway intersection where he'd parted ways with Will. Kids were running so fast at David that it was all he could do to just hold on to the door frame and not get swept away in the flow of bodies.

A hand planted firmly on his shoulder. David turned sharply to see Will looking back at him, his eyes frenzied.

"We gotta get out of here," Will shouted.

Will was completely bald, and it was a jarring sight. If his brother hadn't found him, David didn't know if he would have even recognized him.

David pulled Will close. "Are you okay?"

"I think so. What the hell's going on?"

David didn't have an answer. All he knew was that he had to get the two of them to safety. He tried to keep a tight grip on Will, but the surging river of bodies kept separating them. Each time he lost hold of Will, David had to fight the current to make it back to him. It took them ten minutes to make it to the three-story front foyer that led to the parking lot. Bald kids rushed out of the front entrance of the school. Everyone screamed, pushing and pulling to be the next ones out, but the crowd was bottlenecked again at the front doors. David and Will tried to force their way forward, but the crowd was too thick.

The glass of the entryway shattered with an odd series of pops. Then there were more. *Pop-pop-pop!* A piece of white brick exploded from the wall behind David. He yanked Will behind one of the six wide pillars that ran the full height of the foyer.

"What was that?" Will shouted at him.

"Somebody's shooting at us!" David said.

David peered around the pillar and saw the front lawn outside. A line of soldiers was advancing up the hill with assault rifles drawn. They fired on the fleeing kids. David recognized one of them, a kid who'd been in Mr. Meyer's English class last year. He was dashing right at the line of soldiers. When the kid got three feet from the line, the two soldiers nearest to him coughed out geysers of blood and dropped dead, just like Mr. Meyer.

"Oh, my God," David muttered. Will was looking out at the scene now too. David pushed him back behind the pillar again.

Out on the lawn, some lucky students made it to the tree line and disappeared into the woods. The unlucky ones got mowed down by a fresh wave of soldiers, who kept a much larger distance between themselves and the school.

"They're going to kill us," Will said.

David grasped his brother's shoulders and said with as

much authority as he could muster, "Everything's gonna be okay. Okay?"

Will nodded, but he didn't look convinced.

The gunshots stopped. Kids were taking cover now and screaming at the soldiers, pleading to be let out. The soldiers held their ground and kept their guns trained on the students. An amplified voice echoed from a PA somewhere outside.

"All students: remain inside the school! It is not safe for you to leave at this time. Stay back!"

Stay back. Those were the same terrified words Mr. Meyer mouthed at David before he died. And they were the last words any of them heard from the outside for months.

4

IT WAS TWO WEEKS LATER. DAVID HELD MR.
Meyer's ankles; Will walked in silence by his side. They both
wore wet rags tied over their mouths and noses. The smell
of rotting meat was overpowering. David looked down the
ruined hall. He still had to drag Mr. Meyer's corpse another
thirty yards.

The lights above were mostly broken; half of the lockers
were bent and warped from the impact of the explosion. The
hallway ended where the collapsed ceiling formed a dead end
of rubble. There was no more school beyond that. The myste-
rious explosion had amputated the rest of the East Wing, and
this hallway was one of the stumps that remained.

David was sweating. Mr. Meyer was heavier than he'd
expected. Will had offered to help, but David wouldn't let him.

He felt responsible for Mr. Meyer. David was with the man in his last moments, and that felt like it meant something. His corpse made a dull hiss as it scraped against the fractured tiles of the floor. David refused to look down; he couldn't bear the sight of his old teacher's rotten, bloated face.

The teachers had started to smell. Every adult in the school had died the same way Mr. Meyer did. Now there were hundreds of stewing corpses scattered across the building. The students decided as a whole that they needed to do something about it. They couldn't wait any longer for outside help. There had been no contact with the outside since the day of the explosion, since the military welded every exit shut and covered the quad with a translucent, gray plasticlike canopy. No one had been able to get a signal on their cell phones, the landlines were dead, and the Internet was down. The thousand or so students locked inside were going to have to deal with things like this themselves.

Dragging a corpse across the school was nasty business. But at least the effort kept the nagging questions at bay. What the hell happened to them that day? Why did it happen? And what was going to happen to them next? Those were the things that David wouldn't let himself think about. The kids who did dwell on those mysteries drove themselves crazy. They ended up wailing in the halls like lunatics, pleading for answers.

"Fuckin' reeks," Will said.

David looked over to Will. He had white stubble growing all over his head. He looked like an elderly marine. Every student's hair had begun to grow back, all of it white. Something bad had happened to their bodies. They were altered. Sick.

"I know this sounds crazy," Will said, "but this isn't that different from Wild-Trek."

"Oh, yeah?" David said. He'd heard this many times already but was happy to go through the routine again. Anything to keep Will's mood from spiraling down.

"It's just a challenge we have to face. If we dig deep and push past our limits, we'll make it," Will said.

"I think you're right."

Will's voice sounded more hollow than usual. It upset David that, each day, Will's speech lost a little more volume, a little more conviction. At this point, it was less like a conversation and more like Will was reciting a prayer.

"To keep a lamp burning, you have to keep putting oil in it. You know who said that?"

"Mother Teresa," David said.

"Yeah, Mother Teresa," Will said. A loud metallic *klang* made Will flinch.

Behind them in the hall, a tiny white-haired boy with raw, red knuckles sat against a dented locker with his head in his hands. Will's eyes lingered on him. David was afraid he was losing Will.

"But you're right, it's the same situation," David said. "It's just a challenge."

David readjusted his grip on the cold flesh of Mr. Meyer's ankles and shuddered.

"It is the same, except . . . ," Will said.

"Except what?"

"Except I don't know when this situation is going to end."

David dragged Mr. Meyer over to two seniors who stood by an open locker. They wore rags over their mouths, and they had duct-taped their shirtsleeves closed so their hands wouldn't have to touch dead flesh.

The seniors lifted Mr. Meyer without a word. They tried not to look at the body while they pushed it into the open locker and shut the door. They sealed up the vents and the seams of the locker with duct tape, to keep the stink in. A lock went on as a last step. David led Will back down the hallway and tried to ignore that the walls all around them were stuffed with dead teachers.

David and Will lay in the quad. They'd been locked up for almost a month. Electricity and running water still flowed. They had heat. It meant that they weren't entirely forgotten, but it was a small consolation when there was no food left. The cafeteria had been picked clean. They were all starving.

David thought he knew what it meant to be hungry. He was

wrong. This wasn't peckish, this wasn't stomach-growling, this was a transformative, gnawing hunger. He felt as though his brain was shriveling. His eyes would lose focus, his mouth was perpetually dry. He felt mean, like a rabid dog.

Hundreds of other kids lay scattered around in the quad as well. They were all limp, like dead fish. No one wanted to spare the energy to move around. The quad's translucent cover deadened the sun's light, but it was still the cheeriest place in the school. The grass was still green underneath them. The slight heat of the sun felt like a trickle of nourishment to David.

"We're gonna get out of here, Will. You know that, right?" David said.

David made sure to tell him that at least twice a day, whether he listened or not. Will ignored him and looked up to the canopy. There was a distant sound, a light thudding. Moments later, it was a thundering. Everyone heard it now, and everyone was looking up. A seam in the canopy opened that David had never noticed before.

It was the first time they saw the helicopter, the black angel that would drop food and supplies to them every two weeks from then on. When that first school bus–size care package slammed down to earth, its securing cords breaking loose and spilling out boxes and cellophane-wrapped bundles, all any of them could do was stare. After they tore away at the cheap crating and industrial wrap, they found canned food, military ration meals, freeze-dried meats and vegetables, drink powders, energy bars, plastic utensils, water bottles, water, blankets, camping rolls, sleeping bags, first-aid kits, second-hand clothes, soap, detergent, trash bags, and antibiotics.

Kids sprinted into the quad from the rest of the school after hearing the commotion. When they saw the supplies, they joined the surging horde, grabbing whatever they could get their claws into. David found energy he didn't know he had. He and Will split up, running around the pile, through the colliding bodies, assembling armfuls of loot. David saw Will in little flashes as they would pass each other in the scramble. Will had a joyous, almost drooling, smile on his face that matched David's.

The supplies had all been scooped up, but kids were still pouring into the quad in droves. David saw Will near the quad's south wall. They both had a great haul. David could barely hold on to everything as he ran up to his brother.

"Look! Look!" Will said, digging his hands through cans and packets piled up on the ground in front of him. "Can you believe it? They want us to live!"

David wanted to hug Will. But as he got close, Will's smile stretched and contorted into something painful. David heard a gurgling rattle of air escape from Will's clenched throat.

Will flopped to the ground. His face was the purple of a blossoming bruise. Veins popped out from his temple, and his eyes bulged, bloodshot. His hands were splayed and slapped flat against the ground. One leg was raised and bent while the other jerked away like it wanted to detach from his body.

"What's up with him?" David heard a girl whisper.

David moved instinctively, dropping down beside his younger brother. He wrapped one hand gently around the back of Will's head. David tore his belt from his pants and placed it in Will's mouth. Will clamped his teeth down on the belt as he flailed. Urine darkened the front of Will's pants. David placed solid pressure on Will's flailing arms, holding them in place. He stroked his brother's head, doing his best to lull him.

"Sshhh . . ."

In his periphery, David could sense people moving toward him. Anonymous hands reached in and stole a package of blankets that David had snagged in the drop.

"Hey!"

More hands reached in. David couldn't leave Will's side, and the kids around him knew it. More were still piling into the quad, angry that they got there too late.

"Leave us alone!" David shouted.

David kicked and thrashed and yelled at the anonymous looters, but it did no good. They darted in, snatched Will and David's things, and darted back out again. They took and took, and by the time Will's flailing slowed and his breath became more regulated, David had only a lone can of beans left, sandwiched between his belly and the ground.

Will's face was spattered with a froth of his own saliva. His eyes cleared and met with David's. David was devastated by the confusion, the fear, the crushing embarrassment that he saw in Will's eyes.

"You had a seizure, okay?" David said as calmly as he could. "You're gonna be fine."

Will pushed David away and propped himself up on one shaky elbow. Not one of the surrounding kids made a move to help or asked if anything was needed. They watched.

Will pulled himself up.

"Don't get up. You need to—"

David tried to stop him, but Will batted his hands away. Will peered back at his audience and then glanced down to see his piss-soaked pants. Someone in the crowd snickered. Will opened his mouth to speak but didn't. David saw what looked like tears in Will's eyes. Will ran across the quad, through the white-haired crowd. David ran after him. He blocked out the smirks and the grimaces and the looks of pity from the scavengers around him.

He had to catch up with Will. He had to tell him everything would be all right. He had to keep him calm, even though their worst fears had been realized. Will's epilepsy medication had run out weeks before, and this, the first episode in well over a year, was bound to be followed by many more.

Sixty-eight seniors were now dead. No one knew what it

meant. They had gone the same way as the teachers, in fits of gruesome vomiting that spilled their very life onto the floor. Every passing week claimed more seniors. The ones still alive, about three hundred or so, had become erratic and volatile out of fear that any day could be their last. Assaults and robberies became things the student body now had to fear. The seniors acted crazy. They wanted to live it up, to have sex, to gorge themselves on food, to pick a fight and win it, but the next moment they'd curl up into a ball and yank on their hair. Their manic weeping was the school's new soundtrack.

David waited for Will in a janitor's supply closet. They had been sleeping in this eight-by-seven-foot rectangle for a week. The walls were lined with empty metal shelves; pillagers had picked the room clean except for a lone mop head without a handle.

In the beginning, everyone slept close together. The large rooms of the school such as the cafeteria, the commons, the auditorium, and the gym, were communal sleeping areas. It felt safer to be with a large group. It wasn't that way anymore. The cutthroat struggle for supplies didn't end when each food drop ended, it was all the time now. Nothing truly belonged to anyone, and once you had something valuable in your hand, you had to start looking over your shoulder.

The door to the janitor's closet opened, and David braced himself for a fight. Will walked in. David relaxed. Will had torn horizontal rips all down the legs of his jeans. Since the seizure in the quad, he'd cultivated a bad attitude to make him seem more intimidating. David knew the truth. Will was scared shitless. He'd had two more seizures in the past month, and there was no way of predicting when the next would be.

"Where were you?" David said.

"Out getting this."

Will dropped a box of tampons on the floor.

"Feelin' a little moody?" David said.

"They'll trade high."

"And how'd you get those?"

"I went to the drugstore. Leave me alone," Will said.

Will flopped down in a metal folding chair.

"I told you to stay here," David said.

"Yeah. I heard."

"It's not safe for you to go out alone."

"I don't want to hear it, David."

"You think I want to sit here worrying that you might have seized somewhere? You could get robbed, or worse."

"It's not your problem!"

Will got out of the chair and paced around the cramped room.

"I'm running at the next drop," Will said.

"No, you aren't."

"I am, and I'm not going for the bare minimum, like you. I want the good stuff."

"It's too dangerous for you," David said.

"This whole place is dangerous. We're stuck here. We're not getting out. I'm gonna get my loot before my time is up."

David hoped Will didn't really think he was going to die in this place.

"They're going to let us out, Will."

"I'm running."

"No, you're not, and that's final!" David said.

Will stormed off into the hallway. David followed him through the doorway, but when he got to the hall, Will was already running around the far corner.

"You're gonna die in here," said a voice from a nearby classroom. It sounded familiar. David paused. A window shattered in the same room. He flinched.

"You'll die in here. . . ."

Kerrang. The sound of metal striking metal.

David edged toward the room.

Kerrang.

The light from the hall glinted off metal as a figure swung a chair against the steel plating the military had secured beyond the window frame. *Kerrang.*

The figure dropped the chair and tumbled away from the sealed window. The person threw himself prostrate onto the floor. He let out a low, defeated moan and sobbed. Maybe he'd gone stir-crazy, like so many. Maybe he was a senior who knew he was about to die. If that were him at rock bottom, or

Will, David would want someone to reach out and help.

"You okay?" David asked, and stepped into the doorway. The person jumped like he'd been jabbed by a cattle prod, and looked up. It was Sam Howard, his eyes stained red from crying. David tensed up. Sam scrambled back into the darkest corner of the room.

David hadn't seen Sam since everything had gone bad. Did Sam want revenge, or was that ancient history now? In the wake of such a huge tragedy, Sam and Hilary hooking up hardly seemed important anymore. Even still, it did make him happy to see Sam acting so pathetic.

"Everything's going to be all right," David said. Then he couldn't help himself. "You don't have to cry, man."

Sam charged out of the blackness at David. He was fast. He shoved David, and David fell to the ground. Sam stood over him.

"You stay away from me, Thorpe. Me and my team. Nothing's changed."

Sam disappeared around the same corner Will had turned earlier. David punched the floor in frustration. He couldn't believe he'd tried being nice to that prick.

David would never forget the arc of blood that sprayed from Danny Liner's neck as he clutched the wooden shard planted deep in his throat. That was when the school truly changed.

It happened following a violent drop in which David saw a freshman get his leg broken so severely that a jagged piece of bone tore out of his shin. Two sophomore girls had clawed deep grooves into each other's faces over a rare bottle of moisturizer.

When the drop was over, everyone had retreated to the sidelines to go hide their haul somewhere. Sam and six other guys from the football team had joined forces that day. They'd gone so far as to give their little gang a name, Varsity. Working together, each Varsity member secured twice as much as they would have alone. Varsity was the talk of the quad. Everyone was already forming little groups of their own to run with in the next drop.

The Varsity guys were carrying their shares toward the exit, but Sam lingered by his own pile, right in the middle of the quad. He was eating a strip of beef jerky. Torn cardboard and trampled packaging littered the area around him. It was a brazen act to eat in public. No one did it anymore, unless they wanted to get robbed.

"If you distract him, I can get his food. We'll be set till the next drop," Will said.

"Are you nuts? We're not stealing his food."

"It's not his food, Dave," Will said. "He's just standing next to it."

David watched Sam tug on the jerky with his teeth. He hoped he choked on it. David was still burning from their run-in, but that didn't mean it was okay to rob Sam. Slashed jeans were one thing, but Will thinking assault and robbery was a swell idea troubled David. Danny Liner, one of the remaining seniors, strode across the quad and planted himself between Sam and his food. They were too far away for David to hear their conversation, but the situation was clear soon enough. Danny slapped Sam across the face with a heavy hand. Sam toppled backward onto the ground, amid the fractured wood of the supply pallets.

Will clutched his stomach and laughed loud enough for the entire quad to hear. Sam's face flushed red. He got up, with a shard of wood in his hand the size of a railroad spike, and he buried the thing in Danny's neck, right under the Adam's apple.

"Whoa," Will said.

All noise stopped. Conversations died midsentence. People forgot what they were doing or thinking or saying, and they watched Danny squirm and twitch on the ground. His neck was a fountain of blood, spraying a raspberry stream with each heartbeat, each stream arcing lower in the air than the last. Moments later, Danny Liner was another corpse lying in a blood puddle.

No one spoke. There had been ruthless competition, fights, robberies, and injuries, but never murder. Sam looked nearly as surprised as everyone else. He stared at Danny's body with confusion. There was a line of Danny's blood across Sam's face, like a drizzle of chocolate syrup over a scoop of ice cream.

Sam's gaze moved from Danny to the disturbed crowd, who still struggled to make sense of this. Something switched. Sam began to stalk around Danny's body and stare into the crowd like he was challenging them to meet his eyes.

"That's right!" Sam said.

David moved Will behind him out of instinct.

"Nobody takes my food! You hear me?"

Sam panned across the gaping faces until he settled on David. He held his stare.

"Nobody!"

"This is all your fault," Will shouted at David as they ran. Five members of Varsity chased Will and David through a dirty, cluttered hallway. David ran by a crying girl who threw a brick into the last functioning ceiling light above him. The fluorescent tube burst into a puff of glass powder, and that section of hallway went black.

"It's 'cause of your bullshit."

"Shut up!" David said.

David yanked Will into a girls' bathroom by the collar of his shirt. Inside, three girls crowded around a fourth who was sitting in a desk chair and had her hair soaking in a sink full of yellow liquid. Lemon Kool-Aid packet wrappers from the drop littered the floor.

The girls' heads turned as one. David could hear their pursuers run past, down the hallway. The fourth girl lifted her head up from the sink. It was Hilary. Her wet hair was a vibrant yellow.

"David?" Hilary said.

She looked into his eyes. God, he missed her! She was the only one he could ever really talk to. He wanted time to stop and everyone else to fade away. The other girls began to shout.

"Help!" they screamed.

Will pulled David out of the room, back into the darkness. The five Varsity guys ran at them from the far end of the hall. David and Will sprinted past four classrooms and rushed down a flight of stairs.

They took every odd turn they could, doubled back, and ended up in the foyer of the school, on the main staircase. They stopped, hearts thumping and legs ready to quit. There was no sign of Varsity on their tail. The glass front wall that once let in brilliant sunlight, now mostly shattered, looked out to a cold wall of steel sheets welded together. Will slumped down against the wall of the main staircase, while David checked all exits.

"I think we're good."

"Screw you. They want you, not me."

Will was right. Sam had been using Varsity to terrorize David in the weeks since he'd killed Danny.

"I'll get us into one of the other gangs," David said.

"Wake up, David. Sam's got it out for you. No one is going to take on Sam as their enemy just to let you in. He straight up killed somebody."

David was tired, and he was sick of Will's attitude.

"Don't kid yourself," David said. "Nobody wants you either."

"I'd have a lot better shot if I wasn't hooked up with you."

"Then be my guest. Go ask one of the gangs. Just try not to piss your pants while you're doing it!"

Will jumped on him. David knew he'd taken it too far. Will hated to admit it, but no gang wanted him with or without David. His epilepsy made him a liability. Will got David in a headlock and tried to squeeze the life out of his neck. It was a solid hold, and Will was giving it everything. He was stronger than David thought. David slammed Will hard against the wall, and his brother's grip popped loose. David slipped out.

Will grabbed a shard of glass off the steps and thrust it in front of him like a knife. He pointed it at David. David stared at the shard.

"What the hell are you doing?"

Desperate anger contorted Will's face. Blood dripped from his tight grip on the shard. His breath sputtered like he was about to cry. Three Varsity guys ran into the room from the first-floor hallway. David and Will ran up the stairs but stopped halfway when the other two gang members appeared at the top of the flight. Will swung his glass shard wildly at them. The Varsity guys closed in on them from both sides, taking one slow step at a time.

"Don't worry, guys," one of them said, laughing. "Sam's got a real fun game set up for you in the gym."

A hissing-popping sound rang out. David took his eyes off the Varsity guys. Sparks flew from a central metal plate at the school's front entrance. A molten red line was being cut through the steel in the shape of a doorway. When the sizzling red line met the floor, the metal cutout toppled inward, sending dust whooshing up in a filthy cloud. Outside, it was dark. It must have been night.

The Varsity guys forgot about David and Will entirely when twenty soldiers, armed with machine guns and wearing black haz-mat suits, hustled into the foyer. With military efficiency, they secured the entrance in a semicircle formation, guns ready to fire at any sudden movement. Their faces were shielded by the tinted lenses of their masks. Students who had wandered in shouted down the halls for everyone to come quick.

The soldiers said nothing as they erected a set of heavy, hinged steel doors to the outside. More and more students flooded into the room and onto the stairs, staying a good thirty feet from the soldiers until it was standing room only. Each new gang was represented: the Geeks, the Nerds, the Sluts, the Skaters, the Freaks, the Pretty Ones, and Varsity, which was now made up of every male athlete in the school.

No one spoke to the soldiers, for fear of getting shot at again. The more kids who appeared, the faster the soldiers worked. Within a half hour, they erected a single-occupancy booth equipped with an identification scanner and a video screen above it. It was stationed off to one side of the steel doors. One of the soldiers powered up the booth. The screen flickered to life, and a man in military fatigues appeared on-screen. He was in his forties, with hair so thin on top it looked like a brown mist hanging above his scalp. The skin under his drooping eyes was dark and sunken. The crowd of students collectively leaned forward for a better view of the twenty-inch screen.

"I don't know where to start," the man said through the tinny speakers in the booth. The speakers' feeble volume put a hush over the crowd. No one could bear to miss a word.

"I'm Colonel Bernard Richards. I'm here for the day to oversee the installation of the equipment you're watching me on right now. Your government would like me to express its—"

The man paused to swallow.

"*Our* regret that you've been left alone so long with so many unanswered questions. I will try to explain the current situation as best I can. You are carriers of a contagious, parasitic virus. In the simplest terms, the virus thrives only in the bodies of pubescent teenagers, and it makes you fatally poisonous to everyone else. Any adult or any young child who comes within a few feet of you dies almost instantly. The toxic pheromone you now produce attacks the tissues of the lungs, rapidly breaking them down. It would be the equivalent of inhaling a highly potent acid. Your virus was engineered, illegally, by the labs of the nearby weapon manufacturer, Mason Montgomery Technologies. You may know it. Some of your parents may have even been employees there. A military task force was sent in to investigate the illegal activity and shut them down. There was a raid. They found teenagers held captive as test subjects for the virus."

The man stopped. He took a long drink of water and kneaded his eyes like he was working a knot out of a muscle.

"The raid," he said, "did not go as planned. One of the infected teens escaped. Once outside, he stole a car. He was chased and very nearly caught. But he got away on foot, and he ran into your school. Knowing the catastrophic repercussions of an entire school becoming infected with this virus, the decision was made to destroy the East Wing of your school."

The crowd gasped. People began to talk, stirred up by the implications. Others hushed the talkers so that the rest could be heard.

"We fired a missile. The hope was that we could minimize the casualties, destroy the virus, and spare the lives of the rest of you. The virus was not destroyed, as you know. Despite our efforts, many infected students escaped that day, and they have infected other teenagers. It spread far faster than we could contain it. More than three thousand died in the first forty-eight hours. Colorado is under evacuation orders, but as you can imagine, that has been an extremely challenging and complicated process. Meanwhile, the virus continues to spread, and casualties are mounting. We hope to reach containment of the virus soon, but there is no way to know when. The situation changes every day."

People around David were starting to panic as the impact of those statistics settled in.

"Do you think Dad—" Will said to David.

"No," David said, cutting him off. "He was traveling that day, remember? He was in—"

"California!"

"Right. He's fine." That seemed to be enough for Will, and David was glad to have a believable answer for once.

"I do have . . . good news," the man continued. "As puberty declines, the virus will leave your body. When it has completely left your body, you will lose your immunity to the toxic pheromones, and any exposure to infected teens will be fatal. What you see before you is an automated testing station. To operate it, place your thumb on the scanner. Press firmly and you'll feel a slight prick, but be patient. If you are transitioning out of infection, the screen will display your scheduled release time, which could be immediate, or somewhere within the following twenty-four hours. At such a time, return to these doors, and scan your thumb again. The doors will open, leading you to a containment chamber, and from there you will be transitioned back to the world outside."

Excited whispers danced out of the darkness. The man cleared his throat. "The telltale sign of the virus leaving your body is a bloody nose. It could happen two or three times in one day. Do not wait to schedule your release. The further you get into that second day, you will be plagued by headaches and then dementia. On the third day, you will have a hacking cough, and death will come quickly."

He loosened his collar and let out a weary sigh. "I wish I could tell you that more improvements are on the way and that we will open up communications between you and the outside. But there are a lot of people who want your school destroyed. The nation is divided on what should be done with you. We are stretched beyond our limits, and all of our efforts must be directed at the management of the epidemic outside. Hang tight in there. We're doing the best we can."

The screen went dead, and one of the soldiers muttered into his headset microphone. The steel doors swung open from the outside. One by one, the soldiers backed out of the school with swift precision. There was a sudden surge of sound as kids shouted every possible question they could think of, all at once. But within seconds, the soldiers were all gone, and the doors were securely shut. Kids rushed the entrance. Some went straight for the doors, bashing against them in the hope they would give way. They didn't. Most gathered around the testing booth, pushing and pulling for a chance to get their finger scanned.

Will looked to David. He smiled with excitement. It was the first happy moment David had shared with his brother in months. David imagined those steel doors in the foyer opening up for them both.

A Nerd and a Freak fought over who could use the scanner next. Both of their gangs got involved, and the area around the booth became a messy brawl. A Varsity was hit by an errant elbow meant for a Freak, and the rest of Varsity joined the violent tumult. David tugged Will away from the spectacle, and they rushed back to their supply closet home.

David and Will sat and talked for hours. They dreamed of the day they'd get out. They each made big plans for their first day back on the outside. They convinced themselves the outside would be safe again by the time they transitioned out of the virus. They talked about how differently they'd live their lives once they had a taste of real sunshine, fresh food, and natural air again.

All they had to do was stay alive.

5

DAVID LEAPT OVER A BLUE-HAIRED FREAK.

The drop was in full swing. Red, blue, black, and yellow heads of hair swirled and collided with each other all around him. A mound of boxes, packaged supplies, and glinting silver bags of powdered soup sat in the middle of the dead brown grass of the quad. People tore away at the edges of that central pile as fast as their hands could grab the items.

A fight erupted between a Skater with a triple Mohawk and a stocky Geek whose black hair had a thick orange stripe down the side. They fought over a box of salt and tumbled into David's path. David roll-dodged around them and kept sprinting. He felt like he was back on the football field, running it all the way to the end zone.

A red-haired Slut to his left got cracked in the head when

she stooped to pick up a package of men's briefs. There was a lot of blood. Scalp wounds always bled a lot.

David doubled back to face the central mound again. The multicolored battle in front of him looked like a blood-soaked Skittles commercial. David actually liked that each gang had its own signature hair. It helped him gauge danger. If there were too many of any one color, he knew to steer clear of that area.

Know what you want, grab it, and get out. That was David's rule for the drops. He kept running, swaying with the sea of lunging bodies, and scanning the ground for neon-green boxes of detergent. Most people went for food and clothes and blankets and the like before they worried about laundry supplies. David's livelihood depended on things staying that way.

A string of bulky figures in stained white athletic jerseys and football helmets advanced in unison, creating a moving wall toward the densest group of boxes—the food. Varsity laid claim to most of the food, every time. The shrink-wrapped clusters of military rations and canned goods shimmered in the dim sunlight that passed through the gray canopy. When a pint-size band Geek tried to dart through an opening in the jock blockade to get to the food, the nearest Varsity member reached out and clotheslined him. The kid dropped like a sack of rocks, then gasped for air on the ground.

David heard a chain reaction of laughter to his right. He

turned to see a group of girls jumping up and down, clapping and letting bloodthirsty screams rip. Their hair was the color of lemon sherbet, and it undulated with the bounce of their bodies.

"Kick that Geek in the face!" yelled one.

Their skirts swished side to side with every gleeful cheer, giving anyone who dared to look a peek at their perfect legs.

"Make him bleeeed, Varsity!" squealed another.

David loved and hated the Pretty Ones. His body wanted them, they were the prettiest after all, but his mind knew it was smarter to fear them. They were partnered up with Varsity, and David still made consistent daily efforts to fly under Varsity's radar.

David spotted a fellow Scrap on the sidelines, another white-haired kid like him, with no gang. The Scrap's face was gouged with scars, and two thirds of his right eyebrow was gone. The kid ran into the fray as fast as he could with his limp. He made a grab for two shining soup bags on the ground. A pack of Freaks sprinted past, knocking him down and trampling his hand. The kid barked in pain and abandoned the soup. He scurried back to the sidelines, holding his bent claw with his good hand.

David needed to keep his mind on the game, but he couldn't. That Scrap would probably starve if that hand didn't heal right. He ran an arc around a cluster of people who fought over a new pair of jeans. He snatched up the soup packets and tossed them to the Scrap. The kid picked them up, smiled at David with genuine surprise, and staggered away. Whatever grungy mouse hole that kid was crawling back to, at least he'd have something to eat there.

David caught a glimpse of neon green through the flickering of running legs. A box of laundry detergent sat perfectly on top of a hot plate. He sprinted toward it.

As David wove his way through the fray, a giant Varsity was doing the same from the other direction, his eyes fixated on the hot plate. David could try to snag the hot plate too. It would catch a good price in the market. But a broken leg could cost him everything, and then Will would have no one to look after him. David plucked up the detergent and kept running. The trihawked Skater from earlier, his box of salt locked under his arm, pounced on the hot plate. He had it in his hand for only an instant before the Varsity steamrolled him into a concrete bench. The Pretty Ones erupted into more cheers as the Varsity did an end-zone celebration dance.

David made one last circle around the edge of the drop. One box of detergent was all he needed, but if he could get another, or a replacement sewing kit for tailoring jobs, that wouldn't hurt. There were fewer people fighting now, and the bigger items were already taken. Skaters loaded their loot into their cage on wheels, constructed out of sprinkler pipes and duct tape. Most of the movement on the quad came from the writhing of the wounded.

There was nothing left to grab. David peered to the southeast corner, his rendezvous point with Will. His brother wasn't there. Nausea curdled his stomach. He whipped his head back in the direction of the drop, looking frantically for his brother, sweat stinging his eyes.

Finally, he spotted Will, not far from where the Skater met the bench. He was making out with a Scrap girl with tangled white hair. David jogged to them. Their mouths were mashed together. Will was bigger now, thanks to a recent growth spurt. He looked like a young man; there was no trace of boy anymore. His body was lean and wiry, and apparently it was working on the ladies.

"Will," David said with a grin.

The mouth-mashers separated, their lips still wet. David had to stifle a laugh; he knew the girl, she was Weird Peggy. Scratch that big brother pride he'd just felt. Peggy was David's year, and she used to come to school every day in an old top hat, the same one that lay at her feet at the moment. She prided herself on being as unique as possible, but David never really thought she had a choice. Grooming, normal conversation, and pauses that weren't painfully awkward were all things beyond her capabilities. He would have been more impressed if he found Will making out with his own shoe.

"Oh. Wow, I didn't know you two were together," David said.

Weird Peggy brightened at the notion.

"We're not, we're nothing," Will said.

Weird Peggy held a frown for a moment then shrugged, put her top hat back on, and ambled away.

"After everything that's been destroyed, why did that hat have to survive?" David said.

Will said nothing. He wiped his white mop of hair from his brow, shoveled his loot from the drop onto his threadbare sheet, and bundled it together into a sack. Will stood and avoided David's eyes.

"So . . . Peggy?" David said.

"Lay off it."

"Hey, I think it's great you have a girlfriend—"

"She's not my—you listen, you're not allowed to give me shit about this," Will said.

"I don't know . . . see, I kind of feel another comment coming on."

"Oh, yeah? Sure about that? Then I guess you don't want any of this then."

Will produced a plastic jar from his sack with an inch and a half of creamy peanut butter at the bottom of it. David could almost smell the nuttiness through the jar. Thick, oily, and dense but still dripping, oozing. Pure fat packed together with so much body it might as well have been meat. He imagined it coating his mouth, working its way between his teeth, spreading its sweet butter over the back of his tongue and leaving a film that would linger on his taste buds for days.

"You traded for this?" David asked.

"Guilty," Will said with a smile.

Will popped the jar back in his sack and strutted away. David remained under the peanut butter's enchantment for a moment, before he caught up with Will.

"What did you trade, a kidney?"

Fifteen minutes later, David pulled his tools from a rolling backpack and laid them out on the crusted bathroom floor: the new detergent, two buckets of soapy water, one ripped yellow dishwashing glove, three toothbrushes for heavy stains, a penknife for gunk, a plunger handle, an eyedropper, chalk dust for grease, salt for blood, and a soda bottle of ammonia. David took a bundle of white clothes out of the backpack and plunged it into one of the buckets. He agitated the garments with the plunger handle.

Laundry was David's daily routine. It wasn't what he wanted to do; nothing about it was fun, and there was no end to it. It was what he had to do to keep them alive; this was his job.

Naturally, Will did nothing to help. He did push-ups in the corner. Again.

"If you're not watching the door, help me wash," David said.

"I'm watchin' it."

"You're staring at the floor."

Will groaned.

"What good does it do anyway? Not like there's a back exit," Will said. He sprang to his feet. "If a gang finds us, they'll jump us. If they don't, they won't."

"Right, right. If we starve, then we starve, why worry?"

Will stayed silent. He interlocked his fingers behind his back and stretched his chest.

"Do something for once. Humor me," David said.

"On it," Will said. He flexed his triceps at himself in the mirror.

David sighed. Will was never going to learn. He bore down on a brown stain, scrubbing the blouse's fabric into itself and grinding in the gritty salt.

"When I graduate," David said, "you're not gonna have anybody to mooch off of."

Will rolled his eyes.

"You're gonna need a trade. Lemme teach you my system."

"I don't want to learn your system."

But he sure loved eating the food David's system bought.

"You gonna flex for food?" David said.

"I'll come up with something. Something good."

"One person can't survive off only what they get at the drops. You're not Gonzalo."

"Whatever I do," Will said, "it won't be washing blood out of other people's clothes."

David stood. Tossed the garment aside. He got in Will's face.

"Hey," David said, "straight up. I want you to answer me."

Will tensed up, ready to defend himself.

"Was it the top hat that turned you on?" David said.

Will curled his lip, faking a laugh.

"Yeah, fine. Fine. I hooked up with Weird Peggy," Will said. "You happy? It's your fault."

"Interesting. Explain that to me."

"Tell me who I'm supposed to date. Can't date girls in gangs. And that's pretty much every girl. Off limits. Whose fault is that?"

He didn't say it like a joke; his words had teeth. David wondered if Will would ever forgive him for the life they had to lead.

"So," Will continued, "there's Scraps. Weird little losers scattered through the school, hiding in their holes, probably eating flies, and hoping no one hits them that day. That's who I get to pick from. Thanks."

Will returned to the corner and dropped to the floor to knock out reps. David's desire to win the argument died somewhere during Will's speech. David faced himself in the mirror. He examined his white hair, the stained clothes in his hands, the filthy bathroom behind him; it was just nasty enough that no one else would want to use it, a place where he could feel safe that no mob of kids would wander in and rob him. He could handle these indignities for the handful of months he had left. But he knew Will couldn't, he knew Will wouldn't try. And he was scared of what Will would try when David was no longer around.

6

THE WET CLOTHES WERE HUNG UP TO DRY where no one would find them, and David's dry deliveries were folded and packed into his bag, ready to be exchanged for food and essentials. Will and David stood at the mouth of the bustling market.

It was a wide hallway, with classrooms on either side. Each gang transformed their own room into a trading post, in which they offered their particular goods and services. The floor was marred with dirt, tracked in from the quad. All the ceiling lights worked, a rarity in McKinley. Other than in the trading rooms, the gangs did not mix. Each stayed with their own and traveled in large groups from room to room until their shopping was done.

David had deliveries to make to the Geeks and the Sluts. He

strode into the market, with Will a step behind. A surly group of Skaters stepped out of a classroom and crossed the hall in front of them. A pack of Freaks crossed too, from the other direction, making it impossible for David and Will to pass. David got a good whiff of the toilet bowl cleaner they used to dye their hair blue. He'd never understand how they could live with the chemical smell.

The two groups slowed as they passed each other. They bared their teeth, cracked their necks, and walked far too close to be friendly. One Freak's face was badly busted up. He shoved a Skater. Both gangs tensed for a fight. David kept his eyes on the Skater. If he attacked, David knew both gangs would go at it. He recognized the kid, Jason he thought his name was. David remembered that Jason and the busted-up Freak were really tight before the quarantine; they always ate lunch together, just the two of them. Jason spit at the Freak and walked away. His gang followed him. David relaxed.

He and Will approached the guard outside of the Geeks' trading post. The guard had his hair dyed in multicolored stripes.

"Laundry for Zachary," David said.

The guard nodded them in. There were tables of drawings from art Geeks on offer, all too expensive unless you were a Varsity or a Pretty One. A girl with caramel skin sat on a stool and sang her own take on a ballad that was on top of the charts right before the quarantine. A bucket drummer and a kid with a three-string guitar accompanied her. David watched her push out the high notes as she rocked her hips back and forth slower than pouring honey. All the Geeks dyed their hair black with charcoal as a foundation, then added touches of loud color by dying sections of their hair or weaving colored things through it. They dressed in bright colors as well, with carefully chosen items of individual flair. As a group, they were boisterous, bawdy, and generally hard to miss, which was probably the point. They wanted all eyes on them.

But no one commanded as much attention as their leader, Zachary. The guy wore a cape. It was made out of two school flags sewn together and slathered with gold poster paint. That would have won the battle for attention right there, but he was the only boy in school to buy the wigs the Pretty Ones sold. Today his hair was long white braids, with ribbons of brightly colored paper woven through each one.

"David!" Zachary said, and clutched David's hand melodramatically. "I knew you'd come."

"Got your laundry here."

"Why are you really here? Let's talk about that."

"Laundry."

"You tease and you tease." Zachary squinted at David and smiled. "That's probably why our first kiss will be so electric."

"More likely, that would be a Taser I'm hitting you with," David said with a smile, and pulled a stack of Zachary's clean clothes out of his rolling bag.

Zachary chuckled, loving it. "You could be an actor, David. Think about it. I'll write a scene for us. It could be in the next Geek show."

"I'm shy," David said with a grin.

Zachary held out six Geek show tickets, but drew them back when David reached for them.

"Do you love me?"

"Oh, Jesus," Will said. He shook his head and walked over to a table where tattoo designs were displayed.

"David, what's with him?" Zachary said. "I know he's your brother but . . . attitude adjustment, please!"

"He's jealous of your hair, which looks fantastic today, by the way," David said.

"Mmm. I'll have more clothes for you tomorrow, pretty lips," Zachary said.

Zachary handed him the tickets with a wiggle of his eyebrows. David collected Will from the tattoo area and hurried to the hall.

"Are you sure you're not gay?" Will said. "I can't believe you go along with that stuff. I wouldn't have."

David ignored him. He held up a bundle of black clothes for the tall girl on guard duty at the Sluts' doorway.

"Go 'head," she said.

Before David could enter, a herd of eight blonde Varsity linebackers trudged out of the room. David spun his back to them. He whipped his black hood over his head. He hoped his body blocked their view of Will. They sounded drunk. He could almost feel a hand about to thud down onto his shoulder, but then their footsteps faded.

He opened his eyes. Will was looking at him with a face like he'd just sniffed rotten milk. David dared a look over his shoulder. Varsity was gone. Why were they here? Did they not go first today? They always demanded to trade first. That was why David had spent so much time washing clothes earlier, to avoid them. But this was an awful reminder that no matter how many precautions he took, he was never truly safe. Will shook his head and walked ahead of David into the Sluts' trading post.

Inside was an expanse of red hair. You could tell what flavor of Kool-Aid the girls used, cherry here, fruit punch there, a faded pink that probably was strawberry but needed a re-dye. Two Sluts slap-boxed just inside the entrance. Nearly all of them wore tight black pants, and there wasn't a sleeve left attached in the whole room. The Sluts were not a rich gang, they had no special item or service, but they traded almost everything. If you wanted it, they probably had it, which was great for anyone who didn't want to, or couldn't, get their supplies from Varsity. The Sluts were the only gang with an open-door policy. As long as you were female and you were willing to fight tooth and nail on the quad, you could have a place in the Sluts.

David spotted their founder, Violet Kelly, behind a trading table nearby. She went by the name Violent now. Violent wore football shoulder pads with broken pencils sticking up out of them like porcupine quills and a necklace made of sharpened cafeteria cutlery. Violent had the reddest hair in school, and her eyes were icy blue. She had shaved off her white eyebrows and replaced them with fake ones made of carefully cut pieces of black electrical tape.

David approached her. She was counting out condoms for a Geek girl, who traded them for a three-pack of fresh athletic socks.

"Got your order," he said.

Violent looked up at David, her face pinched in aggravation. "What?"

"Delivering your stuff."

"Oh. These better be spotless, Jacob."

"It's David, but yes, don't worry . . . they're clean."

She stayed suspicious as another Slut collected the laundry. David could never tell if he really had remained a stranger to Violent week after week, or if she just wanted him to think so.

"Didn't I call you 'Ragman' last time? I like that. That's your name, Ragman."

"You could call me David," he said. Violent didn't laugh. He pushed on. "So, we're looking for the usual, a week's food, whatever you got. We have six Geek show tickets and these items for trade." Will lifted his sack of loot from the drop onto the table. Violent looked through Will's items and fixed him with a direct look that made him blush. She grinned.

"Kathy, bring me five days' worth, on the light side."

A Slut girl brought over a small collection of canned fruit, canned tuna, refried beans, dry soup, and two bottles of tomato juice. As David stuffed those items in his bag, Violent stared at Will with increased interest.

"What's your name?"

Will met her stare with a look of defiance.

"I'm Will."

"That's not a lot of food for a week, Will. And there's two of you."

"What about it?"

"Ooh, he's got a little fight in him," Violent said to the other girls. "I'll tell you what about it. I could help you. I have a lot of food, I got everything. Maybe you should come visit me some night. I'll make it worth your while."

David stopped putting the food away. He watched Will stand there, frozen on the edge of a response.

"What do you say, girls?" Violent said to the entire room. "Would he make a good rent boy or what?"

Sluts converged from around the room, circling Will,

looking him up and down, squeezing his arms, giggling, and detailing their opinion of each part of him, like they were buying a horse.

"Rock hard," one of them said with a flare of her nostrils.

Will shrank under all the female attention, overwhelmed.

"All right, all right. That's enough, back to work. Show me some hustle," Violent said.

The girls dispersed. Will's breathing was heavy and fast. David zipped up his bag and led Will away from the table.

"Think about it, Bill!" Violent called out after them.

"I can't believe you went along with that stuff," David said as they entered the hallway. "I sure wouldn't have."

"Shut it."

They had nothing left to deliver and nothing more to trade, but David spotted a medic table set up outside the Nerds' trading post. There was a line of injured people in front, wearing filthy clothes, freshly stained with blood and dirt. Could be good for a quick buck.

David led Will over to the medic table. The Nerds had a couple first-aid kits open and medical books from the library laid out on the table. The Freak at the front of the line was writhing in his seat, getting a V-shaped cut in his arm stitched up with lavender thread. David rooted through his bag to find the mini cleaning kit he kept in there. He approached a couple people who were waiting.

"Get your clothes cleaned before those stains set. I can do it right here for half price. Who wants to save their clothes?"

A few people in line looked over with mild interest. Will hung by the door and peered into the Nerds' room like it was a girls' shower. He stroked his cell phone in his hand. It was caked with layers of duct tape on the back for protection. Inside the classroom, Nerds had refurbished laptops and phones laid out on tables. David could almost hear Will's requests already: *David, can you buy me a charge? Can I get one of their genre packs of MP3's? I need my left earbud fixed.* Will said that kind of stuff every time they passed a Nerd.

"If you don't have a stain," David said to the line, "maybe you have a torn shirt or pants? I can mend that for you."

A frumpy Nerd, who obviously spent no time thinking about his appearance outside of dying his hair plain black like all Nerds, came out of the trading post and planted himself in front of David.

"No panhandling. Come on, you gotta get out of here."

David buried his frustration, put his kit away, and walked. He ignored the heat he felt on the side of his face from people in line staring at him. He hated how low he'd had to bring himself to survive. How far was too far down? He wasn't that Scrap in the quad, but he was close. He was ready to call it a day.

"David, wait up," Will said, jogging after him. "You're just going to leave me there?"

"Oh, sorry," David said. He hurried toward the market exit, past Varsity's classroom. David wouldn't look into it. Not that he was afraid Sam was inside: He knew Sam would be back at the gym at the Varsity drop party by now, drunk on homemade moonshine. David didn't look in because he couldn't bear to see it. He didn't want to see the piles and piles of food or the lines of traders from each gang who stood in there, all at Varsity's mercy. If Varsity was happy with you, the price of food would be low; if they were upset, it would be high. There was always someone walking away from the trading table in tears.

The Pretty Ones' classroom was a different story. David always got an eyeful of that before he left the market. Their room seemed to glow from its pristine white walls. They were the only clean white walls David ever saw anymore. Inside the room was the greatest injustice in McKinley. All of the school's most gorgeous, luscious, kill-yourself-for-them girls belonged to one gang, and they only dated Varsity guys. They wore white dresses. They played with their yellow hair.

David would have gladly done their laundry, but the gym and athletic facilities where they lived with Varsity was equipped with washing machines. They had white-sheeted tables of beauty products on offer, along with hair extensions and wigs. But like all boutique products, they were expensive. Girls from the other gangs had to save up for months to buy a Pretty Ones' product.

As David and Will got close to the doorway, he stopped. He

saw a Scrap girl in a chair on top of a black garbage bag drop cloth. He knew her: Belinda Max. David guessed Belinda had weighed more than three hundred pounds before the explosion, but a year as a Scrap in the shadows had changed her. She'd lost at least eighty pounds, but she didn't look any more confident for it. All David really knew about her were the taunts he used to hear in the halls: "Maximum load!" Belinda shivered in the chair. She had long curly white hair with a bright luster to it.

"Damn, she must be hungry," Will said.

Hilary slid up behind Belinda with a pair of electric clippers in her dainty hand. David still couldn't see her as the head of the Pretty Ones, or maybe he didn't want to. Hilary clicked on the clippers and made one buzzing stroke down the top of Belinda's head. It revealed a wide stripe of scalp. Belinda wept and hid her face. Hilary continued, stroke after stroke, shedding shiny ringlets of white hair down onto the black square.

The school knew Hilary as cruel, even evil. The hottest girl in the hottest gang, who showed no mercy for anyone and never lifted a finger. David couldn't stand that he was still attracted to her, but he was, even while she shaved a poor fat girl's head.

Hilary looked up, right at David, as though she could smell his eyes on her. He tried to read the expression on her face but couldn't. He wanted to talk to her.

"Are we goin'?" Will said.

David turned his head. Will was twenty feet ahead of him, at the exit. He looked back to Hilary one more time, but his view of her was blocked.

Sam stood in the doorway.

His blond eyebrows were bunched up like train cars in a horrible accident. David only met the wrath in Sam's eyes for a moment. He instinctively looked down and scurried out of the market, feeling like the slave who had dared to look the king in his face.

7

THE FOYER SMELLED LIKE A DIRTY OVEN.

The floor was charred from a trash fire that had gotten out of control a few weeks earlier. The linoleum tiles had warped and scarred like a burn victim's back. Dim light glinted off scratches on the steel entrance doors. They were names. All of the students scratched their names into the metal when they graduated. Beside the doors was the graduation booth, as it had come to be called. The small screen above the thumb scanner, inside the booth, played a loop of a health video from the military.

David hummed one of the cheesy jingles from the video as he waited for Will to finish up in the bathroom. Even though it was barely audible from this distance, he knew it well. It would be stuck in his head all day now.

Only minutes before, a large crowd of Freaks had gathered to see their gang mate graduate. The kid had scanned his thumb and been verified. The doors opened for him, and he entered the containment cell on the other side, which was a coffin-shaped capsule big enough for only one person. The doors closed, and he was gone. It was a near daily routine. Only a handful of Freaks remained in the foyer, telling stories about their friend who made it out and forecasting their own graduation day. David couldn't wait to be out either, for all the same reasons as anyone else, but at the moment, it was just so that he'd never have to back down from Sam again.

"Hey!"

David jumped. He turned and saw Dickie Bellman standing behind him. Dickie had been student body president at the time of the quarantine. He still wore his tie and jacket from the day of the explosion, but now they were stained and rank. His eyes sparkled with excitement, but his teeth were so yellow, it looked like he slept with a mouth full of coffee every night.

"Jeezus, Dickie," David said. "What do you want?"

Dickie presented a clipboard with a frayed, water-stained notepad clipped to it and a pen dangling on a string.

"I've got a petition going to get our cell phone service and Internet switched back on. We really need your support on this one," Dickie said with an insistent nod.

"No, thanks."

Dickie stared back, baffled. "We've all got to work together, David. Don't you want to call people on the outside? Your parents? Doesn't the student body have a right to communicate with the world? We are very close to getting this issue handled."

Dickie leaned in as if he was about to let David in on a big secret. Up close, any semblance of competence dissipated. As he whispered, his breath hit David's nostrils, smelling like pure ass.

"I've got 'em on the ropes, David. I mean, we're talking about maybe a couple more months. If that."

"A couple more months . . ."

"Until they let us all out. All of us. I've got their word."

"Their word? The military? You're talking to them?" David asked.

Dickie nodded. "Every day. They trust me, David."

David grinned and signed the petition. Dickie beamed and patted him on the arm.

"You won't regret it. You're a friend to the cause, David. Remember to vote for me again next year," Dickie said.

"I'm graduating."

"Right. Well, I'd appreciate it if you put in a good word with your brother for me," Dickie said, then trotted off, petition in hand. Sometimes David envied Dickie. Physically he was locked in there with the rest of them, but mentally he was somewhere else entirely. In Dickie's mind there had been more contact with the military since that lieutenant explained everything to them. There was more than just food every two weeks. For him, there was a dialogue happening with the outside, and it gave Dickie constant hope that things were changing for the better. Must have been nice.

David's eye was drawn to a girl by the stairs, beyond the Freaks. She had the lightest skin he'd ever seen. She stood out against the blackened backdrop like a dove in a storm cloud. She wore a tattered white dress and clutched a white leather pocketbook in her hand. Her hair was yellow. She was a Pretty One.

David found himself wandering closer to get a better look. Something didn't feel right. The girl was alone and inching toward the graduation booth. She looked around nervously, stepped inside, then laid her thumb on the scanner. Moments later, a buzz echoed out into the foyer, and a message flashed on the screen in large block letters:

VIRUS ACTIVE. NO RELEASE SCHEDULED.

The girl blankly stared up at the screen. She placed her thumb on the scanner again as if she hadn't even seen the results. Another buzz rang out. This time, she winced at the sound. The remaining Freak stragglers watched her and chuckled.

The girl started to whimper. This was not the place for a breakdown. Her eyes were wide and heartbreakingly vulnerable. David thought she had a face like the angel statues in the cemetery where they'd buried his mother, minus the bird shit.

David looked for the cursive letter *P* that was stenciled onto every Pretty One's white sweater. It wasn't there. Instead, there was an ugly rip that exposed the skin of her chest.

He scanned the foyer again. One of the Freaks whistled in her direction. David didn't like the look of any of them. They must have seen her torn sweater and made the same assumption he did.

She had no one protecting her anymore.

Everyone knew that if you messed with a gang member, you had their whole gang to answer to. But if your gang tossed you out, you were back to square one. This girl was too beautiful to just blend into the background. She would always be noticed. If she bluffed that she could handle herself, she might have been able to walk past those Freaks without being bothered. But she was trembling, and they had stopped talking to each other entirely. Their eyes stalked her.

The girl looked from face to face for a friendly one. With each look, she lost more hope until she locked eyes with David. He looked away; he couldn't help it. David glanced back to the bathrooms. Where was Will?

The girl clutched her bag to her belly. She searched for a way out of the foyer, but there were Freaks between her and every exit. She backed toward the booth again, terrified.

David tightened his grip on his overstuffed backpack. It was filled with everything he had to eat. He'd get a bit more for laundry during the next two weeks, but this was most of it. He couldn't risk losing it all to help her.

She tried the thumb pad again. The speakers buzzed. It seemed louder this time. All the Freaks in the foyer pushed off their respective walls at once, like foxhounds who'd just heard the hunting horn.

This wasn't David's problem.

The guys crept toward her, hungry grins on their faces. He wanted her to run. This was her last chance to get away. She huddled farther back into the booth instead and pulled the glass door shut. The guys collectively surged forward. The fox had trapped itself.

"Whoa. What do we got here?" a voice bellowed out of the shadows. Everyone turned to see Brad Hammond in his football jersey and Nantucket red shorts, party cup in his hand. His thick calves crisscrossed as he trudged down the stairs, drunk.

"These guys bothering you, sweetie?" Brad slurred as he stepped into the foyer. The comment prompted the Freaks to back off, fast. They wanted no trouble with Varsity, especially Brad. He was Sam's best friend.

"You guys think you're gonna get something going with a girl this hot?" Brad broadcast as he approached the graduation booth. He stared down every single guy who had been moving in on her.

"Nah, none of you little bitches got the ca-HO-nays," Brad grunted.

Brad waved them off and spun back to the graduation booth. He peered through the glass at the girl, who had not moved, her back still pressed against the farthest corner. Brad studied her with the curiosity of a kindergartner staring at a hamster in a cage.

"What's the matter?" he said in a softer voice.

"I'm fine," she said.

"Why don't you come out of there?"

The girl didn't move. So Brad opened the door for her. She jumped.

"Relax." Brad grinned. "You think I'm gonna hurt you?"

"No." She shook her head. Brad squinted his eyes. The big rusty gears in his head were clunking into place. He looked back at the Freaks, still frozen in place. His face darkened with ominous intention.

"Get lost," Brad said, and the onlookers scattered. He didn't seem to see David. Brad turned back to the girl. As soon as he did, the Freaks crept back around the corners to watch. None of them wanted to miss what was bound to be major gossip fodder. They might even be able to spin a trade out of their story.

"You're like a little bird," Brad mumbled, taking a step into the booth. He tried to stuff his empty plastic cup into his pocket, but it slipped out of his hand and rattled onto the floor.

David's view of her was completely obscured by Brad now. His chest tensed, and he edged forward. Brad's voice devolved into a drunken murmur. He was so wasted. How was he even standing up?

"No, Brad," she said. "Leave me alone."

David had moved close enough that he could hear their hushed conversation. He was out of the shadows now, much closer than any of the other spectators dared go. He didn't really know why. What he did know was that he couldn't fight with a Varsity.

"No? Who do you think you are?" Brad said.

"I'm a Pretty One," she said, with a sudden burst of confidence.

"Oh, really? 'Cause word is you got kicked out."

He's not going to rape her. He's just trying to scare her. David looked back at the rest of the spectators and prayed that one of them would intervene. As a group speaking out, maybe they could diffuse the situation. Some of them looked upset, but the gleam in their eyes was sadistic. They weren't going to stop this spectacle. David felt a drip of sweat slide down his temple.

"C'mere, party girl," Brad cooed as he pawed at her.

"Get away from me!"

She threw all her weight against Brad in a moment of bravery. He wasn't expecting it, and the booze slowed his reaction time. She squeezed out of the booth.

"You're not going anywhere," Brad said. He was angry now.

Brad yanked her over to him by her sleeve. His hand flopped down on her thigh, and he roughly tugged her dress up toward her hips. Her eyes locked with David's. Something gave way inside him. David let go of his bag. His feet broke into a run before he'd even decided to do anything. His whole body flashed hot. In five steps he crossed the foyer and clumsily kicked Brad in the side with all the momentum of his run. Brad shouted in pain and fell away from the girl. He looked up at David, shocked and angry.

"Walk away, Brad," David said, standing in front of the girl, shielding her.

"Oh, did you decide to get brave now, washing machine?" Brad said as he pulled himself off the floor. His face convulsed with rage. "I'm gonna break that neck."

Brad swung at David's chin with bad intentions. David ducked, but Brad's fist glanced off the crown of his head. It threw him off balance, and David knocked the girl onto the ground behind him. A burning pain flared across his skull. Brad cocked his other fist back, but David was faster. David threw everything he had into an uppercut. It connected with Brad's chin, and David felt something pop in his own shoulder. Brad staggered back. He slipped on a pile of ash, fell, and cracked his head on the industrial steel of the graduation booth. His body went limp.

David was in an adrenaline haze. Baring his teeth like an

animal, he spun around to face any other attackers in case one of the shadow kids had suddenly gotten bold. The first face he saw was Will's. Will was rushing into the foyer twenty yards away. His face was a mask of confusion. He looked from the girl to David to Brad, like it was a puzzle he couldn't make sense of.

"What's going on?" Will dashed over to the girl, who was still on the floor, and grabbed her by the shoulders. "Lucy, are you okay?" he said.

Will shook her when she didn't answer.

"Lucy?"

The girl wasn't listening. She was staring right through Will, up at David.

David floundered, trying to catch his breath. A voice floated in from what seemed like an ocean away. He couldn't hear the words exactly. David turned to see one of the Freaks who had been hiding in the shadows. He was now kneeling over Brad.

"What'd you say?" David asked.

"Brad's dead."

8

THE HALLWAY WAS DARK. THE ONLY SOUND was the shuffling of the girl's and Will's feet behind David.

"Hurry up," Will whispered.

David realized he was creeping along at a snail's pace. He couldn't be too careful. There were plenty of witnesses to what had just happened. Word would travel fast. Distant fluorescent light from an adjacent hallway gleamed off the aluminum of the bashed-up elevator doors at the end of the hall.

The girl coughed. Her name was Lucy. Will knew her somehow. He insisted she come with them. It was the last thing David needed now, a third wheel. David waited for a moment in case the cough prompted any hidden attackers to step forward. Nothing happened.

He waved for Lucy and Will to follow. He tried to move

slowly, but with every step toward home, he couldn't help but speed up. By the time the three of them reached the end of the hall, they were all running. David threw open the door to the electrical closet, a few feet right of the aluminum elevator doors.

"Get in," David said. Will gently took Lucy by the hand and led her inside. David made one last scan of the hall for any sign of approaching intruders and ducked in, pulling the door shut behind him.

Inside the closet, Will was already climbing up chunky machinery to a small ventilation duct, the width of a large pizza box. He slid himself in feetfirst, then turned back to Lucy and extended his hand to her.

"I've got you," Will said. There was a good-natured smile on Will's face that looked foreign to David. Will hoisted Lucy up into the vent, and David followed. David crawled blind through the cold metal air duct. His mind flashed bright with images of the scene in the foyer. The furious uppercut. Brad's head cracking against the metal of the booth. The awful silence that followed. The Freaks all stared at David like he was a monster. When he'd stumbled away from Brad's body, some kids jumped back like they thought he might come after them too.

David squeezed out of the vent and into the pitch-black elevator shaft. He descended a few rungs of the metal maintenance ladder and dropped down onto the top of the elevator car. It creaked under the weight of three people, and every noise they made echoed as if the shaft had no bottom. He reached up and pulled his backpack after him.

David couldn't see two feet in front of him. Will pulled open the emergency hatch of the elevator they were standing on. A weak brown light drifted up from the car's interior. It illuminated the crisscrossing laundry lines David had rigged all up and down the elevator shaft. Clothes hung down, still damp from the scrubbing earlier in the day.

"Here, let me help you," Will said. He took Lucy by the forearms and lowered her down inside until her toes touched the floor. David didn't like this. No one was ever supposed to know about their home.

"Lucy, I need to talk to Dave here for a sec," Will said. "Make yourself at home. I'll be right down. I can't wait to talk."

Will dropped his smile and closed the hatch. David heard Will clomp toward him. He could just make out Will's face inches from him.

"What the hell were you thinking?" Will said. "You had to do it again. Do you know how much shit is coming our way now?"

"It's . . . I reacted to the situation, I didn't know he would . . . We'll figure something out."

Will's face was barely visible, a dark, judgmental blur. David felt Will's finger jab between his ribs. David shuffled back and caught himself at the edge of the elevator car. One more step backward and he'd plummet.

"You're not dragging me down again."

"She can't stay here," David said.

David heard Will back away. Will opened the hatch and dropped down inside.

David had killed someone. He had to steady himself on the elevator cables. His hands felt numb, but his nerves buzzed. How the hell did that happen? It was just a punch, and now Brad was gone. A whole history, a whole life. Done. He was probably being stuffed into a locker somewhere near the gym, with all of Varsity in the hallway, watching, and pacing, and hatching bloody plans to make things right.

David walked toward the light of the hatch. He lowered himself down inside.

When David landed in their crowded box, Will was wearing that good-natured smile again and lighting candles. Lucy looked all around at her new surroundings. The low voltage emergency lights cast a straw-colored glow onto the six-by-six-foot space. Shelves made from the tops of classroom desks lined the walls up by the ceiling. The lowest shelf contained all of David's and Will's food supplies and two sets of clothes for each. The upper shelf housed everything else: makeshift weapons, knickknacks that David and Will had salvaged from their lockers, library books, and everything else they owned.

David's laundry supplies were gathered in a cinched sack that hung from the ceiling to save floor space. Their beds took up most of the floor, makeshift mattresses that were just piles of discarded clothes. There was about two square feet of clear floor space left. That's where Lucy sat, her knees pulled in close to her body.

Will finished lighting the candles. They were precious supplies. Normally, David would get mad that Will was wasting them, but what did it matter now? Will pressed a button on the control panel, and the emergency lights turned off. The elevator car was dark and warm by candlelight. Will fished out a piece of dry bread from his loot sack, broke it in half, and handed half to Lucy. As she took it from him, their fingers touched. David noticed that Will let his fingers linger on hers longer than necessary.

"Lucy, you have nothing to worry about, okay?" Will said.

The tears collecting in Lucy's eyes threatened to spill over, but she tapped them dry with a square of white cotton from her purse. She took a bite of bread and tried to settle herself.

"I like your place," she said.

The sensation of his fist connecting with Brad's jaw flickered through David's knuckles again. For an instant, he reveled in it. No matter what he told himself, he had enjoyed knocking Brad to the ground. Before that Freak said Brad was dead, David had felt a rush of pride filling his chest.

"Thanks," Will said. "I can't believe you're here."

"Well, I was in the neighborhood. Thought I'd just drop by," Lucy said.

Will laughed. David looked up at Lucy. He was surprised. It took a certain strength of character to crack a joke after what she'd just been through. Lucy met his gaze. It seemed she wanted to say something to him, talk about what happened probably. David looked away—he couldn't bear that. He needed to do something. He got up, grabbed a crumpled bottle of water off the shelf, along with a toothbrush and detergent. He fished a T-shirt out of his sack and sat back down on his mattress. David set to work, scrubbing wet detergent into a soot stain.

"You look so different," Lucy said, still eating.

"Oh, yeah? You look great. So great," Will said.

"I've seen you at the market," Lucy said. Then, as if she was apologizing, "I wanted to say hello."

"Me too," Will said.

David felt Lucy's eyes on him. He didn't look over.

"The last time I saw you, you were wearing those ripped-up pants," she said.

"Yeah," Will said. "Those were cool."

Lucy laughed. "Do you measure cool by how much thigh hair you have showing?"

"Maybe I do! Got a problem with that?" Will said, and chuckled.

She laughed again, but it was wilting and quiet.

"We're going to get through this," Will said. "It's just another challenge. Just like Wild-Trek."

David stopped scrubbing. It all clicked. That's why Will insisted this girl come back to the elevator. This was the girl he met on his camping trip in Utah. He and Will had been joined at the hip for over a year in this place, and Will had never mentioned that Lucy went to McKinley. Why hadn't Will told him?

"You're right," Lucy said. "Thanks, Will. You're a good friend."

"So . . . what happened?" Will asked.

"Hilary kicked me out of the Pretty Ones."

David looked up at her.

"Yeah, she's a bitch," Will said, knowing it would piss David off.

"Bitch doesn't cover it," Lucy said. "She's psychotic."

"Psychotic how?" David said. Lucy looked him in the eye.

"She tells every girl who they're expected to date. The Pretty Ones depend on Varsity. We—they wouldn't survive if Hilary didn't keep Varsity happy."

"She made you do that?" Will said.

"She tried. I found ways to avoid the arrangement, y'know? I stayed busy. I worked the door at the girls' showers and helped make beauty products. I actually developed a new shade of lipstick using a box of red pens I found."

Lucy brightened for a moment.

"I flirted when I knew Hilary or one of her suck-ups was watching. And then I'd—" Lucy suddenly laughed. Will sat up, moving closer. The candlelight lapped across her face.

Will took Lucy's hand in his. "What? What did you do?"

"When the girls weren't looking, but I knew Varsity was, I'd always try to throw in a belch or a snot rocket. The grosser it was, the better. Anything, just so they'd leave me alone."

"Ha!" Will said, and hooted. "I love that."

Lucy gave the faintest of smiles.

"About a month ago, I was changing in the girls' locker room. I thought I was alone, but I wasn't. A Varsity guy snuck in and was watching me. He was one of Brad's friends."

David clenched his jaw. Lucy looked to the ground as soon as Brad's name escaped her lips.

"Scumbags," Will said.

"I screamed, and he ran off. But after that, he started asking around about me. I knew it was only a matter of time. Hilary approached me and said I had to be his girlfriend."

"She said that?" David asked. Lucy nodded. She maintained eye contact with him as she spoke. Her version of Hilary was ugly, and he didn't like it.

"When I told her that I wouldn't, she got this freaky look on her face. It was scary. I thought she was going to stab me. But she just walked away. At first I thought maybe everything was fine. But then the other girls stopped talking to me. Then no one would let me into the bathrooms. And eventually, they wouldn't let me have food. Hilary made everyone freeze me out, even girls I thought were my friends. For a week I was invisible. I was dirty and hungry. She wanted me desperate, I know she did. And I was. She came to me again and asked me if I felt like dating that boy now. I probably would have said yes, I don't know, just to eat. But she brought him with her, and he was so . . . He looked at me like I was his property. I couldn't do it. I said no again."

"Damn right you did," Will said.

"What did she do then?" David said. He'd placed the stained shirt aside.

"She dragged me in front of all the girls. She tore the Pretty Ones insignia off of my sweater. She said I was dead to them. I kept looking at my friends in the crowd, but none of them would look back at me. And then Hilary made an announcement to all the Varsity boys that I was not protected by the Pretty Ones."

Lucy took a deep breath to steady herself. "She said they were free to do what they wanted with me."

"I hate her," Will said. "I always did."

David looked at Will, but Will wouldn't look back. David clenched his eyes shut and rubbed his temples. He wanted to forget everything he'd heard. He wanted to forget that Brad was dead too, but he couldn't.

"I ran out of there. And a bunch of Varsity guys chased me.

All over the school. They kept yelling they were going to . . . use me up. They acted like it was funny. I finally got away from them when I made it to the foyer. I knew I wouldn't be eligible for release, but I was so scared I couldn't think straight—"

Lucy finally crumbled. She couldn't get any more words out without crying. "You saved me," she said between sobs. "I'm sorry. I'm sorry that happened. And that Brad—"

Lucy's tears took her over again. David was glad. He'd heard enough.

"Sam's gonna go crazy," she said.

David stood. He was fed up. He put his tools and the shirt away and snuffed out the candles in his corner.

"I'm going to hide out here for as long as I can stretch out our supplies. You can sleep here tonight. Stay away from the food. I'm going to bed."

He lay down on his bed with his back to them both. He could hear Will say that Lucy could have some of his food. Will could say what he wanted. She couldn't stay.

David imagined Varsity swarming the corridors in search of him. He pictured himself staying in this elevator for months, gripped with fear that the hatch door could be torn open at any moment. That they'd come crashing down through the ceiling, stuffing themselves into his secret home until they blocked out the light. Then they'd stomp him into the floor until he stopped breathing.

David clung to the belief there was a chance of survival. If the elevator stayed hidden and Will found a way to bring him food. . . . If he could trust Will to keep his mouth shut, and if the girl kept quiet, and if no one saw Will come and go and no one caught him while he was out there. If all that, maybe he could last until his graduation. He could find a way to sneak all the way to the front door without being noticed, scan his thumb, and get his walking papers. He might be able to last. In the hour it took him to fall asleep, David's mind whirled with nightmares to come. He did his best to stay focused on the hope that he could do it, that he could get out, without ever having to answer for what he'd done.

9

WILL WASN'T SLEEPING. HOW COULD HE?
Lucy was there. There was only two feet between him and the girl he'd dreamed about since Wild-Trek. And there weren't two inches between her sleeping body and David's. It made him crazy. Before Lucy went to sleep, Will tried to persuade her to take his bed. She insisted on the floor. She said she didn't want to be a burden to anyone. Once she was asleep, it was as though her body was magnetized to David's. She tossed and turned, moving an inch closer here, two inches there. Will could count on his hand how many times Lucy had looked at him since they got back to the elevator. She had spent the rest of the time staring at David.

She was almost entirely on David's mattress now. Was she really asleep? It would be almost worse if she was asleep.

Then she'd be subconsciously trying to spoon his brother. It was torture, and Will couldn't take it anymore.

Will rose to his feet, quiet as a burglar. He looked down at David and Lucy, still curled up together. He knew David was asleep, his snoring had started right on cue. Will monitored Lucy for any more movement. The tear in her sweater revealed the butter-soft skin of her chest as it gently rose and fell with each breath. Were all girls this beautiful when they slept?

He could've stood there and watched her all night, but if he was going to leave, he had to do it now. He slid his fingers up her shoulder. He just needed to make sure that she was asleep first. She didn't stir. He did it again, but much slower, just in case. He could still feel the summer breeze slip through the tent the night they spent together; her head on his chest; the stars twinkling through the mesh skylight overhead; the tart smell of lemon juice in her hair.

Lucy murmured and shifted her body closer to David again.

Ugh. Why did he have to go to the bathroom after the market? He'd been kicking himself for the past year that he never made a move, never took things to the next level with Lucy. Will had planned to ask her out on the first day of school. When the East Wing exploded, it threw his plan off the rails, and it never seemed like the right time after that. How do you ask a girl out when the world's ending? He wanted everything to be perfect when he asked, but once the gangs formed it was too late.

Now, out of the blue, he had a real chance, and David was trying to take it from him. Will should have been the one to save her. He would have done it. And probably wouldn't have killed someone in the process. She should have been looking at him the way she'd been looking at David all night. It wasn't fair.

David didn't get to have Lucy just because Will had to take a dump.

Will pulled one of David's buckets off the shelf and laid it in the center of the floor, upside down. He placed his toe on the bucket and stepped up as quietly as he could. He pulled himself out of the elevator. He'd been sneaking out for months without David knowing. Usually he was satisfied just wandering around, getting into trouble, but tonight he had an actual mission. It was the beginning of a plan that would keep David alive, and keep him away from Lucy.

First step, Will had to get to his locker.

He wasn't dumb. He knew he had to nip this David-the-hero business in the bud. It was just the kind of thing girls melted over. David didn't deserve her; he didn't even know anything about her. He didn't know that she makes amazing quesadillas. He didn't know that she does a hilarious French accent. But Will did. He knew everything about her.

Will stepped out of the elevator electrical closet and into the dark hallway. An uneasy smile stretched his lips. Venturing out now, after what David had done, was idiotic. Danger tickled his fingertips, vibrated through his arms, and sent a shiver rippling up his neck. He couldn't stop smiling. He felt electric.

Will sprinted softly down the hallway, gaining confidence with every footfall. He hated being cooped up in that elevator. Running through the empty halls, all alone, while everyone else slept, he almost felt like he was outside again.

Something rumbled toward him out of the darkness. He jumped into the nearby stairwell. A Skater with a spiked Mohawk bombed past on a longboard, with three full garbage bags slung over his shoulder. The skateboard's rumble came to a stop. Will peeked around the corner. The Skater dropped his bags on the floor and jumped up to place an adhesive label on the high wall clock. It had a ballpoint pen drawing of a duck on it. The Skater picked up his bags, got back on his board, and kicked his way down the hall. Will exhaled with relief. If Will wanted to pull this off, he had to remain unseen. It was a real possibility that some gang could kidnap Will, trade him over to Varsity, and maybe use him as leverage to lure David out of the elevator.

Will ran and fantasized about his plan. He would return to the elevator with enough food for David to survive on for weeks, then announce that it was too dangerous for Will and Lucy to keep coming and going from the elevator. The two of them would have to move out and find somewhere else to live. Together. He pictured the look on their faces when he returned with arms full of food. Both David and Lucy would realize that Will had risked his life to get it. David would flip out, but that would only make Will look more brave.

He snatched up an apple-size hunk of concrete from a pile of rubble and chucked it. It smashed into a PA system speaker, knocking it loose. The speaker hung by a wire and swung from side to side, scraping the wall. It was stupid to make this much noise. There were hundreds of kids sleeping in the classrooms all around him.

Let them come out here and take me on, Will thought. *I'd like to see them try.*

Will took off again. Ten minutes later, he'd reached his locker. It was always a small relief to see the door still there with the lock attached. A lock was a sign of valuables. Will had written *RIP Emmett Dorn* on the front of the locker in Wite-Out. Who would want to open a locker that might have a corpse inside? He dialed the combination, and the lock popped open.

Will's locker was full of months' worth of stolen goods. Sometimes he'd steal something from the market, but most of his best finds were the products of his night walks, when he snuck around the perimeter of gang territories looking for anything left unattended. He'd occasionally find something valuable, but the bulk of his stuff was small things: school supplies, old clothes, books, an occasional laser pointer. But when he'd accumulated enough of this stuff, he was going to trade it all to buy the phone charger that David refused to rent for him. He hadn't listened to his music in months and he wanted to look at his pre-quarantine photo galleries, but tonight, things had changed. Getting Lucy all to himself was way more important than old songs and dusty memories.

Will moved fast, grabbing a garbage bag and stuffing the locker's contents into it. He locked it up and hurried off to where he knew Smudge would be.

Will and Smudge had been friends since middle school. For as long as Will could remember, Smudge had been frail and bony, but now his face was creased with wrinkles that a kid shouldn't have. Will had gone through a growth spurt, like most kids their year had at this point; Smudge hadn't. He was still the size of a child, and he looked about as healthy as an old woman's finger. But he was a survivor. The kid was a cockroach.

Will found him in his usual place, the closet of a first-floor computer lab that no longer had any computers in it. A single candle lit up the closet, casting long shadows up Smudge's gaunt face.

"Willy! How goes it?" he said.

"Same old. Got some big-ticket items to trade tonight, man. You're in luck."

"Same old, my ass. I heard what happened."

"What did you hear?" Will said.

"Varsity is going crazy. They want your brother bad."

"It'll blow over, probably."

"I don't know, they're all having a funeral for Brad in the quad right now. Your bro is suicidal, man. It's retaliation, right? 'Cause Sam shut you fools out of the gangs?"

"No, it's not like that at all."

"Maybe that's not what he tells you, but if I was some football star that got knocked down to being a washing machine, I'd want a little revenge."

"Yeah, laundry this, washing machine that, it's always the same stuff with you," Will said.

"They want to kill him. Straight up. I heard they're gonna cut his head off and play soccer with it in the quad."

Will pictured David's severed head sailing through the air.

"Hey, you okay? You're not gonna spaz out on me, are you? I don't want you peeing everywhere," Smudge said with a flickering grin.

Will tolerated Smudge's shithead comments; he'd known Smudge long enough to know that he was all right underneath. His meanness was his armor. Smudge mimed a seizure, sticking his tongue out and rolling his eyes.

"I'm fine," Will said. The truth was Will hadn't had a seizure in a month, and it was making him antsy. He was due for one. He wished there was a way to induce it himself. Then he'd be able to relax.

"Yeah, but you guys both gotta be crapping your pants, right?"

"Anyway . . . you know who's living with us now?" Will said. "Lucy."

"What! For real?"

"She got kicked out of the Pretty Ones. So we're helping her out."

"How much you charging for rent? A grope a day?"

"Don't be such a scumbag," Will said, and then realized what a pointless request that was.

"You lucky bastard. Seriously, congrats. It's high time you closed that deal."

"It's not about closing a deal, man."

"Oh. My bad. What's it about? Love?"

"No," Will said.

Smudge laughed so hard that drool spilled from his mouth. He shook his head and wiped the errant spit off his chin.

"You actually think you love her!"

"Screw you. Just show me what food you got."

Smudge shrugged and spread a bunch of cans and shrink-wrapped packages of food across the floor between them. He hooked Will's garbage bag with his other hand and picked through it. Will looked over the food. It was enough for David to stretch out for a good two weeks.

A gleam of gold caught Will's eye from inside the closet. He looked closer. It was a grime-covered gold necklace with a sparkling pendant draped across a pile of stolen goods. Will fished it out of the closet. He held it up, the candlelight glittered up and down its gold links.

"Where did you find this?" Will asked.

"Found it in a clogged toilet in the ruins."

Will grimaced at the necklace and dared to sniff the grime. Vile. He gave the necklace another look. If he could polish it up and make it sparkle, no one would know where it came from. He could see the look of love on Lucy's face when he placed it in her hand.

"What do you want for this?" Will asked.

"That's a real top-notch item. I could sell it to a Pretty One for some major loot."

"It smells like a vulture's ass," Will said.

Smudge shrugged. "Well, since you might not be around much longer, I'll make you a deal. I'll give it to you for everything you brought."

"Are you kidding? Just the necklace? That's three months' worth of snatching right there!"

"Hey, listen. We don't have to do the deal. I'm sure whoever you were gonna give this to wouldn't mind a can of collard greens instead."

Bastard. Will felt stuck. It was either the necklace or the food. His brother couldn't leave that elevator; he needed food. Food was the sensible choice.

"You got a deal," Will said.

"You got a necklace."

Will pocketed the necklace, then reached over and grabbed his garbage bag. He turned it over and emptied all the contents on the floor.

"Hey, what the hell are you doing?"

"The bag wasn't part of the deal," Will said as he scrunched up the bag and stuffed it into his back pocket. "Good tradin'."

As Will turned to leave, Smudge piped up. "Hey, where are you guys living now?"

"Ha! Where do you go during the day, Smudge?"

Smudge smiled. Neither of them would be revealing any more.

"Keep your ear to the halls for me," Will said as he walked out.

"I hope she likes it, Willy boy," Smudge called out.

Will chipped the filth off the necklace with his thumbnail as he bopped down the hall. The necklace would put him over the top. No one could get their hands on a new gold necklace in McKinley—they didn't exist. Lucy would be floored. He ran faster, with no other purpose but to run, to pump blood through his veins.

He skidded to a stop when he saw the west entrance of the gym. How had he run that far into Varsity territory without noticing? He nearly darted off the other way, but he noticed the gym was silent. They must've still been in the quad. Will had always fantasized about going to one of Varsity's legendary parties. The drinks, the girls, the food. A brilliant idea bloomed in Will's mind, and he shivered from the sheer danger of it. He fingered the crumpled plastic garbage bag hanging out of his pocket.

Varsity had a giant stockpile of food in the gym.

If Will returned with a garbage bag of food on top of the gold necklace, that would be the killing blow. Lucy would forget all about David, wouldn't she? He had an idea, and before he could decide if it was a wise one, his hand reached out and knocked loudly on the door. He ran back into the shadows. All was still. Will gradually stepped back into the hall. His heart walloped in his chest. He crossed the hall, put his hand on the gym door handle, and pulled open the door. Will stepped inside. There wasn't a soul in the gym.

Holy shit. He was inside Varsity headquarters. The place was a mess. Party cups were strewn all over the basketball court. Individual areas were partitioned by hanging sheets; free weights littered the ground; there was a lounge area; and on the opposite end, a gigantic pile of food cascading down the extended bleachers. Will guessed the pile could have fed the entire school population for a week. It was obscene. Will's pulse pounded with fear and with a raw hatred for Varsity.

He bounded over to the food. He had to work fast; who knew how much time he had left? He shoveled food into his bag. His hands shook. His breaths were short and shallow. It was taking too long to fill the bag. He shoved bread in there, jam, sugar, salami, cookies, canned chili. He couldn't believe it. There was so much. The bag ran out of space. Will cinched it up and dashed toward the exit.

A basketball in the middle of the court caught Will's eye. He stopped. He knew he shouldn't. It was stupid. Pointless. His luck couldn't last forever. But then again, who could say they shot a three pointer in the middle of Varsity's home base?

Will ran to the basketball and picked it up. As soon as he touched the ball, he felt a surge of bravery. He checked the main entrance. Nothing. He dared to dribble the basketball once. The *thwap* of the ball on the floor exploded like a cherry bomb, sending tinny shock waves of sound to the farthest corners of the gym. It sounded too good not to do it again. Will dribbled. Then again. Each loud bounce was like a middle finger in Varsity's face. His heart beat faster with each *thwap*. He took a moment to line up his shot. One more long breath. He let it fly. The ball arced gracefully toward its target. Just as it swished through the hoop, savage bellows echoed in from the market hall outside the main entrance.

Varsity.

Before the ball even hit the ground, Will grabbed his heavy bag and launched himself toward the west entrance. The voices were approaching too quickly. He shifted his momentum, reversed, and dove behind the bleachers. The main entrance doors flew open. The entire gang thundered into the gym. They raged, kicking chairs over, tearing down whatever they could lay their hands on. Will braced himself and stared out at them through the slats of the bleachers.

He watched as the Varsity guys started punching each other and smacking themselves in the head. They howled. A pack of them ran up the bleachers and stomped and kicked all around Will's hiding place. He had seen video footage on the Internet of a zoo where all the monkeys went crazy in their cage at once. This wasn't much different.

"I WANT BLOOD!"

Will's stomach twisted into a knot. He recognized Sam's voice. Varsity roared in response. Will spied Sam through the slats of the bleachers. He was standing on a chair with his arms outstretched, looking down at his gang like some crazed preacher. His yellow hair looked unnatural against his skin. He looked bigger than Will remembered.

"We won't let this stand!" Sam said.

Varsity cheered louder.

Hilary glided over to Sam and entwined her arm around the inside of his leg. She looked up at him with a soft smile and said something that Will couldn't hear. Sam's expression lost some of its menace. He held up his hand, signaling that he needed a minute. He climbed down from the chair. The gang entertained themselves with vicious conversations about David. Sam and Hilary walked over to the bleachers. Will lost sight of them, but he could hear their conversation; they were very close.

"Are you sure about this?" Hilary asked.

"What are you talking about?"

"What if you captured him and kept him as your prisoner?"

"He has to die," Sam said.

"But if you locked him up in the equipment cage and kept him there, he'd have to pay for it day after day, and then, baby, he'd end up wishing you killed him."

There was a pause.

"Why do you want this?" Sam asked.

"If you kill him it will spook the other gangs. They'll want to take us out."

"They're not strong enough to take us out."

"They could band together," Hilary said.

"Together, they aren't strong enough! What are you up to?"

"Strategy, baby."

"You still love him."

"No, that was forever ago. You know that."

"You don't want your boyfriend to get hurt, huh, bitch?"

"Sam, don't."

"Say another word. I dare you."

Hilary said nothing. Sam stormed back into Will's view and stepped up on top of the chair again. He shouted to his gathered flock.

"David dies tomorrow! Everyone will see. They'll all see what you get when you cross us. We'll get our blood in the morning, you can be sure of that!"

One Varsity echoed Sam. "We'll get our blood in the

morning!" The chant caught on. "WE'LL GET OUR BLOOD IN THE MORNING!"

The gym reverberated with the threat. The senior Varsity members escorted their Pretty One girlfriends to their respective sheeted cubicles. The Varsity underclassmen all climbed onto the bleachers above Will to lie down.

"WE'LL GET OUR BLOOD IN THE MORNING!"

Will stared up, petrified. He lowered himself to the ground, amid the trash and giant clumps of dust. He shut his eyes and tried not to make any noise, as a nest of his enemies piled up above him.

10

DAVID WAS FIVE YEARS OLD. HE LAY ON THE couch eating a bowl of cereal. He could feel the warmth of his mother lying behind him. The living room of their old house was bathed in an easy morning light. He felt safe, nestled in against his mother's body. He could smell something sweet baking in the kitchen. His mother placed one of her arms over David, squeezing his belly with affection. It all seemed too perfect.

Just as that thought entered his mind, David knew he was dreaming. Everything started to slip away. He tried to hold tight to his cereal bowl, to the couch, to his mother, but he couldn't get back to that perfect moment no matter how hard he tried.

David opened his eyes, and he stared at the cold brushed

steel of the elevator wall, only inches from his nose. There was an arm around him, but it wasn't his mother's. It was Lucy's. Lucy's body pressed firmly against his back. He could feel every curve and swell of her, the slight pant of her breath on his neck. David strained to keep any movement minimal. He didn't want Lucy to wake up. As he inhaled, he smelled the sweet scent from his dream. It belonged to Lucy. She smelled like cookies or something. How did she do that?

He knew he should throw her arm off of him and stand up. He should tell her that he wasn't her protector, and it was time for her to go. But she was so warm.

He sighed and placed his hand around Lucy's arm. He contorted his body to slip out from underneath it. Her skin was seductively soft but goose-bumped from the endless cold of the elevator car. David and Will had adjusted to it long ago, but Lucy must have been freezing.

He sat up carefully and looked over to Will's corner hoping that he hadn't seen any of the cuddling. It was dark, but it looked like Will's bed was empty. He strained his eyes to see more sharply.

Will wasn't there.

Any fogginess from sleep burned off in a flash. He saw the bucket turned upside down in the middle of the floor. He looked up to the emergency hatch. The little bastard snuck out? Was he out of his mind?

David stepped over Lucy with as much speed as silence

would allow. Before hoisting himself up to the top of the elevator car, he snagged a blanket from Will's bed and placed it over Lucy.

David tugged a Geek's dirty green hoodie out of his materials sack; he didn't want to wear his own. He grabbed a can of tuna and stuffed it in the sweatshirt pocket. He might need to barter his way in or out of something. He pulled himself up to the hatch and disappeared into the pitch-black above.

"Will?" David whispered into the darkness of the elevator shaft. All he heard was a stunted echo. Damn it.

David reached over the edge and located a two-foot-long metal pipe he kept duct-taped to the side of the elevator car. It was thick and heavy; the thing could definitely break a bone. David hoisted himself into the vent that led to the hallway.

When he emerged from the elevator electrical closet, he pulled on his hood, keeping it low over his brow. He concealed the pipe up the loose sleeve of his sweatshirt. His shoulder still hurt from punching Brad, but if he ran into any trouble, he hoped the pipe would make up for it.

The elevator stood at the corner of two perpendicular hallways. David stared down one, then turned to the other. Right now, his brother could have been anywhere. He had no idea where to start looking, and he wanted to panic. David grabbed his forehead as if he was trying to squeeze out a single clear thought.

The Skaters . . . if Will had been taken, the Skaters might

have heard something. They spread gossip at every stop on their trash route. It was a safe assumption that they had already broken the story of Brad's death over the PA in his sleep. But David could offer them a scoop. He could trade on his side of the story in return for info on Will. He started for the administrative offices, where the Skaters lived.

He didn't get far before he was spotted. A white-haired kid was creeping out of a classroom dead ahead of him. David accidentally locked eyes with him. He was the Scrap kid with the trampled hand from the quad. The kid's eyelids peeled back when he saw David's face. He waved David over with his bent fingers. The kid took off down the hall, limping fast, then stopped and looked back. He waved David forward again, with more urgency this time. What did he want?

A racket snapped David out of his head. It came from the hallway behind him. It sounded like kicking on lockers. Then there was male laughter, a lot of it. It could've been a Varsity posse looking for him. He didn't want to find out. David ran toward the Scrap.

The kid limped down the long hall and into a math classroom that stank of sour armpits. David shut the door behind him as gently as his fear would let him. The room was a dumping ground. There were piles of junk, bloodstained rags, tied-off plastic bags with God knows what inside, and a puddle of oily brown liquid on the floor that David wanted nothing to do with. The Scrap moved an unhinged, ruined door and revealed a hole that had been burrowed through the wall.

The kid smiled with pride—he was almost giddy.

"I'm Mort," he said. "Remember me?"

Mort wasn't the least bit out of breath, but he was soaked with sweat. It dripped off his nose; it slicked his hands. "Don't worry. Come on."

Mort crawled through the wall. David followed, still fearful of the locker kickers in the hallway behind him.

The room on the other side of the wall had a malfunctioning fire sprinkler in the ceiling that spit an uneven drizzle of water over the room. The constant flow of water had bubbled the paint on the walls and buckled the floor tiles. One fluorescent bulb in the far corner cast a sickly light on six Scraps before him. Their conversation stopped dead when David entered.

David didn't know the effeminate Korean kid with his eyes cast down. Next to him were a gangly set of twins, one boy and one girl, both with long white hair. David had never seen them before, but they seemed young enough that they couldn't be more than sophomores. They each kept a finger hooked through the other's belt loop. They looked like the dirty hillbilly kids you wouldn't want to meet if you hoofed it too far into the mountains.

Nelson Bryant was a year below him. He was a ruddy runt of a kid who looked like he was born in the wrong century, like he should be wearing suspenders and knickers. David always felt sorry for Nelson because he was mostly deaf and wore the biggest pair of old-school hearing aids he'd ever seen. Nelson must have ditched the hearing aids when they ran out of batteries because he held a plastic chem lab funnel up to his ear like an ear trumpet.

The last Scrap was Belinda Max. The ceiling light glared off of her wet scalp. David wondered how much she'd gotten in return for giving Hilary her hair. She bounced over to him.

"Mort! You found him?" Belinda said.

"Sure did," Mort said with a laugh like a panting dog. He placed his sweaty hand on David's shoulder. David shrugged the nasty thing off.

"Why are you looking for me?" David asked.

"Leonard, get him something to drink. Would you, um, you know, like something to eat?" Belinda said, and the Korean kid began frantically searching the room.

"Here, let me get you a dry chair," Nelson said.

David's discomfort grew with his impatience. He looked back to the hole in the wall that Mort now blocked.

"I don't want a chair. What . . . what do you guys want from me?"

"Oh, no, you have nothing to worry about," Belinda said. "Not from us."

"We want you to be . . ." Leonard started, his words losing all volume halfway through his sentence. He blushed and looked away when David met his eyes. He held out a bottle of dirty water. David shook his head, and Leonard backed off.

"You're safe here," Belinda said. "You're with Scraps." Belinda's eyes filled with tears. David was confused about whether she was happy or sad. This crew of weirdos wasn't getting him any closer to finding Will. Every second he was out of the elevator his chances of surviving until graduation were in a nosedive.

"I have to go," David said. He figured the locker kickers must have been gone by now.

"Yeah, but . . . let us help you," Belinda said, spilling tears from her eyes but smiling.

"Okay. Have you seen my brother? Will Thorpe? Do you know him?"

Belinda bit her lip. She looked on the edge of a nervous breakdown.

"What?" David said, suddenly worried by her tears. "You saw him? What's wrong?"

"It's just . . . I'm so glad to have you here."

"Here's your chair," Nelson said, and scooted a chair behind David. It hit his knees, and he sat without thinking.

"Nelson, have you seen Will?" David asked.

"Ooh, no, I don't have any pills. Do you have a headache?" Nelson said.

That funnel didn't seem to work very well. David's chair was anything but dry. This was enough. He had to get out of here.

"Mort, thanks for the hiding place, but I'm leaving," David said.

The mountain twins burst out laughing. They were having a murmured conversation. The girl snickered and gripped the boy's arm like she'd fall over without his support. While she doubled over laughing, he picked things out of her hair like a mother baboon.

David turned to crawl back through the hole. Belinda rushed in front of him, pushed Mort out of the way, and blocked the hole with her bulk. David tensed up. This was more than weird, it was getting dangerous.

"No, but you can't go!" Belinda said.

David tightened his grip on his pipe.

"And why's that?"

"We need you," Belinda said, her voice choked with emotion. "You're the one we've been waiting for."

David realized he'd walked right into a trap. He let the pipe slide out of his sleeve and lifted it up, ready to swing. Belinda cowered.

"You lookin' to sell me out to Varsity? Huh? I'm not your meal ticket," David said.

"We want you to lead us. Our gang," Belinda said. David lowered the pipe a little.

"Huh?" He would have laughed, but he was too on edge.

"A gang for Scraps," Belinda continued, tears welling up

again. "So we can have rights, fight for our fair share together, and y'know, protect each other."

The look on her face had no hint of humor to it.

"I've got bigger problems right now," David said.

"Yeah, but . . ." Belinda's voice jumped to a desperate octave. "No, but that's the whole thing. If there was a gang for us, then you wouldn't have had to do what you did yesterday. That girl woulda had someplace to go."

David could admit that the idea was nice—safety in numbers, a team of people he could trust to take care of Will after he left, a place for Lucy as well. But how? Take on Varsity and every other gang with these six misfits at his back? They'd never stand a chance.

"I'm not your guy. I'm nothing special," David said.

"Yeah, but no, but you are. You're the one! You stood up to them. If other Scraps knew you were doing it, they'd join. They'll follow you, David," Belinda said.

He looked over to the twins. The boy had his head tilted back and his mouth open, trying to catch droplets from the sprinkler. The girl twin held her dirty hands like a gutter to catch more water and funnel it into her brother's mouth.

"I'm leaving," David said, and tucked his pipe into his sleeve. He gently moved Belinda to the side. She grabbed his hand with both of hers and held on to it as he crouched and entered the hole.

"No, but please," she said.

David looked back at her and saw a pain that he recognized, the frustration of giving your heart and soul and watching everything still go to shit anyway. For a moment he wanted to say yes, that he would be their captain, that he would take on the school, that he'd prove her right, but he didn't speak. He let the moment pass.

"I'm sorry."

She let his fingers slip from hers as he crossed into the stinking math room. David opened the door to the hallway and poked his head out. Totally empty. It was still early. He knew Varsity was up and lurking, but most of the school was still asleep. He might have time. He had to find out if Will was okay. He jogged in the direction of the Skaters once again.

David hit the stairs fast. He ran for a couple minutes. He was in Geek territory, not far from the auditorium. David stared down a long hallway. Geeks slept in the rooms on either side. He ran down it, hoping to reach the end as fast as he could. A third of the way down the hallway, the ceiling lights flickered on.

It must have been later than he thought. David poured on the speed, but Geeks began to spill out of the classrooms, ready to start the day. He drew his hood even farther over his face, kept the pipe at the ready up his sleeve, and slowed to a brisk walk. He felt sure that, past the green fabric of his hood, every eye in the hallway was pointed right at him. He was completely exposed.

He kept his eyes glued to the floor and only looked up when he had to. He passed a pair of kids chatting on his left side. He waited for a comment. A shout. The clapping of footsteps after him. But nothing happened.

Another pair of Geeks approached, lugging jugs of water. David held his breath. They passed without a word.

Halfway down the hallway, more students began stepping out from classrooms. And then more. And more. It seemed like they were never going to stop. Like a nightmare. David hunched over and picked up the pace. He nearly collided with someone and got a peeved "Watch it!" thrown his way. He kept walking, but just as he rounded the corner, a voice rang out.

"Hey, it's you!"

The voice sounded like it had come from directly in front of him. David flinched and looked up, expecting the worst. The source was a scruffy band Geek with a sharp nose and pockmarked cheeks. But he wasn't shouting at David. He was pointing at another kid next to David who held a Frisbee.

"I knew it was you! What, were you just never going to give it back?"

David glanced at the Frisbee thief next to him, who was fumbling for a response. The thief made eye contact with David. Recognition flashed in his eyes. David aimed his eyes back at the floor and strode forward, but it was too late. He heard the noise of a phone camera shutter behind him. In two seconds, the Frisbee thief was at David's left side, walking in unison with him.

"Hey, you're David, right?"

David ignored him and lengthened his stride. The kid backed off for a moment, then matched David's new pace.

"Yo, what's your problem, man? Back off," David spat out, mustering faux anger. He didn't want to look at the kid, but it was tough to achieve a scary "Back off!" when he was looking straight at the floor.

"You're him! I was in Spanish with you," the kid said. "Taylor. That's my name. Remember?"

"I didn't take Spanish," David lied. But he remembered Taylor. "Tayloroso," he used to call himself. Every time Señora Pérez went around the room asking each student "*¿Cómo estás?*" when she got to Taylor he would answer with a spicy flair, "*¡Yo siento muy . . . Tayloroso!*" The kid was annoying.

Tayloroso held his phone up, trying to get a shot of David's face. David broke into a run.

"Hey! Hold on! I want to talk to you," Tayloroso shouted, running after him. When David didn't stop, Tayloroso yelled at the top of his lungs, "Hey, it's the kid who killed that Varsity!"

David pushed hard and gained a slight burst of speed. He heard shouts of recognition from the other students. Someone pulled David's hood off. It didn't matter now. He had to keep moving. He flicked his head back to see just how many kids he was dealing with. Five more were running beside Tayloroso.

"That's him! That's the guy!" Tayloroso hollered.

Groggy kids poked their heads out of classrooms. Some of them grabbed at his sweatshirt and laughed. They swarmed behind him. His legs wouldn't move fast enough; it felt like a nightmare. David let the pipe slide down out of his sleeve and into his hand.

Someone snatched the pipe away from him. He looked back at the mob again as he rounded a corner. His vision flared white. He hit the floor before he realized he'd been punched. David blinked through the haze and the pain and saw two Varsity guys towering over him.

A third person stepped between them. It was Sam. His voice was the last thing David heard before an incoming Varsity fist smashed his vision to black.

"Tell everyone. The execution of David Thorpe starts in ten minutes."

11

DAVID AWOKE WHEN SOMETHING LONG AND cold and rubbery coiled around his neck and choked his throat shut. The white-hot light of the market seared his eyes at first. A crowd of people stared at him. That thing that gripped his neck, it yanked him up, it bit under his jaw and bent his head down; pain cut up through his neck like a cleaver. He had no air. David dangled by his neck, toes scraping for the floor, fingernails raking at his windpipe. He tried to suck in a breath, but it only hollowed his stomach.

He was being hanged. David thrashed his feet, which twisted him around to face the other end of the hall. He saw Fudgey, the football team's kicker, and three other Varsity guys holding an orange extension cord that was looped over a sprinkler pipe above David and cinched around his neck.

They gripped the cord and leaned back like it was a game of tug of war.

"All right, let him on his feet."

The noose went halfway slack, and David found the ground. He gagged. Blood rushed to his head, and he felt his sense of balance slip away. Another pair of Varsity guys wrenched his arms behind him and held him up; David's legs were just noodles in shoes.

"You all know why we're here," Sam's voice said from behind him. "Yesterday David Thorpe murdered my friend Brad Hammond."

David's vision came back into focus. The market was packed with people, except for a fifteen-foot-wide circle of clear floor around David. Each gang was represented. The crowd was riveted, almost excited, as they waited for his life to be taken in front of them. He remembered seeing a lot of those very same faces in the stands on a Friday night, during his final season, cheering him on.

"There aren't many rules in here," Sam said, "but I'm making one today. No one kills my friends."

David's breathing settled into a rhythm, and he was able to lock his legs straight underneath him; he felt somewhat solid again. Solid and scared out of his mind.

"You don't kill us," Sam continued. "You hear me? You try anything, and what's about to happen to him . . . I'll make sure it'll happen to you."

"He hit his head!" David shouted.

All eyes snapped to David.

"It was one punch," David went on. "Brad fell and hit his head. I didn't murder him!"

"Liar. You liar!" Sam said, "Fudgey, shut him up,"

Fudgey let go of David's right arm and clamped his hand over David's mouth. David bit down on the Fudgey's finger. Fudgey screamed and fell back. David spun and drove the point of his elbow into the other guy's ear. It was Anthony Smith, a linebacker who'd always hated David. To his right, the Varsity guys holding the extension cord dropped it and ran at him. David dashed forward.

He got a good five feet into the crowd before he felt the noose yank on his neck. It stopped him dead just as he came face-to-face with a Nerd girl in the crowd. She had dry, frizzy black bangs that nearly covered her eyes.

"He was going to rape her!" David said.

The Nerd girl froze, terrified. Her eyes shook as she looked back at him; she looked like she was being mugged. Conversations burst out through the room. His noose jerked up and back, pulling David off his feet; he crashed to the floor, onto his back. The crowd towered over him. The noose pulled again and dragged him back through the thicket of legs. Lit from above, the faces of the crowd were lost in shadow.

She was all alone! She had no one to protect her! That's what

David wanted to yell to the crowd but the cord around his neck kept him silent.

Once he was pulled back into the clearing, five Varsity guys jumped on him. They pinned his arms behind him again, throttled him around, and forced him back into place, underneath the sprinkler pipe.

"Guys, listen to me," David said to them. "You know me. I wouldn't do something like that!"

Sam grabbed a fistful of David's hair and cranked his head back. Sam's eyes were flared open so wide that David could see white above his corneas. He spoke in a raspy hush that only David could hear.

"You just had to start it back up, didn't you?"

"Sam, don't do this."

A scraggly vein inflated across Sam's forehead.

"You did this to yourself."

"Just—just think for a second, Sam. What are you doing?"

"Lift!" Sam said.

David heard a collected heave of effort from behind him. The cord clenched his neck so hard his head wanted to pop off his body. They were going to lynch him. Again, his feet couldn't find the floor, his lungs were stuck empty. His hangmen heaved again, and David rose farther above the heads of the crowd. His feet chopped at the air.

He couldn't scream. He looked into the crowd. Someone

needed to help him. They had to. But each person he looked to looked away as though he wasn't being lynched right in front of them. They did nothing.

The sound of his own gagging became muffled, like he was hearing it through a pillow. The world darkened. He was an anvil dropped into the ocean, sinking away from life, down into the dark and the cold.

But then saw Will.

His vision was dull, but he opened his eyes wider. Will charged into the far end of the hallway. He lugged an over-stuffed black garbage bag over his shoulder. Within seconds, a stampede of hollering Varsity guys rushed into the hallway after him. Will ran into the dense crowd, and the stampede barreled in right after him. The smashing of bodies sparked a ripple of violence as opposing gangs careened. When Will broke through to the open circle, he swung the bag around. Food flew out in a wide arc and scattered onto the floor. The hallway went berserk.

Fights erupted everywhere. People punching, yelping, falling down below him. The tumult overtook the clear circle of floor underneath him. Fudgey and his other hangmen were knocked to the floor. David heard the noose zip over the pipe. He felt air rush down his throat and his body lose all weight for a moment before he smacked down onto the floor. The feet of the brawlers above kicked him and stepped on him.

Someone picked him up. It was Belinda. She had her arms

around his hips, holding him into her plush flank. Mort's sweaty hands held his head and shoulders. Together, they rammed their way through the thrashing crowd, carrying him. Leonard, Nelson, and the weird twins crowded around, shielding David from view. They carried him away from the hallway riot, out of the market, and into a dark hall. The roaring chaos in the market faded until all David could hear was the huff and wheeze of Belinda's breathing.

12

WILL TOOK THE CORNER FAST. FEAR TICKLED the back of his neck, making him run harder. There easily could have been fifteen of them still after him. He covered the next hallway in seconds and hooked a right at an intersection. It didn't matter. His pursuers were the best athletes in the school; he was never going to outrun them.

He saw a locker grave. *RIP* was scratched into the paint in tall letters. Someone had broken the duct tape seal, and the stench of death permeated the air. He whipped the locker open. A rotting body stared down at Will's shoes. Its arms were snaked through the straps of an old blue backpack that hung on a coat hook. The reek fouled his stomach. The growling pack of Varsity goons neared the corner. He plugged his nose, covered his mouth, and stuffed himself into the locker, closing the door behind him.

He heard Varsity run past the locker. His hand brushed against a knob of dry, shrunken flesh. He didn't breathe. The Varsity guys were talking to each other, but he couldn't hear the words through the door. Something was poking him in his back. It could have been an elbow. Or a broken rib. He heard the sound of locker after locker being opened down the hall. He wanted to take a breath. They opened more lockers, right by Will. He let a little air out and took a quick breath in. He stifled vomit, and the acid burned his throat. He was sure that he'd just inhaled particles of death. He heard the locker next to his open, then slam shut. He braced for an attack. But his locker didn't open.

He didn't hear any more noises.

Were they gone?

He couldn't hold his breath any longer.

Ten seconds, maybe he could last ten more seconds.

By five, he was ready to die. After seven seconds, Will pushed open the door and fell to the hallway floor on his knees. He looked down the hall, expecting Varsity eyes to be staring back at him. There was no one there.

Will laughed. He'd single-handedly ruined Sam's big show, and his brother was saved. As soon as he'd heard the announcement over the PA system about David's execution,

Will couldn't hide under those gym bleachers any longer.

Who were those kids that carried David off? Scraps, clearly, but he'd never seen Scraps band together bravely like that before. And where did they take David?

As long as David wasn't in Varsity's hands, Will was pretty sure David could take care of himself. He had to get back to Lucy in the elevator. He was dying to tell her everything that had happened. He was tingling as he relived the glory, his lips moving slightly as he rehearsed his delivery.

Buoyant conversation and laughter echoed down the hall. Will ducked into the nearest stairwell and pressed himself against the wall. He had a clear view of some Freak girls. They had smudged ash mascara and matching blue bobs. They were returning home from the market.

"That was literally the sickest thing I've ever seen."

"In a good way?

"Totally. I'm in love."

Will grinned, psyched to hear about his handiwork.

"David's cute, huh?"

What? Will's grin flattened.

"Is it wrong that the cord around his neck got me hot? I just wanted to crawl on top of him—"

"Omigod, you are mentally ill!"

The girls laughed.

"People are saying he planned the whole thing. Like, he let

them capture him so he could make Varsity look stupid."

Will curled his lip.

"Whoa. Really? Wow. It totally worked."

"That sounds so like him. I used to know him. He's kind of a genius."

How could they call David a genius? He didn't plan dick.

The Freak girls walked toward the stairwell. Will had enough time to run up the stairs and disappear, but he didn't do it. He stuck his hands in his pocket and leaned against the wall inside the stairwell with his coolest pose. These girls were going to get all flustered when they saw the guy who saved David's life. The girls stepped through the doorway.

He smirked at them. "'S up?"

"Ew . . . Scrap," the first said.

The second girl pulled her friends along, up the stairs.

They had to be joking. Did they just not see what he did?

"David stands for something. Like, he's a really good person," the third said as the girls continued up the stairs.

"I know," her friend said. "He's, like, a saint for taking care of his little brother with all those problems. It's so sad."

"You're sad!" Will shouted.

The girls flipped him off and disappeared up the next flight.

Unbelievable, Will thought. *Freaks suck.* He rolled back into the hall to go home.

Ten minutes later, he was at the elevator. He slipped into

the electrical closet and then up through the vent. After a few rungs of the ladder he hopped into the darkness, knowing just where his feet would land. They made a brassy *boom* against the metal of the elevator. The sound hung in the air. There was no light on inside the car. He dipped his head down inside, gripping the sides of the hatch hard. No one was inside.

Will pulled himself back up and sat on the roof of the elevator shaft. He tried to make sense of her absence. He was starting to panic about David too. Things might not have gone as smoothly as he thought after David escaped the market.

No. Everything's fine, he thought. *Lucy just left out of curiosity, but she's smart. She wouldn't go far. She'll be back.*

He decided to stay cool and wait. He dropped back into the elevator, lit a candle, and picked up a book of short stories David had been reading. The creaking of the elevator's steel cables reverberated up and down the shaft, sounding like a fingernail slowly scratching down the string of an electric bass. Will tried to concentrate on the story but couldn't. He tossed the book aside and just sat, staring at the candle. He tapped his fingers. He didn't know for how long.

I gotta get out of here.

Will pulled himself out of the elevator and climbed the ladder to the vent. There was no way he could sit still, and he figured that if he kept moving he'd eventually run into either Lucy or David. He crawled through the vent to the closet and pushed open the door to the hallway.

A pale boy and girl, who looked like inbred hicks with long white hair, stared back at him.

"Gah!"

Will stumbled back into the closet and pulled the door shut. He held firm on the knob. He waited for the invaders to tug on the door. Or knock. Anything. But nothing happened. Will leaned close to where the door met the frame.

"Hello?" he said.

"Is—is—" a boy's voice began.

"You Will?" a girl's voice finished.

Will crinkled his nose, confused. "Yeah," he said.

"Got a letter for you."

"Slide it under the door."

A scrap of paper appeared at his feet. Will picked it up and opened it, straining to read it in the darkness. He pulled a lighter from his pocket and sparked it. The lighter was almost empty and produced only a blue nub of flame. On the scrap was written: "Lucy's with me. These kids will take you to us—D."

Will relaxed when he recognized David's handwriting. He pushed open the door and came face-to-face with the ghoulish twins. They shared the same cringing smile; it revealed more nostril than teeth.

"We don't bite," the boy said.

The girl covered her mouth and giggled. Will turned up his nose, crumpled up the paper, and pocketed it.

"You two are weird-looking," Will said.

The boy kept a straight face, but the girl sneered at Will and spit to acknowledge the insult. The saliva landed on her own shorts. The twins turned in unison and walked away from Will. He figured that was his cue to follow.

"Oh, I wanted to ask . . . How long have you been dead? I think I bunked up with a friend of yours in a locker a little while ago."

They giggled. Will craned his head, surprised at their response. But they weren't listening to him. They were communicating with each other through barely audible whispers and slight hand gestures. Another flourish of giggles and a glance back at Will. They were talking about him. Will sped up to see if he could hear what they were saying.

". . . ehse ogto suey-sus . . ."

The girl giggled hard this time. A mucous bubble expanded from her nose and then popped. Part of the bottom of her oversized T-shirt was crusted into a point. She lifted it and wiped her nose. Will stifled a gag.

"Let me guess? Single?" Will said.

"The dump," Will said to himself. "Shoulda seen that coming."

Will stood at the top of a wide staircase. At the bottom of the stairs were two open doors that led to the basement. Trash bags were scattered around the doors. The twins trudged their way through the doors. It smelled rank, not rotting-corpse rank but enough to piss Will off.

Will groaned, took a deep breath, and waded into the trash and debris. He passed through the doors into the basement. The room was as big as a basketball court. Before the explosion it had been the school's storage area, but everything worthwhile had been raided. Piles of black plastic trash bags, ruined furniture, and debris filled the room. There were hundreds of piles, some knee-high, some almost to the ceiling. To Will's surprise, every light in the room except one was still working. Not that it helped anything. The lights cast a bluish tone across the wall-to-wall junk.

There was a small crowd of white-hairs gathered at the wall to Will's left. They stood around the door to the boiler room. Will recognized most of the group—they were the ones who pulled David out of the market. There was Leonard and the runty kid with the funnel, but there was no sign of David or Lucy. Without acknowledging Will again, the twins settled at a small three-legged table, pulled out a dirty pink string, and started playing cat's cradle with each other.

"Yeah, okay, later . . . nice hanging with you . . . and your snot shirt," he called after them, but they ignored him.

Will walked to the boiler room door. Leonard Jong stood guard. He still couldn't get over the fact that Leonard was one of the ones who helped get David out of the market. In middle school, Will once saw Leonard scream and run away crying when a squirrel got too close to him.

"Leonard . . . hey. You remember me, right?"

Leonard shrugged. It was sort of a yes, a shy yes.

"I'm looking for David."

"He's inside."

Leonard's voice was quiet and melodic.

"Thanks," Will said as he reached for the door handle. Leonard pushed Will's hand away.

"Nobody go—" Leonard said, and then Will couldn't hear the rest.

"What?"

"Nobody goes inside," he said, this time only slightly louder.

"Yeah, but I'm his brother."

"I—don't know that."

Leonard's voice dropped an octave midsentence. Will wasn't buying it.

"I saved him in the market. You were there. Let me in."

"A lot of people want to see David right now."

Will rolled his eyes and grabbed for the door handle again. Leonard grasped his wrists. Will shook him off and raised his fist at Leonard. Leonard squeaked.

"Looks like you're B-list around here, Spaz," someone said.

Will scoured the huddle of Scraps nearby for the speaker and saw Smudge leaning against the wall, smirking back at him. Will sank. If there were a worse witness to his rejection at the door, he couldn't think of one.

"What the hell are you doing here?" Will said.

Smudge thumbed at the Scraps beside him. "These stalkers

came for protection. I came 'cause . . . well, I just wanted to see what happens next."

"Protection?"

"Yeah. Your bro's, like, the next Moses or something."

Will glanced back at Leonard and the four Scraps who came to David's aid. They eyed Will suspiciously.

"I think he's changing clothes in there," Will said in an attempt to sound off the cuff. "That's why they won't let me in."

Smudge's smile widened.

"Lucy's in there."

"Oh. Yeah?" Will said.

"They might be taking clothes off, but I'm not sure they're putting 'em back on," Smudge said.

"Shut up."

"Hey, man, I'm just saying. He saves her life one day, goes toe-to-toe with the most powerful guy in school the next. I'm not imagining any dry panties in that room."

Will remembered the fantasy painted by the Freak girl he'd overheard in the hall. *Just be glad David's alive,* Will thought. But he could feel jealousy rising up in him.

"I rescued him," Will said.

"Not the way I heard it."

Did everyone have their eyes closed when he saved the day? This was unbelievable.

"I don't believe you," Will said. "Lucy's not in there."

"What'd she think of the necklace?"

Will pressed his hand on his pocket. He could feel the links of the fine chain through the worn denim. He had forgotten all about it with everything that had happened. And suddenly, it seemed much less special.

"I—I haven't seen her yet," Will muttered.

The door that Will wasn't allowed go through opened.

"Well, here's your chance," Smudge said.

Belinda emerged from the boiler room. Everyone went quiet. Kids gathered around like band groupies. There were ten of them.

"He's ready to speak," Belinda said. Her voice warbled with reverence.

"You gotta be fuckin' kidding me," Will said under his breath. Belinda stepped aside, and David appeared in the doorway with Lucy next to him. Will tensed up. Lucy had her arm wrapped around his waist, and his arm was around her shoulder. Will needed them to stop touching each other. Immediately.

Lucy was supporting David, walking him gently as he winced with every step. His neck was purple, and he had a swollen eye. Lucy was so tender with him. Will remembered her sweet touch in his hardest moments of Wild-Trek, her kind words, her total belief in him. And now it was all for David.

This wasn't the heroic return Will had been hoping for. He turned away and stepped into the shadow of the nearest trash pile. He didn't want to be seen by them yet. He was sure David hadn't noticed him, and Lucy had her eyes on David, but Will knew Smudge was watching him, probably loving it.

David spoke. His voice rasped from the abuse to his throat. It only made the Scraps listen more intently.

"It's been a hell of a day."

Nervous laughter bounced around the clearing.

"A lot of you know about Belinda's idea of forming a new gang, so Scraps like us could be fed and protected. I know that's why you're here right now. I don't know if I can be what you need, and I'm sure things will get harder before they get any easier, but none of us should have to fight alone. The gang begins now with all of you. I am officially accepting Belinda's offer to be your leader."

Everyone burst into cheers. Will didn't make a noise.

13

WARM COPPER LIGHT SPLASHED AGAINST
Lucy's bed. She watched it sparkle like raindrops on her
dress. Lucy smiled. Over to her right, beyond the fort of broken school desks that carved out her sleeping area, Leonard
was unfolding an emergency fire blanket. The light from a
halogen work light beamed off its crinkled metallic surface.

Lucy drew in a deep breath and let it all out. It had been
nearly a week and a half since David's escape from Varsity.
Today, for the first time, she felt at ease. She sat up and looked
at her area. She was grateful for her pillow. Old socks in a zip-
lock freezer bag. She had taped it shut with an airtight seal.
Every day here was an unending battle against stink. Lucy
had scrubbed every nook and cranny around her area.

She had to. She'd started to feel like the filth was infecting her dreams. Nearly every night for the past week she'd had nightmares about Brad. She was there in the booth again, trying to get away, but David never showed up. What happened next was awful. She fought with everything she had, but Brad was always stronger. It didn't matter what she did to him. She'd tear out his tongue. She'd kick his knees until his legs bent backward, but he'd still keep coming. Lucy never thought waking up in a pile of trash could be such a relief.

Lucy stretched. She opened her white leather pocketbook and pulled out a brown glass bottle of pure vanilla extract. She dabbed a little behind each ear. From inside one of the desks she pulled a shard of mirror with the edges ground down. It belonged to Dorothy, an ex-art Geek, who'd joined up with their group last week. Dorothy had held her own photography show months ago, full of naked pics she had taken of other art Geeks without them knowing. She'd said she was trying to confront people with the nude human form to start a dialogue about how similar and how vulnerable they all were, no matter their gang affiliation. The Geeks kicked her out instead.

Lucy checked herself out in the mirror. It was marred with gouges, but it let Lucy see enough to know whether she was walking around looking like a ghoul. Her lemon blonde coloring had faded. Her hair would be white soon. She tied it up in a high bun. There was no point in checking out her dress. She'd worn it every day and slept in it every night for weeks. She knew what it looked like. Bad. She put the mirror back in the desk. Her sweater was as dirty as her dress. Her fingers traced the hole where Hilary had torn off her Pretty Ones emblem.

She hated them. Early in the quarantine, when Hilary offered her a spot in the gang, it just made sense. Her family had only moved to Pale Ridge that summer. She didn't really know anyone. Hilary approached Lucy because she was "pretty," but Lucy never fit in with the Pretty Ones. She couldn't bring herself to blindly follow orders. All the other girls went along with Hilary's demented rules without question because she had them convinced that they couldn't survive without her protection.

"We made a great haul today," someone said.

Lucy peeked her head around the cluster of desks and saw Mort limp through the basement doors, backed by the twins. They wove their way through trash piles to the heart of the camp, which was hidden behind the largest pile in the room. They each carried trash bags and dumped the contents out on chairs for the other Scraps to see. Mort's bag contained food. Both the twins' bags contained dirty laundry. Belinda, bucket in hand, scooped up an armful of clothes. Will poked through the food and held up a bottle of vinegar with a puzzled look to Mort.

"Vinegar? Seriously? What, does the Army think we're pickling eggs in here?"

Lucy smiled. Thank God for Will. Will had been there for her every day, since her ordeal, helping her feel at ease. He was a good friend. There was a time, back on their Wild-Trek trip, when Lucy hoped they could be more than friends, but Will never made a move. He just didn't think of her that way.

A kick ball rested on the ground near Will, inside the chalk outline of a four-square court. Nelson had found the ball in the trash. He'd organized a four-square tournament that had really helped to bring people together. The only precaution was being sure not to make too much noise when they played. That went for every aspect of their life down here. They'd managed to keep their little camp secret so far by hiding in the boiler room whenever the Skaters rolled in and dropped their trash at the end of their runs. The Skaters never had any reason to venture this far back into the trash.

Lucy stepped out of her quarters. So far, she'd opted out of group activities like four-square because she needed time to herself after what had happened with Brad. But she was starting to have an odd feeling that no one liked her. She was probably just being paranoid.

Belinda was washing a sweater in a mop bucket. She wrung it out. Lucy approached her.

"I can hang stuff if you just want to wash," Lucy said.

Belinda ignored her, hung the sweater on a turned-over chair, and turned back to her sudsy bucket of gray water. Lucy bit her lip.

"Would that help at all?" Lucy said.

Belinda slapped down the wet laundry in her hand with a huff.

"Or . . . not?"

Belinda grumbled down into the bucket. "The little princess finally wants to help."

"Excuse me?"

Belinda looked up and jutted her jaw. "You heard me. Just because David thinks you're so special doesn't mean we do . . . Pretty One."

Lucy felt a surge of anger at the comment. She searched her mind for a biting comeback.

"Hey, Haunches, you got a problem with Lucy?" Will said.

Lucy turned to see Will. He wore a cocked sneer, and his eyes were squeezed to slits. Something about the way he was holding his head, his shoulders back, made Lucy notice how muscular he was now. Belinda must have noticed too, and she backed up with a startled whinny.

"Will, don't. . . . It's okay," Lucy said. She'd wanted to say something mean to Belinda, but she never would have called her fat.

"No, it's not okay. You're trying to help," he said, and turned to the rest of the room. "Hey, listen up, anybody that's got a problem with Lucy has a problem with me. Got it?"

"Will, stop . . . ," Lucy said with a blush. She tugged on his sleeve, and he put his arm around her and gripped her hip. The rest of the Scraps stared at her.

The door to the boiler room swung open, and David stepped out. Lucy felt hot all of the sudden. Every time David entered a room, she practically got a fever. She smoothed out the wrinkles in her dress.

"What's going on?" David said. He looked perturbed.

"Nothing," Lucy said. "It's fine."

"He called me Haunches," Belinda said.

David looked at Will and sighed. "What are you doing?"

"She's trying to freeze Lucy out of the group," Will said.

"Hey," David said, projecting his voice for everyone to hear. "Let's try to get along, okay? All we got is each other. So let's make it work."

David looked exhausted by the whole squabble.

"Okay?" he said.

He clapped his hands and strode back to the boiler room. Will walked after him.

"That's it? She was a total raging bitch to Lucy," Will said.

David grabbed Will's arm and pulled him into the room. Lucy followed right behind them. The giant industrial boiler took up half of the room; a tangle of pipes led off the top and sides of it and reached across the ceiling. Raw heat pressed in all around Lucy.

"I don't know how this got so out of hand but I don't want this to be a big deal." Lucy said.

"I know you don't," David said. "Will, do me a favor just play nice. We need a hundred and ten percent from everybody right now, and if you're calling people *bitch*, it's gonna fall apart."

David looked pained. He massaged his jaw. She wanted to massage it for him. With her lips.

"It's going to fall apart because we live in a trash pit, man," Will said.

"I'm working on that."

"Maybe it's just better if me and Lucy split."

"No," Lucy said, a little more forcefully than she meant to.

"But they don't understand you," Will said. "They're calling you a Pretty One, and you're not. They've got no respect. It just makes me want to—"

Lucy put her hand on Will's arm to calm him.

"It's okay," she said, then looked to David. "I can change their minds. This is where I want to be."

Relief eased the wrinkles in David's forehead. He gave her a little nod of thanks and focused on his brother.

"Don't bail on me yet, okay?" David said. "I can still make this work. If we can bring in more Scraps like us, we'll have something. You'll have a gang, man."

"You gotta pick up the pace," Will said.

Lucy took Will's arm before he had the chance to say anything worse. "Let's go," she said, then turned to David. "Bye."

"Bye," he said. They held eye contact until the door closed between them. Whoa. That look was loaded. Lucy's heart fluttered at the thought she might have a chance with David.

She and Will walked back into the camp. Mort and Nelson

were in the midst of stashing the new food out of sight. An idea gave her a little rush.

"Will, I know what we need to do," she said, gripping his hand in both of hers. She jumped a little, getting herself excited. When Lucy moved to Pale Ridge, she'd been bummed about being in a new town, in a strange house, but it was that first meal with her family that made the place feel like home.

"We need to get out of here," Will said. "I was serious in there. If just you and me went back to the elevator, we'd be fine on our own. You don't belong in this nastiness. This is David's thing."

Lucy frowned. "Will, David's your brother. He loves you, and he's asking for our help. We're not leaving."

She eyed a large sheet of plywood. "Help me with this," Lucy said, and pulled him toward it. Dorothy, the ex-art Geek, pushed her stringy hair off her face and poked her little beak of a nose toward them.

"I'll help," Dorothy said.

"No, thanks," Will said.

Lucy gave him a soft punch and waved Dorothy over. "We'd love it."

David paced in the heat. He was slick with sweat. He hadn't left the boiler room since he'd spoken with Will and Lucy. Thank God for Lucy. She was the only thing keeping Will here, and David knew it. He'd tried to thank Will for saving his life several times over the past week and a half, but it didn't seem to make a dent. Everything David did seemed to piss Will off.

This boiler room was hell, but he couldn't leave until he came up with a plan. Nothing changed the game like a good strategy, but he'd been racking his brain for too long. It wasn't just Will; everyone was starting to get anxious. He knew what they were thinking when they stared at him: *If David's our leader, then when's he gonna lead? What's the next move?*

David had no idea.

He didn't even know how they were all still alive. Everyone seemed to believe that the fact that Varsity hadn't attacked this whole time meant that no one knew they were down here, or that Varsity was scared of David. David didn't buy that. He knew there was no way Sam would let things end like they had in the market. Every day that Sam didn't attack, David grew more wary. What was he up to?

David tripped over his laundry bucket. The dirty water splashed onto his browned sneaker. He'd thought the laundry business could be a trade for the whole group, but it was a miserable failure. Will and David had barely eked out a living doing laundry before. There just wasn't enough business to spread the profits between fifteen people and have it be viable. The pathetic amount of food they'd managed to get in the past week and a half was proof of that. On top of it, they couldn't keep running a laundry service out of a dump.

Everything smelled worse on the way out than it did on the way in.

There was no trade in McKinley that wasn't already accounted for. And if the fifteen of them tried to fight in the upcoming food drop, Varsity would take them out in five minutes.

David's stomach growled at him. His neck was still sore from the attempted lynching. He tried not to think about how he was as hungry and afraid as the others. Maybe more. He couldn't be. He was the one they were depending on. He had to be fearless.

He heard the excited voices of his gang outside the door. Then there was a knock. David stared at the door. Maybe they would just go away if he didn't answer.

"David? It's Lucy. It's dinnertime."

"Uh . . . that's okay. I'm not hungry," he lied.

"Oh," she said. "But Will and I have a surprise for you."

Shit. A surprise. Only an asshole turns down a surprise.

"Okay . . ."

He opened the door. The stench of curdled trash bit the inside of his nose. Lucy was wearing a scarf over her nose and mouth, but he could tell by the crinkles in the corners of her eyes that she was smiling.

David did a double take as he stepped into the camp. No one was around, or so it seemed at first glance. A brand-new structure stood behind the largest trash pile—a twelve-foot-long tent made out of black garbage-bag plastic. Conversation emanated from the tent.

"You ready?" she said, and reached for David's hand. "Everyone's inside. Now, when we go in, be quick. So far, I've managed to keep the smell out."

"Then I guess the twins aren't in there."

Lucy laughed. It made him feel a little better. She pulled apart the layers of hanging black plastic, and they ducked under it.

Inside, everyone sat around a plywood table. The only light came from three flashlights, sitting pointed up, like a centerpiece of candles. One had a weak set of batteries, and it flickered like a dying flame. If hobos had banquets, this was what they'd look like. The others quieted upon David's entrance. Nelson stood and saluted him. Leonard tugged on Nelson's sleeve, signaling him to sit back down.

Everyone watched as David took a seat at the head of the table. Lucy sat to his right. Will had positioned himself at the other end of the long table. As a result, he was barely visible to David, just a pair of eyes in the darkness.

David breathed in deep for Lucy's benefit. He was amazed by the legitimate lack of stink. Instead, there was a distinct, familiar scent.

"Do I smell pickles?"

"Vinegar." Lucy pulled down her scarf and said, "We used it to scrub everything clean."

David looked down at the place setting before him. His plate was made from the square cover of a binder. An anarchy symbol and other ancient classroom doodles were scrawled onto it in ballpoint pen. A spread of crackers and a few cuts of salami were scattered across it. He took a deep breath, then looked to the gang.

"Hi, everybody," David said. "Um . . . I guess, first, I want to thank Will and Lucy for putting together this dinner—"

"It was Lucy's idea, not mine," Will said abruptly.

"Well, all the same, I think it's just what we needed. Right?"

There were a few nods, but for the most part, the faces he saw echoed his fear. They wanted answers. A state of the union. He had to tell them that he didn't have a clue.

"Anyone have any news?" David asked.

"A Skater threw his trash bags at me yesterday," Nelson volunteered.

"I think we might be losing trades because we smell bad," Mort said.

"No shit," Will said.

"Do we have more food coming in, 'cause I might want to save this if we don't," Dorothy said, looking at her plate.

"Well . . . ," David said.

"What are we gonna do, David?" Will said. It was more of a challenge than a question. David stared down the length of the table at his obnoxious brother. Will was leaning into the flickering light now. "I don't know about the rest of you, but I'm sick of living like a rat."

The table gasped and muttered about Will's insolence. They waited for David's swift and strong response, which would put Will in his place. Seconds passed. Smudge laughed. David's anger over Will's comment was making it hard to think straight.

"Unfortunately, the situation is—"

In the middle of David's sentence, a Varsity tore the tent open. The whole table sprang to their feet at once and scattered. The tent was torn to pieces. Someone smashed into David from behind. He tumbled forward, got caught in the tatters of black plastic, and fell to the ground. He dug his way out of plastic to see the camp under a full-scale attack.

Varsity was destroying everything in its path. Three of them were pulling down the desk wall of the girls' quarters. Will was wrestling with a Varsity on the ground. He saw the boy twin yank his sister out of the way, just in time to miss the swipe of a Varsity pipe. He saw Nelson get knocked into a trash wall. Nelson held his chest and grimaced in pain. A Varsity stood over him with a lacrosse stick.

David spotted a file cabinet drawer in a pile of trash by his feet. He grabbed it and swung it hard into the Varsity's head, catching him in the ear with the drawer's metal corner. The Varsity crumpled to the ground. Half of his ear was torn away.

David reached out to pull Nelson up when a sharp pain dug

into his ribs. He dropped to one knee. He jerked around as fast as he could manage. His attacker was already running the other way, holding a field hockey stick in his hand. David looked up to see that all of Varsity was retreating to the double doors that exited to the stairwell. It didn't make sense. Most of David's gang was strewn across the clearing, groaning from their injuries. What were they up to?

A plume of brown smoke rose up from trash clustered by the exit. And then, the first lick of orange flame.

"Fire!" David shouted.

David ran toward the fire. Will and Mort were on his heels. Others pulled themselves to their feet. David stomped on the first small fire he came to, a flaming, stuffed garbage bag. He kicked it toward the exit, but the doors were closing.

David ran to stop them. In the brief moment before they closed, David locked eyes with Sam on the other side.

"You're not coming out until the food drop!" Sam shouted. "I'll be waiting in the quad!"

With a flick of his hand, he signaled the Varsity members to follow him up the stairs. The doors closed. David wrenched his hands around both knobs and pulled. *Please open.* Nothing gave. David pulled and yanked. He pressed one foot on one door and jerked on the other. Didn't even budge.

David spun around to face the basement. Will was shouting orders to everyone. People were smothering fires wherever they found them. Noxious smoke the color of dirt clouded the lights above. It took twenty minutes before every flame was out. People were coughing and hacking. They were smeared black with soot and sweat. Ghostly ash hung in the air. Piles of trash bags were now misshapen hills of black magma.

Will looked up to David, who leaned against the door. He didn't even want to say it, but there was no denying it.

"We're trapped."

14

WILL CLOSED HIS EYES AS LUCY'S FINGERTIPS

slid down his cheek. Soft. Gentle. She stroked more paint on.
It was cold, but the warmth of her fingers radiated through.
She drew a jagged line down his jaw.

It had been Lucy's idea to do the war paint. She concocted
it out of a mixture of watered-down glue mixed with ash,
and she'd devoted the entire morning to painting everyone's
faces. This was Lucy's contribution to the battle effort. She
hoped that if they looked like savages, maybe people would
believe they were. Nobody argued with her plan; they needed
whatever help they could get.

He looked at her. She looked at his cheek. He could feel
her warm breath touch his nose. The last time he'd been this
close, really this close, he was too young and stupid to know

what to do. He'd just lain inches from her all night in that tent in Utah, their noses almost touching, their hands clasped. Why didn't he kiss her then?

Lucy bit down on her plump lip. Will could barely handle how adorable she looked when she concentrated. The fierce painted lines on her face couldn't betray her beauty. Her skin glowed especially white against the muddled black of the war paint. She was perfect.

Will's hand was in his pocket. He rubbed the fine gold necklace between his fingers. He wanted to pull it out. He wanted to tell her everything he felt about her. Lucy's fingers trembled as she painted a stripe down his nose. She was scared. They all were. They were hungry and rattled after four days and nights of Varsity pounding on the locked doors, taunting them, telling them they were going to die when the food drop came. It was no way for Lucy to have to live, terrified, scavenging trash for forgotten crumbs wedged in wrapper creases. He'd tried to comfort her, but she said she was fine. She said they needed to focus on keeping everybody else's spirits up. He didn't care about the rest of them, only her.

"Lucy . . ."

"Yes," she said, her voice caught in her throat.

Will pulled his hand out of his pocket with the necklace clutched in his clammy palm.

"There's something I—"

David stepped into view behind Lucy. He held the thick

wooden leg of a desk in his hand. A heavy metal L-bracket was still bolted to its end. Will paused.

"They're going to open the doors soon. Let's get ready," David said.

Lucy looked up at David, and her chest heaved. She nodded quickly. David gave her a pat on the shoulder before walking to the doors. She leaned toward David's touch. She'd never responded to Will that way. No gift, no matter how nice, was going to outweigh everything she thought David had done for her. If he was going to get Lucy to see him for who he was, it would have to be from something he did, not something he bought her.

Will stuffed the necklace back into his pocket. *Too much, too soon,* he scolded himself. He'd been playing everything wrong. How did he get her to sleep in that tent under the stars? He'd been crazy that day. He'd sprinted all the way across Devil's Spine, that narrow rock bridge, without ever touching the guide rope. Chazz was pissed at him, saying it was a stupid risk, but Lucy . . . she looked at him differently after that. He had to do something that brave again. He had to be her hero today.

"What were you saying?" Lucy said.

"Nothing."

Lucy promptly finished Will's face paint. She pulled away from Will and walked with David to where the group was gathered by the locked doors. Will lifted himself to follow, but someone grabbed his arm.

It was Smudge.

"It looks like a dog dumped on your face," Smudge said.

"So now I know what it feels like to be you."

"You scared?"

"No."

"I'm not going," Smudge said.

"What? You have to. We need everyone we can get."

"You're crazy if you think you got a fighting chance in that drop. It's suicide, man. I'm not dying for your brother."

"Yeah, but—"

"What about your girl? You gonna let her die too?"

"I'm not going to let her fight," Will said.

"Dude, there's gonna be, like, a hundred Varsity out there. It's a joke. If you go out there with them, you're gonna die. You're all gonna die."

David faced his tiny gang of fifteen in front of the locked doors. The food drop would be starting soon. Blackened faces looked back at him. The paint couldn't cover their fear.

"We're gonna make it," David said.

It was a lie. This food drop was a fixed fight. Sam had trapped them in the basement without food for days. He wanted them tired and hungry. He wanted to break their spirits, so they'd be easy to take down. David had no choice but to play Sam's game.

David heard the shuffle of footsteps down the stairs outside the double doors. He turned to face them, slapping on a mean face. The handles moved, and the doors were pulled open from the outside. Trash scraped against the floor. The Varsity doormen remained hidden in the shadows. His fellow Scraps crowded close behind him, and David took the first step up the stairs.

They all wore at least five layers of ruined clothes they'd found in the dump for extra padding. Some had even poked holes in linoleum floor tiles and tied them to their bodies for added protection. Each of them carried a weapon, if not two: pipes, shivs, lengths of chain. The twins each carried a pair of scissors, broken apart, one blade in each hand. Belinda hefted a book bag full of bricks. The slashes of black paint marring their faces were dry and cracked now. They stank like hell.

David's stomach felt like it was turning inside out.

"Keep walkin', Scraps," a Varsity said from the darkness.

They ascended the stairs and reached the first floor. Two Varsity guys, in full pads with lacrosse sticks, stood on either side of entrance. They were Rhodes Dixon and George Diaz. There was a time when David had laughed hard with these guys about stupid stuff, farts and nicknames for ugly girls. Today, they were laughing at him.

"Ooo, check it out, Rhodes, look at their faces."

"I can't, Diaz," Rhodes said with a mocking shiver. "I'm too scared."

Both guys cracked up. David ignored them and waved everyone forward.

"You're gonna die, Thorpe," Rhodes called out like a song after him.

The hallway ahead was long. Nelson hyperventilated behind him. Belinda mumbled calming words into Nelson's funnel. David looked at Lucy. She forced a smile, but it ended up being nothing but a flat line. David checked on the rest of the group.

There were only eight of them.

David's fear nearly sank him. Including him, that made nine against a hundred. He hated the six deserters for jumping ship, but he couldn't blame them.

"They're not coming," Will said from beside him. "Smudge and Dorothy and some of the other ones . . . they never left the basement."

David scanned past Will. A Varsity in a football helmet with a tinted visor stepped into the hall from a classroom. David glanced to the other side of the hall where another one stood, holding a position beside the opposite row of lockers. It was the same all the way down the corridor. Bulky figures stepped out from classroom doorways and from adjoining hallways.

They barked and hissed and spit as David and the gang walked past. David's gang huddled closer together. Each Varsity they passed joined the growing pack, led by Rhodes and George, that followed at their heels.

David stepped through the wide open doors to the quad. Every gang was represented: the redheaded Sluts in their spikes and chrome; the Nerds in their khakis; the Freaks in black with their blue hair; the Pretty Ones in their pristine whites. The band Geeks wore their ragged regalia and set up their instruments in one corner to score the bloody affair. Some were there to fight. Most were there for the show.

Conversation burst through the crowd when they saw David. What had they come to see? A bloodbath? He wanted to run. Like a coward. He wanted to hide in the trash like Smudge and Dorothy. David walked forward instead, making sure his strides were long and confident. The crowd hushed. Hundreds and hundreds of eyes were on him, riveted by his presence. What did they think? That he was an idiot for even showing up? That he knew something they didn't? Behind David, the sound of Nelson's breathing changed to the sound of Nelson throwing up. Some Skaters laughed. David kept walking.

He saw a small clearing along the perimeter where no gangs stood. He led his crew to it. They stood close together in that spot, their backs to the wall. As David faced the quad, he realized that their spot being vacant was no coincidence. Varsity was assembled directly across the quad from them.

Varsity's front line was bashing helmets and thudding each other in the chest. There were so many of them. David couldn't see Sam. Every other gang looked from Varsity to David and back again, ready for something to pop off.

"Look at the fat one!" a voice declared from the Varsity crowd.

Laughs.

"No fair! Elephants aren't allowed to fight at the drop!"

Varsity laughed louder.

People in other gangs covered their mouths, embarrassed for them but still laughing. Sam's voice cut through the crowd's rabble.

"I heard there was a new gang!"

Sam lazily swung a length of steel chain in his hand.

"I could have sworn I heard that. I'm looking, but I don't see one," he said.

Varsity laughed right on cue. Some of the crowd did too.

"All I see is nine Scraps with a death wish."

The *thup-thup-thup* of helicopter blades floated in from far away. It was almost time. Varsity readied themselves for attack. David's only thought was that he could make them chase him. Sam only wanted him. If David ran out of the quad and into the school, maybe he could lose them, maybe he couldn't, but Will and Lucy and the others would be spared. David scanned the Varsity line, focusing on their best runners. He knew Keith Anderson was definitely faster than him. And Wesley James was at least equal his speed, probably faster with David's lack of sleep and nourishment.

Sam signaled Anthony Smith and the other linebackers. They hustled to each exit and stood guard. Shit. Sam knew just what he was thinking. David wasn't getting off the quad. He was going to die here.

A new sound drowned out the distant noise of the helicopter. It was the rhythmic crack of Varsity's baseball bats on a brick wall. They'd be cracking David's head next.

David turned back to his gang of eight. They didn't deserve to die because of him.

"This is not your fight," David said. As he looked from face to face, his words became more urgent. He didn't want any argument. "Stay against the wall. Then, split up. When other gangs are leaving, get lost in their numbers and sneak out. Run and hide. This whole thing was a mistake—"

A heavy hand slapped down on David's shoulder. He almost jumped out of his skin. He turned. It was Gonzalo. Gonzalo was huge. Six foot nine. Stout and round. He carried a fire ax over his shoulder. He had long, dry, white metalhead hair that covered his face. Back when David had been captain of the football team, he'd tried desperately to get Gonzalo to join the team, but the guy couldn't be bothered. He was the epitome of a loner. Gonzalo was the only student who was able to thrive at the drops fighting all by himself. Every two weeks he walked through the drops unchallenged, picking up what he wanted. No one wanted to mess with him, and there was never a good reason to. He only ever wanted enough for himself.

"Heard they tried to hang you in the market," Gonzalo said. "That ain't right."

David was in shock. Gonzalo towered over him. He could only nod slowly in response.

"Is it true you're starting a gang that won't stand for that shit?" Gonzalo asked.

"Th-that's right," David said.

"Then I'm in."

"You're shitting me," Will said. David couldn't have put it better if he tried.

Gonzalo took his place beside David and faced the crowd, ax in hand.

The sight of Gonzalo threw the crowd into disarray. Everyone was shocked. The bats cracked faster. The blades above thumped louder. One white-haired Scrap came running out of the crowd and stood in front of David and Gonzalo. He was a little guy, wiry. His face was latticed with crisscrossing scars.

"Name's Ritchie. I want to fight with you guys. Is that cool?"

David nodded again. "Yes. I'll owe you forever."

Nelson handed Ritchie a hammer. Ritchie refused it and cracked his knuckles.

"No, I'm cool."

Then more Scraps came. It was just a few white heads of hair trickling through other gangs at first, but within moments Scraps converged on him from all over the quad. Some he didn't think he'd ever seen before. They were loner kids who lived in the shadows, who haunted the edges of the school, who had long ago been forgotten.

The helicopter roared overhead. The canopy was opened, and the giant pallets were lowered through the hole.

David was encircled by white hair. There had to be eighty of them now. He had no idea this many kids were without gangs. A familiar feeling flickered inside of him. He had a team behind him again, one with a fighting chance.

"Listen to me!" David screamed. "You're not alone anymore. We fight together!"

They raised their fists and cheered.

"This is your gang! And that"—David pointed to the heavy pallets swinging above—"is OUR food!"

The pallets dropped.

With a wooden *crack*, the pallets hit the ground. Food erupted from the broken containers. David's gang charged. Varsity and the rest of the school did the same. The quad was a vortex of bodies, all grabbing for loot. Everyone slammed into each other. David swung his club into the forearm of his old teammate Rhodes and heard a crunch. Rhodes clutched his wrecked arm and fell.

Someone blindsided David, tackling him into a pileup. Anonymous fingers hooked the inside of David's mouth, threatening to tear his cheek off. David chomped down on the fingers. Whomever they belonged to screamed. George Diaz rushed toward David wearing a lacrosse glove with nails sticking out from it. George swung at David with looping punches. The nails whizzed by his nose. David threw a lucky punch and caught the underside of George's glove, driving the nailed side into his face. George screamed and tumbled off, the fat glove still fastened to his cheek.

David lifted himself to his feet. He saw Hilary bolt from the Pretty Ones and into the mix. Sam was one thing, but Hilary never left the sidelines during a drop. David tracked her path to Lucy, who was hefting food toward the exit with Belinda.

Hilary grabbed Lucy by the hair and flung her to the ground. David pushed off to stop her, but Will was already ahead of him. David ran up and kept pace with Will. He was afraid of what Will might do to Hilary.

"I got this," David said, putting his hand out to block Will. "Focus on the food."

"Get off me." Will shoved back. "I'm serious."

David stumbled, and Will took the lead. Ahead of them, Lucy flailed underneath Hilary, who had both hands in Lucy's hair, pulling her around like a dog by the ears. Will got to Lucy first and grabbed hold of her. David ran to Hilary and clutched her by the waist. David yanked Hilary off of Lucy and spun her away. He held her firmly in his hands. It was the first time he'd touched her since the night she'd broken up with him. He didn't want to let go.

Lucy broke free of Will, and kicked Hilary in the stomach. Hilary yelped and doubled over in David's hands. Will, smiling, dragged Lucy away again.

"Are you okay?" David said. Hilary's eyes were still savage from the fight, but David's voice seemed to tame her.

"Don't touch me," she said, and jerked free of him.

When David reached out to take her hand, a rock hit him in the forehead. He clutched his eyes shut and bent in pain. When he opened them again, Will was already hurrying Lucy off the quad. All around, rocks, bricks, pencil sharpeners, staplers, and other small objects rained down from above.

David looked up to see white-haired kids throwing those objects out of second- and third-floor windows. Their target was a large group of Varsity guys who were dragging a huge unbroken pallet of food toward the gym. The Varsity guys were pelted over and over, bricks ricocheting off their helmets. The ones without helmets bailed until there weren't enough of them to haul the pallet. Ritchie was on their trail and moved swiftly with a pack of white-hairs to reverse the pallet's path. After ten minutes, the remaining supplies on the quad had all been scooped up.

"Scraps!" David called out as the last fights died down. He raised his hands victoriously in the air. "Let's roll!"

As David turned toward the southern exit, he saw Sam tromping toward him, his heavy steel chain dangling from his hand. David panicked. He'd lost his weapon in his last scuffle. Empty-handed, he didn't stand a chance against Sam's chain.

Sam was closing in fast. Scraps, eager to prove themselves to David, stepped into Sam's path to stop him. Each one received a vicious slap of chain for their trouble. But they still piled in. Five feet from David, Sam was consumed by vengeful Scraps.

They hated Sam. They fought each other for the privilege of

hitting him. They kicked his face, they pounded his ribs, they tore at his skin. They were going to kill him. David caught glimpses of Sam's face through the writhing heap. Sam was in agony. He met David's gaze. Sam was scared. Truly, honestly scared.

"Get off him!" David shouted.

No one listened.

"I said stop!"

The mob backed off, leaving Sam on his back, bloody and moaning. David stood over him. Seeing the tyrant who had tormented him for a year lying broken on the ground in front of him was better than any trophy he could ever win. David crouched down and got in Sam's bludgeoned face.

"You lose," David said.

He stood and walked away.

Varsity members swooped in fast and carried Sam off.

David led his gang off the quad. No one blocked their path. He saw awestruck grins and nods of begrudging respect from the other gangs. David's gang regrouped near the foyer. The initial nine were now nearly a hundred, their faces blood-streaked and smiling. Each one had their arms full with food.

"Let's go eat," David said.

David walked toward the West Wing with an army in his wake.

15

THREE FOOD DROPS HAD PASSED. DAVID stood in front of a metal door, with twenty-two of his gang members behind him. They all wore makeshift armor and carried weapons. They called themselves the Loners now. Ritchie and Gonzalo flanked David. David held a machete he'd made by hammering a radiator cover flat. The hallway had no functional ventilation, so the air had a dead, dusty quality that made David feel like he was inhaling someone else's exhale.

David pounded on the wide metal door with three solid knocks, then dragged the tip of his machete across the width of the door. The Loners behind him clutched their weapons tight and kept their eyes on the hallway behind.

The door opened a crack, still fastened shut by a heavy chain on the inside. Leonard looked out.

"Welcome back," Leonard said, but the rest was too quiet to hear. He still lost heart midway through sentences, but Leonard was coming out of his shell bit by bit, now that he worked the door.

Leonard pulled the door open. The twenty-two Loners followed David into their home, a three-story stairwell they had dubbed the Stairs.

David hung his machete up in the armory, a triangular alcove under the bottom flight of stairs. The others did the same, adding their armor and weapons to the piles.

With the door locked behind them, David felt safe. It was a feeling he was still getting used to. He took to the first flight of stairs. About fifteen of the now ninety-four Loners were hanging on those steps, talking quietly and playing games. Being in a gang was an adjustment for all of them. They were learning that they didn't have to run from every noise. They could eat more than a palmful of food every other day. And they could trust each other. Each of the fifteen lit up as David walked by. The girls reached out and touched him with affection. He smiled.

David heard a rumbling of anticipation up the stairs. People knew he was coming, it made him feel like a celebrity. He reached the first landing of the staircase. It was packed with white-headed Loners eating dinner. They stood, clustered onto the twenty-by-thirteen-foot space that served as the gang's food storage and kitchen. More sat on the next flight of stairs up, chatting and chewing. Nelson doled out rations of canned mandarin oranges and cold hot dogs. David could already taste the mouthwatering combination of salt and syrup on his tongue. Nelson waved to him. He was the ideal choice to put in charge of splitting up the food equally, mainly because he never heard anyone's complaints.

"Everybody, huddle up!" David said as he stepped onto the landing. They stopped eating and looked to him. He couldn't help but love that feeling, the respect they showed him, the gratitude.

"So, we just got back from a meeting with the Sluts. I got some pretty good news. As of today, if any Loner runs into trouble on the east side of school, you can go to the cafeteria, and the Sluts will take you in until backup arrives."

The Loners cheered through mouths clogged with food.

"But I'm talking about serious, end-of-the-world stuff here, guys. Please don't go knocking on their door just because you want to use their bathroom, okay?"

There was a smattering of laughter. He'd caught them at the right time. Food always put people in a good mood.

"I don't know," Ritchie said. "They do keep those bathrooms spotless."

David grinned. He slapped Ritchie on the shoulder.

"This guy took a cast-iron dump in there. Almost ruined the whole deal."

The crowd broke out in real laughter this time. David always ragged on Ritchie in his speeches. It was becoming a popular routine.

"Seriously, Ritchie, we eat the same food. How does your ass smell like that?"

More laughs. Ritchie hung his head, playing along as usual. As David scanned the elated faces of his gang, their laughter filled him with purpose. He wanted to do right by them. Everything that happened before was worth it for this feeling. He punched Ritchie playfully on the arm. Having Ritchie and Gonzalo around was great. He'd forgotten what it was like to have solid people with him that he could count on. They knew what it meant to be part of a team.

Will walked down the stairs, through the crowd, shirtless.

David's smile faded. Will paid no attention to David, didn't even look at him. He maneuvered through the crowd of attentive listeners, grabbed his share of dinner, then tromped back up the stairs. David forced a smile for his audience.

"Anyway, the point is, we've got friends on that side of school now, and we're gonna do the same for any of Violent's girls who come to us for help. Sound good?"

They cheered in response.

"Solid. Have a great dinner, everybody," David said, and he made his way to the second flight, through back pats and high fives. He took his tin-can dinner from Nelson and headed up. He had one thing on his mind: crashing. Two more flights and he could fall face-first onto the sofa cushions in the corner of his room and check out completely. It'd been a long day. Running the Loners had been a privilege so far, but it left him exhausted.

"David?"

David turned to see Dorothy. Her greasy, white hair hung to one side, her shirt was wrinkled, and she had ink stains on her fingers.

"Oh, hey, what's up?" David said.

She held out her hand to reveal a perfect paper square with a tiny portrait on it. She placed it in David's hand.

"It's you," she said.

"Hey . . . cool. I love it. Thank you."

She had been giving him tiny homemade gifts every couple days. He was starting to feel she did it out of guilt.

"Listen, Dorothy, I just want you to know that no matter what went down with the drop, it's in the past. You're a Loner now—"

A look of horror twisted Dorothy's face and had gotten worse with each word David said. She turned and bolted down the stairs.

"Okay," David said.

He studied the miniature portrait. The lines were light and wobbly. The look on his face was stern, and he stared off into the distance. What was he supposed to do with these things? He tucked it in his jeans pocket and rounded the banister to the second-floor landing, the lounge.

Ten class chairs sat in an imperfect semicircle; piles of

library books on loan from the Nerds were scattered around the room. Mort sat on one of the piles, reading a paperback, probably staining the pages with sweaty fingers. Belinda was checking her hair growth in the gang's only mirror, mounted on the wall. There were a dozen Loners crowded together in the corner watching one cell phone screen. They leaned forward in a huddle to hear the audio from its little speaker. It was one of three phones in the whole gang. By now, it was hard not to know every song and every video on those three phones by heart, but they kept playing them anyway.

Will came bounding down the stairs into the lounge.

"Boom," Will said. He held out a double-wide power strip with four phone chargers plugged into it, their cords hanging down like dead snakes.

"How sweet is this?" Will said.

The dozen cell phone watchers nodded and *ooh*'d.

"Where'd you get those?" David asked.

Will's face grayed at the sight of David.

"Don't you worry about it, boss. All you need to know is they're ours now," Will said.

Boss. The word dripped with sarcasm. He'd given Will plenty of space since the gang formed; he wanted things to cool down between them. He thought a little time apart and the camaraderie of a gang would fix Will's attitude. No such luck.

"Four chargers. Kinda seems like overkill, doesn't it?" David said.

"Yeah, now. But if we wanna be legit, we're gonna need a phone for every Loner."

David saw the faces of all the kids in the huddle bloom with hope.

"C'mere," David said to Will with a hook of his finger. Will followed him to the barricaded entrance to the second floor. David cleared his throat and dug in with a hard whisper.

"We're barely getting by as it is, don't put pipe dreams into people's heads about personal phones."

"We're all cooped up in this staircase with nothing to do," Will said. "We need somethin'. Just food and a place to sleep isn't enough."

"So, hang out. Tell stories. Sing your camping songs, I don't know. But don't say 'phones for everybody.' You say it, and then I gotta deliver. You get that? You're not the one who has to answer for it. They're all looking at me."

"Yeah, and you just hate that, don't you?"

Will was always going to act like a little shit to him, no matter what David provided for him.

"Did you steal them?" David asked.

"What, like that's a sin? Don't pull the whole golden boy thing with me, man. I know you."

Will was baiting him. He wanted David to flip out in front of everybody.

"No phones," David barked, loud enough that the whole landing heard him. They groaned. He wasn't going to deal with this now. He left Will by the door and charged up the next flight. Only one more set of stairs after that, and he'd be home.

He high-stepped it across made and unmade beds on the next landing. This was where most of the gang slept. It was first come, first served for floor space, the rest had to take a stair. The stairs were only a foot wide and weren't comfortable to sleep on, but you could fit if you slept on your side.

On the last flight up, a lot of Loners were working hard. They stacked wooden planks, salvaged from food-drop pallets, onto each stair until it was flush with the stair above. It effectively doubled the width of each stair. Eventually, with enough planks, the whole gang could have a double-wide stair to sleep on. Lucy was on her hands and knees, helping place planks. He climbed the steps up to her.

"Hi, David," she said. Her voice gave him a surprising little rush.

"Hey."

She stood and dusted off her hands, her brown eyes as big and hypnotizing as ever. The blonde was long gone from her hair now; it was a pure white. The tips of it stroked her soft freckled shoulders. She wore a new dress he'd never seen before. It was pale blue, and somehow she'd kept it impossibly clean while doing this manual labor project.

"Did, um . . . did Dorothy find you? She was looking for you," Lucy said, stepping after him and letting her hand slide along the banister behind her.

David pulled the hand-drawn portrait from his pocket. He'd given Lucy a glimpse of Dorothy's other gifts in the past. Lucy covered her mouth with a little gasp, and her eyebrows parted sympathetically. "She loves you," Lucy said.

"Oh, God, don't say that," he said.

"But it's so sweet. I hope you're keeping them safe."

David nodded, but he didn't know what he'd done with the last couple pieces—the paper-clip medal and the index-card diorama.

"I wish I could make things like that. I'm just not creative," Lucy said.

"That's not true," David said, pointing to the wooden bunks. "You're doing a great job here."

Lucy flitted her big eyes in that pretty-girl way that reminded David of Hilary.

"David," she said, "industrious is not the same as creative."

And then, when she said something like that, David remembered how little Lucy was like Hilary. That seemed like the kind of worldly wisdom a grandmother might've wielded. David had been learning a lot about Lucy over the past few weeks. She wasn't just the delicate flower he'd thought she was when he saw her by the graduation booth. She was happy to get her hands dirty and chip in. Every once in a while, she'd throw out a comment that cracked David up. She was . . . cool.

"Oh! So I figured it out!" Lucy said as she stretched her arm up the railing and behind David's thigh.

"What?"

"What we were saying this morning . . . best slope in the Rockies? It's Point Peak. Hands down."

In a gang full of snowboarders, Lucy had discovered that she and David were the only skiers. David agreed about Point Peak, but he squinted his eyes and faked uncertainty. Her jaw dropped.

"Oh, my God!" Lucy said. "I can't believe you even have to think about it! I'm right. You know I'm right."

"Maybe."

Lucy punched David in the chest, her mouth still agape. He nearly fell backward.

"Maybe?"

David laughed, "Easy! I gotta weigh all the factors. Besides, a guy's entitled to his opinion, isn't he?"

"Not when you're wrong! David, even if there's a double black diamond like it, nothing beats that view of the mountains. Nothing." Then her eyes went wide, suddenly inspired. "That's where I'm going to visit tonight."

"Visit?"

"Yeah, right when I close my eyes to go to sleep, I pick a place or a memory, and I try to hold on to it as long as I can."

Lucy closed her eyes and moved up another step, getting close to David. "I walk through every part of it. I look at every little detail. Until I fall asleep."

She opened her eyes and breathed in. "It helps keep away the nightmares."

The air between them felt hot. David's room was only few stairs away. He had the third-floor landing all to himself, closed off from everyone by a pair of heavy blanket curtains. Once he was behind those curtains, no one could see him. He could bring Lucy in there, and they would have total privacy to do whatever they wanted.

Will's laugh echoed up from the stairs below. It was sharp and had a malicious edge to it.

"I should . . . ," David said, pointing back toward his room.

"Oh," Lucy said, looking down. "Right."

David didn't look away though. He knew Will had a thing for her. But she was the hottest girl in the gang, and she wanted to flirt with him. How much could it hurt to flirt back a little?

"I'll see you on the slopes," he said.

"I'll wear something hot," Lucy said.

She blushed right afterward, then laughed and skipped down the stairs.

David climbed the last few stairs and ducked into his room, to sit down at last and eat his meat and oranges.

16

LUCY COULDN'T SLEEP. TRYING TO VISIT Point Peak in her mind had been a bust. She pictured every bit of it, every inch of her descent down the slope, but she couldn't stop smelling the kids sleeping around her. She couldn't ignore the hard stair against her back. No matter what she pictured, no matter how vivid, she couldn't get there. She was stuck in the Stairs.

She wanted to crawl up those fifteen stairs to David's curtain door, past Belinda's snoring, past the twins' midnight murmurings, past the wet squelches coming from Gonzalo's two-zipped-together sleeping bags, where his four foot ten girlfriend, Sasha, was somewhere inside, doing something that should've been done anywhere else but there. Lucy wanted to disappear into David's room, to be wrapped in his sturdy arms, feeling him. It wasn't just that he'd saved her life, David was the first person she'd met in this place who was willing to risk his own life to help other people. He was good, and that was a rarity.

"Wanna get out of here?" a voice whispered.

Lucy looked to the landing below. Will stood amid the sleeping bodies that packed the floor. He stared up at her with a tilted smile. She narrowed her eyes at him.

"What do you mean?" Lucy said.

"Out of the Stairs. Let's go for a walk."

"We can't. David said no one leaves the Stairs in—"

"In groups of less than fifteen. I know what he said. But I'm losing my mind in here. I feel like I'm sleeping in a beehive."

"I know the feeling," she said.

"So come on."

Lucy stared at him. She shouldn't. She should stay, keep on smelling her gang mates and twiddling her thumbs.

"It'll be a thrill," Will said, his smile getting wider.

"Just a short walk."

Will held out his hand to her.

She took it. He was right, it was a thrill. They moved together, totally in sync, tiptoeing between the slumbering bodies, down the next flight, past the lounge, past the kitchen, and down to the bottom landing, all without saying a word. Will quietly plucked a club from the armory, a broken flagpole with a big brass eagle on the end.

Leonard had fallen asleep on guard duty. For such a quiet person, he snored like an old lady. Will very carefully lifted the chain from the door. Every movement of his hand was controlled but quick. The door popped open with a soft click. Will looked back to Lucy with a wiggle of his eyebrow. She knew this was stupid, so stupid. But it was fun. The air in the hall was warm and gross, but it felt so good to be out of the Stairs that she didn't care.

"Don't worry," Will said, "I know my way around at night."

Lucy had never been walking at night. It felt sort of naughty. She strolled down the hall next to Will. It was odd, the halls were so quiet. Every tiny noise was amplified. Someone must have been hearing them.

"Are you just saying that to sound cool?" Lucy said.

"Nope, I'm out at night all the time."

"What for?"

"I don't know. Why shouldn't I go out, if I feel like it?" Will said.

"You're not scared?"

"Of what?" He said it so matter-of-factly, like being afraid was a waste of time and energy.

It reminded her of the day they hiked up to Devil's Spine. It was a narrow rock bridge. On either side was a seven-hundred-foot drop to a churning river below. Lucy was scared to death, everybody was. Chazz warned them that the extreme wind conditions meant that they would have to cross it on their hands and knees, but before he could finish his instructions, Will charged out onto the bridge. Lucy's heart stopped—she was sure he was a goner. Chazz screamed after him to stop, but he didn't. Will ran all the way to the other side and threw his hands up in victory. She'd never witnessed anything so daring in her life, and it turned her on.

Being with Will, out in the halls, breaking the rules, Lucy couldn't help but feel the tug of old feelings. Will rounded the next corner. Before following him, Lucy glanced back to the door of the Stairs, now a hundred feet behind her. She got a stab of anxiety. She could almost feel Brad's hands closing around her neck. She hurried up next to Will.

"Will . . . I'm not sure we should do this," she said. "David's rule is sounding pretty good right now." She stopped walking. Will sighed.

"David doesn't get it. He doesn't know what it's like for us," Will said.

"What do you mean, for us?"

"He'll be out of here in months. We've both got years to go," Will said.

Years. She focused on the new long hallway ahead. The air was dirty. There was barely any light. The lockers were littered with dents. Each month the lockers were more dented, the walls more scrawled with cuss words. Lately, people were taking the walls apart to use the wood and drywall. The walls. What would be left of the place by the time she got out?

"It's fine for him to play it safe," Will continued. "He's almost out. But we have to adapt to living here 'cause—well, we have no choice."

Lucy didn't want to think about the idea that David was going to leave.

"I know what you need," Will said. He smiled and wagged his eyebrows up and down again. It was cute. "You need to run."

Each doorway, each corner Will pulled her past frightened her. But it was all in her head. There was no one hiding in the dark waiting to attack. She let go of Will's hands and took big breaths and full strides. It felt good watching the school fly past her so fast. She never got to run anymore. She either stayed in the Stairs, or she walked at a regular pace inside a tight group. That was the only thing that looked good about the food drops: those kids got to run around.

Will wasn't kidding, he did know his way around. Some corners he barreled right around, then at others he would make her stop and he'd peek around first. The longer they went, the more she felt fast and slippery, like no one could catch her. She bolted ahead of Will.

The only reason she stopped on the third-floor balcony of the foyer was because she was out of breath.

"Wait." She panted and leaned against the railing that looked down on the graduation booth below. Will stopped and bent over with a smile, resting his hands on his knees.

"Check it out," he said, and climbed up onto the balcony railing.

"Will!" she gasped. "What are you doing?"

It was a forty-foot fall to the foyer floor. Will stayed focused on the three-inch-wide metal path in front of him.

"Shh," he said gently. "I'm trying to concentrate."

He took a careful step forward.

"Hold my hand," Lucy said. She reached up to Will. He ignored her hand. She wanted to grab hold of him and yank him down to her, but what if that made him slip and fall the wrong way?

"Watch this," Will said with a wild smile. He closed his eyes.

"Will, don't! Cut it out."

He took another step. Bigger this time. He lifted one knee up and stood wobbling on one foot.

He was going to die right in front of her.

"You're scaring me," she said.

Will dropped his foot, stumbling forward a few steps. His eyes snapped open. He jerked his hips to keep his balance. Lucy squealed. Will shot his arms out to his sides and steadied himself. He looked at her, his eyes wide with astonishment.

"Did you see that?"

"Yes, I saw it! Will, I swear to God, if you die . . . !"

He cackled with delight.

"What is wrong with you?" she said.

"Oh, I don't know. A lot of things."

Will hopped farther down the banister, landing on his other foot again. Lucy gasped.

"I'm epileptic."

Another hop. Lucy cringed.

"I got it bad for a girl, and I mighta missed my window with her."

Lucy looked Will in the eyes. Was he talking about her?

"I've always had bad luck."

Will jumped, but his foot missed the mark. He slipped off the side, the bad side. His armpit landed hard against the top rail. He clamped down with his whole body. He hung by the hook of his armpit, and the rest of his body dangled over the foyer below.

"No!" Lucy said.

She lunged for him, grabbed his arm, and pulled. She pushed off the balcony wall with her foot. She could hear his feet scurrying for a foothold. He threw his weight over the top of the banister, and they landed on the balcony floor next to each other. She whacked him in the chest.

"Don't do that!"

"I'm sorry," he said with a chuckle.

"It's not funny," Lucy said. "You scared me to death."

She pushed away from him. The smile vanished from his face.

"Don't be mad," he said. His voice shook. "You're everything to me."

Lucy stared at Will. He blushed and looked away. She realized her mouth was hanging open, she was so surprised. She was the girl he had a crush on.

On the walk back to the Stairs, Will tried to start up more conversations, but she pretended to still be mad. She needed time to process all of it. Had Will liked her since Wild-Trek? She glanced at him when she thought she could get away with it. He was handsome, and tonight had been such a thrill. She couldn't deny that they had fun together, but maybe that was because they were such great friends. Could she risk ruining that friendship just to see what dating Will would be like?

As they neared their home base, Lucy saw a smallish figure in an oversize McKinley sweatshirt by the entrance to the Stairs, about to knock on the door.

"Hey," Will said. "What do you want?"

The figure jumped in surprise and turned to Will and Lucy, a strand of blonde hair curled around the lip of her hood. The light caught her face. Lucy knew her.

"Tara?" Lucy said.

Tara was one of the more athletic girls in the Pretty Ones and she was Hilary's right hand. Tara had once slapped Lucy across the face for talking back. She could still feel the sting of it on her cheek.

"I'm here to see David," Tara said.

"Why?" Lucy asked.

"I have a letter to deliver to him," Tara said, her hands

clutching something in her sweatshirt pocket. "And I'm only supposed to give it to him."

That letter had to be from Hilary.

"Give it to me," Lucy said.

"No. I'm only supposed to—"

"You're not getting in here," Lucy said. "I don't know what you thought or Hilary thought, but you're not going to see David. It doesn't work that way."

She could see Tara's confidence slip a little. Lucy pounced. She got right in her face.

"I know you don't want to go back to Hilary with that letter in your hand." She spat her words out, sharp and nasty. "I mean, I can't imagine what she'd make you do. But I'll take it. I'll give it to David. And you can go back to Hilary and tell her you placed it right in his hand."

Tara looked at Lucy, still unsure. She picked at her lip as she weighed Lucy's words. *Give it to me,* Lucy thought. *Give it to me, you little bitch.*

"No."

Lucy lunged for Tara's stupid, oversized pocket. Tara ran.

"Don't come back! You hear me? You're not welcome here!" Lucy shouted.

This was her gang, her home, and Hilary didn't get to stick her skinny little fingers into it. And what the hell was in that letter anyway?

17

A WINDOW SMASHED BEHIND WILL. HE
couldn't run any faster. They were coming up hot behind him.
Will pushed a rolling cart; it had a flat-screen TV and a DVD
player on it. The dangling power cords twisted and tangled
and lashed at his legs. One wheel of the cart was stuck, and
it flapped around like a flag on a car antenna, shaking the
entire cart. The TV began a tap dance off the side, but Will
caught it.

He looked back. Freaks. A herd of them, clutching splintered two-by-fours. Fifty feet away. Blue hair whipping above
their furious faces. They screamed. The sound of it bounced
off the hollow metal lockers of the long hall and vibrated in
the air all around him like the crash of a symbol.

Don't seize.

He could have a grand mal seizure. Right now. But then again, he could anytime. Eating breakfast was just as dangerous. He could clench up, choke on a piece of bread, and die. He pumped his legs harder. He felt alive. The danger, the chase, the psychos at his heels, it all coursed through him like an electrical current.

Will rammed the A/V cart smack into the door of the Stairs.

"OPEN THE FUCKING DOOR!" Will screamed.

He pounded and kicked it. The screaming mob barreled toward him like a runaway semi.

"It's Will!" he shouted. The door jerked open a crack, security chain still in place, and Leonard peeked out from the gap.

"What's going . . . ," Leonard trailed off.

"HURRY!" Will barked, and Leonard jumped.

The chain fell away on the other side, and Will shoved the cart into the door. It swung wide, he charged inside. He let the cart roll away and smash into the armory. Will spun around and slammed the door shut on a Freak's forearm.

The Freak's hand writhed and twitched and clawed around for Will. Will drove his shoulder into the door and pushed with everything he had.

WHAM! Something heavy hit the door on the other side and cracked it open three inches wider. The Freak got his whole arm through the gap. The disembodied arm grabbed Will's hair and yanked on it.

"Leonard, help me!"

Leonard stood still as a statue. Three Loners ran down the stairs and pushed Leonard aside. One of them was Gonzalo. Gonzalo dug in and planted his wide hands on the door. His arms were as thick as legs.

"Who's out there?" Gonzalo shouted.

"Freaks," Will said. "A lot of them."

WHAM! WHAM! More Freaks against the door. Gonzalo filled his chest and pushed. The hand let go of Will's hair. A scream for mercy soared louder than the rest of the mob, and the arm jerked back. With a painful twist, the hand slipped back through, and the door slammed shut. Will quickly looped the chain and locked the door.

WHAM! A last-ditch effort from the other side. Some muffled conversation, then . . .

"You're dead, Loners! Dead!"

They clomped off, back from where they came. Will dropped to his ass and struggled for breath. Loners poured down the stairs. They packed the first flight, scared and curious. The crowd parted for David.

"Shit," Will said.

Gonzalo chuckled under his breath.

"What the hell just happened?" David said. He rushed forward.

"I got us a TV," Will said, holding his gaze.

In the armory, Leonard tipped the TV back onto its stand and wheeled the whole rig out for the gang to see. The room gasped and clapped as though they had just seen a magic trick.

"You got us a TV, or you stole a TV?"

"I stole a TV, David. You think those Freaks were just doing a free delivery?"

David glared at him, but Will stared at Lucy. She flicked her eyes between Will and the TV, like she couldn't believe what he'd pulled off.

"You want to start a war with the Freaks over a TV?"

"And some movies," Will replied.

"What movies?" Gonzalo said, pushing off the wall and shuffling toward the cart.

"I don't know, there was a stack of them—"

"Forget the movies! We don't need any more enemies."

David was acting like he was Will's dad again, but Will wasn't going to look like a chump in front of Lucy.

"They hate us already for moving in on their action on the quad, just like the Skaters. If you don't want trouble, you shouldn't have started a gang."

"You want Loners to get killed so you can watch DVDs?"

David looked desperate. Deep down, Will knew his brother had a point. Maybe he'd taken it too far, to impress Lucy. He felt a twinge of regret, but then again, he'd already taken it this far.

"Are you telling me we have to give this stuff back?" Will said.

The whole gang leaned forward. David scanned the room. All eyes were on him. David looked down at Will again, and with a face as cold as a corpse's, he said, "Take the TV up to the lounge and hook it up."

Exhales all around. David was angry, angrier than Will could remember. It raised the hairs on Will's neck. David turned his back on Will and walked back up the stairs. Will had won, but he'd played dirty to pull it off. Guilt needled at him, but the crowd's murmured conversations grew once David was gone. People crowded around him, they patted Will on the back and thanked him. Then they walked to the cart, all bunching around it and stroking the TV like it was a new-born baby. Lucy was the only one to stay put. She watched Will, concerned.

Will pulled out a DVD he'd wedged in his waistband behind his back. It was a documentary on wildlife in the Caribbean. He tossed it to Lucy.

She caught it, looked up, and smiled.

Will bit on his tongue to keep from smiling back too hard. He wanted to look cool. That was the smoothest thing he'd ever done. He noticed his tongue was sore, a sign that he had seized in his sleep. Maybe last night. Maybe the night before. He didn't know for sure, and he didn't care. He felt phenomenal.

"Yeah, she picked you over David today," Smudge said. "You know why? Because she felt like it. Tomorrow, maybe she won't. Maybe she'll do something so fucked, you'll want to jump out of a third-story window and splatter your head onto the quad, 'cause at least then you could stop thinking about her. And she'll stand there looking all pretty and innocent, she's gonna go, 'Oh, that's so sad. Poor, poor Will.' That's the way these bitches work. See, they know they can get away with murder, so they do."

"Jeezus, Smudge."

Will sat against the wall in Smudge's little closet apartment. The only light source was a lone ceiling light at the far end of the computer lab. It was weak and cold, and it muted all the colors around Will. The closet reeked of soiled clothes and dried beans. Smudge's stolen items were usually neatly organized, but now they lay scattered on the floor, intermingled with garbage. Smudge sat across from him in the closet, picking at a scab on his neck.

"Just warning you," Smudge said, his voice trembling.

"Are you all right, man?"

"I'm great."

Smudge wiped his cheek. Will squinted through the dim light. Was that a tear?

"You know, Dorothy came back," Will said. "You could come back too. Be a Loner. Those phone chargers were a big hit. They'd love you if they knew you supplied them."

"Ugh, shut uuuuup," Smudge said.

"I'm saying, we'd like to have you. Why not? It would be fun."

"I like it here."

Smudge ate raisins off the floor.

"Well, anyway. . . . I'm gonna take her on a date," Will said. "I just need to come up with somewhere great. I'm out of ideas."

"Oh, I got it."

Will sat up, excited for the big idea.

"In my pants," Smudge said.

"Come on. I'm serious."

"So am I. Do yourself a favor. Don't fall for a Pretty One. Just don't. They smile at you, but they don't mean it, they just want the attention. The moment you go for it, they'll laugh at you."

"She's not a Pretty One anymore."

"No? You think that shit just goes away? Trust me, she's a tease."

"Lucy's not like them," Will said.

"Yeah, well, none of us are like we used to be, are we?"

"She's different. Don't say that shit about her."

Smudge picked up a laser pointer and started flickering it on and off, beaming the sparkling red light into Will's left eye.

"Willie, she's another bitch like the rest of 'em."

Will couldn't stand to look at him, the little worm, hunched over in the corner of his dirty box. What did he know about girls? Will shot to his feet.

"Fuck you, man. Why do I even hang out with you?" Will said.

Will stomped away, toward the exit.

"Hey, wait!" Smudge said.

"Go to hell."

"I didn't mean it."

Will kept walking. "Yeah, well, you look like a fetus. I don't mean that either."

Smudge caught up with Will by the door and gripped Will's elbow with his dry, chicken-bone fingers.

"Hey I'm sorry! You don't have to leave," Smudge said.

"Why can't you be happy for me?"

"I went too far, okay? It's probably gonna be fine with Lucy. You're right, it could be it, y'know? She could . . . like you."

"Whatever, man. You're still being dicky, even when you apologize."

Will pulled his arm away and walked out the door.

"I know a place you could take her on a date," Smudge said.

Will stopped. He turned back. Smudge's eyes were quivering.

"A place no one else knows about. Would blow her mind, for sure," Smudge continued.

"Is this a joke?"

Smudge shook his head. His forehead wrinkled with worry.

"Can you vouch for her?" Smudge asked. "Can you guarantee she can keep a secret?"

Will couldn't think of anyone he trusted more than Lucy. And this was starting to sound really good.

"Yeah. Definitely."

Smudge fished a folded-up sheet of paper out of his pocket,

along with a pen. He scrawled something along the top edge, then tore that part of the paper off.

"You'll keep coming by, right?" Smudge said, eyes downcast.

The torn ribbon of paper dangled from Smudge's fingers. Will ached to know what was on it.

"Why? So you can make fun of me more?" Will said.

Smudge looked up.

"You're the only one who talks to me," he said.

Will cringed. Smudge talked so much shit, sometimes Will forgot how sad and lonely he was.

"I can maybe stop by tomorrow?" Will said.

"Sure, whatever," Smudge said.

He handed Will the paper.

"All right, dumbass, see you later," Will said, and walked away fast.

"Yeah, later, prick," Smudge said.

Will rushed around the corner, and when he got to the first functioning ceiling light, he opened the paper. It was the combination to a lock. And underneath the combo, in large, scratchy letters, it read:

Locker 733

18

DAVID'S MACHETE CLAPPED AGAINST HIS
back with every step. He'd fashioned a sheath for it out of
thick, folded cardboard and fastened it to his back with string.
He looked over the chaos of the market, at all the flapping
mouths, the bared teeth, and the grabbing hands. He didn't
want to be here long. Get in, get out. Thirty Loners stood
behind him carrying goods for trade; the rest he'd sent back to
the Stairs with the food they'd need until the next drop came.

"Ritchie, take Nelson and your team to the Sluts. Try to get
the bulk of supplies from them. Toilet paper, soap, the usual.
Everybody else, make your free trades, but stick close to each
other."

"Loners!" somebody shouted over the crowd. David didn't
have to look up to know who it was: Bobby Corning, the

Freaks' leader, who now insisted on being called Jackal. He painted his face white. He thought it made him look undead. David couldn't bring himself to call Bobby Jackal. Before he'd decided to reinvent himself as a satanic singer-songwriter, Bobby had spent his freshman year in pastel polo shirts. That was hard to forget.

"You picked a good day to die!" Bobby said as he cut through the market with a swarm of Freaks behind him. Other gangs stopped what they were doing to watch.

"That's your big line?" David said with a grin that covered up the anxiety churning his insides. "I hope you didn't spend all day on it."

Bobby's face soured. "No, I just came up with it right now!" he said. He flipped his blue bangs out of his eyes with his sharpened black nails.

David relaxed a little. He already had the upper hand.

"You owe us a TV, bitch!" Bobby said. He got in David's face.

Will lunged for Bobby. David barely caught him by the waist of his pants. He yanked Will back beside him.

"You want that TV? You come and get it! Bring all your poser friends!" Will said, trying to fight David off in the same breath. David motioned for Gonzalo to intercede. Gonzalo wasted no time picking Will up and walking him away to the back of the group. But he still got one last jab in. "They can watch me beat your face in, toilethead!"

"It's Jackal!" Bobby shouted after Will, spit flying from his mouth. He turned sharply to David. "Who the hell are you, huh? The Loners? You're not a gang, you're nobodies."

The Freaks creaked forward in their shoes, waiting for Bobby to say the word. *Grab your machete*, Bobby's eyes seemed to say. David had only thirty people with him; the rest were on the other side of the school by now. That's why Bobby had picked the market instead of the quad to face off. Bobby had at least sixty Freaks with him now. The Loners would lose.

"Just take it easy, Jackal," David said.

"Stay outta the drops, Loner. You're messing with our livelihood," Bobby said, getting louder so other gangs could hear. "You're messing with the whole food chain! I want to hear it, right now! I want to hear you say the Loners are off the quad for good."

"Fuck off," David said. His hand crept up toward his machete.

The Freaks raised their weapons, but they didn't have a chance to use them. Varsity surrounded the Freaks. Bobby's nose crinkled in confusion as Sam stepped out from the forest of his guys. David was shocked. Everyone was. Sam hadn't made a public appearance since he was nearly killed by the Scrap mob in the quad.

Sam looked sickly pale; the natural ruddiness of his skin was gone. Sam's eyes seemed darker too, like his pupils had spilled and stained his corneas. Sam rushed toward Bobby and David. David sped up his reach for his machete, and as he wrapped his fingers around the hilt, Sam grasped Bobby's hair.

With a single yank, Sam pulled Bobby off his feet and dragged him to the closed door of a classroom. The door had a two-by-two-foot window in it, at head level. Sam slammed Bobby's head into it. David heard the glass crack with a pop. The Freaks lurched forward, shouting, but Varsity held them back. They watched as Sam pressed Bobby's face hard into the cracked glass, and leaned close. He whispered in Bobby's ear, but he kept his eyes locked on David. Sam's eyes quivered with rage.

POP.

The single crack in the glass grew longer, reaching up from the bottom corner toward Bobby's face. Bobby was staring straight at it, like he was face-to-face with a rattlesnake. Sam pressed Bobby's face harder and harder into the glass, whispering all the while. He sneered at David. If the glass gave way and his head went through, the glass would filet his face. David pictured Bobby trying to pull his head back out and leaving his cheek behind, hanging from the shards like a wet leather glove.

P-POP.

The crack splintered off into smaller ones. One touched Bobby's nose. He whimpered. The Freaks pushed at Varsity. They were upset now, yelling and punching back. Bobby's eyes bulged. Sam wasn't whispering anymore. He bore down on Bobby's head.

Sam pushed off of Bobby and stepped away. Bobby didn't

move at first. He just kept his face to the glass, staring at the cracks that could have disfigured him. The Freaks ran to him. He wouldn't look any of them in the eye and he scurried out of the market.

Everyone watched as the Freaks had no choice but to follow, with their tails between their legs. As Sam walked in David's direction, David finally pulled his machete from the sheath. He held it down but ready, and the Loners flanked him. Sam walked like he was going to pass David right by, but stopped. He stood in profile but slowly lifted his head and turned it toward David. There was dirt on his face. He must not have washed it in days.

"Nobody gets to kill you but me," Sam said.

Sam walked on, and the rest of Varsity followed.

David spent the next twenty minutes in a fog. He had gotten too comfortable with Sam not being around. Varsity had attacked them repeatedly in the halls, but they were unfocused without Sam's leadership. Loner-Varsity scuffles had become routine, but Sam's return was a bracing reminder that this was personal and always would be until one of them was dead. David sank. Whether it was tomorrow or in a month, the only way David could stop this vicious cycle was to kill Sam.

Could he do that?

"We're good to go," Ritchie said, his team behind him with a full load of supplies from the Sluts.

David nodded. "Good. The rest of the team is at the Nerds'. Let's get the hell out of here."

David stepped away from the wall and into the flow of market traffic. Someone in the crowd took his left hand for a moment and squeezed it. It was a Scrap girl David didn't recognize. Her white hair was gray with filth, and it hung over her face. Her feet were wrapped in rags. She wore a ratted-out down jacket two sizes too large for her, and a slash in the nylon fabric left a trail of down feathers behind her. She must have been one of the Scraps who'd lost their minds.

David pulled his hand away out of instinct, and the Scrap girl kept walking without flinching or looking back.

"I didn't know there were any more Scraps left," Ritchie said.

"Some people just want to be alone," Will said with a shrug.

David felt something stuck in his palm. He opened his hand to see a folded rectangle of paper in the middle of his hand and flipped it open with his thumb. "Follow me," it read. "H."

H.

David knew the handwriting. Hilary. He looked up and frantically scanned the crowd for the girl. He spotted her as she slipped between a bunch of Skaters and a troupe of Geeks promoting their next show. She ducked into the Nerds' trading post.

"U-uh," David stuttered, "W-w-why don't you guys meet me at the market entrance. I'll get everybody else."

David didn't wait for their responses. He cut through the crowd. Hilary wanted to talk to him, and he'd been waiting to talk to her for more than a year. It wasn't smart. She'd cheated on him. She'd dumped him. She dated the guy who wanted David dead. She didn't make a move to help him when Sam strung him up. She had a hand in all of this misery. It could be a trap. There were so many reasons for David to stop walking, but he didn't.

He caught up to Hilary at a table of electronic goods at the Nerds' trading post. Behind her haggard bangs, her face was smeared with soot, but her eyes were vibrant. She pretended to look at a battered laptop for sale. David stood beside her and poked through some used phone batteries.

"What the hell is this about?" David said.

"I know this is crazy, David, but I'm desperate. I didn't know how else to get your attention. I tried to send you a letter, but it got turned away."

Turned away? Who did that? Why didn't he know? And why was she desperate? What did Sam do? Her frantic tone tugged at his emotions. But he kept still. Stoic.

"Why should I trust you?" David asked.

He wanted to trust her. He knew that any reason, even a thin excuse, would have been enough.

"You know me, David. Don't you? I mean, I'm still me."

David looked up and studied Hilary's face. Now that he was only inches from her, he could see that her dirty white hair was a wig. Her lip quivered. Part of David wanted to reach out and cup her face in his hand and whisper that everything was all right, like she had done for him after his mom died.

"Don't look at me," Hilary said. "Somebody might see you."

"Hil, what do you mean desperate, what's happening?"

Hilary looked up at David for the first time since he entered the room. Her face was flushed, even through the gray and black of the soot. She needed him. He didn't know why, but he knew that look. He wanted to tell her that he missed her. A few Varsity guys entered the room, and the yearning in Hilary's eyes was overtaken by fear. David reached out and took her hand. It was still soft. If anyone else had touched her skin they would have known for certain that this was no Scrap.

"David, let go," Hilary whispered, barely convincing.

"Talk to me," he said.

She tried to pull her hand away, but David wouldn't let go. He'd hold on until he got an answer.

"We'll meet tonight," she said.

19

LUCY WISHED SHE WAS A NERD. BEST SHE
could tell, they got to hide in the library and read books all
day. It sounded wonderful. She wondered if the Nerds organized salons to discuss great fiction or the pertinence of
historical events to the present. Were they living out some
utopian existence two floors up, musing over philosophy or
quantum physics, while the people below them smashed their
heads together?

It didn't matter. She wasn't one of them. She was a Loner,
standing in a cluster of Loner girls, at the Nerds' trading post,
sifting through their bin of bargain books. Like Will said, she
would be here for two and a half more years, maybe more.
Either she was going to need a whole heck of a lot of books,
or she would have to adapt and figure out a way to make

peace with her surroundings. Sasha, Gonzalo's girlfriend, stood next to her. She was a Persian girl with a smattering of freckles across her olive cheeks. Everything about her was miniature, except her attitude. She could be downright mean when she got riled up. Lucy usually kept clear of Sasha, but maybe it was time to start making friends.

"I heard this was pretty good," Lucy said. She held up a rust-colored paperback. She didn't know if it was good. She did remember seeing it on her mom's beach-book shelf though, and she needed a way into the conversation.

"Hmm," Sasha said, considering it for barely a second before moving on. Conversation failure. Sasha didn't need Lucy. Sasha had Gonzalo, and that was enough to survive. Belinda was on her other side, and she didn't even bother to look up. Belinda had been the hardest nut to crack. They hadn't had any more clashes since the incident in the dump, but they weren't exactly friends either. Lucy was sure that if she could just get Belinda to warm up to her, the other girls would ease up too.

"Really?" Dorothy said with a dreary tone from behind her. "I heard it was trashy."

"Of course it's trashy. That's why it's fun," Lucy said.

"I'm sick of trash," Belinda said.

Lucy wanted to throw up her hands. So much for her having girlfriends. In Belinda's eyes, Lucy was beneath Dorothy. She was worse than the girl who turned her back on the Loners when they needed her most, and then groveled her way back in.

"Lucy."

Lucy looked up from the beach book in her hand. A tall Asian girl with crimson hair stared back at her. The tip of her nose had been horribly torn away. It was Julie Tanaka, and she was flanked by six Sluts. Belinda, Sasha, and Dorothy clambered to attention and eyed the Sluts' weapons.

"Um . . . hi?" Lucy replied. Julie lived on the same street as Lucy, and they had hung out once at a neighborhood barbecue before school started.

"I didn't know you were a Slut," Lucy said, in an attempt to make the moment less awkward. But it didn't sound so friendly. No matter how she tried to say it, it always sounded bad out of Lucy's mouth. The big Slut. The Asian Slut. The Slut without a nose.

"Can I talk to you for a second?" Julie said.

"Okay," Lucy said, staying put.

"Like, in private?"

Lucy looked to her gang mates. It didn't seem like the right thing to do, Lucy didn't have a good reason to trust this girl. Who knows what they had in mind for her? Most of what Lucy heard about the Sluts came from rumors among the Pretty Ones. All the Sluts were lesbians, and they beat each other up all the time just to get more scars on their faces. Lucy didn't believe any of it, but she couldn't help but doubt herself as she stared at Julie's nose.

Julie sighed, fed up with waiting, "Fine. Anyway, we're all new recruits and we're each supposed to bring in one prospect. I saw you kick Hilary in the gut a while back. I thought you'd be a good fit."

"Oh, well, that was nice," Lucy said.

Julie sneered at Lucy's gang mates, then dropped her eyes back to Lucy. "Well? You want in?"

"Want in? I don't get it. I have a gang."

"Yeah, but wouldn't you rather have somebody who can back you up?" Julie said, and she looked Belinda up and down. Lucy didn't know how to respond. She'd never had a chance to consider the Sluts as an option. She'd left the Pretty Ones and gone straight to the graduation booth, where David had swooped in. Lucy had to admit, it was nice to hear that there was a group of girls who actually respected her and wanted her around. The Loner girls only seemed to put up with her because Will and David vouched for her. Lucy turned to Belinda. Belinda met her eyes, just as interested in Lucy's response as Julie Tanaka was.

"No," Lucy said. "No, thanks."

"Um, yeah, get lost," Belinda said, quick on Lucy's heels.

"Yeah, 'fore I kick you upside your funky nose," Sasha added.

"Be that way," Julie said. She flipped Sasha off and waved her Sluts off.

Lucy let out a long breath she didn't even know she was holding. "Um, that was awkward."

"Does this mean we can't hide out in the cafeteria if we get attacked?" Dorothy said.

"Who cares?" Belinda said with a frown at Dorothy. "They started it. They're asking for trouble, trying to poach Lucy."

"Yeah," Lucy said with a pump of her head like she was outraged. She wasn't. She was thrilled. It was the first time Belinda had ever said anything positive about her.

"I'm gonna tell you something," Sasha said, and wagged her finger. "I don't like those girls. I think they got bad attitudes, all of them. And that red hair has got to go. They look like used tampons."

"Ugh, Sasha," Belinda said.

"I think Violent's freaking out," Dorothy said. She was thumbing through the beach book that Lucy had put back. "She's got way too many seniors, and I heard she lost, like, eight people to graduation this month."

"Yeah, but no, you don't steal members from other gangs," Belinda said, and shook her head.

"I guess I'm just not enough of a Slut," Lucy said.

Belinda giggled. "You know why Violent named her gang that, right?" she said, then she lowered her voice. "I heard she got . . . raped."

Lucy felt light-headed at the thought. It was the worst nightmare for all of them, definitely Lucy's, and if it happened to the strongest girl in school, it could happen to any of them. Lucy knew that well enough.

"I heard it was bad," Sasha continued. "It was before the gangs formed. Some senior guy did it, he beat her up bad. A few weeks later, she got a bunch of girls to come with her and find him. They were gonna kill him. But he was already dead. The virus got to him before she could."

They all stayed quiet. What was there to say? It was ugly, just one more nasty story they'd have to carry around in their brain. It made Lucy want to take back her smart little crack about not being a big enough Slut. She hunted for any comment to change the subject. A hardback book caught her eye. She picked it up.

"Oh! I'm gonna buy this."

Belinda eyed the book. "*Alexander the Great?*"

"Planning on taking over the school?" Dorothy said.

"I think Will would like it," Lucy said.

"Will? I thought you were wet for David." Sasha said.

"Sasha! Ew," Lucy said.

"Oh, please, girl, I've seen you following David around like stink on the twins. You got it bad."

"I do not!"

"So, you like Will then?" Belinda asked.

"Will's my friend," Lucy said.

"So then, who *do* you like?" Belinda said.

David. The answer was David. But running the halls with Will the other night, she'd felt brave and dangerous and alive. She didn't know what to tell them.

"Guess it's gonna have to be Will, 'cause looks like big brother's taken," Sasha said with a wide smile. She was looking at someone across the room. Lucy spun around.

David was at another Nerd table shuffling through a stack of books. Beside him was a weird white-haired girl in a puffy jacket. She wasn't a Loner, that was for sure. She looked more like a bag lady. Belinda giggled again. Even Dorothy laughed at the weird pairing.

"Is that Weird Peggy?" Dorothy said.

"No, she graduated last week," Belinda said.

"Good thing you took yourself out of the running, Lucy. That is some stiff competition," Sasha said with a playful push. Lucy relaxed. "Oh, my God, you shoulda seen your face. You got it bad!"

A warmth filled Lucy as she watched David pick through the pile of books. What was he deciding on? What did he like to read? She wanted to know everything about him. Maybe they could read a book together, discuss it, they could have the salons she imagined were in the library. What was stopping her from doing that kind of stuff with the Loners in the Stairs? And with David.

Lucy's fantasies blew away like dust. David was holding the weird girl's hand.

David's lips were moving. He was talking to her. She looked back to the hand. She knew that hand. She knew those skinny fingers and those manicured nails. The ugliest girl in the room was actually the prettiest one. Lucy felt an overwhelming instinct to run over, yank off Hilary's wig, and expose her. She would have, but the sight of David gently cradling Hilary's hand drained the anger out of her. Hilary pulled away from David and scurried out of the room. Lucy looked back to David. He stared at the exit long after Hilary had already walked through it like he didn't want her to go. Lucy turned away. She couldn't bear to look at him anymore.

"You want to buy that?"

A Nerd was pointing at the hardback *Alexander the Great* book in Lucy's hands.

"Yeah, I think I will," she said.

20

THEY THINK I'M WEAK.

That one thought echoed inside Sam's head. He knew they were thinking it. His own gang. The whole school. Everyone saw what happened in the quad. They saw David and his gang of beggars kick Sam's ass.

"Come on and throw with us, Sammy! Get that blood moving!"

Sam looked down from the bleachers at Alan Woodward, who slapped a football in his fat hands. His round cheeks were red like cherry bombs, and Sam wished they'd explode.

"No," Sam said.

It wasn't that Alan was a bad guy. It was just that he was an idiot. Ninety percent of Sam's day was dealing with idiots, keeping them happy so they didn't gang up and kill him. It was starting to drag him down. But he couldn't slip now. That was what everybody was waiting for.

Alan shrugged and shuffled off. He cocked his arm and threw the ball to a group at the other end of the gym. Sam admired the tight, spiraled throw. It was a nice toss. The guys at the other end elbowed and shoved each other to get a clean grab at the ball. Their shoes squeaked on the varnished floor. It sounded like the squeal a dog made when you hurt it.

When Sam was seven, he had a curly-haired black dog named Trixie. It was a stupid name, because Trixie was a boy. His mom named it. She wanted a daughter but only had sons, so the dog became Trixie. It was one of those miniature dogs that women keep in their pocketbooks. Twitchy. Fragile. Every time he picked it up he could feel its brittle ribs. It used to chase him around the house trying to hump his leg. Nasty little thing. Nothing was more disgusting than its little furry hips thrusting away at his ankle. It scratched at every door he hid behind, always wanting to hump him more. And no one helped him, all the adults just laughed. "Look, Sammy's afraid of Trixie. How cute!" They stopped laughing when he stomped down on the thing and snapped its back. He could still hear the dull crunch. His father beat him for that. "What's wrong with you?" he yelled. No one seemed to understand. The perverted little thing was assaulting *him*.

"Hi, baby."

Hilary walked up the bleachers. She sat beside Sam and slid her hand down his thigh to his knee. Her nails made a zipping sound along the synthetic fabric of his breakaway pants. She kissed him on the cheek.

"How come you're not playing with the boys?" she said.

"Where've you been?" Sam asked. He readied himself for one of her lies.

"Downstairs. I said it was okay for people to have the drop party at the pool. How was the market? Did it make you feel better?"

"Saw your boyfriend."

Hilary pulled her hand off his knee. "Why do you say things like that?"

Sam laughed. "Relax, baby. It was a joke."

"I hate it," she said, her eyebrows digging down deep.

Just what he needed, Hilary pissed at him. He took her hand and put it back on his knee. He touched her face with his other hand and turned it toward him with a little force. She kept her eyebrows angry and her lips tight. She was playing angry, another lie.

"You don't like jokes?" he said.

"Not funny, Sam. Just not funny," she said, doing her vulnerable act. There was still no one hotter than her. Sam leaned in to kiss her but stopped. There was a one-inch smudge of filth on the underside of her jaw. He swiped it with his finger.

"What is this?" he said.

He looked at the dirt on the pad of his forefinger. She looked at it too. Dirt and grime were prevalent in McKinley, but not on Hilary. She was always clean, made up, and smelling sweet.

"It looks like dirt, Sam."

"It was on your face," he said, his words heating up.

"Okay, so?" Hilary said, then let out an exasperated breath. "When are you going to stop acting like this?"

She was avoiding the question. She was covering for something. She was lying and lying and lying.

Hilary lowered her voice. "You're starting to freak people out."

Someone was laughing. Sam snapped his head toward the gym floor where Alan's half-assed game was underway. His team was huddled near the basketball foul line. Alan was braying like a donkey over some joke. He hated Alan's laugh. Sam caught his eye from fifty feet away. That sort of thing didn't happen accidentally. Alan was talking about him. He knew it.

"Would ya come on and play, Cappy?" Alan shouted over the gym. He was trying to cover his ass.

"Go," Hilary said, a little anxiety in her voice. "They need you, Sam."

Sam didn't move. Alan sighed and waved him off, pulling the ball up and nodding to the rest to get started. His boys talked to each other and smiled. They weren't talking about the game. Who cared about games anymore? They all had their little plans for him that they'd kick off when the moment was right.

They didn't think he had it in him anymore. He could still feel the fingernails of those Scraps tearing at him. They never would have stopped if David hadn't called them off. David. As long as David and his gang were walking the halls, no one would forget that Sam had crumbled when it mattered.

"Who's Alan's girl?" Sam said.

"Roberta Fennessey," Hilary said.

"Have her dump him."

"What?"

"We'll hook her up with one of my sophomores."

"I can't do that. She likes Alan. They like each other."

"Do it."

"No," Hilary said. Her tone was firm. Sam looked at her. She'd betrayed him. He didn't know how, but she'd done something. He was slipping. He was asking for her betrayal. He was asking for a coup. Nobody feared him like they used to. His tangle with Bobby in the market meant nothing to them. They all saw it as a desperate move.

"Fine," he said.

Sam stood up. He picked up an aluminum baseball bat. He never went without it in the gym. You could never be too careful. He stepped down the bleachers, reaching the gym floor in five long strides.

"Sam?" he heard Hilary say distantly.

Anthony had just run a touchdown for his team. Alan was acting as his quarterback.

"YES!" Alan shouted, and raised his fists to celebrate. His offensive line was a good ten feet in front of him after the play. Alan turned toward the bleachers, smiling, hoping for Sam's approval. His smile bent down when he saw Sam charging him.

Sam smashed his aluminum bat across Alan's face.

Alan dropped to the floor. He flopped around at Sam's feet. Alan groaned. He was disoriented, reaching for his head, trying to understand what had happened. Blood spouted from his ear. He clawed at the air in front of him.

Sam heard the shouts behind him. He heard Hilary crying out for him to stop. Sam raised the bat over his head and brought it down again. He felt Alan's face give way. Blood and teeth flew. Alan barely looked like Alan by the third swing. He was dead by the sixth. But Sam didn't stop until the tenth.

It was an awful mess. He dropped the bat, and it clanged onto the hardwood floor beside Alan's collapsed face.

Sam turned to the gathered crowd. The Pretty Ones buried their faces in the sleeves of their Varsity boyfriends. None of them dared to meet his gaze. He saw the fear had returned to their faces now.

It had to be done.

21

DAVID SNUCK INTO THE MARKET. EVERY LIGHT
was off. Every trading post door was closed and locked. There was no bustle, no hocking of goods, no fighting. Everyone was gone.

The sounds of his own shoes scuffing the floor made him tense up. If anybody happened upon him, even just a few Skaters, they could overpower him and hold him for ransom. Stupid. The Loners would either have to bend to them, maybe give up all their food as a payoff, or they'd have to fight to get him back. Either way he'd be dragging everybody down, just because he couldn't control himself.

Hilary wanted him back. That was all he could think about. He still fantasized about her, maybe not as much as he used to, but every time he saw her he couldn't help but remember the feel of her hands on his chest, the sweet smell of her neck just below her ear. And now, after all this time, she wanted to meet. Alone. At night. He'd been wishing for something like this for so long.

She's psychotic.

Those were Lucy's words. He'd never forgotten them. Lucy described such a vindictive, nasty Hilary, one that he had no memory of. *Psychotic* sort of matched the Hilary he'd seen shaving Belinda's head, and enjoying it. It definitely fit the girl he saw savagely attack Lucy on the quad.

Lucy.

How could anyone attack Lucy? She was so good. So kind. David understood now why Will thought she was so amazing. As time had passed, David had become more at ease about what happened at the graduation booth with Brad. Brad's death was a horrible thing, but David shuddered to think what could have happened if he hadn't intervened. He felt violent at the thought of someone trying to hurt Lucy. If he had to live it over, he wouldn't do any different. He'd kill Brad all over again if that's what it took to keep her safe.

David reached the door to the Pretty Ones' trading post. He reached out to knock on the door but paused.

Was this really what he wanted? He'd built a gang. He'd come back from being entirely forgotten and had become a real force in the school. And now he was thinking about hopping into bed with the girl who'd treated some of his gang like dirt? If Lucy ever found out . . .

It didn't matter what Lucy thought. He'd wanted this for almost a year and a half.

David gave the door a soft knock and stepped back. She might not have shown. Maybe she'd chickened out. That would settle it. David's eyes wandered up to a sprinkler pipe above him. It was the same pipe Sam had hung him from.

The door clicked open. Hilary peeked out from the crack between the door and the door frame.

"Hey," David said.

Hilary threw the door open and grabbed David by his belt buckle. She yanked him into the candlelit classroom. He closed the door behind him and barely had a chance to lock it before she swung him over to a teacher's desk.

"Whoa, easy," David said.

Hilary didn't say anything. She was all over him. She kissed him. She tore at his shirt. It was his good flannel shirt, and he tried to stop her. She pushed his hands away. She wrapped her legs around him, and her hands locked around the back of his neck. The candles were dim, he could barely see her face.

"Slow down," he whispered in her ear. This wasn't how it was supposed to go. He wanted to savor every moment, he had been craving this for so long. He wanted it to be like it used to be, back in his room, before everything went to shit.

"I need you right now," Hilary said. She tugged at his belt, trying to unfasten it. *Just go with it,* David told himself. *Here she is, in your arms again. What the hell are you complaining about?*

He slipped her dress up and held her firm thighs, pulling them closer to him.

"Mmmmmm," she moaned, and closed her eyes. "I missed you so much," she whispered. She managed to get his belt loose and was working on the top button of his jeans. He was kissing her neck, searching for that sweet spot. She didn't smell the same as he remembered. Maybe he had it confused with something else . . . with Lucy, when they were in the elevator, her arm over him, so close, so warm. *Shut up.*

"Don't stop," Hilary said. He didn't realize he had. She managed to get his pants unbuttoned. She slid her fingers down inside. Her hand was cold, but it felt amazing. David hadn't been with anyone since Hilary. But Hilary had. She'd been with Sam. It turned his stomach.

David pushed Hilary away, which forced her to plant her feet on the ground.

"What are you doing?" she said.

David buttoned his pants and stepped away from the desk. He didn't know what to say.

"David?"

"I need a second," he said. "What are we doing here?"

"This," she said. She pressed herself into him, and went in for an openmouthed kiss. He pulled his head away.

They stared at each other for a moment. Tears gathered on her eyelashes and twinkled in the light of the candles.

"Don't cry," David said.

"Sam killed Alan today."

"What?"

"He killed him. For no reason. He just beat his face with a . . ."

She couldn't go on, she was sobbing too hard. She pushed away from David. A shiver slid through David. Alan. Out of all of Varsity, why Alan? He was one of the most cheerful kids David had ever met.

"Alan's dead?" he said again. It didn't feel possible.

Hilary collapsed into a chair, lifting her feet up onto the seat and tucking her knees underneath her chin. David pulled a chair around to face her and sat down. He leaned forward, placing his hands on her legs.

"Sam's lost it. Ever since you beat him on the quad, he's been worse. He thinks he's better than everybody. He's out of control. I'm trying to act like everything's okay for the Pretty Ones, but I'm scared. When's he gonna swing that baseball bat at me?"

Hilary sobbed again. This wasn't what he wanted. He thought they'd talk about their feelings. She'd tell him everything she'd felt about him for the past year and a half, and he'd do the same. He never thought it would be this.

"He's made me do so many awful things. Things I never would have done."

"Why did you do them?" David said. It sounded cold, but he needed to know. She looked at him like she was offended.

"You don't know what it's been like."

"I think I do," David said. "He tried to hang me."

"Well, we all can't be as noble as you, David."

"That's a cop-out."

"I had to survive!" Hilary said. David realized that she had probably never said any of this to anyone. "And he was my boyfriend."

"He's not anymore?"

"It's complicated."

"He kills people. And lets others starve. Why would you stay with him?" David said.

"You kill people too."

That got David's anger up.

"Maybe this was a bad idea," David said.

Hilary stared at the door.

"I don't know what to do," she said finally.

The excitement he had felt walking into this room was gone. This wasn't the girl he lost back at Sam's party. Or maybe it was, but the feeling was gone. They didn't belong together. But he still cared for her. He didn't want her to live in fear.

"Do you want to join the Loners?" David asked.

"You could kill him," she said. "I could sneak you in. You

could take over Varsity. I'd support you. I have the girls. Everything would be okay. We could be like we were."

David stared at her. Who was this girl? She dumps him, acts like he's invisible all this time, and then asks him to kill her boyfriend?

"I'm not going murder anybody, Hilary."

"Why not? After everything he's done to you? After everything he's done to everybody?" Hilary got angry. "He'll do it to you. He's going to kill you!"

"Well, it sounds like he's really going someplace."

Hilary stood up. She jabbed her finger at him like a knife.

"You're an idiot. I'm giving you a chance to change things, David. Everybody could start over!"

"I already have started over."

Hilary shook her head and pushed open the door.

"I'm sorry," David said. And he was.

She slipped out into the hall and was gone. David let out a long breath.

"Oh, man . . . ," he said to himself. "That went well."

David leaned back and ran his fingers through his hair. He stared at the ceiling. If there was anything to be said for McKinley High, it was that, with enough time, it revealed the truth about everybody.

22

WILL GRIPPED THE HANDLE OF LOCKER 733.

This was the moment of truth. He looked back at Lucy. She smiled at him. But it wasn't her full smile. He knew what Lucy looked like when she was truly happy, and this wasn't it. She said she was fine, but he could tell something was weighing on her mind. He hadn't planned on taking her out tonight. He hadn't even checked out what was in the locker yet. He was going to do that tomorrow. But earlier in the night, when Lucy gave him the book on Alexander the Great, he knew he couldn't wait. She'd told him that Alexander had conquered the ancient world even though he had epilepsy. She wanted to inspire Will, she believed in him, and that meant she really cared about him. Will couldn't hold it in. He told her he had a surprise for her, but they'd have to sneak out again.

He expected to have to twist her arm, but she was all for it, excited even.

Tonight was the night he would make his move.

As he lifted the locker's handle, he panicked. What if there was nothing inside? What if this was all a big practical joke by Smudge? He didn't know what could be in there. Maybe a map to another location? A ring of keys that unlocked a door that no one else could get through? He took a big breath.

"What's wrong?" Lucy said.

"Nothing," Will said. He swung the locker open.

There was a giant hole in the back of the locker.

The metal back wall of the locker had been bent inward, and a hole had been knocked through the drywall behind. There was darkness beyond. Lucy gasped.

"What is this?" Lucy asked.

"I said it was a surprise, didn't I?" Will said.

He hoped she bought that. This was way better than he hoped. It was taking everything he had to hide his shock.

"Ready?" Will said.

"I think so. Where does it go?"

"You'll see."

He took her hand. He stepped into the locker and through the ragged hole. Will led her into the black void on the other side. He clicked his phone on, and its thin light revealed that they were in an interstitial space between the wall of lockers and the load-bearing concrete wall. It was a slim space, three feet wide. He couldn't tell its length, it was too dark. The air smelled stale. Someone, probably Smudge, had drawn a large black arrow on the concrete wall. It pointed left.

"Will, should I be scared?"

"No way. It's gonna be fun."

He prayed he wasn't wrong. He reached back through the hole and closed the locker behind them. It felt like closing a coffin from the inside. The hallway's light barely illuminated the underside of the locker's horizontal vents. Will got a little scared himself. They were inside the guts of the school, heading who knew where. He didn't let go of Lucy's hand. Her palm was the littlest bit damp now, just a trace of sweat.

"This way," he said.

Will followed the arrow and pulled Lucy down the thin passageway. His phone's anemic light only revealed a few feet in front of them.

"How do you know about this?" Lucy asked.

"I know a lot of places in here you've probably never been to."

"Is that so? Like what?"

"Don't worry about it."

Lucy chuckled. "Bullshitter."

The passage came to an end at a wall. A slim hole was knocked through the drywall between two exposed studs. Again, there was only darkness beyond it.

Will squeezed through the hole. By his phone's illumination

he saw a light switch on the wall. He flicked it. Bright ceiling lights sputtered on. Will and Lucy were in a small ten-by-ten-foot room with a metal access panel, sort of a hatch, in the middle of the floor. The hatch was open, revealing a maintenance shaft with a utility ladder that led down toward the basement level. The room had a single door on the far wall, but the knob was missing.

"Is this . . . it?" she asked.

"Yeah, I just wanted to show you a supercreepy room."

She rolled her eyes and smiled.

"Keep your pants on. It'll be worth it," he said.

He had the distinct feeling that he was digging himself deeper each time he said something like that. He was depending entirely on Smudge's good will now, and that was less than reassuring.

"I should tell Sasha about this place. She's always looking for a private place for her and Gonzalo to have sex," Lucy said.

"Maybe you should. I hate having to listen to them go at it."

"I know, right?"

Will peered down the shaft. The metal ladder extended down to a dirty concrete floor. He was getting nervous that this wasn't leading anywhere good at all. Lucy tried to open the knobless door, but it wouldn't budge.

"This way," Will said.

He climbed into the maintenance shaft and took the ladder down one cold metal rung at a time.

"Don't look up my dress," Lucy said as she followed him onto the ladder.

He looked. But she was just a black silhouette against the light of the room above. The shaft emptied into a small hot room full of large humming machines with blinking control panels, and a network of square metal air ducts coming off them. He hopped off the ladder. He spotted another arrow. It pointed to a square hole in the side of a low-lying air duct. The vent grille was missing.

Lucy stepped off the ladder and took in the room. For the first time, she looked genuinely disappointed.

"Now what?"

"It's just through here," Will said, pointing toward the hole in the air duct.

"There? Come on. You're joking. This is my only dress, you know. Can't you just tell me what it is?"

He was losing her.

"I promise it's worth it," Will said. Lucy pursed her lips and waggled them from side to side, weighing the decision in her mind.

"Is it far?" Lucy asked.

"It's super close."

He should just shoot himself now. He had no idea how much farther it was, or how the hell he'd know when he was even there. His big romantic date was going off the rails.

Will didn't wait for her answer. He climbed headfirst into

the air duct. He shined his phone ahead. The duct seemed to extend forever and the air inside was hot and dry. It flowed in the direction he crawled, away from the room full of machines. He could hear Lucy climb into the duct behind him.

"Oh, my God, it's so hot in here," she said.

"It's not that bad," Will said.

But it was. The farther he crawled, the hotter he got. He hoped she liked sweaty guys. The duct metal was hot, and it hurt the skin on his forearms.

"Will, I'm getting burned. I don't like this."

He could hear the aggravation in her voice.

"Not much farther."

With every foot he crawled, Will could feel Lucy slipping away from him. She was probably wishing she had never agreed to come out with him at all. Whatever was at the end of this journey had to be huge. Impossibly huge.

"I want to go back," she said. Will ignored her.

The end had to be soon. Either that, or Smudge had burned him. He'd probably hit a dead end, or pop out of a vent in the middle of the trash dump. Smudge was probably holding his stomach, cackling at that very moment at the thought of Will stuck inside this hot metal esophagus, ruining any chance he'd ever had with Lucy.

"Will, are you going to answer me?"

The duct turned again. He saw a faint blue glow ahead. Finally. He crossed Smudge off his mental To Kill list.

"We're here," he said.

"Really?"

It had to be it. He didn't know what it was, but it had to be.

"Yup."

Will crawled faster. The blue glow was shining through the black slats of a large vent grille. He scurried up and pressed his face to the slats. The vent grille popped right off and clanged down onto a white-tiled floor below. The sound hung in the air.

"Holy shit," Will said softly.

It was the pool. Giant, six lanes. The water's surface was absolutely still. It looked like clear blue glass. He could smell the chlorine. Damn, it smelled so clean. There wasn't a soul in the room. He knew the pool was under the gym, inside Varsity territory. But he didn't care. He had to get out of this hot tunnel and into that cool, serene water. He climbed out of the duct.

Lucy popped her head out right after. The bothered scowl on her face reversed at the sight of the pool. She beamed. Relief drained the tension from Will's muscles. Lucy was finally smiling her full smile.

"The pool!" she said. "Will! You took me to the pool?"

Her voice echoed through the tiled room. Will pressed his forefinger to his lips with a smile. He didn't know if Varsity was lurking. Lucy lowered her voice.

"What time is it?" she asked.

"I don't know, maybe four?"

"That's perfect. Hilary doesn't go for her morning swim until six thirty, and free swim isn't till after that. So nobody's going to be down here."

"Free swim?" Will said, his jaw hanging open. "You guys got to swim every day?"

"Believe me, it takes all the fun out of it when Varsity guys are watching you like sharks trying to cop a feel under water."

"Lucky bastards."

"Will!" She laughed.

He laughed too. This was the moment. She was happy, he was happy. He needed to take her head in his hands and kiss her.

But he didn't. He froze, when right in front of him, Lucy unzipped the back of her dress, and let it fall to the floor.

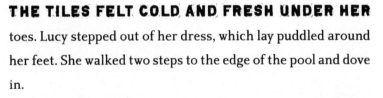

23

THE TILES FELT COLD AND FRESH UNDER HER
toes. Lucy stepped out of her dress, which lay puddled around
her feet. She walked two steps to the edge of the pool and dove
in.

Chilly water caressed every inch of her. She loved being
underwater. She spread her arms out and dug through the
water. Deeper. The pure silence was almost as refreshing as
the water. She closed her eyes, relishing her weightlessness.
She ran her hands down her body and kicked hard.

Deeper still. It was so familiar. Every summer she swam at
her family's lake house. She and her cousins would lie on the
wooden raft anchored near the shore and bake in the sun
until they couldn't stand it. They'd jump into the crisp water
and swim all the way down, racing to be the first one to touch

the silty bottom. Those were some of her favorite memories.

Lucy touched the bottom of the deep end with her fingers. She curled into a ball and tumbled forward, drifting slowly like an astronaut in deep space. She lingered there a moment.

This was the best gift Will could have given her. She finally had some relief from obsessing about David and Hilary together. All the gloom washed away.

Her lungs began to burn. She opened her eyes and kicked off the floor. She loved the drag of the water on her body. She broke the surface and drew in a full, fresh breath. She scanned the room for Will.

He was hopping on one foot as he yanked the last leg of his jeans off. He wore a wrinkled pair of light blue boxers with some goofy pattern on them. There was a rip in the thigh. They were about as ratty and worn out as Lucy's bra and panties.

"Um, what's on your boxers?" Lucy said with a grin.

Will looked down and groaned.

"Uh . . . Santa hats. They were from my grandma. If I knew I was going to be locked in here for years, I probably would've picked something else."

Lucy laughed. It was cute. Will looked around the room. "Pretty great, right?"

"Amazing," she said. "You win the prize."

He nodded. He held his pants in front of him like he was nervous being nearly naked in front of her. She could tell he was tense by the way he was holding himself.

"Well, get in," she said. "It feels great."

Will cast his pants aside and cannonballed into the pool. She hooted and clapped for him. She was having fun. The last time Lucy was in the pool she was surrounded by a bunch of rude Varsity jerk-offs. Guy like Brad would give her butt a squeeze underwater. She remembered being offended, but at the same time she couldn't help feeling excited. She never let on, but some of them turned her on, in a purely physical way. She'd seen things as a Pretty One she'd never seen before. She'd stumbled across couples having sex in the showers a few times. Sex had stopped seeming like that thing that adults did. It could be something she could do if she wanted to. And she did want to. There was just no one in Varsity she trusted enough to try it with.

Will still hadn't surfaced. She wondered if he'd swum past her, all the way to the shallow end. Then hands grabbed her ankles and tugged her down. She got out a yelp just before she went under. Will's fingers tickled her ribs. Air bubbles rumbled out of her mouth. She kicked and twisted back to the surface. Will's head was already above water, and he was smiling. She had not expected that, but she didn't mind.

"Hey!" she said with an exaggerated scowl, and pushed his shoulder.

"Couldn't resist."

"Perv."

"You're the perv for stripping in front of me," Will said with a grin.

"Whatever, I know this was all a big trick to get me in my underwear," Lucy said.

"Worked didn't it?" Will said with a grin.

Lucy splashed him and laughed.

"Well, I'm impressed, but you said you know all these places I don't know about. What are you going to show me next that beats this?"

"The outside," he said. He said it with such certainty that it made Lucy do a double take.

"Yeah, right."

"You never know."

Will was so full of surprises. Who knows? Maybe he could pull it off.

"Yeah, but even so, we can't go out there," Lucy said. "We might kill someone. We just have to wait until it's our turn to get out."

"I bet we could make it to the mountains without getting near any adults. We could get a bunch of gear, hike in, and camp out in the woods."

"For two and a half years?"

"It's doable. It'd be better than this hellhole."

Lucy extended her arms, kicked, and floated on her back. She stared upward. Undulating blue light reflected off the water's surface and frolicked across the ceiling. Maybe they could hide out at the lake house. No one was there in the winter. Lucy sighed, more relaxed than she'd been in a long time. She moved her hands gently back and forth. She slowly realized exactly how much of her body was floating above the water, exposed to Will. Even though she'd never eaten so sparingly in her life, her body felt fuller than it did a year ago. She could feel his eyes slide across her exposed skin and linger on the places kept hidden. She blushed, and there was no way to hide it. She could sense his desire. The power her body had over him excited her.

Lucy glanced over at Will and caught him staring. Her cheeks got hot. She looked away. "I'll be back," he said.

Lucy lifted her head and sank her body back in the water. Will was swimming for the side of the pool. He tore through the water with long, hard strokes.

"Where are you going?"

"It's a surprise."

"Another surprise?"

How many surprises could he have? Will pulled himself out of the pool. His wet boxers clung to him. Will knelt down by his clothes and reached his hand into the pocket of his jeans. Lucy did a little kick in the water and glided left to get a better view of what he was getting.

Will stood up, his fist closed around something. They locked eyes across the water. Will smiled. Lucy watched his closed hand as he walked back to the pool. What was he holding? It had to be a condom.

He eased back into the water.

Lucy's heart fluttered. She took a deep breath to steady herself. Will waded toward her, the water lapping against his chest. He stared at her with purpose. Maybe she shouldn't have let him tickle her. This was happening too fast. Her mind flashed with the question, If Will did try something right then, would she let him? Yes, she would. Will's hands rose out of the water. Draped between them was a glittering gold necklace with a diamond pendant. She wanted to go back underwater.

"What's this?"

Will didn't speak. He leaned close, his cheek touched hers as he fastened the clasp of the necklace behind her neck.

"I just like you so much . . . ," Will said.

Lucy couldn't breathe. She didn't realize Will's feelings were this serious. He moved his mouth toward hers, his lips beginning to part.

I'll only hurt him, she thought. Lucy lowered her head just as Will's nose touched hers. He tried to reach her lips. She turned away. Oh, God. What had she done?

Will stayed frozen, mouth open, as if he didn't want the moment to be real. She saw the hope in his eyes die. It was replaced with a naked embarrassment. He shrank away from her. The water felt too cold all of a sudden.

"I'm sorry," Lucy said. She didn't know what else to say.

24

DAVID LOVED HIS GANG.

If his messy hookup with Hilary had taught him anything, it was that he was lucky to have so many people around him that he trusted. There definitely weren't any Loners asking him to murder someone. They were his family, and he was proud. It was time to celebrate them.

David walked down to the lounge where people had gathered for breakfast and a morning screening of a National Geographic video on Will's flat screen. He passed Gonzalo and the twins sitting on the stairs, eating a black bean breakfast. The twins were mashing their beans into a paste and spreading it onto crackers they pulled from their pockets. He noticed that the crackers had green fur on them. Gonzalo groaned.

"Damn! How long have those been in your pockets?" Gonzalo said.

"A while," the girl said.

"They went bad," Gonzalo said. "Don't eat that shit."

"If they was black, they gone bad," the boy said.

"If it's black, send it back. If it's got fuzz, eat it just becuz," the girl said, then giggled. The boy guffawed through a mouth of beans and crackers and mold.

"Will y'all get the hell outta here?" Gonzalo growled. "You're ruining my breakfast."

The twins laughed at Gonzalo even harder this time, then picked up their breakfast and headed upstairs, arm in arm. David smiled. He liked the twins. They were dirty, rank, and weird as hell, but they stuck together. Half of David's gang was weird. There was Marcy, who prayed to fairies before every meal. There was Colin who could puke on command and loved to show it off. There was Drew; he would take off running at the drop of a hat, and people would have to chase him down to bring him back. There was Sal, who'd eat anything on a dare. David had seen him eat belts, drywall, feathers, and one of Ritchie's scabs. And of course, there was Vincent; he was a compulsive liar. It was harmless stuff, but fun to listen to. He claimed he'd knocked out a cow with one punch. Evidently, his father was the personal drug dealer to the vice president of the United States. And once he'd been run over by a tank.

The Loners were about as far you could get from David's old football friends, but he wouldn't have it any other way.

David moved to the center of the crowded landing and put his arms up, "Hey, everybody! Can I get your ears for a minute?"

All the chattering went quiet. Someone clicked off the TV just as a grizzly bear snagged a jumping salmon.

"Everybody here has worked really hard to turn the Loners into a respectable presence in this school. We've made a name for ourselves. We fight like a team, and because of that nobody's hungry . . . well, you might be hungry, but nobody's starving."

They all laughed eagerly.

"We've got a safe place to sleep at night. We can defend ourselves. And every single one of you is going to graduate, because every single one of you is committed to the gang. You've changed my life, and I want to say thank you. We're going to have to hustle a little harder at the next drop to make up for the expense, but I struck a deal with the Geeks this morning, and . . . you're all going to the Geek show tomorrow night."

Ecstatic cheers cut David off. They beamed like little children on Christmas morning. They were all former Scraps; David was sure that none of them had ever been to a Geek show. He raised his hands to try to quiet everyone down.

"And . . . I'm waiting to hear back from the Nerds on their

phone supply, but we should be able to strike a deal this afternoon. There probably won't be enough for everybody right away, but we'll get there, okay?"

More shouts of approval.

"So, here's the only bummer. Tomorrow night, we're going to have to do shifts for the Geek show. Just like on market days, one group is going to have to stay behind to guard the Stairs, but then we'll rotate through the night, so everybody gets an equal—"

"Everybody but you, right?" Will said.

David stopped. Will walked up from the first floor. He leaned against the banister and ran his hand through his damp hair. Lucy was behind him on the stairs, hesitating for some reason. Her hair was as wet as Will's. What were they just doing together? He felt a stab of jealousy.

"Where've you been?" David asked Will.

"Don't act like you didn't hear the question. Tell the truth. Everybody has to work a shift but you, right? Isn't that the way it goes for King David? We all hustle while you get to take everything—"

"Will, stop," Lucy said.

"You know what?" David said to Will. "I don't care where you've been. Maybe it's best if you just go back there."

Will turned away from David and addressed the gang.

"Don't believe a thing this guy says. His whole 'I put you first' act, it's fake. He acts like he only thinks about you, but I know from personal experience that when everything goes to shit and you need him, he won't be there."

David couldn't believe his ears. Where did he get the nerve?

"Screw you, man. You lived off me this whole time! I do everything for you!" David said.

"Oh, really? Where were you when Mom died?!" Will said.

Will's face was nearly purple, and it was strained. He might seize. David wished he would.

"She died on me too!" David said. "What, you're the only one who gets to hide in your room and cry? You're an idiot. I had my own life that had nothing to do with you, and you know what? I liked it that way."

Will applauded sarcastically.

"Thank you! Thank you for showing everyone what you're really like."

David stomped toward Will. He was going to break his nose. But Ritchie got to him first, standing on his toes to get in Will's face.

"David busts his ass for this gang!"

"Get out of my face, Ritchie. I'm talking to my brother," Will said.

"No, you're talking to our leader, and none of us want to hear any of it, you whiny little pussy."

"Who you calling little, midget? Get out of my way."

Will pushed past Ritchie, but Ritchie shoved him in the back.

Will spun around, furious. He pushed Ritchie. Ritchie lost his footing at the edge of the landing and toppled down the stairs. People rushed to the edge. A girl screamed. David cut his way through the crowd and grasped Will by the shirt.

David cocked back his fist.

Lucy threw herself between David and Will. "Stop!"

Her eyes were wide and pleading. David let go of Will. Everyone was watching them.

David scowled at Will. "You're not going to the Geek show, and you're on guard duty for a week."

"How about a month?"

"Done," David said, and turned to the other Loners. "Fights within this gang won't be tolerated. You heard it right now. Punishment is guard duty for a month. We've got nothing if we're not together."

David walked away from Will.

25

"SORRY, GUYS, YOU'RE GONNA HAVE TO check your weapons."

Ritchie, who had a nasty new gash scabbing up across his forehead, sneered at the Geek like he was crazy.

"It's okay," David said to Ritchie and the mob of Loners behind him. One by one, the gang piled their weapons high on the table in front of the well-guarded box office, and each Loner received a claim ticket in return. By the end of five minutes, the counter was overloaded with blades, spears, chains, pipes, slingshots, and wire knuckles. What the Geeks didn't know was that hidden somewhere on each Loner were at least two shivs.

Someone was going to kill David tonight at the Geek show. That was the rumor. According to the Skaters, Bobby was losing his cool after being publicly embarrassed by Sam. He may have been scared of Sam when he was in the market, but when Bobby got back to Freak territory, David bet he was more scared of what his own gang might do to him. Bobby had to show the school that they should fear Jackal. Offing David would definitely get the message across.

The PA system squawked to life, and a booming voice addressed the school.

"Geek show! Geek show! You don't want to miss this one. Get your butt to the auditorium before we run out of tickets."

David had made a promise to his gang, and he wasn't going to back down now.

The Loners crowded into the auditorium, and David scanned the light rigging for any ominous figures. Colored lights and flashing strobes made it impossible to tell for sure. He'd heard of Freak kids trying to perfect bow and arrows. He didn't want to find out those rumors were true tonight.

David let his eyes wander over the spectacle before him. It was nothing like the dismal gray that lurked outside the doors behind him. The air smelled fresh somehow. The Geeks had frosted the tips of their hair with acrylic paint from the art studios. He saw turquoise, magenta, and tangerine, rare colors for McKinley. He had forgotten how big the auditorium really was. It'd been built to house the entirety of the student body and the faculty for school events for decades to come. A red-curtained proscenium stage, bathed in golden light, took up the entire far wall. Between the stage and where David stood were fifty rows of raked seating. Interspersed along both walls were small, makeshift tents. In front of each tent was a Geek barking the surprises and entertainment that waited within.

It was a carnival, and to David's disbelief, it looked like kids had not only checked their weapons at the door, but also their affiliation. He'd never seen anything like it, probably because he'd never had the opportunity to go to a Geek show before. It put him on edge. Everyone mixed freely with each other. An assassination seemed more feasible than he'd imagined. He noticed Varsity members and Pretty Ones scattered through the room. A Freak gave him a hateful look. All through the crowd David saw potential threats, enemies pretending to be amused by the extravaganza.

"Stay close," David said to Ritchie, who signaled to the rest of the Loners.

David heard a high-pitched scream and feet rushing toward him. He pivoted his body and dug in, ready to fight. He didn't expect a hug. It was Zachary. He wore a blazing orange Marie Antoinette wig, tall as a top hat and full of decorative curls.

"Well, look how far he's come!"

Ritchie grabbed Zachary's shirt and swung him off David.

"Hey, hands off!"

A throng of Geeks broke out of the crowd, and they promptly surrounded the Loners. David put his hands up to calm the situation.

"Whoa, whoa, all a mistake! Let's be cool," David said.

"I think I liked it better when I had you under my thumb," Zachary said.

Ritchie held out his hands. They were covered in a glitter that shimmered with every flash of the lights. Zachary righted himself with a sneer and straightened his black shirt, which was covered in the same stuff, a powder of crushed glass bonded to the fabric with a weak glue. Sparkles sprinkled onto the floor all around him.

"What is this crap?" Ritchie said.

"Fashion, moron. And that before is called a hug. You cavemen don't get out much, do you?"

"We're a little rusty," David said. "But if I recall correctly, partying is like riding a bike, isn't it?"

Zachary smiled and waved for his Geeks to relax. He wagged his finger at David.

"If you didn't spend like a drunk stepmom, I'd throw you right out of here, Davey-pie," he said, and then waved his hand around at the tents. "So here's the deal. The main show and sideshows are free, but games and goodies cost tickets. We've got a couple lovely girls over there who will gladly relieve you of whatever you'd like to trade for a roll of tickets."

Zachary clapped his hands, and one of the Geeks tossed a large roll of tickets to David.

"Here's a few on the house."

"Hey, you shouldn't have," David said dryly, passing them back to Ritchie.

"I know. I really shouldn't have, but hey, we're going to rob you blind tonight anyway. Have fuuuuun, Loners!"

With a twirl and a sweep of his hands, Zachary led his crew on to the next gang of customers. David smiled. Even with a death threat looming over his head, it was hard not to find Zachary's mood infectious. Since forming the Loners, David had paid close attention to the leaders who had gained the true respect of their gang. Zachary was one of them, and he admired his style.

David turned to his gang mates. Eighty of them had come, and twelve had stayed behind at the Stairs. All of them were salivating over a different Geek show attraction. They were dying to cut loose.

"Okay," David said. "I need five volunteers for a security team, and we'll rotate it. That's it. Everybody else, go hang out. Somebody better have some fun, or this is going to be one pricey downer."

Five people stepped forward to stick with David, and the rest of the giddy Loners scattered like mice let out of a cage. A band playing on a tiny homemade stage kicked into a song. A small crowd gathered around. The band used traditional instruments together with handmade ones. Tubas and violins harmonized with desktop wood blocks and nails being scraped down chalkboards. There was a stand-up bass made out of stripped electrical wires and a desk drawer. The clash of sounds made a harmonious racket. Lucy was dancing by herself right up front. There were a hundred different things you could do at the Geek show, but all David wanted to do was watch Lucy dance. "You should dance with her," Ritchie said. "Before I do."

"You're not dancing with her."

"I am if you keep hesitating. Seriously," Ritchie said, moving his head in unison with Lucy's butt, "I want that thing to live on my face."

David laughed. He felt like a goon, standing with five other goons, ogling her.

"I'll be right back."

"Yeah." Ritchie nodded slowly.

"And look at something else, will ya?"

"Just trying to keep you safe, Dave."

David navigated past dancing kids. He felt acutely aware of how hard he was trying to act casual. He sidled up to Lucy and stared at the band, as if that was the real reason he was there. He bopped his head. He tried to shuffle his feet to the beat, but he felt like an idiot. He wasn't a dancer. He glanced over at her as she rotated her hips.

"Have you ever been to a Geek show?" David projected loudly.

The band stopped playing, and the second half of his

question echoed out over the lull. They put down their instruments and took a break.

"Hmm?" Lucy said.

"I said, have you—"

"Yes."

"Oh."

He didn't expect to feel awkward around Lucy. But he did.

"Will you show me around?" David said.

"Are you dating Hilary?" Lucy said.

"Whoa," David said, and reeled. "Where did that come from? I mean, I used to date her."

"I saw you with her at the market," she said.

"Oh, uh . . . okay, well, I did talk to Hilary, but we aren't dating."

Lucy bit her lip and considered David as if he was lying. Maybe he'd left some stuff out, but he wasn't really lying. He gave her a reassuring smile.

"Believe me," he said. "I don't want anything to do with her."

"Come on," she said, then hooked her hand around his arm and pulled him off into the rest of the crowd. Her hand was light but firmly nestled into the crook of his elbow. As she pulled him past a cluster of Freaks, David felt a surge of anxiety. He looked back at the Loners fading from view. They were struggling to catch up, but Lucy was moving quickly. He suddenly felt out of control. Who was watching him now? Did he just bring Lucy into the line of fire?

"Actually," David said, "we should stick by the guys in case—"

"Do you want me to show you around or what?" she said.

Lucy placed her other hand on his arm too and pulled David away from Ritchie and the security detail. They came to a comedian who paced on a rectangle of six milk crates. A small crowd was gathered around him. The kid was painfully short and had a face like a bulldog. Given how he looked, being funny was his only option.

The comedian's eyes lit up when he saw David.

"Uh-oh, look who it is," he said. "Does anyone have any zit creme? I got some whiteheads I need to get rid of."

The crowd chuckled at the old joke. David didn't. He moved to leave, but Lucy tugged him back. She was giggling.

"Hey, what do you call it when two Loners stand together?"

David looked up at the guy.

"I call it my future wife and . . . some asshole."

More laughs. The comedian mouthed the words *I love you* to Lucy, and he got a cheap laugh out of the crowd.

"I'm just joking, David. No hard feelings. In fact, I'm glad you're here. I got a stain on my boxer shorts. Got a second?"

The crowd laughed hard at that one. David pushed out a strained smile. Lucy's hand was shaking on his arm. David looked over to see that her face was red from trying to hold in her giggling. She couldn't stop.

"Oh, come on," Lucy said, tugging him away from the comedian. "It was a joke. You can't take a joke?"

"Hey, if it's funny, I'm the first one to laugh."

"Ooh, I think he touched a nerve."

"Pssh, are you kidding me? I love thinking about all the mornings I spent trying to scrub blood off of some kid I hate's sleeve with a toothbrush."

Lucy looked unsure as to how to respond. David meant it to be sarcastic, but it came out angry.

"That's just not what I am anymore," David said.

"Jesus, the guy was joking. You need to give yourself a break. You've already done more for all of us than anyone could have expected you to. Take the night off, for crying out loud. Let Ritchie do the worrying, because he already is anyway."

Lucy motioned behind David, and he turned to see Ritchie less than ten feet away. He was shadowing them, and he knew he was busted. Ritchie strode up to them.

"So . . . hey, what are you guys up to?"

Lucy arched her eyebrow at Ritchie.

"You know what? Never mind. Pretend I'm not here," Ritchie said, backing away.

When Ritchie was finally gone, Lucy squeezed David's hand.

"So, do we have a deal or what?"

"A deal?"

"Are you going to just enjoy yourself tonight? The world's

not going to end if you have a little fun."

David took in the auditorium. He didn't see one person who was having a bad time. If kids could mingle across gang lines here, why didn't they all the time? He wondered if the school could ever be like this every day.

"All right," he said. He turned to her. "Deal."

Lucy jumped and clapped her hands. She pulled him over to a concession stand that served juice. To compensate for their smaller claims on the quad, Varsity had started selling what was once reserved only for their own drop parties: their homemade apple juice hooch.

"Two cups, please."

Lucy slid two tickets across the table, and the Geek at the stand served up two tin cans full.

Lucy raised her can up to David's.

"To a great night," she said.

"You drink?" David said.

"Not really, but if I'm asking you to cut loose, well, I guess I can't be a hypocrite."

David liked that. He raised his tin can.

"To a great night," he said, and they each took a swig. It burned going down.

"WHOOF!" Lucy yelped. She had to cover her mouth to force herself to swallow. She fluttered her fingers and did a little dance to help it go down. She finally managed and crumbled into David. "What is in that stuff?"

"Good old-fashioned moonshine, mixed with apple juice."

"Moonshine? Is Huckleberry Finn in Varsity?"

David laughed.

"Yeah, moonshine. Anthony Smith used to bring it on the bus to celebrate after we won away games. It's just sugar and yeast, and you distill it, I think. If Varsity can do it, it must be easy."

"You mean, it's sugar, yeast, and fire. I can't feel my throat."

"Me neither. That means it's working," David said, and took another swig.

The juice made him buoyant. Anxiety slipped away. David reached out to take Lucy's arm, but somehow they ended up hugging. She felt so good in his arms. He didn't want to let go.

The night became a dazzling blur. The colors, the sparklers, the flames. David held close to Lucy. Her laugh was fast and childlike. She had one pointy tooth that only showed when she smiled all the way. Her fingers would graze the inside of his wrist. They shared more juice. Wandering performers interacted with the crowd in improvised dramatic scenes. At a game booth run by art Geeks, kids could pay one ticket to take whacks at papier-mâché sculptures of soldiers in haz-mat suits. David demolished one as Lucy cheered. They stumbled from spontaneous sing-alongs to dance performances to rap battles. One Geek took his clothes off and streaked through the auditorium. The music thumped.

The houselights flashed, signaling everyone to their seats.

David and Lucy were ushered to the best seats in the place, a gift from Zachary. As they settled in and the lights went down, Lucy slid her fingers between his. The curtain parted, and the stage lit up. Zachary took the stage to begin the school's most popular ongoing play, *Sunday Morning*.

David was surprised to discover that Zachary was a fine actor. His grandiose personal flourishes didn't exist onstage. He was completely in character. He was Paul, a normal kid from the suburbs, on a lazy Sunday morning. Paul went to the grocery store; he read a book; he walked his dog. David understood why McKinley students never tired of dipping into Paul's world. It was a world with no threats, no danger, nothing but real-world leisure and everyday chores, the things that they ached to be bored by again.

He let himself be carried away by the delicate world onstage. Paul was David. David was Paul. And nothing mattered anymore. He wasn't in McKinley. He was in Paul's living room, then in Paul's backyard, under the open sky.

"Lucy," David whispered.

"Yes, David," Lucy said, her head on his shoulder.

"Is there anything between you and Will?"

Her head lifted up.

"I . . . Will is just a friend," she said.

While David could still feel the breeze of Paul's world on his face, he leaned over and gave Lucy a soft, slow kiss.

26

WILL WANTED TO VOMIT. HE WATCHED DAVID
kiss Lucy. His lips against her lips. His tongue digging in her
mouth. Her hand was on her chest, covering the necklace Will
gave her. He hated the look on Lucy's face; she was in heaven.
Her eyes were closed, and she coiled her arms around David's
body. David held her face in his hands.

"Hey, man," someone rapped their knuckles on the back of
his head. Will spun around. It was Ritchie. He looked at Will,
totally astonished. "What the hell are you doing, dumbfuck?"
he said, then lowered his voice to a growling whisper. "You're
supposed to be on guard duty."

Will didn't have an answer. He looked down where David
and Lucy were seated. Lucy was resting her head on David's
shoulder.

Will found it hard to breathe. The auditorium was immense, but it felt like it was pressing down on him. He broke away from Ritchie and pushed past a Geek guard. Will bolted out a fire door into a raked hall that ran the length of the auditorium. The guard took off after him and shouted to a cluster of costumed drama Geeks at the end of the hall to stop him. Before they could react, Will blasted through them like bowling pins.

He ran past dressing rooms, catching a fleeting glimpse of a make-out session in one, a pile of ragged costumes in another, and in the third, he saw a momentary reflection of himself in a full-length mirror, the biggest mirror he'd ever seen intact. It would have been worth a fortune in the market.

Will careened into art studios. A shirtless guy poured black paint over his face, then rubbed his head against a bedsheet that was stretched across the wall. Will slipped on some paint and slammed his body against the sharp corner of a metal table, cutting open his lower back. He shouted in pain and kept running. He blazed past wire sculptures, reconstituted furniture, burned canvases, and finally a series of charcoal drawings. They were head and shoulders portraits of the old faculty members, but in all of the drawings, they were vomiting crimson blood.

"Get that guy!" A mob of Geeks burst into the workshop.

"You get him, I'm trying to work!" the shirtless guy snapped back.

Will was already out of the room. As he sprinted down the

hall and rounded the corner, the Geeks' shouts faded. A minute later he skidded into the foyer of the school. It was empty. He couldn't run anymore; he wasn't out of breath, he was heartbroken. He dragged himself to an out of the way corner and sat underneath a shattered window. Will gritted his teeth so hard he thought they would crumble.

David knew how Will felt, and he'd stabbed him in the heart anyway. It was cold and calculated. Will's eyes overflowed. He tried to wipe the tears away, but more kept dribbling out.

Will could finally see how much his brother hated him. David had held it in for so long, but now it was all out in the open. And the worst was that Lucy meant nothing to David either. He'd just led her on with his quarterback bullshit act, so she could never, ever really consider Will. That's what happened at the pool, when Lucy pulled away from him. She just saw David's little brother in front of her, the virgin from the trail. David just had to have it all. He always got it all. He was the star. Will kicked the window frame.

He wished Smudge had never told him to go.

An hour before, Will had been stationed at the third-floor door to the Stairs. Everyone had gone to the show, mostly everyone anyway, just Will and a skeleton crew of kids remained in the Stairs, guarding the exits. He was in the middle of telling himself how unfair it all was when he heard a whisper echo in from the other side of the door.

"It's Smudge."

Will stayed quiet. He trotted over to the stairs and leaned over the railing to make sure the guards below didn't hear. He didn't see anyone. He hurried back to the door.

"It's about Lucy. Lemme in," Smudge said.

Will narrowed his eyes. He was curious. He pushed the barricade back just enough so that he could pull the door open a crack. Smudge was right outside, staring back at him. His nose was plagued with blackheads. Smudge looked grave. It didn't suit him. It only made him look uglier.

"I saw something tonight. Something I thought you should know about."

Smudge told him that he had seen David with Lucy at the Geek show. He said they were all over each other, for everyone to see. Will didn't believe him, but the longer Smudge talked and the more details he supplied, the more afraid Will got.

"Trust me, Will. I've watched a lot of people make out. I know what it looks like when two people are about to mash lips. This was, like, a half step away. Who knows what they're doing now?"

The thought of David and Lucy kissing made Will even more ill than realizing that Smudge probably spent hours watching the Pretty Ones from that air vent in the pool room. Probably jerking off.

"He ain't your friend," Smudge continued, "I'm your friend, man. What pisses me off is that you've been so loyal to that asshole. I mean, you could've come with me the day of that food drop, but you didn't. You stuck with him because you guys are brothers."

Will punched the door.

"I'm sorry, man, I shouldn't have told you."

"No," Will said. "You did the right thing."

That's when Smudge offered to cover for him on guard duty for ten minutes. And Will ran all the way to the auditorium. And then he saw them. All over each other. Licking inside each other's mouths. He wanted to die.

Will stood up. His tears were dry now. He knew what he needed to do.

He was going to kick David's ass.

Lucy knew she wasn't in love yet. This was just the beginning, but it felt tremendous. She felt so full with joy that it lifted her off her feet. She'd seen the same joy bubbling up in David too. He'd unleashed his inner goofball. She spent half the night with her mouth hanging open. She couldn't believe David's silly voices or the imitation of a drunk giraffe he did to make her laugh. She wished she could peek into his ear and see everything inside his head.

Lucy ran around a corner and crouched down next to the stripped skeleton of a water fountain. David was chasing her. Her cheeks hurt from smiling, but she couldn't stop. She was breathing hard, her whole body tingled. She poked her head past the water fountain and peered down the hall. There was no sign of David. He could've been anywhere.

She popped up and ran. She'd get to the Stairs eventually, but she was having fun. She looked around every corner. Her heart drumrolled from the anticipation.

She couldn't wait for David to catch her.

She raced around another dark corner. Something collided with her. Unseen arms lifted her off her feet. She tried to scream, but pure fright kicked the air out of Lucy's chest. Her attacker took her down to the floor quickly, but a hand slipped behind her head to soften the impact. It was David's hand. His lips were on hers. The first kiss was soft and gentle, like they were sharing a whispered conversation. But then his body pressed heavy into hers. His lips were firm and hungry, and he made a deep humming noise that made Lucy sweat.

She lost track of time. She felt small and delicate. David pulled away and stared into her eyes. He said nothing. She didn't look away. She didn't dare risk losing the power of the moment. She felt connected to him, bonded to him, vulnerable to him. It overwhelmed her. She was completely lost in him.

David stood and pulled her gently to her feet. They walked back to the Stairs without saying anything. Some of the time he had his arm around her, and the rest of the time he held her hand. She thought he was pretty good at both. Everything was so right.

When they passed through the guards and the barricades

of the Stairs, they paused by the armory. They were jolted from their dream state by the racket of three floors' worth of conversations. The whole place buzzing with talk about the Geek show. It sucked the life right out of her.

She grimaced at David, and he grimaced back. Lucy didn't want to deal with the rest of the gang. She didn't want to walk up there and have to declare themselves an item, but she also didn't want to walk up there and pretend like nothing was going on. And then there was Will. Guilt reached its hands out at her. She pushed Will out of her mind.

"Do you want to go hang out in the elevator?" David said.

Lucy turned to David, filled with relief. She squeezed his hand.

"Yes."

"Wait here. I'm gonna grab some candles. I'll be quick."

David bounded up the stairs. The elevator sounded wonderful. She couldn't think of a more romantic place to hide. Just them, and no one else. Her perfect night didn't have to end just yet.

Behind the curtains of David's quarters, the noise of the gang was softer and more distant. David fished three candles out of a tin can that was nailed to the wall. He rooted around in other cans until he found a condom. Just in case. It wasn't like he had a plan. He'd stopped planning when he kissed Lucy in the auditorium. Lucy didn't need him to be a heroic leader.

He didn't have to act like everything would turn out all right. And he didn't have to be on guard. He just had to be himself. That's all she wanted. It made him happy.

And then there was Will.

David thought he would have passed him on the way up to his room, sulking at his post. But he didn't, and he didn't care. He'd deal with Will tomorrow. Not that there was anything to deal with. Lucy had told David plainly that she wasn't interested in Will. That was that, and everything afterward just happened. Nothing more to say.

He couldn't wait to get back to Lucy.

Something cracked hard across the back of his head. He dropped to the ground in an instant. His head struck the floor.

Hands grabbed at him. Fingernails dug into his skin. He could smell fruit and flowers. Fabric rustled above him. He struggled, but there were at least four figures tugging him around. They flipped him to his back and pinned him to the ground.

Freaks, David thought. This was it. Oh, God. They were going to kill him.

David strained his eyes to see into the dark. Feet shuffled all around him. The closet unit he'd built was open, and clothes spilled out of it onto the floor. That was where they must have been hiding. Why wasn't he paying attention?

Someone slapped his face then clutched his head. He felt his hands being crushed. He wanted to scream, but someone crammed a rolled-up athletic sock in his mouth.

"Daaa-vid," a singsongy voice whispered, "pay attention, you piece of Loner trash."

David widened his eyes to focus on his attackers. He saw six elegant silhouettes in the dim light. They were Pretty Ones. Their legs were like silken columns towering over David. Two stood on his hands. Two held down his legs. Another sat behind him and pressed her palms down on his forehead with all of her weight, keeping his skull planted on the floor. One girl sashayed from side to side lazily like she was listening to a song that no one else could hear. As she moved, her skirt would flit open, and he could see all the way up. David wrenched his arms and legs around, but he couldn't overcome their combined grip. They stared back at him blankly, with plastic smirks like evil dolls.

The girls pried David's legs apart, and Hilary stepped into view. She lowered herself down to her knees and began to crawl on top of him. Her hair hung in front of her face. He felt her leg against his. She was shaking.

"Mmm, hot," one of the Pretty Ones said. The others snickered quietly.

David's heart pounded as Hilary made her way up him. It may have taken only seconds, but they were torturously long.

Hilary pulled her body up and straddled David's rib cage. Her weight squeezed air out of his lungs. The light cutting through the curtain entrance caught Hilary's face as she turned. Her face was slack, and her right eye was purple and swollen. It looked inflated.

She leaned her lithe body forward. Down her dress, he saw the weight of her breast. David pressed his tongue against the sock in his mouth, and it moved a bit. He kept his eyes locked on hers, breathing hard through his nose.

"David," Hilary said, "what happened the other night . . . was a mistake. I was weak, and you took advantage of that." Her voice was flat, distant.

She ground down on her words. "It's your fault this is happening now. You need to learn your place."

She looked off into the darkness as her voice failed her. "All you Scraps need to learn your place." Barely a whisper now. "This school belongs to Varsity."

David worked his tongue against the sock in his mouth. His whole gang was just on the other side of that curtain, only a few stairs away. He screamed, but it was too muffled for them to hear. David kicked and thrashed his legs, but the Pretty Ones held fast.

Hilary held out a shaky hand, and one of her girls placed a slender ivory comb in it. She turned it in her fingers to reveal that the handle had been whittled into a sharp dagger.

Hilary looked out to the darkness again and shivered.

"Do it," said a whisper from the dark.

Oh, God . . . Sam. He was here.

Hilary clamped her eyes shut.

David shook his head violently at her. The Pretty One above him held tight to his head. He pushed and pushed with his tongue, edging the sock out.

"Do it, baby," said the whisperer from the dark.

No, Hil. No!

A drop of water fell on his face. Then another. They were tears, falling from Hilary's chin.

Hilary lifted the dagger high, and her beautiful face twisted into something ugly. David screamed, and some of his voice escaped.

Someone threw aside the curtains and burst into the room. Light from the stairwell spilled in. David's heart soared.

It was Will.

He had a look on his face. It was pure rage. He must have heard David's scream. He looked ready to fight, but then he froze, dumbfounded by the scene.

For just a second, David and Will locked eyes. Then Will had a seizure. He dropped on his stomach, his shuddering face landing inches from David's. David could hear the sputter of his gurgling throat. David looked back to Hilary.

She jammed her dagger into his eye.

27

AGONY. IT WAS ALL DAVID KNEW FOR AN eternity. Pain knifed through his eye, it twisted and scraped inside his skull so relentlessly that it felt like Hilary was still over him, rattling her ivory shank in his eye socket. David swung in the dark to knock her away, but it never changed anything.

Pain permeated his dreams too, making it impossible to know for sure when he was awake and when he wasn't. He could sense that people were trying to help him. He heard words of consolation, but they were unintelligible through the throbbing haze.

In time, pain didn't consume him anymore. He slept more restfully. He'd only awaken for moments before fading to sleep again.

"You had a fever from an infection," Lucy said softly, holding his hand. "You're doing well now, David."

She returned to reading a book aloud. It was rhythmic and soothing. There was talk of a picnic and cold iced tea. Her voice faded away.

He came to later. Lucy's voice came from a different direction.

"Oh, my God," she said. "You're not going to believe this, but I was really jealous of Dorothy. All those gifts she gave you? I actually tried to draw a picture of you one night. You should have seen it, it was horrible. Wow, I hope you're not listening to any of this."

He was, sort of, but he drifted away again.

"If your jaw hurts, it's 'cause I had to knock you out, you were thrashing and yelling so bad," Gonzalo said, chuckling. "You almost took that Nerd's head off when he was operating on you. Jeezus, it was crazy."

David tried to laugh, but he fell asleep instead.

When he awoke, he reached up and dared to feel his right eye for the first time. His fingers grazed the crusty gauze.

She took my eye, David thought. *We were a couple. My mom made her dinner twice a week. I loved her once.*

He gnashed his teeth together. He was angry now. No matter how many times he thought it, it never seemed acceptable. She could have killed him if she wanted to, but no, she wanted to shame him. Scar him. Make him look weak.

Sam made her. Sam wanted all of those things, and he scared Hilary into doing it. He made her feel like she had no choice.

But she did have a choice.

David had asked her to join the Loners, leave the Pretty Ones behind. He would have protected her. She wouldn't do it. She wouldn't let go of the power. David knew then that Hilary never loved him.

No one would ever mutilate someone they loved.

The rage within David felt good. It dampened the fire in his eye. He turned revenge scenarios over in his head, lying on his side, staring at his room with his one good eye. Dull light seeped through the curtain.

His room had been rearranged. A first-aid kit, bottles of water, rags, and a pile of books sat on the floor, next to his bed. A pillow lay scrunched into the corner. That was where Lucy sat when she read to him and kept him company.

She'd talked about episodes from her childhood, things about her family, random thoughts about life. One time, he remembered her singing softly to him. Some kind of folk song or something. He couldn't remember the chorus, but her voice had been so sweet and lulling.

David's mind traveled to the night of the Geek show. It seemed like a dream.

Lucy entered in the half-light, stepping quietly around the room so she wouldn't disturb him.

"I'm awake," David said.

Lucy sat down on the bed beside David.

"I need to change your bandage."

"Okay."

She peeled the tape away from his face. With a damp cotton ball she gently dabbed below his eye to clean the area. David kept his good eye to the ground. He felt ashamed. How could she look at it? It had to be vile.

"It looks a lot better," she said.

David stayed silent as Lucy unwrapped a new bandage, then used a pair of scissors to cut it into a much smaller shape.

"Thank you for treating me so well," David said.

He looked up at her. Lucy was right there, her eyes big and loving. He missed her, even though she'd been right next to him day after day. He felt like precious moments had been stolen from them. He took her hand and held it tight. Her eyes glistened with wetness. Tears threatened to tumble out from his eyes as well. It hurt.

"I wasn't going to lose you," Lucy said. "I swore I wouldn't."

David was overcome by her devotion. He was lucky to have her.

"How long have I been out?"

"Almost three weeks."

David reeled at the thought.

"Where's Will?"

Lucy stayed quiet.

"Just tell me he's okay."

"He's okay. He just . . . decided to leave."

"I don't understand. Where did he go?"

"Nobody knows," Lucy said. "He left not long after the attack, and nobody's seen him since."

"Nobody's seen Will for three weeks? Where did you look?"

"There've been a few search parties for him, but he didn't turn up. It's been hard to persuade the gang to go after him."

"Why?"

"Will left his post the night you were attacked. That's how Hilary got in. Ritchie saw Will at the Geek show."

He knew what it meant. Will saw them.

"It's my fault," Lucy said. "You asked me if there was anything between me and Will, and it was just so complicated, I didn't know how to put it."

"Well, how would you put it now?"

"I may have . . . I did . . . I gave him the wrong signals, when I should have been clear. I hurt his feelings. This is all my fault."

David hung his head. He punched his fist into the bed. Lucy jumped.

"I'm not mad at you, believe me. This is not your fault," David said.

This was all David's fault.

"I tried to stop him from leaving, but he wouldn't listen,"

Lucy said. "He said the Loners would never forgive him. He thought they might even try to kill him."

"They wouldn't."

"Everybody was upset, David. You were in bad shape. You screamed for days straight. I just don't think Will could take it anymore. But we'll find him. I know we will."

Lucy finished the bandage she was cutting and lifted it to place it over David's eye. He stopped her.

"I want to see it."

Lucy gave David an unsure glance. "David—"

"Let me see it."

Lucy got up, walked out of the room. She returned with a small mirror and handed it to him. He took a deep breath and then held it up to his face. His dead eye stared back at him. It was crusted with yellow and red, and the globe itself was deflated and opaque. It looked like a steamed onion.

David lowered the mirror. He was disgusted. He felt weak. He felt violated. He knew that's what Sam wanted, but he couldn't stop himself. Lucy sat down next to him again with a pleading look.

"You're no different, David. Everybody's waiting for you. Everybody believes in you."

How could he possibly think his enemies would take the night off just because he decided to?

"David," Lucy said, trying to get his attention.

David turned to Lucy. She gazed at him, and he recognized the same affection she had in her eyes at the Geek show.

"You're so beautiful," he blurted out. She blushed and looked down.

He wanted her even more now than he did the night of the Geek show.

"David," Lucy said. "There's something else. It's Gonzalo. He's graduating tomorrow."

David laughed.

"What else are you going to tell me? Somebody stole all our food?"

Lucy didn't laugh. David's face dropped.

"That didn't happen, did it?"

Lucy shook her head, then said, "You should be happy for him. He's been a good friend. He got everybody through a tough time while you were hurt."

Lucy took David's hand.

"I'll be right next to you. I'll do whatever you need me to do. We're going to be okay."

Lucy squeezed David's hand.

"I have something for you," she said.

Lucy reached over to the first-aid kit and plucked up a twelve-pack box of chalk. David gave it an odd look.

"Open it."

He opened it and pulled out a white leather eye patch. He smiled.

"You made this? From your pocketbook?"

She nodded.

"Well, let's see it on," she said.

Lucy placed the small bandage over his eye and taped it down. She took the eye patch from David's hand and gently placed it over the bandage. She ran her finger along the white shoelace straps, guiding them through his hair. As she tied it, her dress stretched across her curves, and he could feel her heat.

Lucy leaned back to have a look at David.

"There," she said, biting her lip, seemingly impressed with her handiwork. She giggled. "Ooh-la-la."

David laughed, and afterward he felt exhausted.

"I'm tired," he said.

"You should lie down."

He nodded and lay back. Lucy lay down with him. She wrapped her arms around his body and cradled David. He thought about kissing her, but he didn't do anything. It felt too good to be held by her, and to let someone protect him for once.

David strode fiercely down the hall. It was reckless considering he'd barely mastered his equilibrium, but so far he was doing a decent job of walking a straight line. The Loners struggled to keep pace. He wouldn't slow down for them. He couldn't.

"You know I'm getting out, not you, right?" Gonzalo said.

"Yeah, you sure you don't want to stick around? It'd be a big help. Even if you're dead, I could probably still scare people off with your corpse," David said, forcing a smile. Gonzalo gave him an approving clap him on the back. It nearly sent him into the wall.

Appearance was everything today. It felt too soon for David's first public appearance since the attack. He was still plagued by episodes of unbearable, plunging pain in his eye. He'd slugged back two cups of juice to try to numb it. But that didn't help his insecurity. He felt like a gimp. He'd been mangled and was about to put himself on display for everyone to ogle and gossip about. What could he do? It was Gonzalo's graduation day.

Graduation was the most important event in a McKinley student's life. You'd made it through. You'd earned your free-dom. And it was an important reminder to everyone else that there was still hope, and that life on the inside wasn't real life, a point that he was finding harder and harder to remember. If David had skipped Gonzalo's graduation, not only would he miss saying good-bye to his most trusted right-hand man, but his absence would have been an admission of defeat to Var-sity and the rest of the school.

He prayed they didn't meet with any trouble today. He wasn't even sure he could land a punch, working off one eye. He couldn't afford a fight, but he needed to convince every-one, including the Loners, that he could.

Thunderous conversation echoed out from the foyer. The closer he got, the more it sounded like the whole school was there. He could see students packed into every inch of space. They'd come to see the return of David.

"How are you doing?" Lucy said, sidling up to him. Worry creased her brow.

"I feel like a million bucks," he said. It was curt and insincere, enough to say bad question, bad time without hurting her feelings.

He kept pushing forward to the foyer like an express train. He marched into the area, bumping a few kids out of the way as he did. He didn't stop until he was a good ten yards in. All talk in the room stopped.

He planted himself there like a colossal Roman statue forty feet tall and made of bronze. The Loners flanked him, creating a ring, looking out at the McKinley population. David peered out at the kids staring back at him. What they didn't know was that David was focusing only on their mouths as they whispered. He couldn't bear to meet their eyes yet.

The stitching on his eye patch prickled his face. He ached to adjust it, but he knew everyone had their eyes on it. The slightest acknowledgment that it irritated him would have been Varsity's first small victory.

David scanned the crowd for Hilary. He had intended for hers to be the first eyes he met. He found the Pretty Ones, but there was no sign of her. Varsity was close at hand, and at the front was Sam. Sam was grinning at David and talking out the corner of his mouth to Diaz and Dixon. David felt a magnetic pull toward Sam. He had an overwhelming urge to kill him right there, but that could start an all-out war. How many Loners would die? If David were to strike back, it would have to be definitive. He'd have to wipe Varsity out completely so they wouldn't be able to retaliate. He would have to win it all in one move.

What did that mean? He had to kill them all?

It seemed like an insane thing to consider. But what if they went after Lucy next? What if they found Will before he could?

What if they went for his other eye?

"You need me to murder Sam for you real quick before I go?" Gonzalo said, leaning in.

David couldn't hold on to his steely expression. He broke into a grin.

"Would you mind?"

"Sure, I could do some kind of suplex or an elbow drop super quick. He'll be dead, then I'll bounce. Cool?"

David's grin gave way to an honest laugh. He turned to his friend and appreciatively took him in. Gonzalo had a bittersweet look on his face. Two months ago, David didn't know if Gonzalo felt any emotions at all. He'd been a deadpan giant then. Now he was a close friend, and he was clearly worried. Gonzalo knew the situation. He knew the pressure that was now on David. He also knew that this room was a time bomb.

David thought that Gonzalo probably wished he could stay to fight just as much as he couldn't wait to run out the front door.

David gave Gonzalo a heartfelt squeeze on the shoulder, as if to give him permission to go. Gonzalo walked to the front doors beside the graduation booth. They were covered with the scratched-in signatures of past graduates. He grabbed the car key that was hanging on a string off a door hinge. Gonzalo found a clean spot among the three hundred or so names on the doors and scratched his name: GONZALO. He turned to the booth, stepped inside, and placed his thumb on the scanner. A moment later, the screen in the booth flashed:

PROCEED TO EXIT FOR PROCESSING.

Gonzalo walked to the door and waited for it to open, but nothing happened. The door should have opened for him. Gonzalo looked puzzled. The crowd whispered about it. Gonzalo walked back to the booth, scanned his thumb again, and still the door didn't open.

A sob echoed from the cluster of Loners. It was Sasha. She'd been a wreck all morning, crying and barely able to stand. Belinda had to hold her up now. The graduation booth not working was just too much. Gonzalo looked at Sasha as he tried the scanner again.

"It's okay, Sash. Don't worry, girl."

She nodded, tears pouring out of her eyes.

David heard a dull clunk. All heads turned to see the doors to the outside swing open. The coffin-sized containment cell that had always been behind the doors wasn't there. Instead, the double doors looked out to a large white room. David felt an impulse to run for that room. That was the way to freedom, and it was wide open.

A soldier in a black haz-mat suit and riot gear stepped forward. Thirty more, identical to the first, charged through the doors in a tight formation. Dread seized David. They hadn't seen anyone from the outside for eighteen months, not since the booth had been installed. This felt wrong. David grabbed Lucy on instinct and pulled her away from the doors. Gonzalo ran back with the Loners. Sasha screamed like mad.

"Get back!" David shouted to the Loners. They retreated to the edge of the foyer in a tight formation around David. Every other gang did the same, finding cover behind the prominent pillars of the room.

The students peered out at the soldiers. It was a quiet face-off.

The soldiers held clear bulletproof shields in front of them, with slots in the middle to stick their assault rifles through. They assembled in a line, spreading out to form a wall of shields. Between that front line of soldiers and the door, another team of soldiers broke into two lines that faced each other, with their shields out to form a wide hallway that led to the exit.

"There's been a malfunction in the automated exit process,"

one soldier hollered. "If this is your release day, line the hell up! We will be scanning for infection! If you try to leave without being scanned, we are prepared to use maximum force!"

As if that wasn't clear enough, another soldier shouted, "We'll lay you rats down! Just try something!"

Everything about the soldiers' entrance and their attitude was jittery. They were on edge, and it made David feel queasy.

Gonzalo looked to David, just as unsure.

"What do you think, D?" he said.

"I think you should get the hell out of here before they change their mind."

Gonzalo nodded. He leaned down to Sasha to give her one last kiss, and she jumped on him like he was a jungle gym. She grabbed his face and pressed it against hers.

"I love you so much, baby," Sasha said. "I'm gonna miss you like fucking crazy."

Tears wet Gonzalo's eyes, and he bit down hard on his lip to fight them back.

"I'm gonna see you soon, Sash. Real soon, okay?"

She let go of him and turned away. Belinda and Lucy opened their arms to her. Gonzalo strode toward the soldiers. Graduates from different gangs stepped forward and formed a line down the center of the foyer behind him.

A cube the size of a walk-in closet, made of thick slabs of clear plastic and mounted on a black metal base with all-terrain tires, rolled in from the outside and continued down the hallway of soldiers. Its motor buzzed like an electric pencil sharpener.

"What the hell is that?" David said.

The cube came to a halt five feet in front of Gonzalo.

"It's a fat guy in a little box," Lucy whispered without missing a beat.

A man sat inside the cube, behind a small steering wheel and a set of computerized panels. He was some kind of scientist, or maybe that was overstating it, but he had on a clean white lab coat. His flabby bulk barely fit into the cube. And he was terrified. He shook as he looked around the room. This clearly wasn't in his job description. His eyes were so wide it looked like toothpicks held them open.

"Uh . . . f-f-first student. Step, uh, come forward."

Gonzalo approached the box. The fat man shrank back in his seat.

"Place your hand in the glove," the fat man said.

Gonzalo slid his hand into a long, rigid, rubberlike glove that extended into his box from the outside, like an incubator. The glove sealed tightly around his wrist. Gonzalo waited. The fat man stared at the screen on his equipment and patted the sweat from his round, hastily shaven cheeks.

Finally, the fat man said, "Name?"

"Gonzalo Mendez."

"Take your hand out of the glove."

Gonzalo did as the man asked. There was a slight hum of whirring parts, and then the hand-hole spit out the glove lining that had fit over Gonzalo's hand. It landed with a nasty splat on the ground.

Gonzalo waited for the fat man to say something. The guy seemed to be busy with follow-up procedures on the panel.

"Come on, man," Gonzalo finally said.

The fat man looked up, rattled.

"Oh, uh, you're free. Your processing section is F. Proceed to the exit."

Boos echoed out from the crowd at the fat man's performance.

"YOU SUCK!" someone shouted.

Someone else threw an oily clump of rags from far back in the room. It smacked onto the side of the cube. The fat man jumped in his seat, making the cube rock from side to side on its wheelbase. The man's heart rate must have tripled. Some kids laughed. The soldiers choked up on their rifles. The rag slid down the plastic, leaving a trail of curry-colored goo behind it.

"See you on the other side, McKinley," Gonzalo said.

Gonzalo walked into the hall of shields. His face transformed when he looked through the doors to the white room. Clean, cool light washed over Gonzalo's face. He breathed in deep. His smile was reverent. It was like nothing David had ever seen from Gonzalo. The rest of his life was waiting for him. He stepped through the door.

And then Gonzalo was gone.

David felt exposed and vulnerable again. He felt the focus of the room shift back on him. He'd been maimed by a girl he used to date; he was half blind; his brother was missing; and he'd just lost the strongest fighter in his gang.

Five more students were set to graduate. Dickie Bellman was next in the graduation line. That wasn't right.

Dickie was at least a year too young to be phasing out of infection. Everyone who had graduated so far would have been a senior. Dickie would only have been a junior at this point. A panic fluttered in David.

"What's Dickie doing?" Lucy whispered.

The Freak behind Dickie was trying to pull him out of the line by his shirt, but he clearly didn't want to cause a commotion that would involve the soldiers. Dickie pushed the Freak off and hustled up to the cube. Without prompting, he stuck his hand into the glove. As Dickie waited for a response from the fat man, whispered conversation spread through the crowd. People were making the same observation David and Lucy already had.

The fat man's eyes flicked over his control panel, then looked up, frightened.

"You are not eligible for release," the fat man said.

"Sir, I hate to be argumentative, but you have to be mistaken," Dickie said.

Dickie gestured emphatically, causing the black glove to snap back and forth inside the cube. The fat man yelped, petrified, and pressed as much of his body he could manage against the back wall of the cube, as though he was trapped in a car with a cobra.

"Pardon me, would you mind running the fucking test again?" Dickie said. His voice slid up and down in pitch as he spoke.

"No! Get out of here!"

The hallway of soldiers turned their guns on Dickie, while the others kept their aim on the crowd. Dickie didn't seem to notice any of it. He was focused on the fat man.

David wished Dickie would just walk away.

"I'm just trying to talk to you like a human being, sir, I don't need to be yelled at. If you simply called the Pentagon, they would tell you I've already negotiated this—"

"I said, go!" the fat man yelled.

"Get back, kid!" the commanding soldier barked. It seemed to snap Dickie into a larger awareness. He turned to see the whole school staring at him. Dickie looked back at them all with disgust. He focused on the fat man again.

"I'll have your whole family fired," he said, and pulled his hand from the glove.

Dickie turned and walked away from the cube. The glove

mechanism whirred and spit Dickie's glove lining out after him. The splat of the lining on the floor made Dickie's face flinch.

"Next," the fat man announced.

The Freak who was next in line strutted up to the cube and stuck his hand inside. The hole sealed around his wrist.

Dickie spun around and dashed back toward the man in the box. A soldier fired a single shot. He missed Dickie and shot the Freak in the hip.

The Freak howled. Dickie had no intention of stopping. He sprinted past the fat man and into the hallway of shields. The soldiers opened fire. Blood shot up over the shield line like a blender with the top off. What used to be Dickie fell to the ground, a mangled lump.

The Freak still wailed, yanking and yanking at the glove that held him fastened to the cube.

"Let go'a me! Let me loose!" the Freak yelled.

With every yank, the cube rocked, and the fat man screamed. The front line of soldiers fired on the Freak, executing him. All the Freaks went wild. Bobby led them in a mad rush on the cube. The Freaks barreled into it. The cube tipped over and crashed to the ground. Simultaneously, a surge of kids ran for the door.

The soldiers' roaring guns spit bullets into the heads, chests, and legs of the charging students. Blood sprayed in the air. Bodies flopped to the ground. Screams filled the room. The kids were screaming in pain and rage, the soldiers were screaming orders at each other, and the man in the cube screamed louder than anyone, his wheels spinning uselessly in the air.

"GET ME OUT OF HERE! PLEEEASE! GET ME OUT!"

A few soldiers desperately tried to lift the cube back onto its wheels. They abandoned their effort and resorted to dragging the whole thing toward the metal door while the other soldiers' guns coughed fire into the riot. Three kids took one soldier down to the ground. They clawed furiously at the back of his suit like dogs trying to dig under a fence. They tore rips into his suit, and within seconds his clear face mask flooded with blood and lung. Another Freak ran straight past the discombobulated crowd of soldiers and out the front doors. David heard adults scream beyond the exit.

The Loners were scattered by the chaos. David pushed Lucy toward the hall.

"Go! I'll be right there!" David said.

Lucy nodded, and David did one last scan of the foyer for any Loners who could have fallen behind. He didn't see any. He turned right to run for the hall and smacked hard into someone on his blind side. He spiraled off the anonymous body and landed on the floor.

David scrambled to get up, machine guns blaring in his ears.

He kept getting knocked back down; he couldn't see anything on his right. When he finally got his bearings, he caught sight of a face staring at him through the mob. It belonged to Sam, who watched in fascination as David was helplessly smacked around.

The twins dragged him away from the crowd by his ankles.

If David wanted to make an impression, the job was done.

28

WILL CLIMBED OUT OF A TRASH CAN.

So far, he'd slept mostly in air ducts, some closets, and once in a second-floor girls' bathroom. It had been stripped of its sinks, its mirrors, its stalls, and its toilets. Even the tiles had been chipped out of the walls and floors. He lost sleep trying to think of what the thieves intended to do with those toilets.

Last night had been his first night in a trash can. It was a big one that must have been for the janitorial staff. He'd knocked it on its side, emptied all the contents, and lined the inside with a clean trash bag from his sack. Inside, it was a little plastic cocoon. His legs stuck out, but he camouflaged them with trash.

It sure left him stiff. He stood and cracked his back. He

fished his backpack out of the trash can and looked through it. He had only one can of tuna left.

Will had taken a whole pack full of food with him from the Stairs, but not enough. He figured if he ran out of supplies, he could thieve in the market. But gangs hadn't gathered in the market for a week, because the food drop never came. He knew the gunfire had something to do with it. He ran to the foyer that day to see what was happening and was almost spotted by Lucy and David when the Loners ran out. He hid. It still felt too soon to face them.

The next day he watched from the third-floor balcony as three kids who were supposed to graduate the day of the massacre tried the graduation booth over and over, but the doors never opened. They ended up coughing their lungs out on the foyer floor.

Will decided to save the tuna for later. He rummaged through his bag some more and pulled out a bottle of water, reinforced with layers of masking tape, and a pencil case. He opened the pencil case and pulled out a clean white toothbrush. Will set off down the hallway, dry-brushing his teeth and rinsing his mouth with slugs of water.

Above him, the ceiling lights went out. Will looked up at the fluorescent light panels that ran the length of the hall.

That's weird, he thought.

The lights were out all down the hall. He clicked on his phone to use it as a flashlight, and continued on.

The hallway was wide and emptied into a small area that used to be a student lounge. Two vending machines, pillaged and bashed, were knocked over on the floor. The whole room was burned black, probably by a controlled burn that got out of hand, some moron burning furniture to make ash for black hair dye. No one came here anymore, and that was exactly why Will was here. It was the same reason he'd gone to the suicide room, the old student counselor's office where four different people had killed themselves since the quarantine began. Will was searching through all of the places no one else went.

He kept replaying the night it all went wrong in his head, as if he thought he could change it. He'd whipped open the curtains. David was pinned to the floor, Hilary on top of him, a shiv raised. And then it all went black. When he came to, there was a lot of shouting. The room was full of Loners. He was on the floor. His brother's face was painted with blood. Will thought he'd been slashed. Then David's head rolled heavily toward him. His eye was destroyed.

Will couldn't go back to the Stairs until he avenged his brother. There were only so many places Smudge could hide. Traitor. It killed Will that he had been played so easily. He was sick and tired of losing. It was no wonder Lucy never took him seriously. He was an idiot. Smudge may have opened the door, but it was still Will's fault. He'd put David in that situation because he couldn't control himself. He'd never had any self-control.

He knew he couldn't make it right. David's eye was gone for good. But he could make Smudge pay. Outside of his time with the Loners, Will only ever saw Smudge at night. Smudge lived on the fringe. The only people he associated with, other than Will, were thieves. So far, Will had struck out, but there was one last place to look.

A wicked smell stung his nose. Putrid flesh. A whole lot of it. He'd been here before, a long time ago, with David. It was the teachers' graveyard, lockers upon lockers stuffed with faculty corpses. Will quickly pulled a bandanna from his bag and wrapped it around his nose and mouth. His stomach was doing backflips. Will was entering the ruins, the decrepit East Wing of the school. There was talk that it was haunted by the ghosts of teachers and dead students. The stench only added to the atmosphere. No sane person belonged here. This had to be where Smudge was hiding.

Will climbed a staircase that had an enormous crack separating it in two all the way up to the next floor. By the light of his phone, Will saw the words *KILL ME* scrawled in what looked like dried blood across a wall of the next hallway. He hesitated before taking the final step up. He hated to admit it, but the ruins were freaking him out.

Will needed to calm down. He pulled a smut phone from his pocket. It barely had one bar left on its battery life. He'd found it in a desk drawer in a classroom overrun with flies. Some kid must have stashed it there to hide it from his girlfriend. The Nerds sold beat-up phones that were loaded with porn. They collected all the dirty pictures and videos they could find from laptops and phones that they charged or serviced. The photo was a girl he recognized, a Freak, and she was nude. She must have struck a deal with some enterprising Nerds, because there were tons more galleries of her on there.

That's one way to make some money, Will had thought.

All the hall lights flickered up ahead. They weren't putting out their maximum wattage for some reason, and the quality of the light fluctuated.

A horrible noise came from far away. It was a gut-wrenching scream that slid into a deep belly laugh.

It must have been one of the burnout kids who lived in the ruins. There was a small group that never could hack it in McKinley. They hid in the ruins, getting high off whatever chemicals were left from the science labs. The only time they ventured out of the ruins was at night, to rob people. Kids said their minds were gone, and they were just animals now.

Another scream rolled down the hall at him. It sounded closer than before. Will pocketed both phones in a hurry. He needed to stay sharp. He rounded the corner into the main hall of what used to be the science department. He came to a hall with a caved-in ceiling. Everything smelled like mold. Will figured there was a broken water pipe somewhere, and it probably had been flooding since the explosion. Water trickled down the walls in steady rivulets. The floor was slick. The rest of the hallway was impassable, caved in completely. He ducked into a doorway.

The room beyond had no floor. A ragged, gaping hole took up nearly the entire room. Floor clung to the walls around the room's edges like a shattered window. Will stood on one of those shards, inches from the crumbled edge. Wavy brown stains marked the ceiling and the high part of the walls.

Below, as best as he could make out, were the remains of four smaller rooms, their walls crushed by what used to be the ceiling above them. Will tried to make sense of what they used to be. The obliterated skeletons of computers, printers, and swivel chairs were half buried in the rubble. It was the computer lab for the science department, a part of the school Will never had a chance to see when it was new.

There was a dog in the middle of the room below.

It was a German shepherd with tan-colored fur and a black snout. Will felt like he was dreaming, but he knew he wasn't. He didn't understand how this was possible. Will softened, looking at the dog.

"Hey, buddy."

Will lowered himself into the room below. He held his hand out as he approached the dog.

"Come here, pooch."

The dog cocked its head like it was considering the offer. It sniffed the air.

"Come here."

The dog sniffed his hand.

"What are you doing here, pal? Where'd you come from?"

Will marveled at it. He dared to scratch behind its ears. The dog let him.

"I'm not so bad, right? You like me, huh?"

The dog panted. The corners of its mouth angled up, which made it look like the dog was smiling. Its breath was hot and comforting. It was an amazing thing for Will to be in the company of another creature that meant him absolutely no harm. There was no duplicity in the eyes he saw before him. If he ever got out of McKinley, he was definitely getting a dog.

Will noticed a trail of blood on the floor leading from the dog to a hole in the wall of rubble. The blood was dripping off the hock of its hind leg. The wound was fresh. A set of tags dangled from the dog's collar. As he reached for them, there was a wet crunch somewhere behind him. Will whipped his head around.

Smudge was frozen, standing on the lip of the broken floor above, with his back against the wall. He must have been creeping inch by inch across the room behind Will, trying to sneak past.

The dog barked. The sound battered Will's ear, and he

jumped. Smudge shimmied across the shards of floor above, hurrying toward the door Will had just come through. Will ran toward Smudge. He jumped up and grabbed the lip of the floor above. The dog bounded away. Smudge disappeared through the door. Will pulled himself up and ran into the hallway after Smudge. Will slipped on the slick hallway floor and crashed into a soft, wet wall. The spongy drywall gave way, and Will landed in the sopping space between the walls.

He pushed himself out of the plaster trap and raced down the hallway. As he closed in on the hallway's entrance, he heard Smudge shriek. Will dashed out to the entrance of the ruins, where he'd first heard that burnout scream.

He skidded to a stop when he saw that half of the cracked staircase was gone. The missing half of the staircase had collapsed under Smudge's weight. Smudge was impaled on a ragged piece of rebar from what was left of the top of the stairs. The rebar jutted out through his neck, and his body dangled with nothing underneath him.

Will knelt by him. Smudge clutched his neck with his free hand, desperately trying to keep blood in his body. He was breathing in short, hysterical bursts. It wouldn't be long.

"Will . . . you gotta . . . help me, man."

Will climbed across the debris and grabbed Smudge by the hair.

"What are you doing?" Smudge said.

"You're gonna die," Will said without emotion.

"Will, come on—"

Will didn't move. Smudge's eyes bulged in disbelief.

"Will! We're friends!"

"Not anymore. Why did you let Hilary in?"

"I don't . . . I don't know what you're talking about," Smudge said.

Will shook him. Smudge shrieked.

"Admit it!"

Blood poured out of his neck like the stream of a weak garden hose. The color in his already pallid skin was nearly gone. His next breath marked a significant downturn. He could barely keep his eyes open now.

"I'm tired," Smudge said.

"You did it."

"Yeah," Smudge said. His voice was thin and it warbled. "I'm sorry, Willie. I didn't know what they were gonna do." Smudge tried to swallow. "They told me they were just going to raid the food supply. I didn't know anybody'd get hurt." Smudge shook his head, his eyes fading.

"Why?" Will said.

"There was a girl. Joan. A Pretty One. I loved her. . . ."

Smudge was nearly gone.

"She didn't like me, but Hilary made her make out with me. You gotta understand. . . ."

His last word had no volume, only breath, and it was the last breath Smudge would ever take. "You know what it's like, right?"

Will let go of Smudge and leaned back. He stared into Smudge's cooling eyes. Will began to cry. The lights above him dimmed a little more.

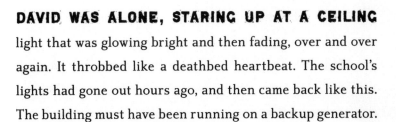

29

DAVID WAS ALONE, STARING UP AT A CEILING
light that was glowing bright and then fading, over and over
again. It throbbed like a deathbed heartbeat. The school's
lights had gone out hours ago, and then came back like this.
The building must have been running on a backup generator.

He reached up and pulled his hoodie tight over his head,
that old comfortable feeling. He wore a pair of cheap sunglasses, with the lens poked out for his good eye. It was his
attempt at a disguise, so he could take to the halls in search
of Will. He went alone. He didn't want to pull the Loners into
his mess.

The halls had become more dangerous by the day as panic
overtook the school. As long as the doors stayed closed, more
seniors meant to graduate would die. And if another drop

didn't come in two weeks' time, they'd starve to death. Now, more than ever, David needed to find his brother. He needed to set things right.

He had a savage headache.

David whisked himself through the shadows, reaching his right hand out to gauge the distance from the wall on his blind side. These night jaunts were good for getting his bearings back. Life with one eye had proved to be maddening. He banged into corners a lot. Doorways seemed to narrow on him sometimes. It was the athlete in him that wouldn't submit to the handicap. He had to master his new, limited perspective.

Thunk, thunk, thunk. He ran his fingers along the handles of the lockers he passed. David had to be strong. He couldn't slip. That's what got him half blind in the first place. The Loners needed their leader now more than ever. They were all scared. David kept telling everyone not to panic, that the military would open the doors again. But it was his job to say that, to get his team through the game. What he should have been doing was figuring out how they were going to get food when theirs ran out. But that was for tomorrow. He still didn't know how tonight was going to pan out.

He turned a corner. David heard a noise up ahead. He stopped. Voices were coming from a classroom down the hall. The door was open. He couldn't make out what they were saying.

David stepped back around the corner and waited, sticking

his head into the hall just enough to have a view of that class-room door. A figure stepped out. It was Kemper, the leader of the Nerds. He had bad posture, unkempt black hair, and he was always cheerful. Violent walked out after him, collecting her mussed red hair into a ponytail. Kemper and Violent kissed. Passionately. David grinned. He couldn't believe what he was seeing. Way to go, Kemper.

David watched as Violent reached up and grabbed a handful of hair on the back of Kemper's head. She turned Kemper around and pressed his back against the lockers. She kissed him deeply. Kemper said something to Violent that David couldn't make out, and Violent giggled.

This was the strangest romantic coupling David had seen so far in McKinley. Now he understood why they were meeting in the dark on neutral territory. It was the same reason he had to sneak out to see Hilary. An affair between two gang leaders stirred up way too much drama. David was comforted by it though. Even when things were this bad, two people who were into each other would still find a way to get together.

They kissed good-bye and went their separate ways. Violent walked away from David, and Kemper walked toward him. David ducked his head back around the corner and clung close to the wall. Kemper, smiling like a goof, passed without noticing David. He whistled a tune that faded off as he disappeared around a corner.

David got moving again. He was wasting time. He'd been avoiding the foyer for the past half hour. He'd just go there and see what happened.

David dragged his feet the whole way there.

The foyer had the same surging and fading light. He exhaled softly, trying to keep his cool, and walked toward the graduation booth. He stepped in. The metal was scuffed from abuse. The booth's walls were plastered with Skater stickers.

David placed the pad of his thumb on the scanner and prayed to hear the buzzer that would mean his time wasn't up just yet.

Sam lay quietly on a towel. He let the water on his body air-dry. He liked looking at his body. He could honestly say it was perfect. That was what four hours a day in the gym created. He worked hard. Nobody could say that he didn't.

He listened to the water lap at the edges of the pool. It was only a matter of time before the maniacs would be shaking down the doors to the gym. They'd be hungry. They'd be angry. And there were a lot of them, a whole school full. They wanted to devour everything Sam had worked for. They wanted to destroy everything he had built.

A light splash from the pool drew his gaze. Hilary glided through the water. This was her nineteenth lap. Watching her go back and forth helped him think.

He could practically hear all of Varsity pacing upstairs.

Idiots. He had to do it all, and if he was wrong, just once, they grumbled. He knew they were up there plotting. They'd try to kill him before the rest of the school had a chance to. Sam wouldn't allow that to happen. Whether it was his own gang or the rest of the school, they were going to lose. He would be the last man standing in here.

Hilary stepped up out of the pool and wrung the water from her hair. Yellow dye splattered on the tiled floor. Seeing her hair nearly white made Sam uneasy. He knew why she'd let it get so light. She was being defiant because he hit her. He admired the dark triangular bruise under her eye. She was so beautiful. She wrapped a towel around her naked body.

"Come here," Sam said.

She walked to him, her face vacant. She knelt beside him, and he sat up. He reached out and touched her temple. His forefinger drifted to her bruise, and he pressed into it. She didn't shudder. She was perfectly still.

"I'm sorry, baby. I didn't want to hurt you."

She didn't say anything. She lay down beside him and rested her head on his chest. She'd been so quiet since the night in David's room. He supposed he understood. She wasn't used to killing.

He had to make her do it. Anthony told him what Tara knew, that Hilary had reached out to David. She admitted what she'd done, but then she thought an apology could be enough. She really could be dense sometimes.

Getting to watch David at the graduation was the most enjoyable thing Sam had done in forever. David was maimed, shaken, faking like he was strong. It was great. Sam had planned on killing David at that graduation. But Dickie Bellman ruined that. His only consolation was getting to watch David flop around on the floor like a drugged cat.

"David's going to come for revenge," Hilary said.

"I know," Sam said.

"I don't want to see David ever again, Sam. You promised I wouldn't have to!"

"I have a plan," he said.

"Well, what is it? Tell me," she said. She was desperate.

"Nope."

Hilary was sitting up now, her face clenched in anger. He didn't like looking at it. He reached out to touch her pretty face, to smooth out the tension. She slapped his hand away and stood up. She flung her towel in his face and marched off naked. Sam grinned.

He loved the way she flirted.

30

LUCY WALKED PAST THE STOLEN FLAT-SCREEN
TV that lay flat on the lounge floor. Empty cans sat on it like a coffee table, and a few kids were using it as a surface to play poker. Dorothy had taken the TV down when the electricity had become unreliable.

Lucy stared at the creation Dorothy had put on the wall in its place. She had removed some hinged windows from the quad, stretched a white sheet behind them, and mounted the whole thing on the wall, with lightbulbs shining through it. It looked almost like a real window, with dawn's dim light shining through from the outside.

Lucy moved close to the window, shut her eyes, and imagined she was at the lake house again, staring out at the water.

Belinda interrupted her mental vacation.

"I'm scared, Lucy. I mean, really. Why didn't they drop the food?"

"I don't know," Lucy said, her eyes still closed, but she could tell that Belinda was choked up.

"Yeah, but no, but—do they hate us? I mean, does the whole world hate us?"

"No."

"It just feels like . . . I mean, who's in charge out there? Do they know what they're doing?"

"Don't worry, Bel."

"Okay."

She was just as scared as Belinda, but she knew Belinda needed someone to tell her everything was okay whether it was true or not.

Lucy tried to get back to the lake house in her mind, but guilty thoughts plagued her. She'd thought she'd left the Pretty Ones behind, but truthfully, she'd acted just like them, and it made her sick. Instead of going after the boy she liked, Lucy sat back and waited for one of them to make the decision for her. In doing that, she'd pitted two brothers against each other. If Lucy was going to survive in here for another couple years, she had to start taking charge.

Belinda piped back up. "I haven't seen Dorothy since Tuesday. When's the last time you saw her? Oh, thank God, David's here."

Lucy opened her eyes, and turned around. David stood on

the next landing below them, in the kitchen. Other Loners gathered around him. Her body tingled with relief. He wasn't there when she woke up in the morning, and she'd been freaked out over it ever since. She wanted to run to him and pull him away, but the group stood in her way. They all needed him so much, she barely got to be alone with David anymore.

David didn't speak until he was sure everyone was ready to listen. Fluorescent light gleamed off his white eye patch.

"I know you have a lot of questions about what our next move is now that there's no more food coming in. I wish I had answers for you today. But this is about something else."

The crowd rumbled with conversation. David raised his hand to get everyone's attention again.

"I got a nosebleed last night."

The crowd erupted in frantic whispers. Lucy felt short of breath.

"The virus is leaving my body. My graduation would have been this morning. You all know what that means."

The crowd quieted. The reality sank in. Lucy reached for the railing for support. Her equilibrium seesawed.

"Sometime tomorrow maybe"—David searched the crowd until he found Lucy's eyes—"I'll die."

Concerned Loners swarmed David. Everything blurred. Lucy's head felt like a spinning plate on a stick. She turned away from David and started pushing people out of her way. She had to get out of there. Belinda called out for her, but she didn't stop. The trek upstairs felt endless. People were staring at her, pitying her. Lucy ran into David's room, sobbing, and flung herself onto his bed.

David didn't enter the room until almost a half hour later. She could hear him answering desperate questions as he made his way up the final flight of stairs. Finally, they let him through. She heard him enter the room, but she didn't look up.

David didn't say a word. She felt guilty. She should have been consoling him, not waiting for him to tell her that everything would be all right.

Lucy opened her eyes and sat up. She looked at him, but she didn't know what to say. She was afraid that if she opened her mouth she might just scream.

"I was never a big fan of having lungs anyway," David said.

She jumped up and ran to him. He wrapped her in his arms and held her tight. She didn't want to cry anymore. She breathed in the smell of him. The heavy scent of his perspiration lurked under the scent of the citrus detergent he used to wash his clothes.

"It was all a joke, wasn't it?" Lucy said.

He stroked her hair in consolation. It wasn't a yes.

"You were joking," she said.

"No, Lucy."

"I don't understand." She let go of him and backed away. "How can you be so calm?"

"I walked around for hours, wishing it wasn't true. I thought

I could figure it out, come up with some solution. But then I realized I was just wasting time," he said. "I've only got a day left. My brain will start freaking out on me soon. I don't want to throw away the time I have left."

She guessed she understood, but she started to cry again, more out of frustration than sorrow. David wiped away her tears.

"Don't be sad. I can't take any more sad," he said.

"I'm sorry."

"Don't be sorry either," he said. "Please. I just want to be with my girlfriend."

"Girlfriend?" she said with a little smile.

David grinned. "Well, it seemed like a good time to make it official."

She laughed and felt a tear slip down her cheek.

David ran his fingers down her hair. He kissed her. She kissed back. All her tension unraveled. He picked her up and moved her back to his bed. She pulled at his shirt. He guided her down.

David was kissing her chest. The diamond pendant slipped down the gold chain around her neck and fell to the side. She pulled David back to her face and kissed him more. She wondered how long she'd actually have him—a day, an hour, only minutes?

Just kiss, she needed to keep her mind on kissing.

She moaned. David's hands were gliding under her dress

and up her thighs. She unbuttoned his shirt. He kissed her neck, pressing against her. His body was warm and heavy. An image flashed in her mind of David coughing out globs of bloody meat onto her. She shuddered.

Lucy sat up.

"I need to stop . . . Just for—"

"Will," he said.

"What?"

David was looking past her. She followed his gaze. Will stood just inside the curtain. She didn't know how long he'd been there. Will's clothes were caked with black muck. Lucy scrambled to straighten her dress. David buttoned his shirt in a hurry. They both stood, keeping a slight distance from each other, guilty but not sure why, as if a teacher had just walked in on them. Will stared back at them, still as a tree.

"Where have you been?" David said first.

Will didn't answer. He watched them calmly.

"We've been so worried," Lucy volunteered.

"You looked it," Will said.

"Look, man," David started to say, but his conviction faded as he struggled for the right words.

"David's going to die tomorrow," Lucy blurted out. She knew David didn't want to dwell on it but she couldn't stop herself.

"Yeah," Will said. "I heard."

David was breathing fast. He got up and walked over to Will with urgency.

"I'm so glad you're here, Will. I was afraid I—"

Will socked David in the chin, knocking him down.

"No!" Lucy said. She ran to David and helped him up. David gestured for her to stay back. He looked up at Will, holding his jaw where he'd been hit.

"I'm sorry it had to happen this way," David said.

"Fine. I don't ever want to talk about it again," Will said.

Will extended his hand to David. David took it. Will pulled him up to standing. Lucy knew that she had caused all this strife between them. She wanted to say something to make it better.

"Will," Lucy said. Will looked at Lucy, his eyes so cold when they used to light up at the sight of her. It made her wince.

"Yeah?"

"I don't know," she eventually said.

Will turned to David.

"None of us are going to die," Will said.

David gave Will a puzzled look. "Why?"

"I found a dog."

ESCAPE.

It was David's only option. Faced with starvation, the Loners wanted out as well, even if it meant putting people on the outside in danger. At this point, it was leave or die.

But it was a long way from the Stairs to where Will found this dog, a lot of different gang territories to cross. All they had was the hope that however that dog got in, they could go the same way to get out. David's chances were slim. He'd probably die before they found this theoretical exit. The idea of spending his last few hours trudging around the ruins and looking for holes in the walls sounded awful. He wanted to spend his last hours in bed with Lucy. She wouldn't allow it. As soon as Lucy heard Will's news, it lit a fire of hope in her that she spread to everyone else. Nearly the entire gang was behind Will's plan. They wanted out of this place once and for all.

"I think if we head through the commons, that'll be the fastest," Will said.

Will was pointing at a school map laid out on the floor of the armory. David's headache was getting worse, and he was having trouble concentrating. Beside Will, Leonard passed weapons out to Loners in a steady flow. David took a baseball bat. He didn't trust himself with one eye and his machete yet.

Will continued, tapping the map: "That means either going through Freaks' territory or Varsity's. I think it's a pretty easy choice."

"We'll go Freaks," David said, massaging his jaw. It still hurt. It was weird. David felt closer to Will now, after the punch, than he ever had before.

"We ready?" David said.

Will nodded. David signaled the twins to draw back the barricade and open the door. David stared at the lit hallway. He took a breath and stepped out of the safety of the Stairs. He'd never step foot in the Stairs again. Will walked in stride with David, and an army of ninety Loners followed. They stuck close to one another, timid but excited at the prospect of reaching their promised land. The hallway was quiet.

They approached the first intersection, and Will placed his hand out across David's chest, signaling him to stop. He did, and all the Loners shuffled to a stop behind them.

David looked down at Will's hand on him. It felt good to have his brother looking out for him. He wondered if the conflict between them was really squashed, or just put on ice.

"I'll scout the next hall," Will said.

Will bounded off to the next turn, twenty feet or so ahead. David marveled at how fast his brother was and how quiet. Will pressed his back to the wall, then peered around it for a good thirty seconds. Finally, he waved the rest of the gang forward. David began the short march.

The school's PA system crackled to life. David stopped. Will looked up at the nearest speaker.

"Wake up, McKinley. This is Sam."

A wave of anxiety washed over David at the sound of Sam's voice. The PA was set to its loudest volume. Every click of his teeth, every burst of breath could be heard. Sam's voice flooded the hall.

"I have an announcement to make. Varsity is offering a one month supply of food from our surplus to any gang that brings us David Thorpe. It's dinnertime, McKinley. Come and get it."

Sam was a bastard to the bitter end. He couldn't even let David die in peace. David knew every Loner was staring at him, maybe even considering how they could profit from Sam's offer. David exhaled in one long, slow breath.

He started walking. He could sense Lucy close behind, but he didn't know how many Loners would follow. He walked a good ten feet before he heard anything. Then, a smattering of footsteps. He couldn't tell how many. If they all ditched, he couldn't blame them. Every gang in school had empty stomachs, and Sam had just left a steaming pie on the windowsill.

David reached Will, then turned to face the gang. Most had followed him. Fifteen kids hung back. They stood frozen, ashamed of their choice. They stared at the floor, shifting their weight back toward the Stairs. He was flattered by all the familiar faces still standing in front of him: Mort, Belinda, Nelson, the twins, Sasha, Ritchie, and Leonard. They'd been through a lot of shit, and they were about to do it again.

David cleared his throat and spoke with an even-keeled cadence.

"If we get separated, stick to the plan. We'll meet up in the ruins at room 1206. Keep your weapons close and your eyes sharp."

"This way," Will said, and they all hurried forward.

It was still slow going. They had to be cautious. Will scouted ahead. The twins and Ritchie checked that they weren't being followed after they rounded each corner. And in between, there were dropped rations, arguments, untied shoes, and piss breaks. At seventy or so heads, they were no stealth operation.

Will stayed on David's right side, covering his blind spot. David would occasionally look to Lucy to check on her.

"I'm all right," she kept saying. He didn't believe her.

They arrived at the wide entrance to the commons. It was

a large two-story student lounge area. Faint mustard-yellow light poured down in intermittent pools from hanging ceiling lamps, and the block columns that held up the second-floor balcony cast long shadows. The outfacing wall had been one big window that looked out on a pristine lawn. Now it was all metal plating, and the glass lay shattered on the ground, forming a jagged creek that ran the wall's length.

"Let me take a look," Will said, eyeing the columns suspiciously.

Will ran into the room, looking behind every column. He got to the other end of the expansive room, gave David a thumbs-up, and waved him through.

"Stay close to each other," David said.

He led them out at a brisk pace. When he reached the column that marked the halfway point, all the lights shut off.

They were in darkness. David wondered if the school generator had finally given out.

"Will! Are you all right?"

"I'm okay!"

David heard a coarse rumbling in the distance, first from the hall in front of him, then from the hall behind. He stuck his arm out to locate Lucy and grabbed at something squishy. Belinda gasped. There was no time to apologize. The growling rumble was coming faster now.

"Lucy?"

"I'm here," she said.

He saw a ball of fire in the distance. The fireball moved fast, circling the room. More flying fireballs popped up around the room. One was coming right at him. It was a Skater on his board, holding a torch.

"Skaters!" David shouted. The Skater swung his torch at him, and David narrowly avoided the blow. The flame revealed a flash of Lucy's terrified face beside him.

More torches descended from the balcony. Skaters were charging down the stairs, joining the flaming parade that poured in from the hallways. They circled the edges of the giant room, their flames too far away to illuminate the area around David. He still couldn't see two feet in front of him.

"If you got phones, use 'em!" David shouted.

David pulled out his phone and clicked on the screen. He held it out in front of him trying to penetrate the darkness. Other Loners did the same, and they bunched together back to back and side to side. The room was a dangerous swirl of fire with a center of dancing white rectangles of light.

David could make out a shadow charging him. He tightened his grip on his baseball bat and swung at the murky shape. He hit something. He heard a body hit the floor. He raised his phone to get a look at his victim and caught sight of a pair of Vans scampering back into the darkness.

Someone jabbed the end of a skateboard into his kidney. The blow knocked the bat out of his hand. David crumpled down to his knees. Other Loners groaned around him as invisible brutes rained down pain on them. The Skaters swung their skateboards wherever they saw a phone.

David fumbled to find his bat, but he heard the squeak of a sneaker to his left. He punched at the darkness. The punch whiffed through the air. He lost his balance and tumbled away from the Loner phalanx. Another skateboard smacked him in the face. He fell flat on the ground. All around him was chaos. He struggled to right himself, peering through the darkness with his one eye. A pair of arms bear-hugged David from behind and lifted him off the ground. He was still delirious, but he kicked at the shadows and tried to pry the hands off of him. Other unseen hands joined in, grabbing David's right ankle, then his left shin. They carried him away.

"Help! They've got me!"

His shout added to the chorus of grunts and screams from the others. No one would hear it. He felt himself be thrown into the air. For a second, he was weightless, then he slammed down on a plywood surface. It wasn't the floor. He flung his arms out to the sides. He felt crisscrossing pipes and duct tape making up the walls on either side of him. He stood and knocked his head against the same grid of pipes above him. He was in the cage that the Skaters used at the food drops.

He tried to find the door. He couldn't. The sounds of battle thrashed all around him. He could feel the cage move.

"It's David! They've got me in the cage!"

But the battle noises and the glow of the torches faded as

the cage was pulled out of the commons. The cage jostled him around. He dug his fingers through the irregular gaps in the cage walls and yanked, but nothing gave.

There was the sound of doors being kicked open behind David. He spun around just as the cage was dragged into a lit room. He charged the other end to face his captors and instead saw Nelson.

Nelson dropped the steering handle of the cage and looked up at David with a goofy smile. He strained to catch his breath. David stared at him, totally confused.

"Did you see that? I took the cage right out of their hands! I gotta go back and help," he said.

Nelson ran back toward the commons. David shook the cage.

"Nelson! No! Don't leave me here! Nelson!"

Nelson didn't hear him. He disappeared back through the double doors to the commons.

"Are you kidding me?" David yelled to no one.

He was in another foyer, another open space that used to be a second entrance to the school. The Skaters must have pulled a fuse in the commons because the lights were still on in this foyer, and David was in plain sight. Anyone could happen across him. There was a price on his head, and he was alone, locked in a cage on wheels. This wasn't good.

David slumped to the plywood floor of the cage.

He pulled his hair in frustration. He stared out into the foyer. Three quarters of the far wall was plastered over with sheets of painted butcher paper that together formed an enormous mural.

"What the hell?" he said.

It was a heroic portrait of David with a sea of white-haired Loners behind him, and a wide-open cobalt-blue sky over-head. The mural wasn't finished. Butcher paper sheets that had yet to be glued to the wall were scattered on the floor below. Dorothy lay dead upon them.

32

LUCY'S FACE WAS COVERED IN BLOOD.
She lay on the ground, bashed and bruised. It hurt to breathe.
There was a huge smile on her face.

There had never been a battle like this. It wasn't like the
drops. It was more cutthroat, and Lucy had fought tooth and
nail. Literally, she'd bitten someone. She'd grabbed a Skater
girl by the hair and yanked her head into a column. Only a
minute ago, she'd stabbed a broken pencil through a boy's
cheek. He'd responded by cracking a skateboard deck across
her head, splitting open the skin of her scalp. Blood poured
down her face like bath water. She was proud. She'd stood
her ground in this mad frenzy and didn't hide. Lucy fought as
hard as any other Loner.

It had been Will's idea to start breaking boards, and it's

what turned the tide against the Skaters. He'd set a broken-down couch ablaze with a Skater torch. All around the commons, Loners had fought to strip Skaters of their skateboards. They would roll them to Will, who would stomp the boards in two pieces and chuck them into the fire. Before losing all their boards, the Skaters had cut their losses and retreated.

The battle was over. Lucy pulled herself up off the floor. She bunched up her dress, lifting the hem to her face. She wiped away her mask of blood, and it left a wide, almost floral, red print on the pale blue cotton. It felt like a trophy.

"Lucy, come on!" Belinda called out to her as the Loners trudged across the commons.

Lucy strode toward her gang, feeling the slightest bit stronger in spite of the stinging on her scalp. She caught up with them as they entered the next foyer.

Some Loners had gathered in a circle around the Skater cage and were helping David out of it. His face was grave and a few tears rolled down his cheek. Lucy followed his gaze to the far wall. She saw it all so fast. A giant portrait of him. Dorothy's body. It was too much.

She went to David's side. He stared up at the mural.

"She fell off the ladder," David said.

A twenty-foot construction ladder lay by Dorothy's body. David wiped the tears off his cheek.

"We're going to give her a proper funeral," David said.

"We don't have time," Will objected.

"We'll make time. Help me lift her into the cage."

David, Will, and Ritchie picked Dorothy up and placed her gently into the Skaters' rolling cage. Lucy had resented Dorothy for months because she'd run away when the Loners needed her most and she'd kept giving David all those presents. It was petty stuff. How could Lucy have forgotten that Dorothy had been the only girl in the Loners to accept her when none of the others would?

Lucy took David's hand. "She let me borrow this little mirror of hers once. She didn't even know me."

"She was a good person," David said, then gasped. "Jesus, Lucy, are you okay?"

David reached out and smeared a trickle of fresh blood away from Lucy's eyebrow. He touched her like she was made of porcelain. His face knotted with concern. She gently pushed his hand away.

"Don't worry about me, I'll be fine," she said.

David pulled hard on her hand and whipped her behind him. Over his shoulder she saw that Zachary and the Geeks had entered the foyer. The Loners picked up their weapons.

There were about twenty of them, lightly armed, and they stumbled into a clumsy formation behind Zachary when they saw the Loners. They looked liked they'd happened upon a stickup and it was too late to walk back out of the bank. The Geeks quickly drew what weapons they had.

David walked forward, putting his hands up to show he meant no harm. Will motioned for the Loners to keep close to David.

"Zachary, what's up?"

Zachary relaxed and smiled at David.

"We heard there was a mural. I wanted to see it for myself. It's . . . kind of unbelievable."

Lucy watched David closely. He wasn't looking at Zachary anymore. He was studying the Geeks. Most of them were from the art clique. They had paint on their clothes and X-Acto knife cuts on their fingers. Zachary stared at Dorothy's body. His head was bowed, and his expression was grave.

"Do you mind if I . . . ?" Zachary gestured toward the mural, and David shrugged.

Zachary walked away from the Geeks to a central spot in front of the mural. He was quiet for a while.

"It's really something, isn't it?"

"It is," David said.

"I don't suppose you'd be all right with it if my people changed it to my face, would you? I'd probably keep the eye patch," Zachary said with a wink.

David smiled and shook his head. "I like it the way it is."

"I want you to know I don't condone this bounty on your head business. Sam is a pig."

"I agree."

"Somebody's got to take a stand against that guy. I think we should join forces."

Zachary pointed toward a far corner, signaling that they should talk privately. David nodded in response.

"How badly do you want out of this school?" David asked.

Zachary shoved David. David stumbled on his blind side, his foot tangled with the rungs of the construction ladder, and he fell to the ground. Zachary pounced on him.

Will and five others broke into a run to intercede, but Zachary was already behind David, his fingers in his hair. Zachary pulled David up by the head, produced a knife, and held it to David's throat.

Lucy choked with dread. She could almost feel the knife at her own throat, its sharp edge denting her skin.

"Stay back!" Zachary yelled at her. He sidestepped toward the Geeks, pulling David with him.

"I'm gonna kill you," Will snapped at Zachary.

"Will, back off!" David shouted. He lowered his voice to talk to Zachary. "Hey, man, this is the wrong move. You aren't a fighter."

"Shuddup, David. You don't know what I am."

David stomped Zachary's foot. Zachary cried out in pain. David pushed the knife away and elbowed Zachary in the face.

David twisted Zachary's hand behind his back and pried the knife out. It was hardly a fair fight. Zachary was instantly overwhelmed. David pressed the knife to Zachary's neck.

The Geeks charged David but stopped ten feet short. The Loners piled in around him, weapons out.

"We're getting out of here," Lucy said, and pulled Belinda in with the Loners.

Belinda stopped cold. She narrowed her eyes at one of the Geek girls with curly locks dyed a rich auburn.

"That's my hair!" Belinda said.

The Geeks were shouting at the Loners, and the Loners were shouting back. David raised his voice above all the noise.

"Move out of the way. We're walking out of here!"

He waved for the Geeks to clear a path. They didn't budge.

"MOVE!" David shouted again. "You want me to kill him? Huh? I'll run this piece of metal right through his brain! You want him to be another Brad?"

Some of the Geeks moved, but others stared David down.

"Tell 'em, Zachary," David said. "You really want to die today?"

"Do what he says," Zachary finally said, and the Geeks parted.

David pushed Zachary toward the hall the Geeks had come from. Nelson dragged the rolling Skater cage. The Loners flanked the cage, and the Geeks kept a five-foot distance on all sides. Will and the twins brought up the rear. Belinda had one arm looped through Lucy's. She felt Belinda's arm slip out. Belinda lunged forward and snatched the Geek girl's auburn hair right off her head. It was a wig. The girl's hair was white underneath, and she covered her head and ran off, embarrassed.

"Get your own hair!" Belinda said.

Belinda pulled the wig over her head and rejoined the Loners. They all backed up through the double doors to the hallway. The twins shut the doors, and Will stuck a pipe through the door handles. It would hold for a little bit. He turned away from the door and locked eyes with Lucy. His gaze fell to her neck where the diamond pendant still hung. He hurried past her.

"Will, wait a minute," she said, but he ignored her.

"Get in," David said from behind her.

Lucy turned to see David holding open the door to the cage, the same cage that housed Dorothy's corpse. Zachary shook his head in disbelief at David.

"David, get real. I can't get in there. She's dead."

David gripped his forehead suddenly and closed his eyes. He cringed. He looked like he was in serious pain.

"You should've thought about that before you pulled a knife on me," David said. "Now, get in!"

"You're an actor," Ritchie said. "Act like she's Paul's new girlfriend and snuggle up."

Zachary climbed in, grumbling.

"I'll let you out when we get to Freak territory," David said. "You've got my word. Now I want yours. If any of your Geeks try to get in our way, you call 'em off."

Zachary nodded but kept his eyes down.

"I want to hear you say it," David said.

"You have my word."

"Thank you," David said as he closed the door.

Zachary kept his word. At every hallway intersection, in every classroom door, there were Geeks waiting for them, now heavily armed. Every time, Zachary motioned for them to stand down. Lucy could see that Zachary was in misery, utterly shamed in front of his own gang. What would happen to him once he was returned to the Geeks? It seemed too easy for people to turn on each other these days.

She looked ahead to Will, again at David's side. She wanted to clear the air.

"Will," Lucy said, hurrying to his side, "I shouldn't have kept this."

She began to unfasten the necklace. He gave it a glance, then looked ahead.

"Keep it. What am I going to do with it?"

Lucy lowered her hands, hurt, leaving the necklace in place. David turned and shouted back down the line, "Ritchie, come up here and swap with Will!"

Will looked at David, upset. "What are you doing? I've got this."

"I need you watching for Geeks coming up the rear. Lucy, will you help him?"

Will sighed and walked back. Lucy gave David a thankful little nod. She caught up with Will.

"You can't avoid me forever," she said.

"I think I can."

"I can be pretty annoying."

Will stopped. "What do you want from me?"

"I want to make it up to you. I don't want to lose our friendship."

"I can't be friends with you."

"Why not?"

"Because"—he hushed his voice as Ritchie hustled past—"because I loved you. Real sorry, but I can't go back from that. You can be as annoying or cute or whatever as you want, but it's not going to change anything. When we get to the outside, I don't really want to see you again."

Will walked away.

"Looks like somebody saddled the wrong horse."

Lucy looked over to Zachary rolling along beside her in the cage. He was sitting cross-legged, his hands draped over the bars. He watched Will walk to the back of the line.

"What?" Lucy said.

"You know, one of my best friends was supposed to graduate last week. She got migraines just before she started losing her marbles. She was holding her head just like David's been doing up there. He's dying, isn't he?"

"No."

"Clearly a lie. You're a very bad actor. Do you want a tip? The key to a good lie is—"

"I don't want anything from you. David's always been a friend to you. How could you do what you did?"

"Hold on, honey. David and I are friendly. Not the same. My *friends* are going to starve if I don't find a way to feed them. Would you do any different?"

Long wrinkles cracked his cheeks. She hadn't realized how emaciated he looked before, but now she was closer. Stage makeup was caked on his face, but it couldn't hide the droop in the skin under his eyes or the hollows under his cheekbones.

"I wouldn't do what you did," Lucy said.

"Oh, I'm just a bad person, is that it? Nobody knows what they'll do till it happens. What are you gonna do when David's dead on the floor?"

He looked her up and down. "'Cause, honey, I think you'll fall apart."

"I will not," she said.

Zachary's lips curled into a smug smile.

"We'll see," he said, and pulled his arms back through the cage. He turned away.

David wasn't going to die. They were going to get out. She and David would be able to go to the lake house . . . Lucy stopped herself. It couldn't happen that way. By tomorrow,

David wouldn't be immune to the virus anymore. He'd have to stay as far from her and any other teenager as he could. Once they were on the outside, Lucy would have to make her way with Will . . . no, not Will, he'd sworn her off. She couldn't live with her parents. She was toxic to them as well. She would have to live on the run until she phased out of infection. That would mean years before she could be in the same room with David again. Years without being touched by him. Could she wait for David? Did she want to? The brutal truth crept into her head: She might not ever see David again after today.

When the gang reached Freak territory, David opened the cage and made good on his word. He let Zachary go.

"We didn't know Dorothy was a brave girl, but she showed us different. She made her mistakes. We all have in here. But what's important is that she kept trying," David said.

David looked at all the Loners surrounding the cage where Dorothy lay. He strained to squeeze out his thoughts, and his head pounded.

"This place has forced us to make a lot of decisions that we shouldn't have to make. And sometimes, doing the right thing just brings you more misery. You start to wonder if there's any point to trying at all. Dorothy's mural reminded me of when I stood in the quad with eight people behind me, facing all of Varsity. I was sure I was dead. But you all saved me. You came to my defense, and together we overcame. We can do it again.

We're gonna get out of here. We've still got trouble ahead, and when we make it outside these walls, who knows what'll be going on. It could be worse out there than we ever saw in here."

"Yeah, but we'll be free," Will said.

"And there'll be food courts," Belinda said.

"And fresh underwear," Mort said.

"And cars. I just want to drive. Like a road trip, across the country," Sasha said.

"And new movies," someone said.

"And parades," Leonard said.

"Parades? What the hell are you talking about?" Ritchie said.

"If I want to see a parade, what do you care?" Leonard said.

"David's trying to say something nice, you guys," Lucy said.

"And hamsters," the girl twin said.

"And hammers," the boy twin said.

Everyone stared at the twins. They twirled each other's hair.

Lucy walked to David, a black row of fresh stitches on her head. He took her hand.

"We're going to get out of here," David told all of them.

They lifted Dorothy's body and walked it to an open locker. They gently hoisted her into her metal coffin. Lucy put her hand on the door.

"Dorothy," she said, "we won't forget you."

33

THE LONERS CROSSED THE LINE INTO WHAT
once was the humanities department. Now it was Freak territory. David needed to be spry and alert, but he was seeing things.

First, it was the mural. He saw clouds drift across the painted sky. Then it was Dorothy. As he closed the locker door, he saw tears stream down from her eyes. Neither of these things was possible. He didn't realize it would start this fast.

David knew what happened to kids who missed their graduation. They stopped making sense. They would lose track of a conversation, then they stopped talking to anybody altogether. And finally, they started talking to people who weren't there. They all cracked in the end.

It was happening to him now, but he couldn't let anyone

know. They were depending on him. Will sidled up to David.

"What's wrong?" Will asked.

"I'm just worried about the Freaks."

It didn't look like Will bought it, but it wasn't untrue. David didn't want any trouble with the Freaks. They already hated the Loners. Sam's ransom was just the cherry on top. When they happened upon two Freak guards, Will and the twins snuck ahead, pounced on them with knives, and threatened to kill them if they made a sound. They dragged the guards off to be bound and gagged and locked away in the nearest classroom closet. The rest of the Loners watched from a distance.

David kept seeing thin, dark fingers flickering at the edge of his vision. He kept thinking someone was standing behind him and reaching over his shoulder. He looked back and saw Lucy.

"What?" she said softly.

I'm losing my mind.

"Nothing," he said. Lucy was depending on him too. He waved the Loners forward.

David looked through the open door of a classroom beside him. He didn't see a classroom. He saw a clean, white hospital room. He could faintly hear the monotonous beep of a heart monitor. He could see someone's arm, an IV taped to it. A curtain was drawn halfway so he couldn't see the person's face. The harder he strained to see a face, the dimmer the room got until what he saw before him was a dilapidated classroom, but with the hospital room still hanging there, transparent, a suggestion of a room.

"David, we should go," he heard Lucy whisper.

All he had to do was get everyone through Freak territory. Once they were on the other side, it was a short trip to the ruins. As long as they could navigate to room 1206, they could find their way to the outside, he hoped. The longer he took, the less immunity he'd have against the fatal pheromones that everyone around him emitted. The less immunity he had, the more fevered his mind would become until the hallucinations drove him insane, and the meat of his lungs would unspool inside his chest.

David was dying, and it was his friends who were killing him.

He walked away from the hazy hospital room. They hooked a right into a wide hallway. The first few yards were shrouded in darkness. After that, the ceiling lights were functional all the way to a T-junction. The last bit of power from the generator barely coursed through the building's wiring. David led the Loners through the darkened section and into the pulsing light.

He heard the footsteps of a crowd. Faraway chatter. Someone was coming. David stopped and motioned for his gang to halt. At the far junction, he saw Freaks, three of them, walking through the intersecting hallway. They passed through the junction without seeing the Loners. He waved the Loners back and reversed his steps as quietly as he could. More Freaks crossed ahead. If the Loners could back up into the dark section of the hallway, they could remain undetected. David glanced at his gang behind him.

They were all Will.

A wide hallway of convulsing Wills stood gagging behind him, their eyes rolling white, a froth of saliva shaking out of their mouths.

David screamed.

"LONERRRRRS!" yelled a Freak.

A horde of Freaks flooded into the hallway and charged. They wore black, and their faces and arms were completely blacked out with some sort of paint. The chemical of their hair looked even more unnatural against their charcoal faces. Some wore swimming goggles. They carried scimitar-shaped shards of shattered blackboard with handles made of desk legs. The Loners sank into fighting stances. David saw an avalanche of blue fall toward him. The Loners ran forward; their white heads penetrated the blue mass. Violence exploded through the hall. David pulled a pipe from his belt. He prayed that whatever he swung it at was real. A blue-hair sliced his blackboard scimitar down at him. David blocked it with the pipe. The blackboard shattered, and the impact rattled the bones in David's hand. The pain in his wrist was no hallucination. David clung to that pain. He swung his pipe into the kid's hip. The kid fell.

David hacked away at whoever came near. He took down a Freak who swung a rope with a brick tied into its end. A blue-bearded Freak wielded a two-by-four that had nails driven through it. He bashed it into the back of a Loner next to David.

David saw a human skeleton weaving through the riot. It shoved people out of its way, throwing its bones into them. It had no jaw. There was a hammer clutched in its fleshless fingers. The skeleton turned to him. Dead, empty eye sockets locked onto David. It ran at him.

A chair smacked into the back of David's knees. He thudded down to the ground on his stomach. He whipped around onto his back. Ritchie was dragging a chair-wielding Freak away from David. David got up on one knee. The skeleton appeared above him, hammer raised high over its cracked skull. A wet, pink tongue extended out from the shadows under its upper teeth. It screeched.

David gripped his pipe with both hands and put everything into one swing, chopping his pipe up into its dead head. The front of the skeleton's skull, its bony face, broke off and flew over the heads of the feuding gangs. The skeleton thumped down on the floor next to David. It took David three blinks for him to see it clearly. It was Bobby. He was unconscious.

Bobby wore the front half of a plastic rib cage from a biology classroom skeleton over his black shirt. The skeleton's bony face had been his mask. David stood.

The battle still thrashed around him. Blue and white hair was now stained with red. The Freaks had pushed the Loners back, into the darkened section of the hall again. Will and Ritchie struggled against four Freaks. Loners were outnumbered by Freaks, twofold. They were giving everything they had in David's name, but they weren't going to last much longer.

"You want me, come and get me!" David hollered to the crowd.

The Freaks all looked at David. Time to run. He bolted away from the Freaks, around a corner and into a narrow hallway. He slammed hard against a row of lockers. His depth perception was jacked. He heard a wailing mob bottleneck through the door behind him.

The hallway was a cluttered dumping ground. The Skaters hadn't picked up garbage for weeks. He tripped over a stack of torn-up carpet and fell into a pile of trash. He fumbled to get to his feet.

Gotta slow down.

But he couldn't. He glanced behind. The Freaks were bearing down on him fast. He collided with a tangle of desks and leapt over a plump garbage bag to keep his footing. He careened off one object and then another, always close to falling over.

The Freaks shouted after him and threw things out of their

way. The hallway narrowed around David as he ran. The walls squeezed in on him.

It wasn't real.

All the doors were swinging open and slamming shut of their own accord. For a moment, he saw a bloodred elk running by his side. The noise behind him sounded like a stampede of screaming elephants. The noise swelled until David thought it was coming from inside his head instead of behind him.

David tripped on a gallon milk jug full of piss, and ate it into a pile of pallets. Pain. He looked back. The churning mass of Freaks was only twenty feet behind him.

David cut left around a corner. There it was: the entrance of the cafeteria. It gleamed for him like heaven's gate. He passed two Sluts taking out their garbage. Two more stood guard ahead of him by the doors.

"Hey!" one yelled.

He couldn't explain. The guards reached out to try to stop him, but he ran through them, knocking the girls aside, and tumbled to a stop inside the cafeteria, in front of a crowd of Sluts. They rose to their feet and shouted at him.

"Shut the doors! Shut the doors!" David shouted.

Violent cut through the crowd to meet David, her face twisted in anger.

"You can't just run past my guards like that!"

"The Freaks!" David yelled, trying to catch his breath. "They're coming!"

The blue-haired army rounded the corner and charged into the cafeteria. The Sluts ran at the Freaks with whatever they could grab, and the two gangs ripped into each other. The cafeteria was pure carnage. David punched at whatever Freak came at him and kept moving. The Sluts fought to get the invaders out. There were too many bodies to discern who was who anymore. He planted his feet. The people in front of him looked like two-dimensional cutouts. He swung his pipe and bashed it against anything solid.

Another entrance to the cafeteria burst open. A hundred Freaks rushed through. The doors of a third cafeteria entrance toppled over. Throngs of Freaks flooded in. The cafeteria filled with blue-haired psychos, hundreds and hundreds of them, charging toward David. He swung his pipe wildly, smashing it into one Freak after another. For every Freak he knocked to the ground, five more would attack. They were on all sides, and they pulled the pipe from his hands. He punched, he elbowed, he kicked. They clawed into him, tearing at his skin, biting his back.

"David!" someone yelled from behind him.

David spun around. Will stood in front of him. The Freaks were gone. Disappeared. In the blink of an eye, there wasn't one head of blue hair in the whole cafeteria. There were Loners and angry Sluts standing all around him. They stared at him like he was a mad homeless man shouting at a bush. He lowered his fists. He felt sick, weak, scared.

"What happened?" David asked Will in a hushed tone.

"We forced the Freaks out. Us and the Sluts."

"And what did I do?"

Will lowered his voice.

"You kept fighting. After they were gone, you fought us."

David looked past the angry people surrounding him. The cafeteria was in shambles. Injured Loners and Sluts rocked and writhed on the ground like maggots in a trash bag. Mort clutched his blood-soaked stomach. He saw a Slut lying on a dining table with a six-inch shard of blackboard protruding from her chest. Violent was sharpening her knives and glaring at David, furious.

"Not part of the deal, David!" she shouted. "Not part of the deal!"

Will stared up at David as though he was expecting an order. David couldn't be trusted to give them anymore.

David pulled Will in close.

"Will. I need your help."

34

WILL WAS IN FRONT, LEADING THE CLIMB
up the stairs to the library. David clung tightly to his arm. His
one eye trembled. Violent and twenty-five heavily armed Sluts
were behind them, followed by the Loners, who carried any
wounded who couldn't walk. Ritchie and two other Loners
carried the Slut with the chest wound. She moaned and sputtered and coughed. Ten more Sluts brought up the rear. They
all climbed as fast as their battered bodies could carry them.

"This sucks," Ritchie said.

Will agreed, but he didn't know what else to do. The old
plan was to cross the Freaks' territory to get to the ruins.
They couldn't go back into Freak territory without another
battle. The only other way was to go to the third floor and
cross over the top of the Freaks' territory, through the

library. David sold Violent on the chance of escape, so she agreed to escort them. She left half of her girls to guard the cafeteria and brought the other half with her to see if this exit was for real.

Will prayed the exit was real. If it turned out not to be, he didn't think he would be able to hold David's hand in those last moments, and tell him everything would be all right, when he knew it was a lie.

"Pick up the pace, David," Violent said behind them.

"Come on," Will whispered to David.

Violent claimed she had an arrangement with the Nerds and could get them through. Back at the cafeteria, David assured Will that he knew, without a doubt, that Violent was telling the truth and could deliver on what she said. Once in the library, they would drop off their wounded and continue through to the other side, then down the stairs and into the ruins.

"So, you saw this way out, Will?" Violent said, walking up beside him.

"I saw a dog that found a way in."

"So, there was . . . what, like, a hole?"

"Yeah."

"Did you go in the hole?"

"No."

Violent grumbled.

If Will couldn't find the exit, or if that dog had somehow

been in here with them since the quarantine, he knew they'd all turn on him.

David spasmed as he took the next step and fell back against the wall.

"I'm gonna die!" David said.

He was shivering. His bulging eye looked like a hard-boiled egg.

"No, you're not," Will insisted. He turned to everyone behind them. "He's not. He's fine."

Will reached out for David, but David swatted his hand away.

"They're crushing me," he said.

"David, just come on. It's okay."

"David, there's nobody there," Lucy said softly.

She reached out and took David gently by the hand. David looked to Will, his eye wide and helpless.

"Am I holding Lucy's hand?"

Lucy looked on the verge of tears.

Will couldn't believe David was this far gone already. It was a strange sensation, taking care of David. He felt like he'd been walking a tightrope and someone just took away the safety net.

The Slut with the chest wound hacked out a wet cough. It sounded bad.

"Let's go! What are we waiting for?" Violent said.

Will pulled his brother forward while Lucy whispered quiet words of encouragement to coax David up the last leg of the climb. Their exchange was intimate, tender, and hard to watch.

Will threw open the door to the third floor. It was a short hallway, a straight shot to the fire exit door that would let them in the library. He was glad they didn't have to mess with the library's front entrance. It was notoriously rigged with a series of deadly traps that had mangled raiders in the past. As far as Will knew, this back hall was safe.

Violent brushed past them and walked to the door. She pounded on it. A metal plate slid aside, and the narrow rectangular window revealed a fat-necked kid with brilliant white teeth. He silently scanned the faces in the hall.

"Get Kemper! We've got injured," she shouted through the door.

Moments later the door opened, and Kemper stepped into the hall. He and Violent engaged in a hushed dialogue. Occasionally, she would gesture back in their direction. Kemper nodded, and Violent walked back to Will, David, and Lucy.

"So, what's the deal? Who's calling the shots now?" she asked in a matter-of-fact tone.

David was staring at the ceiling.

Will stepped forward and cleared his throat.

"Uh, me. What's going on?" Will said.

"They'll let you guys through. But you gotta check your weapons. They'll give them back once you get to the other side. That's the deal," Violent said.

"Uh . . . gimme a minute." Will strolled away from Violent.

It sounded like a bad idea, but it was their only option. Will looked to his gang. Ritchie walked among the gathered Loners, checking on everyone, pepping them up with words of assurance. He strutted around like a mini David. God damn it, he hated Ritchie. Always trying to replace him. Obnoxious little gnome.

"Ritchie," Will said, "can I talk to you for a second?"

Ritchie sneered in response, then swaggered over to Will.

"What?" Ritchie said.

"We need to hand over our weapons to pass through," Will said.

"Get out of my face with that," Ritchie said.

"This is the only way," Will said.

"Yeah, I get that, moron. That doesn't mean we're not walking into an ambush! Unarmed! Are you out of your mind?"

"David swore to me that we can trust Violent's relationship with the Nerds."

"Was that before or after he was fighting people that weren't there?"

"After. But I believe him. Look, Ritchie, we don't have time to argue. David's going to die. Can't you do it for David? He needs your help."

Ritchie wiped his scarred face with his hands, frustrated. "This is such bullshit."

Will couldn't lose him.

"Are you gonna make me say this?" Will said. "The gang

doesn't like me. They won't listen to me. But they trust you. . . ."

Ritchie was shaking his head. There was one last thing Will was hoping he didn't have to say.

"And I'm sorry I pushed you down the stairs."

Ritchie looked back at the gathered gang. He cracked his knuckles. He wasn't budging.

"Look," Will said with a sigh. "If we make it through this and get outside, I'll give you one clean shot at me. I won't even try to block it."

"Head or gut?" Ritchie said.

"Head."

"You're on," Ritchie said, and walked back toward the Loners. He stopped halfway and turned back.

"I'm gonna fuck up your face," Ritchie said, and went to break the news to the gang.

Great, then we'll look like twins, Will thought, but kept his mouth shut. He walked back over to Violent.

Violent nodded to Kemper. There was no going back now. Five minutes later, Will led the Loners into the library.

"Wipe your feet," Kemper said as he slid the barricade back in place behind Will, David, and Lucy.

"Fussy, fussy," Violent said to Kemper with a smile. He blushed.

Will looked down at a maroon rug. He couldn't remember the last time someone had asked him to wipe his feet, but he could hardly object. The library was a marvel. The carpet was clean.

Every book was in its place. It even smelled like a new building.

Kemper clapped his hand on Will's back with a friendly smile. "Welcome. Have you ever come to the library before? Even before the quarantine?"

Will shook his head.

"Well, everything is almost exactly like it was. Pretty cool, right? Nonfiction is over here. Fiction is on the far side. Over there are the computer stations, but obviously, all we have is a local network. Not that we can use it when the power is—"

"We need to get to the ruins," Will said flatly. Will didn't know Kemper that well, but a couple seconds told him the guy was a chatterbox.

"Oh . . . right. I'll take you to the east fire door. From there, you can take the stairs to the science department. Then, which way are you headed? Because—"

"We got it from there, okay? Let's go," Will said.

Kemper clamped his lips, like he was holding his breath. It looked like it hurt him to shut up. He forced a nod and led the Loners through a maze of bookshelves. Will was in awe of the Nerds' little utopia. They'd converted tall bookshelves into bunk beds, four beds high. They passed through the common area where Nerd medics were tending to wounded Sluts. Mort and the other injured Loners joined them. The rest of the Nerds seemed unbothered by the interruption. The majority were reading books. Others were engaged in rounds of role-playing games. Will and Lucy shared a look of wonder.

"This place is amazing," she said.

"Amazing," he replied.

Kemper led them through the stacks on the east side of the library, and they reached the far wall. David grabbed Will and stopped.

"Whoa . . ."

Will turned to see David staring through the window of a study room. He pawed at the glass with wide eyes. The central desk was cluttered with the innards of electronics and looping wires. It looked like some sort of two-way radio with a microphone. Thick cables ran from the main box up the wall and into the ceiling. Kemper quacked a laugh.

"Cool, right? My masterpiece. It's a ham radio," Kemper said with a nod. "We're trying to make contact with the outside."

"It's real?" David leaned in and asked Will.

"Totals," Kemper said proudly. "Now all I have to do is make it work. I had a really cool idea the other day. I'd like to get the phones working again, just between the gangs. It would be great for negotiations. It'd be so much safer around here. Shouldn't be too hard. The phone lines are already there. The hardest part really would just be everybody's cooperation."

Kemper continued prattling on as he led them down a long corridor of eight-foot-tall bookshelves. Will was in front with David and Lucy and Violent. Seventy Loners followed behind them. The corridor of shelves ended at a barricaded red fire door, identical to the one that got them into the library. A line of Nerds stood in front of it, each holding one of the Loners' weapons. Kemper gave his people a casual wave.

"All right, guys, open it up."

A black-haired kid with an infestation of freckles shook his head.

"We want David," he said.

Will clamped his hand tight on David's arm. He shot Kemper a furious look.

"What the hell's going on, man?" Will asked.

Kemper furrowed his brow and shook his head.

"No, no. This is not . . ." Kemper clucked, trying to make sense of what was happening. "Henry, what are you doing? Is this some sort of joke?"

Will could see it for what it was. Mutiny. Nerds filed out from the stacks on either side of them. They were stone-faced. Their earlier distractions, reading and gaming, that was all a ruse. Nerds clutched thick, heavy dictionaries in their hands, ready to swing.

"Give us David now!" the freckle-face said again, with more bass in his voice.

Kemper stomped forward and stretched his arms out as if he was protecting all the Loners.

"Henry, this is unacceptable. Put that bat down right now—"

Henry planted his bat right in Kemper's gut. Kemper stared

at his gang mate in confusion and crumpled to the ground. Violent growled and socked the freckled kid.

"Push!" a voice shouted.

Bookshelves behind Will toppled over, crushing the majority of the Loners underneath them and raining books down on their heads. The Nerds attacked. Will fled, pulling David and Lucy with him. Nerds poured out from every corner after the trio. Books sailed through the air after them. One smacked directly into Will's temple. It was a hardback encyclopedia, and it knocked him off his feet.

"Will," Lucy cried out.

He lost his grip on David and fell to the ground. He was in pain. He rolled over and struggled to his feet, still woozy. He saw a cluster of Nerds tear David away from Lucy. She shrieked. It took four Nerds to hoist David up and push him onto a rolling book cart. They ran fast, wheeling David through the common area and back toward the west fire door.

He couldn't lose him.

But he did. Will tried to run, and he fell, still dazed from the book to the head. By the time he pulled himself back up, David was gone. He had spent years protecting Will, and Will hadn't lasted an hour in David's shoes.

35

LUCY RATTLED THE HANDLES OF THE LIBRARY
doors and yanked with all her weight. The Nerds had forced her out, but she had to get back in. David was running out of time.

Behind her, Violent fought a hulking Nerd with a droopy face and giant hands. Three other Sluts stood and watched as the Nerd threw a punch at Violent. It connected with her ribs, and she stumbled back. She shook it off and swung a swift kick into his kneecap. Instantly, his leg buckled. He squawked and collapsed to the ground.

"Wait," Lucy shouted. "He can help us get back in!"

Lucy ran to intervene, but one of the other Sluts stepped into her path and shook her head. It was Julie Tanaka.

"Keep out of this," Julie said.

"Get up," Violent said to the Nerd. He struggled back up, keeping his weight on his good leg. "You fuckers messed up big. You're nothing without Kemp."

"No, he messed up when he started making out with you. . . . Slut."

The Nerd hopped forward like he was going to attack. Violent kicked him in the chest. He stumbled back down the hall. He looked up to the ceiling, and his face flashed with panic.

"No . . . ," he said.

A rain of bricks fell out of the ceiling and pummeled his skull. He dropped to the ground. Lucy jerked her eyes to the ceiling above her, terrified that the same thing was about to happen to her, but no more bricks fell. Violent stepped toward the Nerd's broken body and knelt. Blood oozed from his head onto the chunks of ceiling and fallen bricks that piled around him. She placed her fingers under his jaw to feel his pulse.

"Dead," Violent muttered coldly.

Lucy looked up, above the dead body. An entire line of ceiling panels had broken away. A heavy curtain that had been holding the bricks and rubble hung down.

Lucy's stomach sank. She stared at the short hall before her. Ten yards down, it cut right. The floor was covered in dust. No one had walked through in ages. This was the main entrance to the library, where all the traps were.

"Why did you do that?" Lucy shouted at Violent. "We could have held him hostage to get back in!"

"Hostage, huh?" Violent laughed and arched one of her black tape eyebrows. She kicked the dead Nerd's shoe and said, "Well, he's kind of useless now."

"We're not getting back in the library, that's for sure," Julie said. "Those doors won't budge."

"What happened in there?" Lucy said. Every second she was away from David made her more angry with Violent. "I thought you had an understanding with the Nerds. You said we'd be safe."

"This is Lucy, that girl who turned us down," Julie said with smug grin.

"Yeah, because I have a gang. And you set them up."

"You should watch your fucking mouth, girlie," Violent said. "I didn't set anybody up."

Julie rolled her eyes. "Can't believe I thought you were Slut material."

It was a comfort to know that Lucy and Julie would have never been friends. She could scratch that off the bottom of her list of regrets. Violent looked Lucy up and down with a sneer, then turned to Julie. "Let's get out of here."

"Yeah, that's the thing," Lucy said. "How?"

"It's a hallway. We walk out," Violent said.

"But the booby traps . . . there's gotta be more. Do you know anything about traps? 'Cause I sure don't."

"No," Violent said, "I don't know anything about traps! Who the hell does? I grew up in Hillcrest."

Lucy had assumed that Violent grew up someplace rough, like an evil orphanage or some war-torn foreign country. Maybe in a jungle. But not Hillcrest. It was one town over from Pale Ridge. It was full of yogurt shops and golf clubs and had wide black roads that were repaved every two years. People from Hillcrest weren't tough.

Violent edged forward. Lucy stared at the ominous hallway beyond the Nerd's body. Behind every surface lurked hidden pockets of death, coiled up and waiting to burst.

Violent picked up a brick and chucked it. It scuttled to a stop at the end of the hall. The other three Sluts liked Violent's plan. They chucked brick after brick down the hall to try to trigger any traps ahead. Nothing happened.

"Let's go," Violent said, then turned to Lucy. "Unless you're too scared."

Lucy held eye contact with Violent and walked past her, taking the first steps into the hallway. Her heart was a hummingbird. Violent laughed and stepped out after her.

Violent screamed. Lucy jumped.

Violent's leg had gone through the floor. She was grabbing at her leg and shouting. Julie tried to help her pull her leg out.

"Spikes!" Violent screamed.

Violent peeled back the broken floor tile to reveal the hole in the floor.

Her leg was in an aluminum mop bucket that was lodged into the innards of the floor. The interior of the bucket was lined with whittled wooden spikes extending down at a forty-five-degree angle. It was easy to get your foot in, but any effort to pull it out drove the sharpened spikes farther into your flesh. The rough-hewn spikes were plunged deep into Violent's calf. She was literally nailed to the floor.

"We have to get the bucket out," Lucy said.

Julie nodded. They dug their fingers into the floor and pried at the bucket. With a few minutes of work, Violent was able to lift her leg out, bucket and all. They marched ahead. Violent dragged her bucket foot in long scrapes punctuated by painful grunts. Lucy couldn't understand how Violent kept from crying. Pretty damn impressive. They reached the turn in the hallway.

The long hallway ahead was mostly dark, except for a few broken lights that spotlighted small sections of the floor, making it look like a suburban street at night. Junk was piled up along the sides of the hall. Halfway down it, the doors to a row of lockers on one side were bent and torn. Sharp metal edges stuck straight out from the wall like thresher blades.

"We need more bricks," Violent grunted out.

"Let's go back and get some," Lucy said.

One of the Sluts walked over to a nearby pile of stuff. It made Lucy nervous how casually she kicked through the pile. She wrenched a desktop from the junk.

"This'll work."

Lucy heard a click. A locker next to the Slut sprang open.

Inside there were three spray bottles full of liquid. Their squeeze triggers were tied with strings that ran through a series of pulleys, to a stack of books. The books dropped down the length of the locker. The bottles drenched the Slut, high, low, and middle. When the books hit the bottom of the locker they triggered the spark of a lighter. An aerosol can blast shot a plume of flame at the girl. It ignited her soaked clothes, and fire engulfed her.

The Slut howled and ran toward Lucy. Lucy could feel the heat coming off of the girl's burning torso and head. The Slut was blazing white. It was run or burn. Lucy and the others fled into the rigged hallway.

CLANG! CLANG! CLANG! Violent's bucket-foot clapped against the floor as she ran.

Ahead of them, a tile popped out of the ceiling. A sharpened broom handle dropped out of the ceiling. A block of bundled library books the size of a guitar amp was duct-taped to the top as a weight. The heavy spike sank into the second Slut's torso, right behind her collarbone. The flaming girl was gaining on them, baying and dripping fire. She cast a blazing orange light on the hallway that made Lucy and Violent's shadows stretch out long before them.

CLANG! CLANG! CLANG!

Julie had managed to get ahead. She was staying a safe distance from the mangled lockers up on the left, but a trip wire snapped loose by Julie's foot. An overstuffed duffel bag detached from the ceiling, swung down on a rope, and crashed into Julie like a wrecking ball. It launched her into the bent metal teeth of the mangled lockers.

Violent yanked Lucy to a stop. Lucy whipped her head to look back, expecting the burning Slut to crash into her. Instead, the girl was smoldering on the floor, crushed under a set of five weighted lockers that had fallen out of the wall.

Lucy heard sobbing. Violent was crying, holding her face in her hands, and staring at Julie. Julie's spine was folded in half. Her body hung over a twist of metal like a wet towel. Violent collapsed. Lucy stumbled to catch her. They fell against the wall together in an awkward embrace, both out of breath. They sat in silence. Clumps of gray dust floated in the air, blown upward by the swing of the heavy duffel bag that had rammed Julie into the locker doors. Bricks spilled out of a rip in the busted bag. The dust fell like dead snowflakes to the floor.

Violent shuddered as she cried. Lucy didn't know what to do. She felt awful for Violent. She wanted to comfort her, but she was afraid Violent might punch her for trying. Lucy dared to put her hand on Violent's. Violent crumpled under her touch. She leaned into Lucy, and Lucy stroked her hair.

Five minutes passed, maybe ten. Violent rolled her head right to look at Lucy. Sweat had grown cold on her forehead. She pushed Lucy off her.

"You believe there's really a way out?" Violent said.

Lucy nodded. "I believe Will."

"You think the two of us can make it to the ruins?"

Lucy looked at the bucket on Violent's foot. Blood dripped out onto the floor.

"I think we should deal with that first," Lucy said.

It took them ten minutes to get the spikes out of Violent's leg. When they did, Lucy helped Violent to her feet and carried as much of her weight as she could. The pair walked cautiously to the end of the hallway. They walked past an upturned table. Looking back they could see it was a warning sign, a message from the Nerds vigorously scratched into the dark faux wood surface of the table. It read: *Past this point = DEATH.*

36

EVERYTHING WAS GOING TO HELL.

Will ran down a hallway, and Nelson followed. All of the hallway's linoleum floor tiles had been ripped up. A hardened squiggle of glue remained for every missing tile, the color of peanut butter mixed with blood. Nelson huffed and puffed; he kept wanting to stop. Will wouldn't let him. There wasn't time. David would be gone soon.

All of this was Sam's fault. And now Sam had David, probably locked up in a trophy cabinet. After the ambush, Will had tried to run after the Nerds who'd carried David off. He couldn't catch them. He was able to find Nelson and Belinda. He sent Belinda off to room 1206 to meet up with Lucy. Will had a plan, and it required a little muscle. Nelson was going to have to do.

As he and Nelson ran toward the school's administrative offices, Will could feel the tension building in his gut. He had to control it. Now was not the time to lose himself. He had to keep a clear head. Will laid on the speed, hoping that Nelson would keep up.

Within minutes they reached the door to the teachers' lounge. Will trotted down to a walk. Nelson panted his way over to him. Nelson had a smear of soot across his face. His pants seemed like they were about to fall down. He bled heavily from both nostrils. If Will looked anything like Nelson, they were in trouble.

"Can you look meaner?" Will asked.

"What?"

Nelson had lost his ear horn. Will spoke directly into his ear.

"I said, can you look meaner?"

Nelson tried to sneer his lip and bare his teeth like a wolf. He looked more like a worried troll doll.

"That's all you got?"

Nelson kept his face frozen like that and nodded his head. Will sighed.

"Okay."

Will shook his arms to get his nerves out. He knocked on the door and backed up. After a moment the door opened a sliver. A Skater with a shaved head and a fat lip peered out. He instinctively recoiled at the sight of Will's white hair and slammed the door shut again. He heard the kid send an alert out to the rest of his gang.

"Loh-ners!"

Will felt a chill.

"Let me do the talking," Will said quietly to Nelson.

"What?" Nelson said, still holding the same ridiculous expression, except now he was bugging his eyes out. Will didn't know what that face was, but he had to admit it looked weird as hell.

The door flew open, and Skaters poured out, surrounding them. The fat-lipped Skater held the jagged edge of a broken skateboard deck to Will's neck, pinning him against the wall.

"Where's David?"

"I want to talk to P-Nut," Will said.

"I said, where's David?"

"Sam's got him."

Fat-lip eased off on the skateboard, sparing Will's throat. The Skaters grumbled at the news.

"Sam caught David himself?" Fat-lip asked.

"No. The Nerds," Will said.

"The Nerds?"

"Come on!" one Skater said. "God damn it!" said another.

Fat-lip looked at Nelson, who stared back with his *I'm worried and I'm in an electric chair* look.

"What's wrong with this kid?"

"He's crazy," Will whispered. "Don't look him in the eyes."

Fat-lip followed Will's advice and looked away from Nelson. Nelson was pulling it off. Will got a surge of confidence.

"So, if Sam's got David, what the hell did you come here for?" Fat-lip said. "You gonna pay us back for our boards?"

"Like I said," Will said, "I need to talk to P-Nut."

Fat-lip laughed.

"Your funeral, kid. But your friend stays here."

Will turned to Nelson and shouted, "Try not to kill anybody."

Nelson nodded, his nostrils flared in faux anger. The Skaters kept their distance.

Fat-lip and his friends grabbed Will roughly by the shirt and shoved him into the teachers' lounge. A half-pipe skate ramp dominated the room. The surface of the ramp was covered in the missing linoleum tiles from the hallway. It formed a seamless surface. The ramp was at least eight feet tall, and they'd torn out the ceiling to access about three feet more of headroom. But no one was skating. They didn't have many boards, thanks to Will. Every Skater in the room stared daggers at him.

He was pushed into the next room where they'd created a mini skate park, full of school benches and wall-mounted handrails pulled from the stairwells, all marred with black scuffs.

Fat-lip pounded on a heavy wood door on the far end of the room. There was a placard on it that read *PRINCIPAL WAR-FIELD*. The name *WARFIELD* was scratched out. Underneath it, *P-NUT* had been scrawled in silver marker.

The door opened, and a cute Skater girl in a bikini top stuck her head out. The sides of her head were shaved, but the hair on top was long and black and fell to one side. Fat-lip whispered something in her ear. She gave Will a once-over and opened the door wide. One of Will's other escorts gave him a halfhearted pat down and shoved him into the room.

P-Nut lounged on a brass-buttoned green leather couch. He had all sorts of angular designs shaved into his short black hair. The bikini girl sat next to him, and there was another hot girl curled up on P-Nut's other side, with a shaved head. P-Nut smiled at Will. He was a white kid, but somehow he maintained a light tan when none of them had seen the sun in more than a year. Will heard he was part Native American. He always looked like he'd just come back from vacation. Maybe that's why the girls liked him. Or maybe it was because he was always smiling. Whatever it was, they liked him. And he liked them back. P-Nut was known as the horniest guy in school.

P-Nut got up and sat on Principal Warfield's huge oak desk, which was covered with hand-drawn stickers. Behind him, numerous photos of Principal Warfield, some with his family, one with the mayor, hung on the wall, but they had been rehung upside down. P-Nut swung his legs casually back and forth and sized up Will. Will shifted his weight, self-conscious.

Will cleared his throat.

"My name's Will Thorpe."

"I know who you are. You're the one who broke my board."

The bikini girl whispered something into P-Nut's ear.

"Bummer," P-Nut said.

P-Nut sat down and grabbed the microphone for the school's public address system from the center of the desk. He pressed the button at its base; Will could hear different sets of loudspeakers squawk to life in the distance.

"Hello, kiddies, this is P-Nut. Got some breaking news. David Thorpe has been caught by the Nerds. The turkey hunt is off. If you're hungry, you might want to think about eating your shoes."

P-Nut let go of the button, and the speakers went quiet. He looked back to Will again.

"So what did you want?" P-Nut said.

"I'll get to that. But first . . ."

Will pulled his smut phone from his pocket.

"Do you like Freak girls?"

P-Nut smiled.

37

IT WAS ALL FOOD. A HILLSIDE OF FOOD. IT cascaded down the bleachers. This was Varsity's greatest achievement, a symbol of their power in McKinley.

David watched the food in this brief, tranquil moment. As gruesome as his hallucinations had been, they could also be awe-inspiring. The food flowed down the hillside and disappeared once it touched the gym floor, like a giant fountain. Occasionally, some of it would spout up into the air in a kaleidoscope of color. It was beautiful. He would have been content to stare at it until his time ran out.

Heavy ropes tied David to the front of a football tackling sled. His hands were bound behind him. The ropes bit him under the ribs. The dummy cushioning on the sled had been torn away so that his back lay flat against metal bars. His whole body was tilted forward so he had to struggle to lift his heavy head if he wanted to see what was coming at him.

David dragged his head up. At the other end of the gym, Anthony Smith was down in a three-point stance. Other guys lined up for their turn. Anthony broke into a run, straight for David. With his first step, it looked to David like he was a mile away. With the next step, a quarter mile, then fifty feet. David closed his eye and wondered if this was the last hit he would take; if Anthony would smash into him and lung muck would rocket out of his mouth.

David snapped his eye open. Anthony was right there, running at full speed. His shoulder rammed into David's chest with all the momentum of his run. Vicious, worming pain dug its roots down into David's chest. He lost all of his air. David's vision went crimson, as if the ceiling had bled on everything in the gym. He heard the gritty rasp of the tackling sled as it scraped across the wood floor. It skidded to a stop. Anthony pushed off David and let out a victory scream. He raised his fists. The Pretty Ones cheered.

"That was for Brad," Anthony said with a slap to David's chin, and jogged away.

David took in air. The red faded from his vision. He stared at a white candy wrapper on the varnished maple floor. The white wrapper tumbled across the floor and then flitted up, caught by a breeze. It twirled and blew away. He could feel the cool breeze on his face.

"You're okay," a voice said.

David looked up. Lucy stood before him. The breeze was coming from her. Her dress was clean and luminescent, the color of moonlight. She laughed, but he couldn't hear it. Her smile crinkled the skin under her eyes. David loved that. He wanted to know what she was laughing at.

"I'm back in your room," Lucy said. "I'm waiting for you . . . naked."

She smiled again. David felt blood drip out of his mouth as a goofy grin spread across his face.

A sprinting linebacker in a scuffed football helmet ran right through Lucy. She burst into a thousand shreds like confetti. David felt his chest collapse. The pain dug through him. His world went red again. The sled scraped. He heard the linebacker grunt then walk away.

He'd never see Lucy again. He knew that now. It wasn't that he didn't care about living anymore. It was that he couldn't care. He had no fight left in his body, and he was in Sam's world now. The game was over. Sam won.

"That's enough," Sam said.

David rocked his head right, his eyelid heavy. Sam was sitting on a folding chair, getting his hair re-dyed yellow by a Pretty One. He was watching David. He pushed the girl away as she dried his hair. David heard another Varsity come running from the other side of the gym, feet clomping on the hard floor. Sam stood, still wearing the towel around his neck from the dye job.

"I said enough!"

The clomping slowed to a stop, and the line of would-be tacklers dispersed. Sam dragged his folding chair out in front of David. David breathed through the discomfort. Sam casually sat down in front of him. He stared at David and considered him as if he was a piece in a museum.

"Why didn't you kill me?" Sam asked.

"What?" David replied.

"Back on the quad. When all your Scraps were trying to tear me apart, you stopped them. Why'd you do that?"

"Why?" David said. "I don't know, I felt bad for you."

"You felt bad?" Sam asked.

Sam scrunched his face up. He was flabbergasted.

"What would it have proved?" David asked.

"Proved? It wouldn't have proved anything. It would have gotten rid of me. You had to know I wouldn't stop, that I'd keep coming for you."

"I'd already won," David said. "It seemed . . . too cruel."

Sam scoffed. "That's a loser's attitude if I've ever heard one. Guess you're regretting that one now, huh?"

Sam smiled then looked upset when David didn't react.

"What do you want from me, Sam?"

"I don't want anything from you. Look around. I have it all."

Pain flared through David's head. His patience for whatever little game this was had come to an end.

"You sent the whole school after me. For what? What did I do to you? I hit you once for stealing my girlfriend," David said, raising his voice. It hurt his chest to talk so loud.

"Oh, that," Sam said. He stood up. "I sent the whole school after you just to keep them occupied. They all want to kill me for my food. But now, instead, they're killing each other to get to you. They're hungry. They'll do anything. They'll kill their best friends. All I have to do is dangle some food in front of their noses. I don't even have to give them any. I stiffed those Nerds who brought you in," he went on. "Later tonight I'm putting a bounty out on them. And then I'll put a bounty on the ones who bring them in, on and on, and by the end of the week, the whole school will be so weak and hungry that even if they all banded together they wouldn't have the strength to knock on my door."

Sam laughed. The noise of it expanded in David's ears like high-pitched thunder. He felt his eardrums tear open. He screamed, "GET AWAY FROM ME!" but he couldn't hear it over the wretched sound drilling into the back of his eyes. He cried. He screamed. The noise stopped dead, but the pain still thudded in his head.

He opened his eye. Sam stared at him, perplexed.

"What are you, nuts?"

He thought about not telling Sam the truth, but what did it matter now?

"I'm dying."

Sam plopped back down in his chair. He gaped at David.

"I mean . . . how long do you have left?"

"Not long."

Sam's posture, his tone of voice, confused David. He almost seemed concerned. David wondered if somewhere deep down in his crooked mind there was a nugget of compassion, a speck of humanity remaining that David could appeal to.

"Sam. I know a way out. Let me go, and I'll show you. We could escape together. This could all be over."

Sam studied David's face, considering the offer.

"I don't think I want to escape," Sam said. "I like it here."

Shoes clapped hard against the gym floor. Hilary stumbled over to Sam. Her eyes were lazy slits. She carried a squeeze bottle full of juice, and there was a wet stain all down the front of her dress. Sam turned to face her, and his lip curled in disgust.

"You're drunk," Sam said.

"Yup," Hilary slurred.

"What are you doing up here? Go back to the pool."

"Hi, David," Hilary said. "I miss you real bad."

She lost her balance, and Sam had to catch her to keep her from falling.

"Get off of me," she said, her words falling clumsily out of her mouth. "I don't want to be with you, I want to be with David."

"What did you say to me?" Sam said, so loud that it echoed through the gym.

Hilary hung off Sam but peered into David's eye.

"I'm sorry, David," she said slowly, trying not to slur. "Sam was a mistake. I never should have broken up with you."

Sam threw Hilary to the ground. She landed face-first. When she rolled over, one of her teeth, her right cuspid, was gone. Hilary fumbled her hand to her bloody mouth.

"You broke my tooth," she said.

"Why the fuck would you want to be with him?" Sam screamed. "Look at him. He's dying, he's got nothing. I've got it all!"

"You don't have shit," she said. "Everyone hates you. Your own gang wants you dead. You haven't got one friend in the whole school."

"Shut up!"

"When do you think one of your guys is gonna take you out? Tomorrow? Today?" Hilary said.

Sam paced back and forth, yanking on his own hair. He whipped back around and thrust his finger at her.

"Is this a suicide attempt? Is that what this is?" Sam asked. "You want me to kill you?"

She smiled at him. Blood and saliva wet her lips. "I don't

want to date a loser anymore, that's what I want."

Sam picked up the metal folding chair. He stomped over to Hilary and swung the chair up over his head.

The school's PA system squawked to life.

"This is Will Thorpe. Are you listening, McKinley?"

Sam halted his swing; the chair stayed frozen in the air.

"This is a message for that big pussy, Sam Howard, who's so scared to leave the gym, he has to send his girlfriend to attack people while they're asleep. That's the guy I want to see in the quad in fifteen minutes. If you want to see a real fight, everybody should come on down. But don't blame me if the big pussy doesn't show."

Sam threw the chair into the bleachers and howled.

David laughed. He couldn't stop. It was so perfectly Will.

WILL STOOD IN THE CENTER OF THE QUAD.

The rest of the school watched from around the edges, waiting for the show. Will felt the singe of every stare. People were hungry and volatile. The sun had set, but the exterior flood lamps were on. The generator was on its last legs and chugging. The harsh spotlights surged bright, casting sharp shadows, and then faded nearly all the way out again, like a drunken strobe.

"You're gonna die," Nelson said from behind him.

"Not helping," Will said.

"I said, you're gonna die!" Nelson shouted at the top of his lungs.

"I heard you! Everybody did."

"Oh . . . sorry."

It didn't matter that the crowd heard him. They were already thinking it anyway. They all came to watch him lose, badly. Every gang was there. If Sam didn't kill him, there was a good chance that the Freaks might.

"I just hope David's still alive," Nelson shouted.

Will cringed. He had to push that out of his mind. If he thought about all the holes in his plan, he'd be sunk. He just prayed that Sam would come soon. He was already late.

Will had no backup. Nelson was against the whole idea, and the rest of the Loners stood in the far corner of the quad. He would have liked them behind him, at least as a show of support, but they had lost faith in him after the debacle at the library.

Will understood. They had already joined in on one of his crazy plans, and it got them ambushed, injured, and demoralized. None of them even believed the exit was real anymore. This was on his shoulders, and he would have only one chance to get it right.

A Freak in the crowd wore black sunglasses. She grinned at him and slowly drew a finger across her neck. Will swallowed hard. He was thirsty. His chest felt tight. He looked back to Nelson, whose teeth were gritted like he was watching a car accident in slow motion. No matter what bullshit he'd told her, Will wished Lucy was there.

The crowd came alive. All heads turned as one. Varsity had arrived.

The Freaks moved aside so that Varsity could enter the circle of gangs. Varsity wore full pads and uniforms like it was a Friday night game. They jogged onto the quad and took a regimented formation across from Will. There were a lot of them, and the other gangs looked like packs of starved dogs in comparison. Varsity was well fed and at full strength. Sam stepped through the front line.

He knew he had a fight coming his way. That was the whole point, but somehow he didn't ever have this bad a picture in his head. If he did, he probably would have never gone this far. Sam was fuming. He seemed repulsed by the sight of Will. He pulled off his jersey. Sam's upper body bulged and flexed. He was huge. Will felt like the idiot everybody thought he was. Will clenched his fists and raised them. His fists were trembling, and there was nothing he could do to hide it. Snickers rippled in from all around him.

He wanted to run, but he didn't think he could. He didn't feel in control of his body anymore. He was all nerves. His mind was plagued with visions of all the ways he was going to screw this up.

Two burly Varsity guys broke through the front line. They were holding David up between them. David's toes dragged on the ground behind him. His head hung down. His clothes were stained brown with dried blood. The crowd gasped at the sight of him.

"All we did was slap your brother around a little, and look

what happened. You sure you wanna go through with this, little boy?" Sam said.

If Sam wanted to get inside Will's head, it was working.

He saw David's foot move. His right toe fumbled forward until he laid his foot flat on the ground. Then the other one. His legs locked straight, taking on the weight of his body. David raised his bloody and swollen head. It looked like a white eye patch tied tightly around a purple water balloon.

David's one eye wandered up until it found Will. David smiled. Will couldn't believe it. It was a broad, genuine smile. His inflated face looked even uglier with the smile, but it was irrepressible. Even after such a terrible beating, David was still defiant. It filled Will with pride, and he smiled back. A calm came over him.

"Well?" Sam shouted for the crowd's benefit. "What's the matter? Did you swallow your tongue?"

Laughs echoed across the quad.

Will flipped Sam off.

Sam charged him. He was upon Will in seconds, and he buried his fist in Will's stomach. Will crumpled forward. It felt like Sam punched a hole through him. With Will bent over, Sam tried to knee him in his face. It connected with his chest instead. Will fell backward, and his feet scurried to stay underneath his weight. He barely stayed upright before Sam kicked him in the bladder. Will fell to the ground and landed on his ass bone.

No tussle at a drop, no scuffle in the halls had ever hurt like this. Will couldn't tell which pain belonged to what. He was losing control. Will struggled to breathe. Things were happening too fast. Sam came at him. Will winged a wild punch at him first. It dinged off Sam's shoulder like a pebble off a car window. Sam grabbed him by the shirt with one hand. His other hand was a fist. He drew it back, winding up to deliver the final strike.

Then, Will seized.

His body stiffened. His eyes rolled back in his head. His feet kicked out from under him. Sam held him up by the shirt. He hung there, rigid and convulsing. Sam let him go. Will dropped like a sandbag and knocked his head against the ground.

There were laughs in the crowd. There were just as many gasps.

Through fluttering eyelids and jerking vision, Will saw Sam towering above him, colossal. Drool fell out of Will's mouth. His body shook. All pretty convincing. Will had gotten plenty of practice from all the times he faked seizures to mess with David.

He rammed his foot up into Sam's crotch, and Sam crashed to the ground. Will pulled himself up. The crowd's laughter stopped. Silence. Will wound his leg back and soccer-kicked Sam in the balls again. Sam bellowed in pain. Everyone stared in disbelief, including Varsity.

"Listen up, hungry people!" Will shouted. "All of Varsity's fighters are here. No one is guarding the food!"

The gaunt faces in the crowd turned in the direction of the gym.

"The food belongs to all of us!"

The crowd barked and whistled and hollered in agreement. Will could feel the tension bristling all around him.

"GO GET IT!"

It was a stampede. The Freaks, the Nerds, the Sluts, the Skaters, and the Geeks all dashed toward the gym at once, like they were trying to catch the last train out of hell. Varsity tried to block them, but the momentum was too great. Varsity's formation was smashed apart. The two Varsity guys holding David cast him aside to go protect the gym.

Sam got to his feet, holding his crotch. For a second he looked at Will like he was about to kill him. But he stumbled backward, suddenly scared. Will was peripherally aware of someone behind him. He turned to see the Loners standing in a semicircle, staring Sam down. Sam yelled out of frustration and ran after the riotous mob.

The generator finally gave out, and all the lights died. The quad was overtaken by darkness.

David was a barely visible, gray lump on the ground twenty feet away. He was faced away from Will and wasn't moving. Will limped over to David as fast as he could. He dropped to his knees and turned David over tenderly. He cradled his brother's head in his hands. David's face looked like a misshapen tomato.

"Dave? Are you okay?"

David smiled.

"I think I'm hallucinating . . . ," David said. "I thought I just saw you kick Sam Howard's ass."

Will laughed so hard it made him cry.

39

LUCY AND VIOLENT ENTERED THE RUINS by the light of Violent's torch. Violent had retrieved it from one of the many lockers full of weapons that she maintained throughout the school. A vicious stench hit Lucy's nose.

"Teachers," Violent said. She handed Lucy the torch. She unhooked a shiv from her necklace of hanging silverware. Using Lucy's shoulder for leverage, Violent reached down and grabbed the hem of Lucy's dress. She stabbed it with the shiv.

"Hey, what are you doing?"

"We need something to cover our noses. That smell's only gonna get worse."

With a solid yank, Violent ripped off the bottom six inches of Lucy's dress.

"You could've used your shirt or something," Lucy said.

"Yeah, we coulda."

Violent tore the resulting strip of fabric in two, handing one piece to Lucy and tying the other around her nose and mouth. Lucy did the same. Violent put her arm around Lucy. Violent limped, and Lucy carried half her weight.

"How do you think the fight turned out?" Violent said.

Lucy thought back to the announcement they'd heard over the loudspeaker. She didn't understand it, but she had to trust Will had a plan. It was blind faith, but it was the only thing keeping her going. David had to be alive, and there had to be a way out of the school, there simply had to be.

"I think Will beat Sam, and we'll see them soon," Lucy said.

"Want to make it interesting?"

"Ew, like a bet? No, you're talking about my friends' lives."

"Just trying to make conversation."

"Well, try harder."

"You make a good crutch," Violent said.

"Thanks." Lucy laughed.

With every step into the depths of the ruins, Lucy felt more unsettled. The flickering torchlight cast mad shadows down the hall. The ruins were like a memorial to the day everything changed. She could almost hear the rumble of the explosion and the bloodcurdling shrieks that followed, echoing down the halls.

"Have you ever been here before?" Lucy asked.

Violent was quiet for a moment and then, "Yeah. A long time ago. Only bad shit happens here."

They came to the remains of a staircase. One whole side of it was gone. All that remained were broken stairs no more than a foot wide, jutting out from the wall. At the top landing, where the stairs should have been, was a mess of bent rebar.

"1206 is on the second floor," Violent said. "We gotta go up."

"You think you can make it?"

"Ssh," Violent said suddenly, dropping to a whisper. "Did you hear that?"

All Lucy heard was the crackle of the torch in her hand. She shook her head. "What did you hear?"

"Nothing, let's hurry up."

Lucy and Violent hurried to the stairs. Lucy climbed the broken lengths of stair carefully, one hand on the wall and one holding the torch. Violent was always one step behind her, using the wall for support. Each step felt treacherous. It took her a minute to get half of the way up.

Lucy noticed something etched on the wall below in charcoal letters: *RIP SMUDGE*. A narrow mound of rubble stood out above the rest. She had the feeling Will had been where she stood.

When they reached the second floor, Lucy heard soft footsteps skittering toward her. She spun to face the hallway. From out of the darkness came a ghoulish boy. He wore a Pretty One dress tucked into black jeans. His face reminded her of a lizard's, dry and pointed, his eyes black and his skin bluish white, like he'd been drained of blood. His hair was long, fragile, and white like an old crazy woman.

The boy stuttered to a stop. He looked nearly as shocked as Lucy was. He lunged forward and snatched her necklace off her neck. He dashed back into the dark hallway.

"Hey! Give me that!" Lucy yelled.

She sprinted into the hall, after the boy. The torch in her hand purred and dimmed as its flame dragged behind. She heard movement in the classroom ahead. Lucy dashed through the doorway. She was in a chemistry lab. Large, six-station islands with soapstone counters hunched in the darkness like sleeping beasts. Broken equipment and dirty papers littered the floor.

A hand clamped down on her arm and flung her to the ground. She lost the torch. The boy sat on her. He pinned her arms and thrust his face into hers.

"Stay away!" the boy said, the stink of his breath invading her nostrils.

The torch had set fire to a cluster of papers, and in the firelight Lucy could see the boy was scared.

"I want that necklace back!" Lucy dared to scream.

"It don't belong to you," the boy said. His accent was strange. It was thick, southern. "Just leave me alone."

Light flared behind the boy. Violent was behind him, holding the torch. She jabbed it into his back.

"Gahh!" he screamed.

Violent stuck him with it again, and he scurried into the corner and crumpled up into a ball near the growing fire.

"You want to hurt girls? Huh?" Violent said, pushing the torch near his face. "Is that your thing, junkie?"

"I want the necklace," Lucy said.

"It's mine!" the boy said. "It belongs to me!"

"Hand it over, creep!" Violent said.

"It belonged to my momma! It's all I got left of her. Please, don't make me. Please don't."

Violent pulled the torch away from him. He pressed his back to the wall like a frightened animal. Lucy ran to the paper fire and stomped it out.

"What are you talking about?" Lucy said, spinning back around to face him.

"He's high. He's been huffing," Violent said, kicking at rags by a dirty, half-empty jug. "Look at this crap."

"No, leave my zip alone!" the boy said, lunging for the jug. Violent got to it first, holding it out of reach suggestively. He looked down, then thrashed around in anger. He moaned, then threw the necklace at Lucy. It skidded to her feet, and she picked it up. Violent tossed the jug into the boy's lap, and he dumped some of the liquid onto a rag. He clasped the wet rag to his face and breathed in deeply. He exhaled with a sob.

"Let's go," Violent said.

Lucy looked at the necklace in her hand, then to the huffing kid. He rocked as he cried and punched at the floor. His anguish seemed so genuine.

"How do I know this belonged to your mother?" Lucy said.

"It's all she ever had," the boy said, through a chemical haze. "They tried to take it from me at the labs, but I hid it from 'em. Them metal bedposts were hollow. Them doctors didn't know that. That's the only reason I'm alive, that necklace. I went back for it when I shoulda run. That's how I got lucky. Ev'rbody else got snagged. I got out . . . lucky. . . ."

At first Lucy tried to make sense of his rambling. It sounded like crazy talk. Labs. Doctors.

"You're the one," Violent said. "You're the infected kid they were trying to catch."

"Lucky," he said again, his face pinched with pain. "They shoulda left us in the mountains. They shoulda left us alone." He scrambled to dampen his rag with the jug. Violent ripped it from his hands and threw it across the room.

"Give it back! Give 'em back to me!"

Violent threw the torch aside. She dropped to her knees and grasped him by his soiled dress.

"You made this happen. You ran into this school when you knew what could happen?"

"They was gonna kill me," he said. It was barely a whisper.

"You brought all this on us?" Violent said, spitting her words like bullets.

The boy shook his head, moaning, frothing, crying.

"YOU DID THIS?"

"Violent . . . ," Lucy said.

"YOU SHOULD HAVE DIED!" Violent screamed. She punched him in his mouth. His eyes fluttered back, and his lip split. She punched again. And again. Long, arcing punches that cut his face, and puffed his eyes, and bent his nose.

"Stop it!" Lucy shouted. "Stop it!"

Lucy pulled at Violent. She wouldn't stop. She was a jackhammer. She was going to kill him. Lucy hiked up what was left of her skirt and kicked Violent in the head. Violent yelped and fell over on her side, holding her ear. She looked up at Lucy, outraged.

"That's enough," Lucy said.

Violent grumbled and stood up. She spit on the boy and limped toward the hall.

Lucy turned to the boy and crouched. His face was mulch. Lucy winced at the sight of him. His breaths were labored, like he was breathing through a snorkel. But he was alive, and he was lucid.

Lucy took his hand and placed the necklace in it. She couldn't imagine the guilt he carried. The deaths, the murders, the brutality, the hopelessness; he'd created all of it. It wasn't his fault, he was just trying to survive. But she still hated him for it. She wished he had died that day.

Lucy stood, and walked over to Violent. Violent still stared at the boy. The two of them walked out the door without another word.

Lucy counted off the room signs when she saw them.

1242 . . . 1238 . . . 1231 . . .

David was so close.

1210 . . .

Lucy and Violent slid into a water-soaked corridor.

Huge chunks of plaster from the ceiling and the walls lay scattered on the floor. Water rained down in waterfalls and then flowed toward a wall of rubble that blocked the end of the hallway. The Loners were there, clustered in the hall; a group of Sluts too. They waited in silence. It was unsettling.

"What's going on?" Violent asked one of her girls.

"Don't know if that dude's gonna make it," one Slut said.

Lucy looked to Violent in a panic.

"Go," Violent said. "Before I kick you in the head."

Lucy let go of Violent and splashed through the wet hall to room 1206. The room had no floor. There was a flash of light from the room below.

"David?" she called out. "Will?"

"Lucy?" Will said.

"Oh, Will, thank God."

Will reached his hands up to her. He helped her lower herself into the ruined room below.

"You made it," he said.

She hugged him and held him tight. She could feel his face turn toward hers. She thought she felt the slightest kiss on her cheek, but she couldn't have been sure. She laid eyes on David.

He was hunched over against a wall, just beyond another thin waterfall. His face was an undulating blur behind the wall of water. She could make out the shape of his arms. They were spattered with dried blood.

Lucy let go of Will and moved toward David. Will stopped her.

"Don't—" he said.

Lucy looked to Will. She had to go to David.

"Get back," David said with a heavy sigh.

"But—" she said, and didn't know what to say next. This wasn't how it was supposed to go.

"We're killing him, even this close. We're toxic to him," Will said.

"No," Lucy said with a whimper.

"David, you have to go now," Will said.

Will gently tossed David his phone. David barely caught it.

"Use the phone's light. Follow the blood trail," Will said to him.

Lucy noticed bloody paw prints on the floor's rubble. They pointed toward a triangular hole in the wall of rubble, where David stood.

"We'll wait an hour, then follow," Will said. "That should give you time to get far enough away."

"Listen," David said. "We don't know what's out there."

David stopped to cough. It took him a good ten seconds to get his voice back.

"When you leave," David continued, "you gotta stay hidden. I'll tie . . . something red to the back door, okay? That'll tell you Dad's not in the house, and it's safe to go in. Just be careful. Take Lucy and go to the basement. Hide there. I'll call."

"Okay," Will said.

"And keep her safe. Promise me you'll keep her safe."

"I prom—"

"I can take care of myself," she said, a little too forcefully.

"Look after each other then," David said.

"David, please, I won't come near. Can I just see you," Lucy said.

David didn't move. He kept his face hidden.

"I can't. Lucy, this isn't the end. I just need a head start."

Lucy couldn't get any words out.

"It's time," Will said.

Tears clouded her eyes. She wiped them away as fast as she could. She wouldn't miss a single moment. The white of his eye patch quivered behind the rushing water, then was swallowed by the dark when David turned away. He cast the phone light on the hole in the wall and climbed through. A small hunk of plaster fell as he brushed up against it, and it landed in a puddle. A moment later, the light of David's phone faded away and he was gone.

She stayed there, staring. Will touched her arm.

"You should sit down. Rest," Will said. "We're gonna need our energy, and we can't go in there for another hour."

The tears still flowed, as heavily as the water from the ceiling.

"You wouldn't believe whose ass I had to kick to get David here," Will said.

Lucy couldn't wait an hour. It felt impossible. This was the end. If she had anything to tell him, this would be her last chance for years. David had risked his life to save hers. He'd given her a home. He'd made her laugh and kept her safe. She loved David. She had to tell him.

She ran to the hole in the wall and peered through. It was a labyrinth of wreckage inside. The *plink-plink* of dripping water resonated through the tunnel. It wasn't a tunnel as much as it was the empty space left between the piled chunks of wall, ceiling, and floor. The chunks rested precariously on one another like a stack of dominoes. She caught the glow of David's phone, then she saw his silhouette.

"David!"

He turned. His face was swollen and bloodied in the phone's light, but his good eye sparkled.

A second later, a chunk of ceiling in front of him fell, pulling an avalanche of rubble down with it.

She screamed. Her legs buckled beneath her; she collapsed into a puddle.

Will ran to her.

The tunnel was gone.

40

DAVID WAS SHAKING FROM ADRENALINE.
He'd almost been crushed. Pain throbbed, everywhere. He
cast the light of his phone back at the passage he had just
crawled through. It wasn't there. Dust and dirt, kicked up by
the collapse, still spun in the air. He pressed his full weight
against the blockage in several places. Nothing gave. It was
solid, through and through.

"Lucy!" he shouted. "Will!"

He pressed his ear to the wall of rock. He could hear faint
shouts on the other side, but he couldn't make out the words.
He heard a whimper behind him. David turned and faced the
path ahead. He held up his phone. It was littered with dogs.
Doberman pinschers with broken backs lay limp over jagged
hunks of debris in front of him. They dangled out of holes

and crannies. They were sandwiched between blocks of wall. David knew they were a manifestation of his fear, but that didn't mean he had to like it.

This school had taken everything from him. His muscles felt like they were slipping off his bones and his bones felt hollow. He didn't want to leave Will and Lucy behind. He wanted to bash against the obstruction behind him until it was dust. It wasn't fair. These fallen rocks had made a liar out of him. He told them that he would get them all out, and now they were trapped again. They would all die of starvation.

He had to get the food drops started again. Graduation too. If he could get out, he could let the world know what was happening inside these walls. He had to try—it was his only chance to keep Lucy and Will alive.

David stumbled away from the obstruction. He heard the sound of a thousand dogs, panting in unison. They were still there. Each dog he passed bared its teeth as he neared. He saw one dried-blood paw print and then another. He prayed the trail would lead him outside.

David careened off jutting rocks, avoiding scratching claws and snapping teeth. He could only see two feet in front of him by the phone's anemic light. He followed the blood trail wherever it led, sometimes having to crawl on his stomach. He lost track of the trail at times and crawled into cramped passages that came to dead ends.

It could've been minutes or hours since the tunnel's

collapse. He had no way of telling the difference. He might have been traveling in circles. He kept going. His vision was savaged by more things that weren't there. They couldn't be there. He saw all the rubble as acne-scarred flesh. He saw his own arms as eels, black and wet and squirming. For a good fifty feet Sam silently followed close behind him, with his arms outstretched, wanting a hug.

But gradually, the hallucinations faded. In time, he didn't feel like his brain was evaporating anymore. He didn't feel like nuggets of lung were rising up in his throat. He just felt like he'd been beaten up by the whole football team, which he had been. It was a good feeling.

David turned a jagged corner. He crawled into a slim space between two horizontal slabs of wall. If whatever was holding those two slabs apart gave way, David would be squashed flat. As he slithered through, David's phone died. The battery was done.

David threw the phone aside and continued on, blind. His hands were his eyes. He felt his way through rocky crevices and disjointed passages. He saw light ahead, a dark gray shimmer in the blackness. He moved toward it as fast as he could. The light forced him to squint. A short tunnel of debris extended above him like a chimney, and beyond it, he saw the gray material of the canopy, just like in the quad. It glowed from the moonlight shining through. He climbed—one final effort. Something scurried down the rocks by him. It was a rat.

David pulled himself out of the tunnel and onto a slanting hill of rubble. He realized that he was on top of what once was the East Wing. The heavy synthetic material of the canopy was in his face; it covered the entire hill of rubble. He could almost see the moon beyond it, a crinkled blur of white. He caught just a whiff of cold, fresh air, but after a year of breathing the recycled, dead air in the school, that whiff was like a spoonful of sugar. He turned his head when he heard a flutter, and he saw a tattered hole in the canopy above him. It was being blown about by a chilly winter breeze. He crawled up to it, grabbed the gnawed and torn edges of the hole, and pulled his head through. A limitless night sky was above him. The stars were sharp and brilliant pinholes, and the silver moon was nearly full. He breathed deeply. The air was rich, like biting into a tomato off the vine.

I did it, he thought. *I got out.*

David climbed out from underneath the canopy. The material sloped up and up above him, over the hill of craggy ruins, all the way to the roof of the remaining building. He looked below him. The canopy ended at the ground, twenty feet down, and beyond it, he saw trees. Real trees. He didn't realize how much he'd missed them until he saw them. He half slid, half climbed down the rest of the canopied rubble hill and stepped onto grass. It was soft under his shoes. The lawn of the campus stretched out before him. He ran to a nearby tree. He just had to touch it. The bark was aged and rough and natural. He savored another gust of fragrant air. It smelled of leaves and grass and rain. He never wanted to be inside again.

Thirty yards away, there was a double line of chain-link fence. It surrounded the entire campus, and razor wire was spooled along its top edge. He saw a guard tower. He saw parked jeeps. Moonlight shimmered across the lawn. There were prefabricated buildings across the campus that he didn't remember. When he looked at the school itself, he saw that the canopy covered the entire massive building, like the school was being fumigated.

He had to get off this campus. The world needed to know what was happening in McKinley. He couldn't afford to screw it up. He knew he should be cautious, survey the scene, make sure no one was around, but he couldn't wait any longer.

David ran for the fence.

41

SAM TRUNDLED DOWN A PITCH-BLACK HALL.

It had been two weeks, and the lights still hadn't come back on. He couldn't see a thing. His muscles spasmed with each step, and his legs wobbled underneath him. His belly twisted and growled. He could taste his own bile on his tongue. The food was gone. His food. The rest of the school had devoured it all.

Those animals. He despised every one of them. They turned on each other like Sam knew they would. Now they all lay out in the quad, starving and helpless. Like babies. Disgusting, pink little babies, crying and waiting for someone to feed them.

He'd show them. There was a gas line to the boiler in the basement. He'd break it loose. He'd let it leak for a day, maybe two. Then he'd drop a torch from the third floor down the center shaft of the stairwell.

The babies would burn. He'd hear their wailing screams as the fire boiled the flesh off their bones. He'd probably burn too, but he'd be dead soon anyway.

Sam saw a pumpkin-colored glow coming from around the corner ahead. It was the fluttering light of a torch. He crept forward, careful to not make a noise, and peeked around the corner.

There in the front foyer, standing by the graduation booth, with their backs to Sam, were Will Thorpe and his skank friend, Lucy. Will kicked at the booth while the skank tried her thumb on the dormant scanner.

Sam slipped his kitchen knife out of his belt. The fire's light glinted off the blade's serrated edge. He snuck toward them. Revenge was only fifteen feet away.

The back of Will's neck was exposed. Sam could see the bumps of his vertebrae nudging out from Will's neck just slightly. He'd push the blade in between them and twist.

Ten feet. They still hadn't heard him. He slunk forward. This was too perfect. He had to suppress an urge to laugh.

Four feet. He tightened his fingers around the knife's handle.

Two feet.

Sam heard the smooth *SHIIICK* of metal sliding against metal. The steel doors to the outside opened. Brilliant light gushed in through the doorway, brightening the entire room. He winced and shielded his eyes.

Sam darted behind a nearby column and hid. He braced

himself for men in gas masks and haz-mat suits. The soldiers were probably coming to slaughter them once and for all. He peeked around the edge of the pillar just far enough to see Will and the skank. They hadn't moved. They stood there, like idiots about to be shot. Sam poked his head out farther. He could see the open door to the outside now.

A teen boy with white hair walked in. Sam couldn't believe what he was seeing. The kid wore dark blue jeans and a ski jacket, and he carried a hunting rifle. He was followed by more white-haired teens, all wearing casual clothes and toting guns. There must have been forty of them.

Sam glanced back to Will and the skank. They were just as dumbfounded as he was.

The kid in the ski jacket homed in on the two of them. His face brightened. He lowered his gun and walked toward them with a big smile.

"You got no idea how long it took us to get that door open," he said. "You okay? You hungry?"

Will and the skank stared back.

"Don't worry," the kid said. "Everything's gonna be okay."

"Where are the soldiers?" Will asked.

"Oh, they're gone," the kid said. "We came to get you out."

Sam felt small fingers touch his wrist. He jumped and spun around. A girl stared up at him. She had a round, wholesome face and long white hair that draped over the shoulders of her down vest. She couldn't have been older than thirteen.

"Hi," she said sweetly.

Sam slowly snuck the knife down the back of his pants.

"Hi," Sam said.

"You want some food?" the girl asked. She pulled a granola bar out of her pocket.

His pulse quickened at the sight of the small pistol clutched in her other hand. He smiled.

"Actually, uh . . . you got any more of those guns?"

WANT MORE OF THE

QUARANTINE

SERIES?

LOOK FOR BOOK TWO FROM
EGMONT USA IN SUMMER 2013!